BEAUTY'S KINGDOM

ALSO BY ANNE RICE WRITING AS A. N. ROQUELAURE

The Claiming of Sleeping Beauty
Beauty's Punishment
Beauty's Release

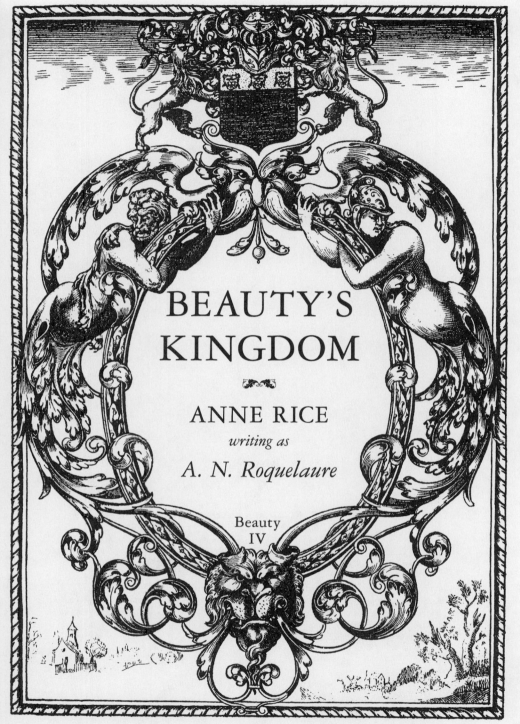

BEAUTY'S KINGDOM

ANNE RICE

writing as

A. N. Roquelaure

Beauty
IV

VIKING

VIKING
Published by the Penguin Group
Penguin Group (USA) LLC
375 Hudson Street
New York, New York 10014

USA | Canada | UK | Ireland | Australia | New Zealand | India | South Africa | China
penguin.com
A Penguin Random House Company

First published by Viking Penguin, a member of Penguin Group (USA) LLC, 2015

ISBN 978-0-525-42799-5

Printed in the United States of America
1 3 5 7 9 10 8 6 4 2

Dedicated
to
Rachel Winter
and
to
the memory
of
William Whitehead
and
John Preston

Love is a smoke raised with the fume of sighs;
Being purged, a fire sparkling in lovers' eyes;
Being vex'd, a sea nourish'd with lovers' tears:
What is it else? a madness most discreet,
A choking gall and a preserving sweet.

William Shakespeare, *Romeo and Juliet*

CONTENTS

Contents

I

TWILIGHT
OF AN
OLD KINGDOM

I

LADY EVA: LONG DAY'S JOURNEY INTO HOPE

i

Ah, such a long and wearying day. And no one in the great kingdom of Bellavalten had heard a word from Queen Eleanor or the Crown Prince in a year.

As the mistress of naked pleasure slaves in the Queen's absence, I had spent hours inspecting all the slaves of the Court and then had traveled to the Queen's Village to make sure that those unfortunates exiled there were being severely disciplined and vigorously worked as always. I loved my duties, loved the training and care of so many beautiful and abject naked royal servants of both sexes who were kept in the kingdom strictly for the amusement of their masters and mistresses, but I was as discouraged as everyone else by the Queen's long absence from the realm and her silence. And I wanted only the peace and quiet now of my own quarters.

I had to stop at Prince Tristan's manor house, however, before returning to Court. And I welcomed a moment's rest and something to eat there as well, and of course I was eager as always to see Prince Tristan.

Prince Tristan had lived for over twenty years in the kingdom.

He was the handsomest of men, tall, robust, with blond curling hair and clear blue eyes, always properly and richly dressed, and the image of

3

the proud and pampered courtier of Queen Eleanor. He welcomed me graciously into his private salon where a cheerful little fire fought the inevitable damp of the stone walls, and I could see wine and cakes laid out on the polished wooden table.

"Ah, Eva, our precious Eva," he said earnestly. "What would we do now without you? Have you had any word from Her Majesty?"

"None, Tristan," I said, "and frankly, though I do all I can—and Lord Gregory and the Captain of the Guard do all they can—the kingdom suffers."

"I know," he said, gesturing for me to take the chair opposite his. "We're the envy of the world for our system of pleasure slavery, but without the Queen, the slaves are anxious, fearful as the rest of us that something may happen to disturb the peace of the realm."

We were alone and Tristan himself filled my goblet. I savored the fragrance of the red wine and then drank. Delicious. Tristan's wine cellar was the best in the kingdom.

"You are so right," I replied. "In the village, Captain Gordon and Lady Julia have everything in hand. She is as good a mayor as ever a man was. I don't mind saying so even if she is my aunt. And Captain Gordon is tireless. But something's wrong, just wrong. I can sense it at Court, no matter how many entertainments I devise. All feel the Queen's absence."

"What can I do to assist?" he asked. He held out the plate of cakes for me.

"Well, this refreshment for the moment is splendid," I said. "I've traveled the entire realm today and I need these moments to recollect myself."

I might have added that looking on Tristan was always a refreshing pleasure.

For years Tristan had lived in his manor house with my uncle Nicholas, the Queen's Chronicler, and Lady Julia, my aunt, and Nicholas's sister. But Lady Julia had gone down to be the mayor of the Queen's Village two years ago. And my uncle Nicholas had gone off into the world a year before the Queen and the Crown Prince embarked on their interminable sea voyage.

Tristan had grieved over the loss of Nicholas miserably. But letters came from my uncle regularly, and though he never promised to return, we maintained the hope that he would do so eventually.

Some months ago, I'd given Tristan a magnificent pleasure slave,

Princess Blanche, one of the Queen's old favorites from the castle. I'd hoped Princess Blanche would delight Tristan, as he had not found his other slaves to be of lasting interest. And Tristan had written notes to me more than once to say that my gift was most pleasing to him.

"And where is my exquisite Blanche?" I asked now. "Are you keeping her quite busy?"

At once he snapped his fingers, and Blanche appeared on her hands and knees moving cautiously and silently from the shadows.

"Come here," said Tristan in a low firm voice, "and stand before Lady Eva for inspection." His cheeks colored slightly as he studied her. How he loved her.

Blanche was a tall princess, with very full breasts and a rounded bottom that was irresistible. She had beautifully turned legs. And though she had fair skin, she did not mark easily, and could be disciplined severely and appear none the worse for it. I'd spanked her bottom many a time, amazed at how the redness so easily faded.

"I work her relentlessly," said Tristan, as she approached. "Kiss Lady Eva's slippers first, Blanche, and then you may kiss mine. You should do that without my telling you."

He sounded stern.

I patted Blanche's head as she obeyed him. "Now stand up, little girl," I said, "with your hands behind your neck and let me have a look at you." "Little Girl" was my favorite endearment for woman slaves, just as "Little Boy" was my favorite endearment for the males. And I'd often observed that this pet name produced singularly good results.

As Blanche rose to her feet, I could see she was flushed and trembling. Inspections are easier for some slaves than others. Blanche had always had a natural shyness to her, a sweet submissiveness that melted hearts even as it invited punishment.

"I find her graceful and polished," said Tristan. "Whenever she is in my presence I have a paddle or strap in my hand. I can't imagine ever tiring of her."

"Come closer, Princess," I said and pinched her smooth plump thigh as I drew her towards me. Blanche was indeed a princess in her own homeland but she'd been sold outright, at her own request, to Her Majesty many years ago. She'd been one of many chosen to serve in the Queen's bedchamber. And in the last few years, she'd suffered from Queen Eleanor's indifference.

"She sleeps at the foot of my bed," said Tristan, "and she kneels at my feet when I dine. I have her punished regularly by her groom if I'm too busy to do it. I adore her."

Blanche stood very still, her eyes down, eyelashes fluttering, hands at the back of her neck as was proper, her exquisite silver hair falling down her back.

I liked her firm shoulders, her shapely arms. I pinched her nipples to make her blush, then told her to kneel. I inspected her pretty white teeth, and then forced her to stand again, this time with her legs wide apart, for a quick, gentle finger inspection of her privy parts which left her in tears of shame and happiness. Her little secret sanctuary under its smoky veil of hair was tight and hot as ever.

Tristan gazed at her adoringly. He couldn't help himself. But that was always Tristan's way, to love and to love deeply. His large blue eyes had a remote yet dreamy quality and again there came that flush to his cheeks as he regarded Blanche. He shifted in his chair uncomfortably.

"You love your master, Blanche?" I demanded.

"Yes, Lady Eva," she confessed. She had a soft low voice, a beguiling voice. Suddenly, her bosom heaving, she said, "Please, please, don't separate me from him."

"Hush!" I said. I spanked both her breasts. "You'll be whipped for making such a request." I looked to Tristan who silently nodded in agreement. "But I can assure you, Blanche, that Tristan may have you as long as he finds you interesting."

She started to cry. She had not been able to control her outburst, and she knew full well it was bad manners. But this is how it had always been with Blanche—small imperfections which more often than not offended no one though of course they had to be promptly corrected.

Tristan snapped his fingers again, and the groom appeared, a fair young man I did not know well, named Galen. He was, like all the grooms and pages of the realm, chosen for his beauty, his grace, and his devotion to the Queen.

"Take her into the bedchamber, Galen," Tristan said softly. "Spank her hard over the knee for her impertinence and scold her when you do it."

"Yes, my lord."

"Then chain her to the bedpost. She's to have plain water and only bits of bread for supper. I'll punish her further myself this evening."

At once the groom took Blanche in hand and led her out of the chamber. She was crying freely.

It must have been an hour that Tristan and I talked softly—about the state of this small realm that was our shared home. Tristan had been my friend since I'd come here—the niece of Nicholas the Chronicler, drawn to the kingdom, to the ways of the Queen, and the ways of pleasure slavery. It was Tristan who had presented me at Court, urging the busy and distracted queen to put the matters of naked slavery in my hands.

We had our little repast now, but before I left I asked for a moment alone with Blanche. As the ruler of the realm, I was exercising my right and duty to see to Blanche's state of mind for myself. Tristan didn't protest.

Alone in the bedchamber, I found her in a flood of tears. She'd been severely spanked and the paddle hadn't spared her thighs or her calves either. Her resilient skin was surprisingly red. She kissed my slippers over and over again.

"Kneel up and talk to me," I said. "I unseal your lips." I took out a lace handkerchief and wiped her face. She had the palest cheeks, and her large drowsy gray eyes burned bright through her smoky eyelashes. Why her hair was silver I had no idea, except that there are people in this world who have this kind of hair, white or silver from an early age, and they are often exceptionally beautiful.

"Now tell me, do you love your master?" I said. "I want to know your secret soul."

"Oh, yes, Lady Eva," she said breathlessly. "I never knew such happiness at Court." And then she let it all slip out again. "I don't care if the Queen never calls me back to the castle. Please, you must let me remain here. I don't want the Queen to come back."

I cradled her bowed head in my hands. "What am I going to have to do, whip you myself here and now? I would never have unsealed your lips if I'd known you were so foolish, so disobedient. You know what is permitted and what is not permitted," I said. "The Queen decides where slaves live and whom they serve. You can reveal your soul to me with a wiser choice of words, you know that!" I lifted her chin. She bit her lip despairingly as she looked at me. I winked at her. "I'll do everything," I whispered, "to see you remain with Tristan."

She flung her arms around me and I allowed it, pressing her lips against my sex which I felt keenly in spite of the thick fabric of my gown.

I gestured for her to rise and I wrapped my arms around her, kissing her deeply. Not all slaves know how to kiss. Some of the most subservient and finely trained simply never acquire the knack of kissing. But Blanche knew how to kiss.

I could feel my own nipples hardening inside my gown and my own sex growing moist. But I couldn't pull away from her. I covered her eyes with my kisses, licking at her salty tears.

"But Lady Eva, why does the Queen stay away so long?" she whispered in my ear. "There is talk. Slaves are afraid."

"Tell me what they say," I coaxed. I smoothed her hair back from her forehead.

"A small group of punished slaves from the village were brought here yesterday by Captain Gordon—to work in my master's garden. Three women and two men. I don't remember their names. At feeding time, they were whispering fearfully that the Queen was sorely missed, that even Captain Gordon and Lady Julia could not keep the village entirely in order in the Queen's absence. They speak of the Queen no longer loving the kingdom. They speak of the Queen abandoning our servitude."

"That's idle foolishness." I sighed. "I'm not surprised, however, that they talk of such things. They miss the Queen's presence even though they seldom ever caught a glimpse of her. Well, I've spent the day in the village. I had at least thirty slaves soundly spanked on the Public Turntable. And I went through the pony stables inspecting every pony for myself. All is well. I suspect those grumbling slaves will sleep well tonight . . . or for the time being. But surely everything will be better when the Queen returns."

"Yes, if she allows me to remain with Prince Tristan," she ventured as she kissed my cheek. "Beautiful Lady Eva," she said.

"Manners, my girl," I said. I pressed my finger to her lips. "I assure you, when the Queen returns, I'll do all in my power to make sure you remain with Tristan. Now repeat that to no one, not even your master, and when he punishes you tonight, if he gives you leave to speak, be contrite for your outbursts."

She nodded gratefully and opened her tender mouth for me to kiss her again, which I did. "But now you let me go, you vixen," I said. "You're too sweet and I'm too tired and must go back to the castle."

I squeezed her warm bottom hard and felt her sigh against me. How hot the flesh was, how deliciously hot.

"Yes, Lady Eva," she said. And I allowed myself one last slow and deep kiss.

ii

It was a short ride to the castle, on a narrow winding road that skirted the Queen's Village. The full moon made the homeward journey all the more easy. And tired as I was, I was glad that I'd seen Tristan.

Tristan had been brought to the kingdom decades ago as a young royal naked slave, and all knew the story. The Queen demanded such tributes from all her allies, and many other realms sent their spoilt and unruly royal young ones to serve the Queen as a matter of course, welcoming the enhancement of their young rebels by their strict pleasure training, and the gold purse that always accompanied the return of such slaves to their homeland. Some noble families did the very same thing, but the majority of slaves were princes and princesses. Oh, what I would give to have seen Tristan then, handsome Tristan, naked and standing ready for service.

But I had not yet been born when Tristan was first enslaved. I was twenty years old now, and it was difficult to grasp that he, with his boyish smile and innocent blue eyes, was actually forty. His story was well known to me.

He'd proved rebellious with his young master, Lord Stefan, the Queen's cousin—a former lover who could not master him—and been packed off to the Queen's Village for harsh punishment for his disobedience. There he'd been bought and trained as a pony boy by my uncle Nicholas, the Queen's Chronicler. Uncle Nicholas had loved Tristan. And all might have gone well from that time onward, given Nicholas's penchant for taming those he loved, if soldiers of the Sultan hadn't raided the kingdom, kidnapping some of the finest slaves for the sultanate.

Tristan had been one of those taken off with the famous princesses Beauty and Rosalynd and Elena and Princes Laurent and Dmitri.

Now the Sultan, long gone from the world, had been a close ally of Queen Eleanor. Her ancestors and his had started the custom of naked pleasure slavery over a century before that time. But in Queen Eleanor's realm it had fallen into decline, and when she mounted the throne, emissaries from the Sultan had come to help the Queen revive it and make Bellavalten once more the talk of the world.

Occasional slave raids were part of a game played by the Queen and the Sultan from time to time. And any slave of Bellavalten learned much under the customs of the Sultan's pleasure gardens. So nobody would have thought much of this latest raid had not it ensnared the fabled Sleeping Beauty. Her parents demanded that Queen Eleanor rescue their daughter and return her to them at once. Servitude to the Queen and her son, the Crown Prince, they could approve but not the loss of Princess Beauty to a foreign lord.

So Captain Gordon was sent with a few handpicked soldiers to reclaim Beauty and what other slaves he might rescue easily with her. Alas, scandal followed. Beauty, and her companions Tristan and Laurent, had not wanted to be brought back; indeed the three of them had fussed, rebelled, and all but kicked and screamed as they were recaptured.

And the beautiful and irresistible Laurent, one of the worst of the rebels, had even been so bold as to kidnap one of the Sultan's most devoted stewards, Lexius, and insist that Captain Gordon bring him back as a trophy to serve Queen Eleanor.

Queen Eleanor had been furious with her recalcitrant brats. Beauty she could not punish further, as she was at once freed to go home to her parents' kingdom. But Laurent and Tristan the Queen condemned to a year in the village stables—to the hardest labor a slave can know: perpetual servitude as a pony. As for the mysterious and seductive Lexius, the Queen was outraged that any slave should presume to offer himself to her as Lexius proceeded to do. Yet she had relented, later making him a favorite as dear to her as her own Prince Alexi, whom she'd famously broken in harsh ways.

Before the end of that year, Laurent had been freed due to the death of his father. Home he had gone to become the King of his realm, and no sooner had he received the crown than he had ridden out to the home of Princess Beauty, who had served naked beside him under Queen Eleanor, to make Beauty his queen.

Ah, it had been another great scandal in Bellavalten as word spread that two former naked slaves were now married and ruling the most powerful house in Europe. Queen Eleanor had thought them brazen and disgraceful, but what could she do? King Laurent was a proud and able ally; and Queen Beauty became the jewel of his Court.

"I will not tolerate talk of them ever," the Queen had famously declared, "and their names must never be mentioned to me." Royal slaves, when freed by her, should return with heads bowed to their kingdoms, never speaking of their naked servitude in her opinion, quick to slip into the demands of royal life. But here were a pair of legendary incorrigibles married to each other and presiding over a glamorous kingdom.

My uncle Nicholas told me that the story of King Laurent and Queen Beauty had not been easy to suppress. Indeed, it spread wildly amongst the slaves of the castle and the village who were heard to comment that it served Queen Eleanor's son, the Crown Prince, right for bringing the awakened Sleeping Beauty here as a slave in the first place and not making her his bride.

Cursed by a wise woman to sleep for a hundred years with her entire family and Court, Princess Beauty had been awakened by the kiss of the Crown Prince—who had brought Beauty naked and submissive to his mother's feet.

The Queen had boldly disregarded the legend, and her son's remarkable achievement, treating Beauty like any other abject erotic toy of the Court, and exiling her to the village for her first real disobedience.

But once King Laurent had taken Beauty as his bride, the Queen sang another song. "If anyone should be the husband of the wench," said the Queen, "it should be my son, not that impudent and unruly Laurent. How did such a thing ever happen with those two disobedient and rebellious slaves! I tell you I am confounded."

"And Laurent was such a handsome prince," my uncle Nicholas told me. "You cannot imagine. Laurent was brown haired, brown eyed, amazingly tall and strong, with features molded by the gods, perhaps one of the most impressive slaves ever to serve at the castle. Lady Elvera was his mistress. Every day she whipped him. Every day she set him to taking two or three princesses in her presence for her delight. He was tireless. His cock was enormous. And when he ran away only to be condemned to the village it was out of boredom. That's what these slaves do, you see, and the Queen never caught on. They pick and choose what they will do and where; and the Queen simply doesn't understand it. She doesn't understand the allure of different punishments for different slaves, or the allure of different masters and mistresses, and that clever slaves have always had ways of defeating her for their own amusement."

This was true. Queen Eleanor did imagine herself always to be in full control. I had seen this as soon as I'd arrived. Old Lord Gregory, the Queen's venerable minister of slaves, fell into the very same error. And so had some of the more rigid and scolding squires and pages, and members of the Court.

Whatever the case, the Crown Prince had never married. It was said he hated his mother for not allowing him to wed the Sleeping Beauty. But that seemed hardly fair. He'd stripped her naked and brought her barefoot and trembling into the kingdom. What had he expected his mother to think or do?

But King Laurent and Queen Beauty had passed out of the Queen's clutches and into history. And there was nothing to be done.

King Laurent and Queen Beauty had gone on to rule for twenty years of unparalleled prosperity until a year and a half ago when, placing the crown upon the head of their beloved son, Alcuin, they had retired to a southern land to live in seclusion.

Queen Eleanor had heard the news as she and her son were preparing for a sea voyage. I had only just been chosen to be head mistress of all slaves in her absence.

"I wonder why the famous pair have retired," she asked. "And whether or not they will come here soon for a visit. Now that young King Alcuin rules in his native land, what will Beauty and Laurent, both in the prime of life, do with themselves?" The Queen had looked at me with her sharp, cruel black eyes. "Do you think they ever speak of their time together here?"

The following day she went on to declare, "You know, Eva, that I had hoped, well, hoped that someday those two—Laurent and Beauty— might come to live at Court here, and inaugurate a new era."

The Crown Prince had been shocked. "What's wrong with things the way they are!" he had demanded.

"Nothing," said Queen Eleanor, "except I'm tired of them and so are you. Just think how very pleasant it would be to give the entire kingdom over to those two and be done with it. I have achieved a great thing here with pleasure slavery, yes, as my ancestors did before me, and as the

Sultan had done in his land before his unfortunate ruin . . . but I am weary of managing anything."

The Crown Prince had grumbled. He'd told Lord Gregory, the elderly minister of slaves, to be ever more strict, charged me to do the same, and then gone to make certain his trunks had been packed properly.

And then they had headed for the coast.

But not before the Queen had given me a sealed letter. "If some misfortune should befall us, Eva, you are to open this," she'd said. And with a cold kiss, she walked out of the castle and towards her waiting coach.

I'd been only too glad to accept the responsibilities given me. I had a knack for governing naked slaves, both male and female, and had used it well since my arrival. By the hour, I'd read my uncle Nicholas's *Chronicles of the Kingdom* and knew the stories of many slaves and how they had been broken and trained and how they had loved and wept when forced to return to the "outside world," as my uncle called it.

I understood slaves. I loved studying them and disciplining them and wringing from each a perfection that the slave had thought impossible. I had a great gift for it. I found their most subtle responses fascinating, and I was thrilled by the endless variety and freshness surrounding me as I wandered the castle corridors and gardens.

At night on my pillow I sometimes dreamed of King Laurent and Queen Beauty; what had they truly been like in their naked servitude?— the King so strong and spirited, and Beauty with her fabled flaxen hair and blue eyes, a dainty slave admired by all? And I dreamed of Tristan too, Tristan who had spent most of his life here.

Of course there had been a time when Tristan did go into the outside world. He'd served out his year as pony in the village as punishment for his disobedience when rescued from the Sultan's palace.

But his family had called him home not long after Laurent was called home. Tristan's older brother the King had been killed abroad in a battle. And Tristan had to take the crown. Such was the way of the world. He had not protested.

Yet three years later, when Tristan's brother had returned much to the surprise and happiness of the family, Tristan had traveled night and day to return to Bellavalten.

It was no longer meet that he should be a naked pleasure slave, of course. Queen Eleanor would not hear of it. And Tristan did not ask for such a thing. But yes, he could restore and outfit the manor house he'd purchased and lodge there with Uncle Nicholas and Aunt Julia. And he might have as many naked slaves as he wished. Queen Eleanor welcomed him as a shining member of her Court. And the Queen's cousins—Lord Stefan, Lord William—and her uncle, the Grand Duke André, were glad to have Tristan in the inner circle.

After all, it was common for royal slaves to become members of the Court in later years. Princesses Rosalynd, Lucinda, and Lynette had all been slaves long years ago and they made up proud and beautiful members of the bored contingent of ladies-in-waiting gathered with their embroidery around an empty throne in the great hall of the castle. From my uncle's pages, I knew their stories, and those of others too numerous to name.

And Prince Alexi, a favorite of the Queen long years ago, had only lately returned, welcomed by the Queen only six months before she'd left. He'd been very happy to rejoin the Court and the royal cousins.

"Is it so surprising that they come back?" my aunt Julia had whispered. "They were happy here when they were nude playthings. And those who've been trained often make the finest trainers." My aunt now ruled the Queen's Village as ably as any male mayor ever had. "I knew," she said, "that Queen Eleanor would forgive Prince Alexi any old offense and allow him to stay." There was some story there which she did not confide.

But she and Prince Alexi often walked out in the evenings together, talking of old times, apparently. Prince Alexi had auburn hair, and small delicate features and dark skin, and what a beauty he was now, as handsome as he'd ever been, said my aunt, who remembered him well as the Queen's favorite. "How she punished him night and day. But then there were rumors . . . and tales . . . but then we can't talk of those things."

Something there that none would confide about Prince Alexi befriending the mysterious Lexius, the steward of the Sultan brought back by King Laurent as a slave, something about Lexius and Alexi displeasing the Queen, but try as I might, I could never get the full story.

And now my uncle was gone wandering the world, and the Queen and the Crown Prince were beyond reach, and I dared not ask Prince Tristan to let me see the *Chronicles of the Kingdom,* which Nicholas had shared with me when I was a girl.

Prince Alexi was still boyishly handsome, with smooth dark skin and quick dark eyes, and an easy laugh, but I found him strangely provocative.

Never did he smile at me without my thinking he wanted me to be his mistress, wanted me perhaps to strip off his fine velvet and gold braid, and smack him hard with my belt. He had a way of lowering his eyelids and looking up at me even though he was taller than me, which many former slaves possess. And when our hands now and then touched, I felt a great shock over all my skin as if he were sculptured from sizzling fire.

One could never know quite what was up with the former slaves who came back to Court.

Had Tristan been the secret slave of my uncle Nicholas behind closed doors in the manor house? And what about Lord Stefan, the Queen's cousin—the indecisive one who had failed to master Tristan years and years ago, prompting Tristan to run away? Lord Stefan had always been here, but how afraid he seemed of his quiet blond-haired slave, Becca, as if she held some secret and immeasurable power over him. I'd caught a glimpse of them in the Goddess Grove one afternoon, that old neglected garden on the western side of the castle that the Queen ignored.

It was late afternoon, and so quiet I could hear only the birds singing. And I'd come upon them in the high grass, the naked Becca with her long flaxen locks straddling the fully clothed lord who lay thrusting and twisting on his back, her oval face upturned and her cold blue eyes on the sky, whispering as she rode his cock, "You will come when I say you can come, and not before! Do you dare to disobey me?"

I had hurried away. The old neglected Goddess Grove had always seemed a haunted place with its vine-covered marble statues and broken arches. And I avoided it after that. Such a shame, for it could have been a beautiful place.

But I had more than ever the sense of the torment of those finely dressed lords and ladies who longed to serve with the abandon of the naked slaves but weren't permitted to do so. As for Becca, she often spanked other slaves for Lord Stefan's amusement. And it seemed it was Becca who picked the slaves Lord Stefan drove with his paddle along the Bridle Path. Did Becca ever shed a tear? No, nor did she ever look unhappy. And it seemed to me that even the elderly Lord Gregory, the archdisciplinarian of slaves, avoided her. I'd been tempted to borrow Becca of an evening for my own amusement. But why disturb what is best left alone?

And now in the Queen's absence all struggled for some day-to-day equilibrium.

iii

It was full dark when I reached the castle, and I hoped to reach my quarters without any further interruption. But I found Prince Alexi outside my door.

His youthful face was contorted with pain, and even in the feeble light from the small lamp in his hand, I could see he'd been weeping.

"What is it?" I asked. I unlocked the door, and putting my arm around him, I drew him into my parlor.

The fire had been started by my devoted slave, Severin, and the candles on the table had been lighted as well. I took the lamp from Alexi's hand and set it on the sideboard. He looked utterly lost.

"Come, sit down, talk to me," I said.

"Eva, this is unspeakable . . . ," he said, shaking his head. He drew a stiff parchment letter out of his velvet doublet. "The Queen . . ." and then he broke off, unable to continue.

At once, I opened the letter and read it.

It had been posted from a distant city in the south seas, and was addressed to the Grand Duke André, uncle of Queen Eleanor. The writing was clear and official.

"It is our sad duty to inform you that your sovereign, Queen Eleanor, and her son, the Crown Prince, are indeed dead, and the search for the wreckage of their vessel has been called off, as their bodies have washed up on our shores, along with several other bodies from the unfortunate vessel and all hope is lost . . ."

The letter went on and on as to the identification of the bodies and that of others, and there was a brief description of the storm in which the ship had been lost. Two early survivors of the disaster, Princess Lynette and Prince Jeremy, who'd been traveling with the Queen, were on the way back to the kingdom now.

Alexi sat with his face in his hands, weeping softly, his auburn hair hanging down over his eyes.

I pondered what I'd always known of him, how he'd been the Queen's favorite slave for so many years, and how he'd somehow displeased her in the end. This was not the time to ask for that story.

"Who else knows about this?" I asked.

"They all know—André, William, and Stefan. They've sent me to you. None of them is fit to take the reins of this kingdom. None of them is willing! As soon as the slaves find out there will be panic. You don't know how many dread the day they'll be sent home free to their families."

"Yes, I do," I said softly.

I looked up. The Grand Duke André was standing in the open door. He was not an old man, though he was the Queen's uncle, and his hair was still jet black for the most part and his rectangular face was still handsome.

"Lady Eva, what are we to do?" he asked. His voice was ragged with emotion.

I rose at once and invited him to take a chair between mine and that of Alexi. And quietly I went to my desk near the window.

There was a lighted candle there as it was often my habit to read or write late into the night, and Severin had set out my ink and quill pens and parchment.

I unlocked a small gold casket that sat on the desk, and I removed from it the sealed letter which Queen Eleanor had given me on that last day before her departure.

I came back to the table and sat down without asking the bereaved Duke's permission. He didn't care. He was comforting Prince Alexi.

"It is the end of our world," said the Duke softly now as he looked at me. He did not resemble the Queen, but he had the same black eyes, which often appeared as cold as her eyes, though they did not now. His heavily lined face was wet from his tears.

"I fear you're right," Prince Alexi answered. And he took the Duke's right hand in his and clasped it. "Bellavalten cannot survive without our gracious Eleanor."

I looked down at the letter in my hand. It was addressed in bold and beautiful script to me with the notation "In the Event of My Death."

I showed it to both gentlemen. The Grand Duke had never learned to read or write, but Prince Alexi was well educated. After they had taken notice, I broke the seal and tore open the letter.

My beloved Eva,

You have been a great consolation to me since your arrival for you have a passion for the realm which I myself have lost. I am well aware that our custom of pleasure slavery is now the vital heart of the kingdom. The visitors whose gold fills our coffers daily come here to see and live amid the spectacle of our well-trained and beautiful slaves. Indeed, many of our finest townsmen, scholars, scribes, craftsmen, and weavers might desert us if deprived of their naked slaves. Our soldiers would likely desert, and even the lowliest of our common people might wander beyond our borders if the old customs which distinguish our realm from all others were abandoned. Even my own great wealth would not sustain the kingdom in such a decline. Therefore, let us pray that I will return from this journey with a new sense of purpose and regard for those dependent on me.

But should I not return, should some accident befall me and my son during our trip, it is my wish that you present this letter, carefully written in my own hand, to my beloved uncle and cousins.

It is my wish that our ways not perish, and that before they abandon Bellavalten to her ever voracious allies and neighbors, they approach King Laurent and Queen Beauty with an offer of the crown and the scepter. If King Laurent and Queen Beauty will honor the custom of pleasure slavery as I have established it, if they will preserve my realm according to those precepts and customs which have made it famous throughout the world and even to the shores of unknown lands, I bequeath to them all my wealth, my property, my castle and my manor houses, my lands, and my entire kingdom.

Eva, I solemnly charge you to approach King Laurent and Queen Beauty yourself, and implore them to take the reins of Bellavalten. And I solemnly charge all my family and all my Court to prevail upon them to accept full authority and to make them welcome.

Only a monarch who has known the wisdom and pleasure of naked erotic servitude in Bellavalten can know the full worth of the laws of our realm. In Laurent and Beauty we have two such monarchs. And it is my hope that they will take the kingdom in hand for the benefit of all who live in it and more—that they may have a fresh view for its continuing prosperity. I am convinced that they will not accept this inheritance if they have no such vision. They are too honorable for that, and too rich to be tempted by wealth alone. On the contrary, it is my belief that Laurent and Beauty have together the force to set a future course for Bellavalten.

If this is not to be, then I leave it to my heirs to disburse the lands and wealth of Bellavalten for their own benefit. All slaves must be freed at once and sent away with appropriate rewards. And Bella-valten shall fade from history as mysteriously perhaps as it long ago entered the written record.

I laid the letter down on the table.

There followed on a second page a long list of plainly small bequests to be made in the event of the Queen's death, but that could all be read later.

And there was her unmistakable signature and her seal.

I looked up into the eyes of Prince Alexi, and then at the Grand Duke.

"You must go to them," said Alexi. "This is our only hope. Eva, you must go, and I will go with you! I remember Laurent well. I remember Beauty!"

"Do you think they could be persuaded?" asked the Grand Duke. "King Laurent is famous for his conquests on land and sea. Why, he's a tireless soldier. Half the world is afraid of him, and half the world is in love with him. Frankly, he made me shiver even when he was a . . . a naked . . . a slave."

"Yes, but the great king is retired now," I said, "weary of war, as all know, having given over his crown to his son!"

"Ah, yes. . . ." The Duke sighed. "There is hope."

"And I've seen King Laurent once or twice in the last ten years," said Alexi eagerly. "Admittedly it was brief, and at a tiresome Court affair in this or that place. We talked for only a few moments. But I know how well he and his queen remember their service here. At least I know how he remembers it. There was something unspoken between us. I wager they've never lied to themselves about how it was." He was becoming ever more hopeful.

"Call Lady Elvera," said the Grand Duke. "She too must go. She was Laurent's mistress. He'll listen to her. And Captain Gordon, he too must go."

Lady Elvera. She was a cold one, very severe, who punished her slaves through aloofness and calculated indifference. And Laurent had served her for two full years before rebelling and having himself exiled to the village.

"What if the King remembers Lady Elvera with resentment?" I asked.

Alexi had to stop himself from laughing out loud.

"He adored her," he said. "He became bored, that's all. Trust me." He leaned forward as if to confide. "He's wined and dined her since at his Court. And laughed about the past. That was about ten years ago. But Eva, I'm surprised at you. You of all people should know the enduring bond that exists between a true mistress and a true slave."

I put up my hand for silence.

"Very well. I ask that you both go to Lady Elvera, and send word to Tristan and summon the Captain of the Guard. But you must, all of you, keep this information from everyone else. No one must know of this calamity until we have King Laurent and Queen Beauty's decision."

"Agreed," said the Grand Duke. "The slaves mustn't hear a word of this, or the people either."

"And no one here at Court must know," I said. "And, Your Excellency, kindly wake your secretaries. We will need appropriate letters and documents for safe travel."

"Ah, I didn't even think of it," said the Duke. "Eva, you think of everything."

I thought to myself, I know, but I didn't reply.

As soon as they had left me, I went into the bedchamber to find that my slave, Severin, had obviously been listening at the door. I slapped him hard for his impertinence. But he'd been weeping and he scarcely cared.

"Lady Eva," he said, kneeling before me with his arms around my skirts, "I can't be sent home. I can't. I'd rather die."

"Oh, do be quiet," I said. "I haven't time to whip you now. Pack my trunks at once, and go to the master of the common wardrobe and obtain clothes for yourself for the journey. You can't very well travel naked. Now hurry!"

"Clothes?" he fussed. "I have to wear clothes?" He was such a pretty boy, with golden ringlets and sweet gray eyes.

But this was the limit. I dragged him to the nearby chair, sat down, and threw him over my knee and spanked him hard until I was tired of it. "And this is just a taste," I said. "When we're packed and ready, I intend to whip you so soundly you'll be sore for the entire journey, and in any inn where we stop, I'll whip you again and likely invite any innkeeper along the way to share the pleasure of same. As for your cock, I'll starve it for the entire journey. Now go!"

2

LAURENT:
BEHOLD SHE
SLEEPS AGAIN

More often than not, my beloved Beauty was like that, sleeping, sleeping as if she'd never wake. This time it was in that bower in the garden, her bed of silk and lace surrounded by fragrant and nodding flowers, her head to one side on the pale rose-colored pillow, a tapestried cover laid carelessly over her, her mouth still.

Had she looked like this when she'd been the Sleeping Beauty of fable?

All knew the old story. When Beauty had been born, the immortal wise women—or fairies—of the kingdom had been invited to celebrate her birth. Each wise woman had offered the baby girl a precious gift—beauty, wit, wisdom, talent, or so the tale went. But one wise woman, overlooked by the King and Queen, came only to curse the infant, predicting that she would someday prick her finger on a spindle and fall into a deathlike sleep—along with the entire Court. Not to be outdone, yet another fairy came who had pity for the tiny girl in her crib.

"Yes, she will sleep for a hundred years," said this wise fairy, "but a prince will come to awaken her with his kiss. She will rise from her slumber, along with the King and Queen and all the residents of the castle. And the spell will be at an end."

Was it a true story? How could I ever know? But I did know that a prince had indeed awakened Beauty from a long slumber, and he had been the son of the powerful Queen Eleanor of Bellavalten, and he had claimed Beauty as his naked pleasure slave, taking her to his mother's Court.

Now why had he awakened her and not me? And why had he long ago passed out of her life, while Beauty had become my happy and contented wife of twenty years?

I wondered if she was still happy and contented, or had that not become a fable too.

She'd sleep like this until evening when I went to waken her—I, Laurent, her king—and to tell her it was time for us to dine together, and maybe after our lovemaking, she'd fall asleep again, into those dreams where I couldn't follow. Beauty, my Beauty, my love.

She was bored. I knew it. Because I myself was bored and found our little retreat here so deadly dull. What had prompted us to choose this path—to leave behind the duties of our royal house, to place the crown upon the head of our young son, Alcuin, and establish him with his sweet queen in charge of the land we'd ruled for twenty years? We were tired of it, that was the reason we'd left it. We were glad to send our daughter, Alcuin's twin sister Arabella, to rule in the land of Beauty's late father, wife to a cousin chosen there to be the new king.

And I was tired of battles on land and on sea, mostly sought for adventure, and of the endless rituals of Court life. Let the younger ones take over. Give the young king the scepter. We'd left the coffers overflowing with gold, and yet taken a fortune with us to secure this fine palace of sorts and this gentle coast.

Twenty years was enough, was it not?

But what were we to do with ourselves now, other than wander this sumptuous residence and these colorful and splendid gardens, and welcome the very occasional guest who came to disturb our retreat? The King and Queen of nothing.

I sat at the window, my elbows on the stone sill looking down on her as she lay there in the garden bower, her lady-in-waiting sewing beneath the nearby pear tree, and my queen not even stirring in her deathlike sleep.

Was she slipping back into enchantment because she had married the wrong prince? I'd been a pleasure slave for years in Queen Eleanor's kingdom when Beauty was brought there.

I'd never quite believed the old legend about her. All I knew was that she was indeed beautiful, as dazzling a pleasure slave as any naked and voluptuous princess I'd ever furtively beheld during my sensuous captivity, and when she was sent home I grieved. When finally, I'd been set free to return to my own kingdom, I'd sought her out in her father's house, and married her and brought her to my royal house to rule beside me, my splendid queen.

The secret memories of Queen Eleanor's pleasure gardens united us; we'd whispered on the pillow of those times—of lush bondage and titillating punishments, of gilded paddles and straps, and delicious rebellion, of stolen kisses our cruel masters and mistresses did not see. I was Beauty's master always; and she was my mistress. There were times when her deft and delicate little fingers tortured me as surely as my firm hands tortured her. But did we ever speak freely in all these years of how we'd loved it, those glorious days of true and inescapable servitude, of sublime nakedness and utter submission, of luxuriant humiliation and sweet shame?

I couldn't fathom it.

More and more of late, I found myself thinking of Bellavalten.

Did I actually long for the realm of Queen Eleanor? Was it something I could not admit? I pondered this a lot lately, and why not, because I had absolutely nothing else to do.

It was the loveliest of spring days, the sky a featureless blue above the fruit trees, and, beyond the battlements below me, the endless sparkling sea. The faintest breeze stirred the old orchards, a breeze that cooled my face and my hands at the window, a breeze that refreshed me only to wonder how I might while away these hours until I might wake her, and tell her, yes, time for us to sup once more before the fire.

I was falling asleep.

I made my way to the bed and collapsed there, turning over on my back, my eyes closing as if I had no control. It seemed I felt and heard the breeze but little else was real to me, and I sank down deep towards sleep with bits and pieces of thought traveling like leaves on the breeze through my mind.

I felt lips touch mine. I felt a hand on my forehead.

At once, I opened my eyes. The world was dark around me, and I could see a sky of endless stars. I scrambled to my feet, but couldn't see where it was that I was standing. The bed was gone, the room was gone, and the darkness around me seemed alive. The figure of a woman rose before me, blazing yet indistinct, suffused with an unnatural light.

It seemed she stood right in front of me suddenly—immense, overwhelming, and magnificent.

"Laurent," she said. Her words flowed slowly and smoothly with a palpable resolution and calm. "You were the one intended all along. Long years ago when my sister cursed little Beauty at her birth to fall into enchanted sleep for a hundred years, it was you whom I chose from the great future for this sweet princess, this tender innocent, whom I would not suffer to sleep forever. It is by my will that she belongs to you and you belong to her as it is now."

I was stunned yet thrilled. My heart was skipping.

I wanted to ask a multitude of questions. The darkness shrouding the woman's image was filled with the roiling motion of smoke. Her shining face was smiling yet indistinct. A vague and enchanting perfume distracted me. I felt her finger against my lips as she continued:

"You were imprisoned in Queen Eleanor's kingdom, were you not, when the time came for the awakening of my charge. And so the Crown Prince became my unwitting instrument to bring your princess to you in the land where you were held hostage, unable to go to her. Defenseless and given over to your servitude, you found each other irresistible as I knew that you would. Slaves together you loved. Free together you married. And trust in me, my king, that a new adventure awaits you both."

For one split second, the figure of the woman blazed brighter and more vivid. I saw her shimmering hair, her translucent veils. Her eyes burned through the clearing mist and she spoke again even more distinctly.

"Fear not. Your lovely queen will waken soon to a new destiny just as you will, and those voluptuous embraces of long ago, stolen from your captors, will be yours again. Bellavalten where you first set eyes upon each other has always been your destiny and will open its gates to you this very day. You must be brave, my beloved king, and trust in the love and bravery of your queen. Remember this. Trust in the bravery of your queen, as you trust in your own bravery. You both must have courage to know once more the freedom and abandon you knew long years ago when you were both enchained."

The figure faded. Again, I tried to speak, tried to see clearly, but the image of the woman was dissolving, the darkness thickening, as if smoke could become the boiling waters of a roaring sea. The light flashed and dimmed. Indeed I heard the very sound of crashing waves. I found myself sinking, turning, falling, and with a start I awoke in my own chamber and on my bed.

I was shaken. Everything about me appeared real and solid. Yet the dream had been real as well. "Bellavalten," I said aloud. It had been so many years since I'd even whispered aloud the name of Queen Eleanor's realm. What in the world could this vision mean?

Only gradually did I realize that someone was knocking hard at my door.

I got up, straightened my rumpled clothes, and turned the knob.

There stood my secretary, Emlin, a young but very capable man, obviously terrified that he'd displeased me by pounding on the door.

"I did tell you not to disturb me for anything, did I not?" I said gently. It was never necessary to be cruel with Emlin.

He held out a letter for me, dripping with ribbons from its wax seals.

I was dazed. I couldn't think. I stared at the letter. I kept hearing the voice of the dream woman. I shuddered.

"Sire, you must forgive me," Emlin said. "Your old ally and friend, Queen Eleanor, has been drowned at sea. Her son was drowned with her, and this is an urgent letter from the Queen's Court begging for your immediate attention. It's been brought here by a Lady Eva who waits below with the Captain of the Queen's Guard for you in the great hall. There is also a Lady Elvera in attendance. And two princes, sire, Alexi and Tristan, who say they are your old friends. All beg that you forgive them for journeying here unannounced."

I was amazed.

I found myself turning around and staring at the empty bedchamber as if I expected to see the magical woman who had only just been talking to me. *Remember this.* For one second, I thought I heard her laugh. I stared stupidly at the letter again and then finally I took it from Emlin's trembling hand.

"Died at sea, have they?" I murmured.

And Lady Elvera, of all people, had come here, the woman I'd served in Eleanor's old Court, the woman who'd many a time . . . I was blushing at the thought of it, of myself down on my knees, naked, abject, kissing her slippers. Of course I'd seen her in the past years, entertained her in our old Court. So formal all of it, so stiff, until we'd been very drunk and alone to laugh together. But even then we had not really spoken freely, but merely through vague allusions and little jokes understood only by the two of us. And now she was here on the official business of Bellavalten!

Remember this. Trust in the bravery of your queen, as you trust in your own bravery.

I laughed. I couldn't help it. So she was here, was she? And the others were here, my fellow slaves! I felt a strange pringling all over the surface of my skin and a stirring between my legs. I heard the crack of the paddle, the smack of the strap. I saw the magnificent Lady Elvera again as she'd been when I first knelt before her, and heard her words as if she were whispering them again in my ear. I saw them all, it seemed, the merciless masters and mistresses of the castle and the Queen's Village.

I tried to stifle my laughter.

"Well, go and serve them food and drink at once," I said.

"Done, Your Majesty," said Emlin. "The Captain of the Queen's Guard begs you to remember him."

"Does he?" I asked, unrolling the parchment. As if I could ever forget him. Oh, I almost laughed recalling the times I'd had with the Captain of the Queen's Guard in Queen Eleanor's realm, and to think he was here, that robust and commanding individual who'd often disciplined me and scolded me and threatened me as he had the most abject of his slaves.

I opened the letter, passing rapidly over all the titles and blandishments to the heart of the matter . . .

". . . our fervent hope that you and your beloved Queen Beauty may consent to receive and rule the kingdom as Queen Eleanor long ago decreed."

I took a deep breath.

"Wake my beloved below," I said to Emlin. "Bring her to me. And tell my guests that we will attend them shortly. They're most welcome under our roof."

My pulse was throbbing. In a jarring flash I saw the mysterious female figure once more and heard her voice. Then she was gone.

I looked again at the letter. ". . . that surely you will preserve the custom of naked pleasure slavery which has made the kingdom a legend throughout the world."

3
BEAUTY:
TO RULE OR
NOT
TO RULE?

Dusk. Beauty had dressed hastily, and there had been no time for her to confide in Laurent about the strange dream she'd had when she was sleeping in the garden. She sat beside the King now listening as the others spoke. What an extraordinary moment this was for her.

Queen Eleanor's letter lay before them all, and in a low but insistent voice Prince Alexi spoke of how the wealth of the late queen and all her power were theirs to claim, if only they would retain the famous customs of Bellavalten. Every syllable from his lips brought back warm memories to Beauty, as did the mere sight of his comely face and his dark, entrancing eyes. It was a pleasure to see Alexi clothed and in full possession of the honors bestowed on him by his birth and heritage. But what were these, she thought, compared to the gift he'd possessed as a naked slave who'd once taken her in his arms in secret?

The presence of all these strange guests filled Beauty with a faint and pleasurable confusion. Captain Gordon, commander of the Queen's Guard, was as alluring as she remembered—his blond hair flecked only here and there with silver, and his quick blue eyes filled with a quiet good humor. How many times had she coupled with him? She couldn't remember. And how many times had he whipped her with delicious precision? She

27

could not remember that either. But it seemed her heart remembered for she could feel it racing.

As for Prince Alexi, who continued to speak, she had never for a second forgotten their one night of stolen pleasure in the closets of the sleeping Queen Eleanor. How she'd melted in his arms, charmed by his soft voice, and silken skin. She could scarcely suppress a faint smile as she studied him, studied his dark reddish hair, and his compact yet strong frame. Yes, he was richly attired, as were they all, but she saw him naked as she had long ago, the respectful and secretive slave of the late queen who seemed to enjoy his subjugation and his secret disobedience completely.

Laurent spoke, interrupting her reverie. As always, her beloved husband had an easy and agreeable air of command.

"And you, Lady Eva," Laurent asked, addressing the exquisite young woman who sat at his left, "have been in full command of the slaves for the last year?"

"Yes, Your Majesty," the woman answered, lowering her gaze deferentially, "but should you accept the crown, I am willing, as are all here, to bend to your will entirely—and to the will of your queen." She glanced at Beauty in the same shy manner.

And no doubt she has been very effective, Beauty thought, and all the more on account of her young age. Lady Eva had full wavy red hair and remarkably clear skin and a well-modeled face with rather luscious pink lips. Her breasts were large and well shaped beneath the silk of her simple gown, and her hands as she gestured were beguilingly graceful. No wonder Laurent was drinking her in with his eyes so boldly. Beauty smiled. Laurent was struggling with all his might not to stare shamelessly at Lady Eva's breasts.

"We place our greatest hope in you," the lady said. "And the royal family is entirely behind us."

Tristan, blond and beautiful Tristan, whom Beauty had so loved, was looking at her from across the table. And when Beauty looked at him now, he smiled without hesitation. There came to her a vivid flash of their time together, naked, their hands bound, in the crude cart that was taking rebellious slaves away from the castle and to hard servitude in the village. How it stirred her blood to remember those moments in which they'd managed to express their love while jostled and tormented among the small gaggle of prisoners! And then there had been that other time, that unworldly time, when, made the playthings of the Sultan's men, they had been pressed together to make love, their skin burnished with gold, and their lips and limbs hungering for each other.

Beauty felt a keen excitement she could not deny, and a little impatience that the same points were being circled again and again by those gathered at the table.

She lifted her hand for silence but didn't wait for Laurent to give her permission to speak.

"I understand the wishes of the late queen," Beauty said, her eyes fixing on Lady Eva who was the obvious leader of the party. "This is all completely clear. And I understand what you've said about Queen Eleanor and her son tiring of the old games, the old rules, yet not wanting to abolish them. And of course, if my lord, the King, accepts to rule Bellavalten we would do it to uphold the ways of pleasure servitude. But surely all of you must realize that we would undoubtedly bring our own refinements to the customs of the past. We would seek to make improvements."

Silence. Then it was Laurent who responded.

"Yes, surely that would be the case," he said as if he hadn't thought of it. He was trying not to smile as he glanced at Beauty and then back to the others. "After all, we would be your sovereigns, and having been slaves ourselves, we may advocate subtle changes with considerable enthusiasm."

"Oh, yes, this would be most welcome," Lady Eva responded. She looked directly at Beauty as she spoke. No fear in her whatsoever, Beauty noted. "But these would be improvements to what has always been so essential to our way of life, would they not?"

"Yes, Lady Eva," Beauty replied. "Improvements to what we all hold dear. Exactly." She looked from Lady Eva to Alexi. "It was my strong feeling years ago that the Queen did not fully understand her slaves, and that at times her slaves played games with her of which she was never aware."

Laurent laughed softly under his breath. Captain Gordon appeared shocked, and Lady Elvera, the most distant of all those in attendance, cold Lady Elvera who had once been Laurent's hard mistress at the castle, remained absolutely impassive.

An awkward pause, yes, and then Alexi spoke. "That's true," he said, looking from Laurent to Beauty. "That is very true. The Queen did not understand fully the personalities or the needs of her slaves, and she was often caught unawares by their conniving."

Lady Elvera looked away as if this were contemptible. Well, so be it, thought Beauty, but it is true.

"Precisely," said Laurent with his easy self-confidence. "We slaves who rebelled did so because we wanted to be sent to the village." He looked pointedly at Lady Elvera, but she did not respond to this. "And our mistresses and masters didn't seem willing to acknowledge that this was the case, as they refused to acknowledge so much else."

At last, a faint smile played on Lady Elvera's lips. And slowly she turned her frigid gaze on the King.

"Yes, Your Majesty," she said under her breath. "There were many things the Queen never understood. And old Lord Gregory—a gentleman who was old already when he was young—never fully understood the tricks played by slaves upon their betters either. And yes, my queen, I think I understand your meaning, when you speak of refinements, improvements. And both words suggest you are in tune with the spirit of the old ways perfectly."

The Captain of the Guard couldn't suppress a short muffled laugh.

"You have something to say, Captain?" asked Beauty. She was enjoying this more and more by the minute. "Speak up."

"Your Majesty," Captain Gordon replied. "We want with all our hearts for you to assume control of the kingdom. Of course you will inaugurate new rules. You will be our king and queen. No one knows better than . . ."

"Yes, Captain?" Beauty prompted. "No one knows better than we?"

"Yes, Your Majesty," he said. "No one knows better than you and King Laurent how vital the customs are and what can and cannot be done to improve them."

"Let me be blunt," said Lady Eva, who was clearly the bravest of the lot. "If Your Majesties do not accept the rule of the kingdom, the kingdom will perish. There will be no more pleasure slavery. And the land will be carved up by the kingdom's neighbors. We are more than willing to accept your complete authority! And as these letters show, so is the royal family."

All agreed to this, it was clear.

Tristan, who had been quiet all the while, spoke up. "Of course you will bring your own ideas to Bellavalten," he said with the air of one who had once been a king himself. "Fresh ideas, innovations, expansions of the old customs, what could be more welcome? This is precisely what the late queen hoped for. She'd lost all interest. She would have given you the kingdom herself while she was living if you had ever come to visit, because she knew that she and her son had nothing further to give to the realm. The kingdom has suffered for many years from her indifference. You'd be appalled if you knew. You knew it in its greatest time. It's been in a slow but steady decline for over a decade."

The others nodded to this.

Tristan went on. "We're eager for a new wind! What we ask is what all loyal subjects ask: that you rule with discretion and full resolution."

"Yes, precisely," said Prince Alexi in a more muted voice. "Discretion and resolution. But you know what it is we want to preserve here. You know! You know why we've come all this way. You know what our hopes are!"

Again all were nodding and murmuring in assent.

There it was again, thought Beauty, Tristan speaking for those who must serve as to the paramount importance of masters being masters, and Prince Alexi showing the old subtlety. How well she remembered Tristan's old story, of how he'd rebelled against the diffident Lord Stefan because Lord Stefan could not master him, and in the village Tristan had found the harsh punishments by Nicholas the Queen's Chronicler very much to his liking. He'd loved the sternness of Captain Gordon as well. And so had her beloved Laurent.

"Well, now, my lord," Beauty said, turning to Laurent. "Let us perhaps discuss this in the privacy of our quarters so as not to keep our honored guests in suspense any longer than necessary."

Laurent gave her the most confidential and amused look. But he rose at once, and all the others rose as well.

"Yes, my dear guests," Laurent said. "My queen and I will have an answer for you tomorrow, I promise you. Until then, please do enjoy whatever comforts we can offer you. But I ask that all of you remain ready to be summoned again by us at any time, singly or together, as we might require this for further discussion. We will not retire until quite late. And again, I assure you, we will have an answer one way or another tomorrow."

Within minutes, they were alone together behind their bedroom door, the vast chamber warmer than the great hall, and empty of all courtiers or servants.

Laurent at once took Beauty in his arms. She could see and feel that he was feverish with passion, his kisses bruising her lips as they hadn't

31

for some time. It took all her will to hold him off, her own blood heated as it was.

"Ah, but wait, Your Majesty," said Beauty, stepping back, trying not to be entranced by the impish smile on his lips. "You are passionate, of course, your usual vigorous self, I understand that. Seeing your old lovers has done its work with you, Laurent."

"Is that so surprising, and what about you?" Laurent said in a low voice, and immediately he kissed her again and again, his lips sucking the breath out of her, his powerful fingers closing on the back of her head, yet she pulled away, pulled away from him and from what she herself wanted to do with him, and she laid a hand firmly on his chest, though he towered over her.

"Yes, what about me, my lord, the very question," she responded, looking up into his playful dark eyes reprovingly.

"Well, what do you think?" asked Laurent. "Surely you're going to give me a quarter of an hour now in that bed before any intelligent discussion can take place! And to rule Bellavalten! Don't tell me you don't want it. I know you. I was watching you in the great hall. I know you in a way they can't know you. You want this, Beauty. Now, must I squeeze it out of you!"

"I want it and I know you want it," she said. "And I wish I had time to tell you of the strange dreams I've had of late, oh, I really do. Such dreams—that something like this was in the offing, so you would realize completely what this will mean for you and for me, for us as king and queen. But there isn't time for all that. However . . ."

"Dreams," murmured Laurent. "You talk of dreams."

"Yes, but I am pressing another point here if you will only listen."

Laurent stood quiet looking down at her. But the smile hadn't left his lips, and his brown eyes narrowed as if he were going to laugh again.

"Your Majesty, pay heed to what I'm saying," said Beauty firmly. "In all these years, I have belonged to you entirely and exclusively."

"Ah."

Beauty studied his face carefully. "I have never asked you what you did in foreign lands," she said gently, "or at sea, or after this or that battle, or even now and then in the bedchambers of our own kingdom. You are the King, yes, and kings will have their way as subjects well know, including that subject of the King who is the Queen. But don't you see? If we rule

Bellavalten, then I must have the very same prerogatives that you have always had. Laurent, that is the way of Bellavalten, that a woman may have what a man has, and men and women must serve men and women."

Laurent stood silent for a long moment. Then he nodded.

"I know," said Laurent softly. A bit of color flared in his cheeks. "Yes, how well I remember."

"And so if we take this step," Beauty said, "we take it together, and I shall rule beside you with all the prerogatives that you enjoy."

Laurent hesitated. Then he smiled again. "I realize this, Beauty," he said. "You will have your slaves, your days and nights of pleasure with them as freely as I will have mine, your days and nights of pleasure perhaps with those who are no longer slaves . . ." It appeared to be sinking in.

"Precisely," she said. "And this is all the more reason why we must reaffirm our vows to each other."

"Yes."

"I will be the only queen of your heart, and you the only king of mine, but the pleasures of the kingdom will be enjoyed by both of us."

Again, there came that cautious pause, but then Laurent smiled and nodded. The mockery and mischief were gone. A dreamy expression softened his face, an expression of love.

"Oh, yes, Beauty," he said. He moved towards her and pressed her close again but this time without urgency and with respect, and gently, he kissed her lips, her cheeks, her forehead. "Yes, you are so very right, Beauty. You are often right. And you are right in this now. And this must be the way; it can be no other way."

Once again she stepped back.

"Do you think I don't respect you?" Laurent protested. "That I don't respect that you took the lead with your suggestions in the hall below? I was so pleased to see it, pleased to see you wanted this, and were already thinking of how it must be. I wasn't merely pleased. I was overjoyed, overjoyed that you remembered the pleasures of our youth, that your mind hadn't rewritten the story of what we knew in Bellavalten together."

"Yes, I know. I knew you were pleased, and of course I might have fallen silent if you hadn't been pleased. But stop thinking about getting into that bed over there just now and let's continue to talk of all this."

"Beauty, I had a dream before the visitors arrived, just before . . ." He moved away for the first time, turning his back to her, and then he faced her again. In a low halting voice he told of the strange woman who appeared to him. "I didn't know whether I was dreaming or awake. It seemed as real as this room is real now. I was lying there on that bed, and quite suddenly, I wasn't, but I tell you she was as real as these walls, or that bed. And the woman said things, said things that I must—"

"You needn't go on," Beauty interrupted. "I had the very same dream, my lord. And I know who the woman was. I know her name. I knew it when I was but a girl and my father and mother told me of her. She is Titania of Mataquin, one of the great immortal wise women or fairies to visit the celebration of my birth. I didn't believe a word my parents spoke on the subject of fairies coming to bestow their blessings. I was like so many children, certain such things as fairies or wise women did not exist. But when I awoke from my hundred years of sleep to the Crown Prince's kiss, I believed everything, and I had known the fairy queen, Titania, in my dreams—yet in such vague ways I could confide this to no one. Well, she has come again to me and she says that this is our destiny."

"Yes, that's what she said to me," said Laurent. He was amazed. "She spoke of *our* destiny."

"Yes, she did to me as well," said Beauty.

"And that it was I all along . . ."

"And indeed it was."

"Then we are resolved, Beauty! But are we not resolved, whether these dreams be shared imaginings or something real, aren't we both wanting this with our full hearts?" He came towards her.

"Stay your passion awhile longer," said Beauty. "You speak of resolve. Well, let's use this night to resolve what small unconfessed doubts we may have about this strange future. I want to be alone now with Prince Alexi perhaps."

He was silent.

"Who knows what I will do or say?" Beauty said tenderly, appealing to him with both hands. "There are delicate questions I would put to Prince Alexi in a whisper, if you will. And there are things I need to know about my own soul. To have been a slave in Bellavalten is one thing. To be a ruler there is another. And I would encourage you, my lord, to do as you please in the same way."

Laurent nodded. "Brave little queen," he whispered. "Courageous little queen." He appeared to marvel.

"I want your blessing, my lord, as I resolve these matters in my heart. I want to be alone, completely alone, with Prince Alexi."

There was no doubt that he had caught her full meaning. Need she resort to cruder words? She thought not.

"Laurent, in all these years," she said coaxingly, tenderly, "you have never failed me."

Laurent's eyes blazed, and for one frightening moment, Beauty thought the cause was lost, utterly lost, but then the brightest smile broke out on Laurent's face. "Beauty, you never disappoint me!" he said.

"Ah, yes, darling," Beauty said. "And if we decide that we are not to accept this invitation, then the heated passions of this night will be forgotten."

"I agree."

"I love you, Laurent."

"And I you, my precious queen, my only queen," Laurent said. "And as always you are wiser than I." He shook his head as if still marveling at it. "The great Titania, who appeared to me, spoke of bravery and courage and how we would both need it."

"Did she?"

He paced the floor, making his way slowly to his favorite chair by the fire and there he sat down and put his foot on the fender. "Yes, you must be free tonight, Beauty, as free as I am. And if we rule, always as free as I am, night and day hereafter. But I think I see the need of yet another true test of my spirit before giving my full blessing to this new path." He paused and gazed into the flames. "Yes, I see it. I think I see exactly what I must do." He looked up at Beauty with a boyish innocence that made her marvel. "Memory can often deceive."

"Yes, it can," Beauty said. "We must use this night well, my lord. Both of us."

4

LADY EVA:
THE FATE OF
A KINGDOM
HANGS IN THE
BALANCE

I'd been writing at my table for over an hour—confiding to the parchment my private thoughts on how the old ways of Queen Eleanor might indeed be improved should King Laurent and Queen Beauty consult me on such a thing. The rooms provided for me in this castle were large and elegant, and so it was with our entire party.

I had remained dressed in the same green Venetian silk gown I'd worn for the earlier conference, but I had let my hair down free over my shoulders. And I was ready at any moment to be summoned for further questions or observations.

Severin, stripped naked once more, was asleep in my bed—a rare privilege which I thought he deserved after the arduous journey. The night before our arrival in the kingdom, we'd stayed in rather luxurious quarters at an old inn on the border of King Laurent's kingdom, and I'd had more than two hours to play with Severin and correct and punish all faults I'd observed in him during our traveling.

Tristan had brought Blanche with him, and last night he'd begged me to discipline Blanche for him, as he was tired and anxious about his meeting with Laurent and Beauty. "After all," he'd said. "How do I know what the King feels at this juncture about my having once coupled with his queen?"

I had no such worries, but had been glad of the opportunity to have Blanche to myself, and she'd received at my hands blows as harsh as those rained down upon Severin. I wondered if Tristan was more at ease this evening as the King and Queen did seem favorably disposed to accept Bellavalten. What was happening between him and Blanche just now?

But more important, what was happening with our gracious hosts?

We could be certain of nothing until they gave us their decision in the morning. But I was hopeful, beyond hopeful, and the future of Bellavalten blazed before me with uncommon brightness. King Laurent was far more handsome even than anyone had ever described him. Words could not do justice to the vitality of his face, or his deep yet lyrical voice, and the way he smiled naturally when he spoke, and seemed to delight in each exchange as if he were unspoiled and eager for it. As for the Queen, she appeared as a girl, as if the fairies had gifted her with eternal youth and sweetness. Yet there were depths to the Queen, lovely depths reflected not only in her fathomless eyes but in her quiet and strong demeanor.

I sat back annoyed. These voluminous sleeves were getting in my way as I wrote, as they always did, and I was tempted to strip off the gown and continue writing in my chemise. But before I could make up my mind there came a soft knock at the door.

I answered at once.

Captain Gordon stood there, and I could see he was anxious.

"Lady Eva," he said. "You must dress and go at once to the King in Lady Elvera's quarters. I'll show you the way. Lady Eva, much hangs on this meeting."

"Well, I am dressed, Captain, but allow me to pin up my hair . . ."

"Oh, no, my lady. Let me suggest that for this you leave it down," he said now taking my measure. "And your slippers, yes, they have raised heels, don't they? I think that is nearly perfect."

"And what concern is all this of yours?" I asked. Captain Gordon had perfect manners. I'd never submitted myself or my costume to him for inspection.

"My lady," he went on. "Did you bring with you certain . . . certain instruments. . . ." He gestured to the distant bed where Severin lay sleeping as deeply as ever.

"What do you mean—for discipline? Yes, I have my paddles and straps, some potions. You know me and my potions."

"Oh, yes, the potions," he said. "I doubt that our gracious king and queen have ever heard of your potions. Allow me to gather up these things and bring them along with us."

I gestured to the casket on the nearby sideboard. It was open. A gilded paddle and a long folded gilded leather strap lay inside, with covered jars and a neat stack of linen handkerchiefs.

He inspected the contents, closed the casket, and lifted it, gesturing for me to go before him.

"You look beautiful tonight, Lady Eva," he said as we hurried along the passage. "Forgive me for presuming to compliment you, but it's true."

"Men are fools for small changes," I said. "My hair is down, that is all."

"No, my lady, that is not all. You shone brightly before the King, and the Queen was also delighted with you." He said all this while looking straight ahead as we moved down the long shadowy corridor.

A torch in a sconce at the far end appeared to be our destination.

"Well, Captain, my personal gifts are not so very important right now, are they?"

"Much more important than you imagine," he said, glancing at me, and then ahead again. "And your lavish dress of silk and brocade is most becoming. And your heels make a nice crisp sound on the stone flooring."

"Whatever are you talking about, Captain?" I asked. "I must confess I always feel smart when I wear these gold-heeled slippers."

We had reached a pair of double doors and the torch that hung beside them.

"Lady Eva," he said in a whisper. "Everything depends on you now, on your youthful self-confidence, and the gifts that have kept the kingdom in order since the old queen departed. Please. Show spirit. Lady Elvera and I have failed in complying with King Laurent's request. Again, everything depends upon your being able to grant it."

Without waiting for me to answer he opened the door and led the way into a vast bedchamber.

Several iron candelabra along the walls gave a soft pleasing light to the room, and there was a healthy little fire going in the great fireplace.

We stood now in a space that was like a parlor, but I could see dimly the great bed beyond and the figure of a naked man kneeling before it, with his back to me. The man appeared young and powerfully built with a mane of thick wavy brown hair. And immediately I felt a stab of desire between my legs as I looked at his naked backside. It was tightly muscled yet pleasingly curved. But this was no young boy.

Lady Elvera stood primly to one side of the naked man, and when she saw me she came forward to meet me anxiously.

"Lady Eva, you must punish the King," she said in a low commanding voice. "It is his wish, and if you fail in this, there may be no new destiny for Bellavalten."

I almost laughed. So you two have failed at it, I thought, but I didn't speak the words.

"Of course," I said. "Captain, put my casket of implements on that small table there by the fire, and both of you be gone from here now."

Lady Elvera drew herself up as if she were insulted. "You remember that this is your lord, the King!" she declared.

"Yes, Lady Eva, please," said the Captain softly. "This is the King."

"And you have disappointed him, have you not?" I said. "Now go, both of you. You who dare to refuse a king's command. I'll send for you when and if I have any need of you."

The Captain at once nodded and moved to the door. Lady Elvera appeared outraged. "Take care, Lady Eva," she whispered under her breath as she stormed past. "This is the King who has all power in his hands."

The Captain hesitated as she went out past him. "Lady Eva," he said in a low voice. "He asks that he be thoroughly mastered."

Then he disappeared and the doors were shut.

I quickly threw the bolt. "Idiots," I whispered.

I moved forward slowly on the great Indian carpet before the fireplace, closer to the kneeling figure which had not moved all this while.

The King. Yes, the King. The warmth between my legs was excruciating. I felt the juices against my inner thighs. I knew I might lose control of that rising, rolling pleasure now and again and again as I proceeded. But I struggled to hold it back, to put my eyes on what lay before me and not let my own passion overcome me.

He knelt still as if he had heard none of this annoying nonsense. His legs were parted, and I could see he'd been beaten not only on his strong tight bottom, but on his well-muscled thighs and calves. His skin appeared golden in the firelight. Smooth. Flawless. His shoulders were large, and the muscles of his back were rather irresistible, as irresistible as the exquisitely curved bottom. I wanted to take hold of his bottom in both hands.

I could see they had delivered a few blows there. But the flesh was for my purposes fresh and virginal, the flesh of a man, not a boy, a man and a king. I could scarcely contain myself.

I'd spanked enough bad boys of twenty and twenty-five and so forth and so on, children still as they groped for manhood. I'd never had a true man before, an older man, a man much older than me, a man who would be filled with inevitable pride and dignity.

My nipples were hardening beneath my gown. I let a deep sigh pass through my lips.

I turned to the casket, opened it, and took out the golden paddle. This one had been made especially for me, with a long handle that felt good to my small fingers, and the thin gilded wood had been well polished by Severin's bottom.

It was a superb instrument for stinging and humiliating.

I drew up beside the kneeling figure. He bowed his head and started to turn away from me. His cock was immense and it was hard, wondrously hard, and gleaming in the half-light.

"Oh, no, you must not do that, my lord," I said, reaching for his chin with my left hand, and gradually turning his face back towards me. "No, you must never turn away from me without my permission. Do you hear? I don't mean for you to speak, I mean for you to nod only. The speaking will come later."

He nodded. His cock jumped. I could all but feel its pain, its hunger.

The scent coming up from his skin was delicious, and it had been so well oiled that it glistened beautifully in the light of the fire. Such powerful arms, such broad shoulders. And every inch of him was polished as if he were made of bronze.

"Now look down as you know you should," I said. "Always keep your eyes down unless I say you might raise them." But I turned his face full towards me. And I could see the tears now clearly, sparkling in his dark lashes, and on his skin. He was trembling.

"You are ready for this, aren't you?" I said the words with low fervor. "You need this so very much, and it's been a long time, has it not, since anyone took command of your desires."

Again, he nodded. But he couldn't keep his eyes from moving over me feverishly before he looked down again contritely.

I grabbed a handful of his silky hair.

"Well, tell me what you saw," I said, "since you could not quite command your impudent gaze, and be very careful that you say nothing to displease me."

"A mistress of great beauty," he said softly.

"And was not Lady Elvera a mistress of great beauty years ago when she whipped you daily?"

"Yes, madam, she was," he replied, eyes down as before. "And she is beautiful now, undeniably, but she is frightened of me."

Perfect answer. His tone was very reverential and polite.

"Well, I am not frightened of you at all. I'm in love with you. Now stand up quickly."

He did as I commanded. Oh, he was surely the most splendid male human being I'd ever beheld, bar none. His shadowy chest and belly were tight and firm, and the cock, though not monstrously long, no, a comfortable size, was exceptionally thick, rising out of its nest of moist dark hair as if a sculptor had made it for the gods, or for me, little Eva, in this moment.

I stood on tiptoe to kiss his face. I kissed his wet cheeks. Ah, this was paradise! I had wanted to do this, so wanted to do it the first time I'd ever seen him. I kissed his eyelids now, felt his eyes moving beneath his lids, beneath my lips, felt his eyelashes against me. I covered him in kisses, sealing my lips to the hard bone of his jaw, to his cheekbones, to his forehead. Rough the shadow of his beard, deliciously rough though it had been shaven close. My left hand played with his hair, smoothing it back, stroking the skin. Dark hair is so soft, always so soft, so much finer than light hair.

I heard him sigh under my kisses, my fingers caressing him. I gathered up his hair in my hand and tugged at it.

"You're afraid, aren't you?" I said. "You've given the order but you're afraid."

"Yes, madam."

"And well you should be," I said softly, lovingly. I turned his face to me and kissed him full on the mouth, my left hand tightening on the back of his neck, breathing into his mouth, stabbing my tongue into his mouth. As I drew back I saw his cock jump again as if it had claimed his soul for its own.

"Your cock knows what you need, doesn't it?" I breathed into his ear. "Now quickly, put your hands on the back of your neck and keep them there, and spread your legs wide."

I stood to one side, my left hand on his right shoulder.

As he obeyed I slipped the loop on the paddle around my right wrist, and felt of his scrotum with my right hand, cupping my hand under it as best I could, and weighing it slowly, then letting it go. With my left hand I lifted his chin. I gave his cock a fierce slap that startled him. He was so ready. I slapped it again, hard, and again and again.

He winced, the muscles of his torso tightening, but he didn't make a sound, and those tears slipped down his face. There was dark hair on his chest, lovely dark hair, curling around his nipples. I hadn't seen it clearly at first in these shadows. But now that I did see it, I loved it. I stroked it, played with it, played with the thin little curls around his nipples.

I slapped his cock right and left and then slapped his face hard.

He was shocked but his cock was harder than ever, dancing superbly.

"You're mine," I said, "and there is no one to interfere, you understand?"

"Yes, madam."

"Now turn around, and get down on all fours in front of the fire, and hurry. I want to see your face clearly by that light as I punish you."

He obeyed at once.

"And your lips are sealed now. Sealed."

He nodded.

"Your rebellious heart drove them wild in the old days," I said. "I've heard plenty enough about it. But you won't rebel against me. You won't dare."

Again, he nodded.

I knelt up beside him. I had his handsome bottom to my right and now at last I kneaded those exquisite fleshly cheeks, felt just how tight they were and how soft and hard at the same time, such a sublime mixture of strength and vulnerability.

I slipped the handle of the paddle into my hand.

And lifting his chin with my left hand, I rained down on him the strongest spanking blows I could deliver. I let loose with all my strength, paddling him again and again with the full force of my arm. At once he struggled to be quiet, helpless little gasps escaping his lips, and as I continued to spank him as hard as I could and as fast as I could, he shifted, struggled, tightened, and finally shuddered all over in his struggle to remain still.

On and on I went with it, giving full vent to my strength, my teeth clenched, but my eyes remained fixed on his face, on his knotted brows and the wet, squinting eyes, my hand keeping his chin elevated mercilessly.

Again and again, I spanked him. He was dancing now, he couldn't help it, his bottom contracting, then loosening, his legs swaying even though he struggled to kneel firmly, but I went on, spreading the blows, smacking him on the right side more and then more on the left, and suddenly letting loose with a torrent on his sturdy thighs. Now he could barely keep quiet. Yet his hands and knees remained firmly on the carpet.

A low delicious groan came from deep within his chest.

"Lips sealed," I reminded him. "Groan if you will, but lips sealed." I put the fingers of my left hand over his mouth. He shivered and then I heard a sob deep in his throat.

But I continued to work with the paddle, going back now to his bottom, slamming it as hard as I could, delighting in the loud, crisp cracking noise that the paddle made.

"You know, Your Majesty, you don't have to be a bad boy to deserve punishment like this," I said in his ear. "You only have to be a boy! And a beautiful boy at that! You do understand that, don't you?"

He nodded as best he could with me holding his chin.

"And I so love to do it," I said. "I have so wanted to do it since the moment I first saw you."

I dropped the paddle on the Indian carpet.

I came round and knelt down in front of him, and pressed his hot wet face against my bosom. He sobbed against me, against the tight green brocade. I stroked his thick wavy hair. I might have come then, just from this, if I had not struggled against it, against my nipples burning, my nether mouth burning.

"You are mine," I said in a low confidential voice. "And now you may speak to me, you may answer, you may acknowledge this."

"Yes, Eva," he said. His voice as low as mine, as confidential. "Yes, Lady Eva!"

"Oh, we'll forgive that little infraction," I said. "Once, but never twice."

I could feel him sobbing harder, feel the sobs cutting loose one after another as he pressed his lips against my breasts. It wasn't the pain that was making him sob. He could take a great deal more pain than that. It was that he felt helpless.

"Tear the cloth, tear them free," I said. "Gowns I have aplenty."

At once with his teeth he bit at the gold border of the tunic, then tore the brocade loose, ripping it down and away from the right sleeve as a beast might tear it, exposing my breasts.

"Suckle them," I said.

I could hear him moan, but he was barely kissing my nipples, the tears shining in his dark lashes.

"Suckle," I said. "The rouge on my nipples is flavored with the essence of cherries. Can you taste it?"

He murmured his assent to this.

His mouth closed on my left nipple and he drew on it with the fierceness of a babe. I sighed, the sudden throb of pleasure so full and huge inside of me that I almost went over the brink. My breasts had always been too sensitive, my nipples connected directly to the throbbing clitoris between my legs.

"But wait," I said, pressing his forehead, moving him back. "Kneel up, hands on the back of your neck facing the fire, and stay there."

I went to the chair. It was time for the golden strap. The strap was wide and soft and not too heavy but heavy enough and plenty long. It felt as good as it looked. Then of course there was the belt I wore, but it was heavy, cumbersome. No. I chose the golden strap.

I doubled it over and whacked my left hand with it. Perfect.

I went back to the fireplace, standing in the wide margin between his kneeling body and the hearth, facing him.

Kneeling down in front of him, I bit at his nipples again, hearing him gasp, bit at them fiercely, and then drawing back, I whipped his chest with the belt, hard, over and over again. He was plainly writhing in misery, and yet his cock, his splendid cock, was hard and shining and dancing to the tune of it. I kept my eyes on his cock as I whipped him, whipped his hard belly.

He bent forward, face tightened with pain, narrow eyes still sparkling with those abundant tears, and I think he tried with all his might to draw away from the belt without moving, but it was pointless of course, and I thrashed him harder and harder with it. I thrashed his thighs.

"Knees wider apart," I said, "wider. Come on. You can do better than that. Wider." I never stopped spanking him with the strap.

I stopped. I stroked his face with my left hand. "Does it hurt more than you remember?" He didn't make a sound. I covered his face in kisses, nuzzling against his neck. "Well, does it?"

"Yes and no, Lady Eva," he whispered.

I laughed, a low full-throated laugh. I couldn't help myself.

"And look what you've done to my pretty gown," I crooned in his ear. "Look."

His eyes moved to my breasts. I could see the pupils dancing.

"Are they pretty?"

"Beautiful," he murmured. He sighed.

I rose to my feet, the belt thrown over my shoulder. I stood just in front of him, but he was so tall that his head was almost to my breasts.

"Kneel up," I said. And at once he obeyed.

Now he was at the right level.

I lifted my skirts. My sex was hot and dripping. I knew that he could see it, see the telltale moisture sliding down my naked inner thighs. I wished there had been a long mirror there so I might see it. I was in agony for him.

"Pleasure me, sire," I said in a low voice. "Do it well."

He needed no urging.

He came forward eagerly and clamped his mouth on my sex, and his tongue went deep inside me. I could scarcely remain standing upright. I struggled not to fall under the onslaught of pleasure, and as the orgasm broke loose, as it rolled like a great exploding flame up through me, I cried aloud as I hadn't once permitted him to do. On and on came his tongue, licking at my clitoris, licking at my vagina, licking, and his hungry lips worked the flesh, my secret most sensitive flesh, sucking at my pubic lips, sucking, and finally I screamed for him to stop. The pleasure had emptied me, taken the breath out of me. Yet the faint echoing shimmers of it would not stop.

I pushed him away.

I wanted to lie down and then I thought, Well, why not? And I did. I lay back on the carpet looking up at him, looking at him kneeling there again near me, over me on all fours, this great strong man, this man who could have overpowered me with one hand, and I looked at his starved cock, and at his smooth perfect obedient face. He seemed ageless, a child and a man, the tears flashing in his eyes beautifully, his strong well-shaped mouth trembling just a little, only a little, the teeth touching the lower lip.

Finally I sat up. I reached out and fondled his scrotum again, leaning against his arm as I did it. "Have you ever been more ready, Your Majesty."

"No, Lady Eva," he said. There was a tiny smile on his lips.

"You think this is finished?" I teased him. "You think I'm going to let that cock have what it wants?"

No answer.

"Take a guess."

"No, Lady Eva."

I rose to my feet. I quickly laced up my dress in front as best as I could, but it was quite beyond repair.

Then I knelt again and took his head in my hands, kissing his eyes again, and running my fingers back through his thick hair. He shuddered all over. Every touch of my fingers, every kiss of my lips, was sending shivers through him.

Perfect.

"Kneel up and turn around. You know where your hands belong. I want to see your backside," I said. "I want to see how well I've punished you."

Ah, it was all quite beautiful, the dark red marks, the patches of glowing red, the white welts and the overall flaming redness of the whole, even to his thighs. But there was so much more to do. So much more.

With both hands, I played with the welts, pushing and scratching at them lightly with my fingernails. I have always had very strong fingernails. And I do not grow them overly long, but keep them filed in perfect ovals. And with these I scratched him idly and not hard, playing, teasing, knowing how this both hurt and pleasured him nearly beyond endurance.

My left hand slipped round in front and felt of the root of his cock. It couldn't get any harder.

"Where did I leave that paddle?" I asked. I rose to my feet straightening my skirts. I saw the paddle, gleaming on the carpet only a few feet away. "Go get it and bring it here in your teeth."

He obeyed more quickly than I had quite anticipated.

He stopped in front of me with his head bowed, and I took the paddle

46

from his teeth. And then suddenly he kissed my feet, kissed my naked insteps, and kissed the toes of my slippers and even kissed my heels, those little golden heels that were an inch high. He stopped, his head pressed to the floor in front of me.

"That was always allowed at the castle, and in the village, wasn't it?" I asked.

"Yes, Lady Eva. Forgive me that I didn't ask." This was said in the simplest most sincere voice. No cowardice and no drama. Ah, I thought, the finest slaves are the honest slaves and the clever ones who grasp all things perfectly.

I gathered up a great hunk of his beautiful soft hair and dragged him up on his knees and after me as I headed for one of the lovely high-backed chairs scattered about the room and I sat down in front of him. Nice down cushion, but quite comfortable. A sturdy chair.

A fresh volley of tears had broken out on his face. I pushed up my skirts until my thighs were naked.

"Come round to this side of me, and when I bend you over my lap, don't you dare let that cock touch me or this chair, do you hear?"

"Yes, Lady Eva." He was shaking all over.

Again, it wasn't the pain. It was the helplessness. He had to obey. He had no choice. And it was the exquisite humiliation of the "over the knee" position that never failed even with the most experienced or well-trained slave.

But what did I care what it was? I threw him down over my naked lap and waled at his gorgeous bottom with the paddle, giving it all my strength again, spanking him and spanking him until his legs were dancing again and those muffled groans were coming over and over again.

I stopped, stroking his bottom with my left hand, parting the cheeks, touching the little pink mouth there, pushing at it, teasing it. His bottom was so hot now, so deliciously feverish and red.

It was so exquisite having him like this, so intimate, over my naked thighs and just taking my time with this warm pulsing flesh. How it must have burned. How it must have throbbed. Even here and there was a very fine bit of dark hair, hard to see in the shadowy light, but not hard to feel as I inspected him, and of course the little pink mouth of his anus seemed to be hiding in its tiny nest of hair, shyly, as if begging to escape humiliation.

I started spanking him again, hard and fast, furiously in fact, sparing no inch of his bottom, giving him the full force of my arm, giving him the full force of my heart.

My juices were flowing again, the little fount in me was sending its waves up through my breasts once more, and I could feel myself almost rising off the chair, pressing my tummy and thighs against his powerful torso, yet spanking him hard all the while.

Finally I pulled him back and stood up and ordered him to crawl to the bed and now.

"Oh, there are so many other games, tasks, tests . . . things that we might do, but I'm hungry for that cock," I said. "I must have it, and what I must have is what must be done. Now up on your knees and rip this dress from me, rip every stitch of it off now with your teeth, hands behind your neck. You dare move your hands and I'll whip your ankles and the soles of your feet. Hurry!"

In a frenzy he obeyed, ripping off my jeweled belt, and tearing the brocade wide open, and dragging it from my arms till the tatters lay in a shining puddle at my feet. Ah, so much for that expensive Venetian fabric, but I would treasure these rags forever.

"Now look at me!"

He did, though it was quite obvious that he might have preferred to look at my sex instead of at my face. He turned his large brown eyes up obediently. We remained still, him on his knees and me naked in my satin slippers, staring at one another, and his eyes seemed filled with curiosity and awe.

"You're so beautiful, Your Majesty!" I said.

A short muffled laugh escaped his lips. "You think so, Lady Eva?" he whispered.

I took his face in both my hands, pressing his cheeks with my thumbs. I bent to kiss him hard on the mouth, but then a wild idea came to me. I glanced at the nearby table. There stood a silver pitcher and a goblet and several linen serviettes. I could smell the wine.

"Open your mouth," I said.

He hesitated but when I slapped him hard he obeyed.

I filled the goblet, swirling the red wine for a moment to look at it in the light, and then I put it before his lips. "Now when I fill your mouth you will not close it, do you hear me."

48

I poured the wine on his tongue, and he trembled all over trying to swallow without closing his lips as I'd commanded, the wine slipping down the sides of his face and down his chin. But he managed to obey, gasping and struggling.

I poured wine onto one of the serviettes now and began to clean his teeth vigorously with it.

Again, he gasped, and he trembled. This had clearly never been done to him before. And as I worked away on his back teeth, he groaned, unable to help himself.

I held his head firmly with my left hand, almost cruelly, as I worked away polishing every tooth in his mouth, his lips trembling violently. Then I lifted the goblet. "Spit in here now," I commanded.

He struggled to obey, spitting out what little wine had been left, pressing his lips together frantically suddenly. I slapped him hard again. "Open your mouth, wide!" I said. "I never told you that you could close it."

It seemed he was moaning for mercy. I kissed his teeth, ran my tongue along the upper teeth and then the lower. I touched his tongue with my tongue. Again, he gasped, as if keeping his mouth open took all his will, and I imagine that it did.

"Close your lips," I said, and I laid mine against his as he did so. The tears were sliding down his cheeks. A long shuddering sigh came from him.

He kissed me back, hungrily, almost desperately. His cock was again dancing wildly. I had never seen a more powerful shaft, a more deeply colored shaft, and he struggled, obviously, to keep it back away from me. Just for a second his hands went loose from his neck, but then he remembered himself and put them back into place. I pretended I hadn't seen it.

I went quickly to my casket on the sideboard, and removed a pot of scented cream, and came back to him, opening the little glass pot and then setting it on the bedside table.

I took a lovely dollop of the cream in the palm of my hand. This was a sweet salve that I'd blended myself with the scent of apricots and sunshine in it, and bits of ground rose petals.

"Stand," I said. I worked the cream all over my hands.

At once he obeyed, as limber as a boy.

I smoothed the thick oily emollient over his enormous scrotum and then his cock, watching him twitch and suffer. He could not hide the trembling now. The tip of his cock glistened beautifully and a thick drop of his own fluid hovered there at the tiny mouth. I was careful not to touch it, not to push him over the edge.

I smiled, wiped my hands on a small linen towel for which I was most grateful, and then stared again into his brown eyes.

They fixed on me and were wet and shining with tears.

"Now into bed," I said.

I climbed up on the bed myself, still wearing my slippers, digging into the burgundy coverlet with my heels, and he came after me and over me. A perfect giant of a man.

"Into me now and hard, and you drive it hard, hard with all your strength, and you come when I come and not one second before, you hear me?"

Without answering he thrust that enormous cock against me like a battering ram. How in the world can that find the little door, I thought with the most exhilarating happiness, but he found it, he ground into it and opened it, parting the dripping wet lips and slamming deep till his belly was against me.

My eyes had closed. I opened them and found myself looking up into his face, into his eyes. Again and again he slammed against me, stretching me, filling me, his arms like pillars beside me, his hair hanging down in his face. I felt the cock fill me up tight, tighter perhaps than I'd ever been filled, oh what cock in the world would ever match this cock, sliding against my clitoris. I started crying out, I couldn't stop myself.

I wrapped my naked legs tight around him, and drove my hands down into the crack of his backside, my first fingers left and right plunging into his anus.

I would have held off for an hour, letting my passion rise and fall, but I couldn't control it. I couldn't. I was writhing against the coverlet trying to control it, riding up with him, slammed down again by him, struggling to bite down against it, but it was useless. My face was burning. All breath had gone out of me. I was nothing and no one.

It was a fire rolling upwards consuming me as I started to come, lifting my hips, crying out, and he let me lift my hips, then forced me down again one final time, coming inside me in one swift glory of jerking movements. It went on and on and finally it was I, I who cried out:

"No more!"

He drew back.

And unbidden, he closed his mouth over mine and kissed me. He drove his tongue deep into me.

"Away, stop!" I sighed. I groaned. No one would call that speaking words.

He fell down right beside me with a long deep sigh and then rolled over on his back. I saw his eyes close.

For a long moment we lay still.

Then I was up and on my feet and inspecting the utter ruin of my garments. I gathered them up as best I could.

I stared down at him. It seemed he was falling into a deep sleep. And on a chair on the far side of the bed, I could see what appeared to be a long robe of red velvet. Surely this was his robe, his dressing gown. He'd been dressed in red when we'd gathered in the great hall. It was his color, red, red trimmed with gold as this robe was.

I put my paddle and strap back in the casket, along with the pot of cream, and stuffed my torn dress inside it and closed it and held it.

"Wake up now," I said.

He opened his eyes and looked at me. He had a vague heavy sleepy look.

"Get up, put on that red dressing gown and slippers if you have them, and take this coverlet off the bed. Wrap me in it as I am naked and without clothes, and carry me back to my chamber."

He obeyed without a moment's hesitation. The moment he closed the long robe around his tall frame, he was every inch the King again, and as he gathered up the coverlet he had an easy graceful air to him as if such a task were nothing.

He held it up for me as if it were a cloak, and as I turned my back to him he wrapped me into it securely and then picked me up as if I were weightless, a light little thing with a casket in her arms, and indeed I was, suddenly cradled in his arms, and staring up at his smiling face.

He carried me out of the bedchamber, easily opening the door, and shoving it back behind us, and then down the long shadowy corridor.

No one was about. If others peeped from recesses in the dark, through keyholes or tiny apertures made for peeping, we didn't know it, and all the while, all the while, he was smiling down at me.

Smiling.

"This is my door," I said when we had reached my chamber. "Set me down on my feet."

He obeyed and then he opened the door for me. A gust of sweet warm air came from my little parlor.

"I'm dismissing you now, sire," I said in a low confidential voice. "With your permission."

"Will you grant me one last kiss?" he whispered, and this time his smile was radiant and infectious.

"As you wish," I said.

He clamped his hands on the sides of my face, and held me captive as he kissed me with as much passion as he had ever kissed me earlier.

"My precious Lady Eva," he whispered.

And with that he turned and walked down the hall without so much as a glance behind him. Such a stately figure with such a sprightly step.

I rushed into my chambers, shut the door, and collapsed at my writing table.

5

PRINCE ALEXI:
BELOVED
QUEEN,
BELOVED
SLAVE

Y ou are to go at once to the north tower. You will see an open
door at the top of the stairs. The Queen will be waiting there
for you."

The page who delivered that message left immediately. And I hesitated only long enough to comb my hair, eat a slice of ripe apple to freshen my breath, and make certain my attire was as it should be. Then I was off, hurrying through the castle, finding the winding stairs of the north tower easily enough and rushing up towards the open door and its promise.

I don't know that I quite believed it until I was inside the room, and the Queen stood before me, her large blue eyes as innocent and enchanting as they had been decades ago when we'd first coupled in a little servants' room near the old queen's bedchamber. She stood staring at me, dressed only in a long full cloak of black velvet, her lovely blond hair loose over her shoulders. She seemed not a day older than she had been in the long-ago time.

"Close the door, Prince," she said. "And please bolt it."

At once I obeyed.

She had moved to the fireplace, and stood with one hand on the heavy stone mantel, looking down into the flames.

To the far right stood a huge bed of dark oak with a paneled ceiling atop its intricately turned posts. It seemed the red brocade coverlet was sewn with hundreds of tiny twinkling jewels, and bits of gold and silver. Chased silver vessels glinted in the half-light on the sideboard. And tapestries enclosed us, of men and women in the Royal Hunt, looking upon us with gentle ever-vigilant eyes.

"My king and I have decided to use this night to ascertain all we need to know for tomorrow's decision," Beauty said, her eyes still on the fire.

I drew closer to her. I marveled at the sheen of her hair in the light of the fire and the dewy freshness of her cheeks. It seemed an agony suddenly to be so near her and so alone with her. Why was she subjecting me to such a trial? I trusted she had her purposes.

"I understand, Your Majesty," I said. "What can I tell you? What questions might I answer?"

"You can take off your clothes and lay them on that table there," she said. She turned and looked at me.

I was petrified. I couldn't find words for what I felt. My flesh was responding to her words as if I had no control over it, no control over desire whatsoever. I was speechless.

"Prince Alexi," she said. "Don't be so foolish. Do you think I would bring you here without my lord's permission? Do you think I would expose you to his wrath? You are a guest under my roof. What happens in any chamber of this house tonight happens with King Laurent's blessing."

"Yes, Your Majesty," I said. I couldn't conceal my relief, or that I was trembling. Quickly, I stripped off all my clothes, my velvet tunic, leggings, everything, and laid all on the table as she had directed me. I felt the warm air moving over my naked skin, and it seemed a riot of memories came back to me, memories of Beauty and me, memories of the kingdom too numerous to assemble in any conceivable order. I felt my face flushed and hot, and with a mind of its own, my cock was hardening. Oh, it was too like the old days, to be naked once more and not hide the subtle and merciless transformation of one's own body, to be exposed and yet to be free, strangely, wondrously free.

I turned slowly to face her.

She had opened her black velvet cloak. She was naked. Her nipples were pink, girlishly pink as they had been long ago, and the golden hair between her legs was gleaming in the firelight. Her soft, flat rounded belly was as beautiful as her smooth thighs. I had always loved her rounded little belly, hard and flat yet part of her voluptuous little body, rounded as were her thighs and her delectable arms. She was a creature of curves and dimples, of wondrously shaped wrists and ankles.

My cock was now fully hard. I had no hope of concealing it or commanding it.

"You are my queen," I said. I couldn't help myself. But I wondered if she knew the weight carried by these words. Of course. She had to know.

We had both been slaves of Queen Eleanor when I had stolen Beauty from the sleeping queen's closet and brought her to a safe refuge where we could make love together. There, I'd told her the tale myself—of how I'd been captured, stripped, brought helplessly to the kingdom, and how I'd been broken by Queen Eleanor through harsh service in the kitchen of the castle for my rebellion. I'd told her how I won Queen Eleanor's favor through the most abject of service, and Beauty had known I was the Queen's favorite.

"Ah, yes, I am your queen now," she said coming towards me. "But we were lovers in that long-ago time when we met. We made a bower together of a servant's straw bed as I remember. A little cell became our royal chamber. And I gave myself to you with triumphant abandon. How I loved it. And we will be lovers here again tonight. That is my wish and my command. You are as beautiful, Prince, as you were then. Your hair, such a color, almost red, and then brown, and so thick, so soft." She reached out to touch it. "And your eyes, your dark eyes as wondering and almost sad as they were then."

She was scarcely six inches from me.

She looked at my erect organ. I could feel her gaze, feel a subtle heat coming from her, and I saw the blush in her cheeks.

She looked into my eyes again.

"I love men with dark brown eyes," she said dreamily. She reached towards my cock but she didn't touch it. I looked down and could see the beads of moisture on the head of it. I felt such a bolt of desire. At the slightest provocation I might come. I wondered if she had any idea what it felt like to be at the mercy of this cock, if she could even guess what it meant for my mind to be emptied now of all will or sense.

What did women feel? What did those little wet hidden pockets really feel? After all these years, these insane ruminations possessed me even when I felt I wasn't actually thinking anymore. I was hard and I was aware.

I didn't know what to say or do, except to remain standing there, waiting for her. A sweet floral perfume rose from her. I stared at her nipples, at the pale pink aureoles around them. I wanted to touch them, clasp them, pinch them, take her in my arms.

She reached up for the gold ribbon at her throat and opened the fragile knot there, the heavy black cloak falling away from her to a puddle of shadow around her naked feet.

"Come to me," she whispered as she opened her arms.

I embraced her tightly, my sex tortured against her smooth flesh. Her mouth opened and I kissed her hungrily, desperately. "Beauty, my precious unforgettable Beauty," I whispered. "Oh, I have been haunted by you so long, my sweet. If only you knew." I was breathing these words, not really speaking them, kissing her hair now, kissing her cheeks, her eyes. All the cruel moments of the old kingdom came back to me, the moment when I'd been told Beauty was gone, condemned to the village, beyond my reach, beyond hope of another night of secret lovemaking. Ah, the anguish of that I wanted never to know again.

Suddenly I took her breasts cruelly in my hands, cupping them and lifting them, and I sucked at her right nipple. She was mine now, once again, here, and I did not care really what happened. I had to possess her.

A low muffled cry came from her.

"Alexi," she said.

I felt her tumbling towards me, weightless, and without will, a bundle of fragrant, delicious limbs, of moist lips and tangling hair.

I gathered her up in my arms and moved towards the bed. I reached to remove the coverlet.

"No, my love, no. Press me down on it, rough as it is, on all those tiny little jewels. I want to feel them against my bottom and my back."

I laid her down with her head on the pillow, her shining hair a tousled nest beneath her.

Her sex was ripe and beautiful as she stretched her legs, the secret lips wet and gleaming in the light of the fire, like a secret rose in a wreath of golden hair.

"That's it," she said, reaching out for me.

I bent over and kissed her belly, and kissed the curling secretive hair, my tongue darting at her nether mouth, licking at it, licking at the petals of the deep dark bloodred rose.

"No, come up in my arms," she said. "I want your cock inside of me. Don't tease me with your tongue."

I obeyed, straddling her on my knees.

"This first time must be quick, for both of us."

I could hold back no longer.

I slid my cock into her, feeling the little mouth clamp down on it hungrily, and the world was nothing but fire. My whole cock was sheathed with her flesh. I could feel her throbbing against me even as she tugged at me with her arms, even as her lips rose to kiss me, her eyes closed, a low moan coming from her as subtle as her perfume.

She writhed against the coverlet, twisting and turning on a bed of twinkling stars.

I clamped my mouth to her lips and rode her hard, thrusting wildly, uncontrollably, slamming against her as freely as if she were a tavern maid, or anyone I had ever utterly possessed.

Her face went bloodred beneath me, her eyes fluttering, her mouth slack as though she were losing consciousness, and then the sheath that held my cock tightened against it in one clamping spasm after another.

"Beauty," I cried out. I could hold back no longer. I shot the fire into her, bucking over and over again. As always, time stopped and the ecstasy seemed to go on forever, to have lifted me forever out of time and out of reason. And then it was finished, and I lay breathless and damp all over, and quiet beside her. Now I felt the prickling of this bed of jewels. Now I felt it biting into my skin and I didn't care.

How long will this last, I thought. She's made a boy out of me, taken me right back down to the boy I was for the old queen, ever hard, ever ready to please, ever ready to do her will, and never able to resist her.

Yet I thought about Laurent, not the mighty King Laurent, but the slave Laurent, the great and legendary slave of long ago. I remembered him vividly. He'd been at the castle as long as I had before he ran away and was sent to the village. All marveled at his height, his strength, the thickness of his organ, and his perfectly proportioned face and devilish smile. The faces of slaves had always mattered. And his expression had been irresistible—so affectionate and generous and yet mocking, yes, mocking, always. What was I by comparison, a more delicate smaller man in every single regard. So be it. Her husband she had anytime she wished. Perhaps I was a spicy dish for a summer night when the regular fare, grand as it was, had grown too familiar. Well enough. I accepted it.

I was too grateful now that we had had this. I turned towards her and gazed at her profile as she lay, as if dreaming, with her eyes closed. Her loose disheveled hair was almost entirely straight, no curl or wave at all, and lovely to look at as it covered the pillow.

I touched her soft pink lips with my fingers.

"I loved you in that long-ago time when we were together," I said. "I love you now. I loved so many who served with me."

"Yes," she said with a sigh. "I loved so many as well. I loved Tristan, and I loved Captain Gordon, and I loved you, yes, you. I loved the cruel innkeeper who punished me with such disdain. Mistress Jennifer Loxley. You never knew her. I loved the strange men and women of the Sultan's kingdom. I loved Lexius, the Sultan's steward who was so strict with us, and yet. . . . We were swimming in love in those times."

"That's why we want it to be preserved," I said. "That's why we have come back to the kingdom, that's why we want to save it now." I did not tell her that I knew Lady Jennifer Loxley very well indeed now. I did not tell her how well I knew Lexius.

"I know, Alexi," she said. "I understand. And surely you know that the decision belongs to Laurent. Oh, I might persuade him not to take the crown of Bellavalten, yes, but I could never persuade him to take it if that was not his wish."

"But what do you want, Beauty?"

"I want it!" She sat up and turned to me, looking down on me, her hand lying on my thigh, close to my cock. "I want it with all my heart," she said excitedly. "But I don't know that I know how to rule or command others when it comes to the old ways of pleasure slavery. I took to submission so effortlessly. I found it voluptuous. Why lie about it? But Queen Eleanor—she was a monarch carved out of ice."

"That's true, but she was not what you are, Beauty. She had none of your mystery, your complexity! Beauty, she was— Ah, I don't want to say unkind things of her now. She was the dark heart of the kingdom. But you bring grace and wisdom to the enterprise. Besides, why would you have to command pleasure slaves yourself? I mean, of course, yes, you and your lord would be our monarchs. But you would have a realm of servants to do the commanding of slaves for you. You would have Lady Eva. You would have old Lord Gregory. You would have a hundred lords and ladies at Court who know how to command the slaves who serve them. You would rule over those who know how to command and those who must obey in whatever fashion pleases you."

"I want more," she said. She was irresistible to me in her seriousness, the deep thoughtful expression on her face. "If I'm to rule, I must be part of what I rule. I must be of the same fabric, not some lofty figurehead gazing on all with aloofness and even fear. I couldn't bear it."

"I think I understand."

She looked girlish and innocent again, her flaxen hair falling down to veil her nipples. "I want to be a true queen if we do it. I want to learn how to be as strict and demanding as the old queen. I want to see from that point of view, which I never truly grasped, you understand?"

"That will come more easily to you, perhaps, than you know," I said. She was such a vision that I had to force myself for the moment to concentrate on the thread of her words. I wanted her crushed beneath me again, helpless and yielding.

"Has it come easily to you?" she asked. "You were such an obedient and near-perfect slave."

"Yes, it did come to me, the ability to command," I confessed. "I found it surprising at the time. But yes, it came to me. You spoke just now of Lexius, the steward of the Sultan, brought back with you from the sultanate by Laurent."

She smiled. "Oh, yes, such a beautiful man. Dark golden skin, gorgeous dark eyes. Eyelashes so thick they seemed unreal. He was our grand master under the Sultan, inspecting us, instructing us, punishing us, and then Laurent made a slave out of him in a flash. Why, Laurent made a slave of Lexius in secret before we were ever rescued from the sultanate. And then in the hold of the ship on our return voyage, Laurent was merciless. Oh, my lord is such a devil! What did happen with Lexius when he was brought before the Queen? I was gone by then, expelled into the 'real' world."

"The Queen accepted him," I explained. "Oh, at first she balked. Slaves were not to choose her, she declared; she was to choose her slaves. How little she understood! But she accepted him soon enough, and he became her beloved plaything as I was. He was magnificent. So stately, tall, so languid in his smallest gestures. He submitted with such irrepressible dignity." I smiled, thinking of it, remembering it, remembering the glint of the light on his dark chest, on his black hair. "He adored her. But . . . we came to have our secrets, Lexius and I. . . ."

"As you had with me."

"Yes, only with Lexius, it was different. After a year, I began to play the cruel master with him in the small hours of the night while the Queen slept." I knew I was still smiling. Bad things had come to pass, but not from our lovemaking.

"It was enslaving Lexius that taught me how to be a master," I continued. "There was something in him I couldn't resist. I think it was his pride. Most of the time when I watched other slaves being punished, I was jealous of their accomplishments. I wanted to be the one punished. It tormented me. But when I watched him being punished, I wanted to be the one with the paddle or the strap in hand. You wouldn't believe how completely I mastered him. He told me once he was as afraid of me as he'd been of Laurent. He poured out his soul."

"And the Queen never caught on?"

"It's a long story," I said. "A long and terrible story. Bad things happened. Bad news from the sultanate. And well, eventually . . . Lexius actually broke the Queen's heart."

"But how? I never knew that the Queen had a heart to break." She looked at me innocently.

I sat up now, facing her. I couldn't stop myself from cupping her breasts in my hands. My cock was stirring again. I bent down and kissed her nipples. I kissed the tender pendulant underside of her left breast. I ran my tongue along the seam where her breast met her chest. Such a lovely place, where the softness and the firmness came together. Rather like the back of the thigh meeting the soft curve of the bottom. Suddenly I had her in a firm grip and I was suckling her savagely.

I could feel her yielding, feel her sweet scent rising again with the heat in her, hear her sighs.

"Stop, wait, you must tell me," she insisted. She broke away. She put her finger on my lips. "How did Lexius break her heart?"

I was burning for her, but I released her and looked into her eyes. She loved brown eyes, she said, but I loved eyes like her eyes that were the color of the sky and the sea.

"If you take the reins of the kingdom," I said, "you and King Laurent, I will tell you the whole story. It is an interesting story, and Lexius and I were sent away from the kingdom together by the Queen and in total disgrace."

"In disgrace?"

"Yes. Because I . . . I stood up for him. But again, it is a long story."

"But you were in the kingdom when word came that the Queen had died. You've come here on behalf of the kingdom, with Lady Eva and Tristan."

"Yes, I came back, but that was after many years. The Queen no longer cared. She forgave me and she allowed me to stay. She was indifferent to me, but I was welcomed as a courtier. I might have had a manor house like Tristan had I wanted the bother. I didn't. She always welcomed the returnees, even more happily in the last years because she relied upon their enthusiasms to fuel the kingdom's fires. And I came back because I didn't want to be anyplace else in this world anymore. . . ." I paused, confronting that truth clearly yet ashamed of admitting it at the same time.

"I know what you mean, Alexi," she said. "Believe me, I know. We knew something there that is intoxicating beyond description."

"Precisely."

"And those who've never known it . . ."

"They can't possibly comprehend. Tell them what was done to us and they shrink in horror. They have no idea what we knew. Sometimes I have to laugh at it, how little others grasped of what pleasure slavery had been. What can they know of the endless pleasures, the endless spectacle of gorgeous flesh, the endless luxury of easy naps, and scented oils rubbed into sore skin, and fingers always stroking, prodding, searching, and kisses without end and the deep soft cleft ever ready for the cock—" I broke off, blushing.

But Beauty was smiling.

"Laurent and I have always shared that knowledge, that private, heated knowledge, shared it as we played our little games, as we came together tenderly and violently in so many configurations, but the kingdom was a world . . ."

"I know. The kingdom became the whole world and we became its most innocent and fortunate of inhabitants."

"Yes."

"I didn't want to be in any other place," I repeated. "Beauty, the kingdom must survive. You and King Laurent must take over."

"Kiss me again, Prince," she said suddenly. "I know Laurent better than I know anyone in the whole wide world, and I am almost certain of what he will decide. Now kiss me, and take me, and do it roughly, as roughly as you can, as if we were riding through an endless night, you and I, you riding me on and on towards the bright lights of the kingdom."

6

LAURENT:
A NEW AND
MORE PERFECT
VISION

I t was noon before we had discussed everything to our satisfaction.
Then properly dressed in all the appropriate finery, we made our way
down the stairs to the great hall where the emissaries of Bellavalten
had been waiting patiently for some time.

Lady Eva looked as delectable and gorgeous as she had last night,
with her lush and full breasts pressing against the dark blue velvet of her
gown, the skin of her throat creamy and clear, as was her radiant face.
And such red hair, such gorgeous red hair, done up now with combs and
pearls yet boldly unveiled. Oh, if only she'd ordered me to brush it last
night. Oh, how delightful that would have been, to brush her long hair
at her command, red hair brushed in the light of the fire. But I wasn't
complaining. Last night had gone very well.

I couldn't help but smile at her and wink at her as I sat down to the
table, and of course this made her blush. I could still feel the cuts and
welts on my backside and thighs and I almost laughed at the secret delicious pleasure of it, a flash of her sweet voice and hands coming back to
me, enough perhaps to make a satyr of me again. But there was work to
be done now and much to say.

Prince Alexi and Tristan were beautifully turned out as though for a
Court fête, and Lady Elvera, though reserved, was her unchangeable and

unchanging self, with a cold grandeur to her pale skin and her hard eyes. As for handsome blond Captain Gordon, he was tentative and obviously ill at ease as if he did not feel entirely comfortable at the table with his betters. But I wanted him there, so this did not matter to me. I knew why they had brought him. He was a pillar of Bellavalten.

"Good day, my beloved guests," I said. "Please do forgive us for keeping you waiting, but it was imperative that we know our own minds on the matters that are so important to us all. We want to give you our decision."

There were nods and whispers, but clearly they were all in a torment of suspense.

"My queen will speak for us both."

"Thank you, my lord," Beauty said softly. She was incomparably lovely in her rose-colored gown with gold embroidery, and her hair was exquisitely coiffed beneath a sheer loose white veil. She flashed her most agreeable smile at me and then turned to the little assembly.

"It is our desire to accept your gracious offer," she said. "But wait, you must hear us out. For we would bring about several key changes to the way of things. And it seems meet to warn you of what those changes would be. For now is the time for you to protest what we mean to say. Once we are crowned as your monarchs there will be no arguing with improvements to the kingdom of Bellavalten that we mean to carry out."

"By all means, do tell us," said Lady Eva. "I speak with the authority given me by the Grand Duke."

How polished and confident she seemed for one so young. But there was a simplicity to her that was beguiling, and neither Alexi or Tristan challenged her in any way. Tristan actually smiled at her lovingly, as though her beauty delighted him, and Alexi was studying Beauty and studying me.

Beauty continued:

"It is my wish that slavery in the kingdom of Bellavalten should henceforth be voluntary, and that no tribute or trophy slaves should ever be demanded from its allies, and furthermore that all those slaves who want to leave the kingdom at our accession to the throne be allowed to do so, with the appropriate rewards."

No one spoke. In fact all seemed astonished.

Beauty went right on.

"And furthermore it is our desire to solicit throughout the world for ripe and beautiful and willing slaves, both male and female, to enter servitude in our kingdom, not only from the ranks of royal and noble families, but from all walks of life, the qualifications for such slaves being physical gifts, vigor, and aptitude, regardless of rank. We would send out our emissaries to publicize our announcement, and to receive applicants whom they would then bring back to Bellavalten to commit to two years of complete erotic servitude and some perhaps for longer if they so wished, and we so wished."

A smile was playing on Eva's lips and I saw Alexi's eyes suddenly crinkle with good humor and Tristan actually sat back with an audible sigh and smiled. Lady Elvera evinced no response whatsoever, and Captain Gordon seemed frankly amazed.

"Imagine it if you will, my lords and ladies," said Beauty. "We are talking now of a call to all the realms of the north, the south, the east, and the west, for those who long for the sweet fetters we offer them in Bellavalten, and no qualified postulant would be turned away. Of course the royal houses may continue to send their princes and princesses for service, but the slaves themselves must consent to it, want it, want to please.

"Now you have told us of many who have returned to the Court—like you, Prince Alexi, and you, Prince Tristan. Well, surely there are enough of you to undertake journeys abroad to all points of the compass to publish our appeal and to review and receive those likely to please and bring them back to our gates.

"And no doubt, as word spreads of a new era of naked slavery in Bellavalten, applicants will come on foot and on horseback and by coach in the hope of being received by us."

"Genius!" said Tristan suddenly. "Of course. You will have more applicants than you can conceivably imagine."

"I agree," said Beauty quickly. "And each and all shall be subjected to six months of probation. Pass that, and one may commit to two years irrevocably."

"Perfect!" Tristan responded.

Alexi's smile was more coy and secretive. Lady Elvera looked aloof and unconvinced.

"And again," said Beauty, "if a fair face and form, and breeding and aptitude, shine in an applicant—no matter how humble—he or she will not be turned away."

She drew herself up and continued, her voice quite soft for all its obvious confidence.

"Now, it is our belief that many slaves presently serving in Bellavalten will choose to remain," she said. "What say you all to that?"

"Absolutely," said Lady Eva. "Without question." Prince Alexi nodded and so did Tristan. The Captain murmured assent under his breath.

For the first time Lady Elvera smiled, but her face was as cold as ever. "Yes, they will no doubt very much want to stay. Rare it was and still is that any slave actually wants to leave at the end of his or her servitude."

"And we shall have time to perfect the rules of the kingdom," said Beauty, now greatly encouraged. "To refine all before the onrush of those who would come of their own free will." She went on, her words running rapidly. "It is our wish that slaves from now on serve in many capacities in the Court and in the Queen's Village, with greater care given to the aptitude of each slave for types of service, so that some may from the first day be trained as ponies, and others for work in the fields and still others for entertainment of the Court—in sum, we want greater care in placing slaves where they will flourish and most fully amuse their masters and mistresses rather than old and tired structures that tempted slaves to play games on their handlers to achieve their ends."

"Yes," said Lady Eva. "This is brilliant. Slaves are like flowers, some wanting sun and some shade and some the mists from the nearby fountains and others the dry soil beside the garden path."

"Precisely," said Prince Alexi.

"Then some would serve at once in the Queen's Village, you're saying?" asked Captain Gordon. "Not because they had disgraced themselves at the castle, but because it was the best place for them—"

"Indeed, yes," said Beauty. "Discipline would be as harsh and as thorough as ever, but the placement would be done with greater care as Lady Eva has just so well explained."

"But slaves wouldn't be allowed to choose," said Lady Elvera sharply.

"Oh, no, never, of course not," said Beauty quickly, "but we would take infinitely greater patience in choosing what is best for them."

"Ponies," said Captain Gordon. "Would you open stables at the castle for men and women ponies, so that the Court might enjoy them as the villagers have all these years?"

"Oh, yes, most definitely," said Beauty. "The spectacle of ponies, both male and female, is too splendid not to be used throughout the kingdom!"

"But wait, my love," I said. "Surely you're referring to men only with this, aren't you? I did once in my time in the village see female ponies . . . but only once, and they were exceedingly rare."

"They were rare, true, sire," said Tristan, "but they were capable and beautiful, believe me. No, we didn't see them much. The mayor kept a stable when we were in the village. But in fact Lady Julia, the present mayor of the village, has kept a large stable of female ponies for years."

"Beloved, it seems too harsh for women," I said. "I can't imagine it. No. I know what it means to have served as a pony, pulling carts, chariots. It's too much."

"Your Majesty, believe me, it is not," said Lady Eva without hesitation. "Do trust me in this. There are princesses now residing in the kingdom who can tell you happily of their voluptuous service as ponies in Lady Julia's village stable. And they would be overjoyed, I'm sure, to help create a huge stable of female ponies at the castle for Queen Beauty's coaches and her pleasure. Why, Queen Beauty could have her stable of elegant female ponies, and you, sire, might have your stable of well-muscled male ponies. You need never, either of you, or anyone for that matter, travel the roads of the kingdom without human ponies."

Captain Gordon nodded at once. "This can easily be accomplished, Your Majesty," he said. "You remember Princesses Rosalynd and Elena who served with you in the land of the Sultan. They were not returned to the kingdom until years after you had left. But they were sentenced to pony servitude by Queen Eleanor to cleanse away all the softening effects of the Sultan's regime, and they served as ponies under Sonya, the head groom appointed by the Lord Mayor of the village in those days. Sonya was the greatest of all grooms of female ponies. . . . Why, Sonya perfected the whole manner of outfitting and handling female ponies." He stopped. His face darkened. He seemed to be remembering himself. "Alas, Sonya is long gone. . . ." He glanced quickly and fearfully at Prince Alexi, but when Prince Alexi merely smiled, he continued, "And those princesses have long been ladies-in-waiting. They can tell you about their service. They speak of it all the time."

"Thank you, Captain," I said. "And do not be ashamed of speaking out here. This is what we must know. I'm finding it hard to imagine, delicate lady ponies, but I shall wait and see, of course, and I suspect you are right in this."

"Your Majesty," said Captain Gordon, "there are ponies in Lady Julia's small village stable now."

"Yes, we must see these female ponies," said Beauty. "We will of course be learning much from what we see firsthand. But I think this is a splendid idea."

I shrugged and looked at Beauty. "If you say so, all of you . . ."

"My lord," said Beauty. "This will be like all else, a matter of aptitude. That will be the very nature of our refinements. We shall choose those who will thrive as ponies. And yes, I can well imagine a splendid stable of male and female ponies, and my own personal royal coach being pulled always by a great team of female ponies."

"And wait till you hear, Your Majesties," said Tristan, "how Princess Lucinda, another former pony, speaks of the splendid gold harnesses, buckles, boots, and plumes in Sonya's time. Why shouldn't there be such lovely stables at the castle? Why, the Court often asked Queen Eleanor for this, but she had no interest in it."

"I always thought the pony life mysteriously seductive," said Prince Alexi. "But then I never knew it, and seldom even caught a glimpse of it. It was almost painful at times, hearing of it and not being able to see it. So what do I know?"

"Oh, poor little good boy," said Lady Elvera, in a withering, mocking voice. "That you were never given the pleasure of being humiliated in the village!"

Tristan laughed and smiled at Alexi in a confidential way.

I couldn't stop myself from laughing.

"Well, one can't have everything in life, can one?" said Alexi as he winked at Lady Elvera.

The enthusiasm was running high all around. Lady Elvera was melting, her eyes dancing as she looked from Alexi to Tristan and then to me. "Ponies for the Court," she mused. "Yes, I do like it. And male and female, yes, quite interesting. But only if it pleases Your Majesty."

"I've certainly heard Princess Lucinda on this," said Lady Eva, "and I think she could draw up rules and pictures of accoutrements for a royal stable of female ponies on her own. Why, with the wealth of the Court, who knows what might be devised?"

Beauty began to laugh, though she tried not to, her hand coming quickly to her lips. "This is perfect!" she said.

"Very well," I said. I knew I was blushing. Female ponies! It was a tantalizing thought. And I well remembered that one glimpse I'd had of the females pulling the mayor's coach. "If you wish. And this will be done in the new spirit, with keen attention to those who flourish in such servitude. . . ."

"Of course," said Beauty. "That's the whole point, the new spirit!"

"But this Sonya," I said, looking at Captain Gordon. "You said she was the greatest of all grooms of female ponies. What has become of her? Is it conceivable she might return to the kingdom if we offered her inducements?"

Again, I saw that shadow cross his face. "Alas, she was dismissed in disgrace," he said. "It's a sad tale." He glanced uneasily at Prince Alexi.

"Yes, disgrace," said Prince Alexi. "As I was dismissed. It was a complicated affair. It involved Lexius. You remember Lexius, my lord, I'm sure, Lexius of the sultanate. But I think Sonya is quite beyond recalling at this point."

"I should like to hear all about this," I said. "Of course I remember Lexius. It was I who stole him away from the sultanate." I tried not to laugh. "It was perfectly outrageous of me to force Lexius to come with us when we were being rescued by the Captain and others." I glanced at the Captain. "But of course, Lexius could easily have gotten away, had he wanted to. Where is Lexius now? What is his story?"

"But not now, certainly," said Beauty. "When we have so very much to discuss. We were speaking of a new spirit."

"In time, sire, I'll tell you all I know of what happened," said Tristan, "of all that was written by Nicholas in the Queen's chronicles. And I can write to Lexius if that is your wish."

"I have already written," said Alexi. "I wrote to him before we left Bellavalten."

"That's good, very good," I said. "I want to know all about what happened with Lexius. Is there any chance Lexius might return?"

"There's a possibility," said Alexi. "But Lexius is far away, in the land of his birth, and it will take some time for our letters to reach him."

I could see that Lady Eva and Lady Elvera were both fascinated. So was the Captain, as the matter of Alexi writing to Lexius had surprised him. I had to know more of all of this.

"But come now," said Beauty, "to the discussion of the new spirit."

"Any good mistress or master," said Lady Eva, "can play a good slave like a harp."

"Yes, and it my wish," said Beauty, "that there be slaves of different ages. In the past most were very young, and with reason, but now and then the kingdom might receive older slaves whose gifts rival those of the young ones, and whose stamina is undiminished, and whose will to serve burns bright."

"Ah, yes," said Prince Alexi with a long sigh.

Captain Gordon nodded approvingly. "There are some male ponies in the village now who are older," he said. "There are some so accustomed to that life that they don't welcome any other."

"This doesn't surprise me," I said, though I had to confess I didn't remember any older ponies. On the other hand, there had been some very rough ponies in those days indeed, and I never really saw all of the others, only those who were in our teams, or near us in the stalls, or took their recreation when we did.

I caught Lady Eva gazing at me with girlish admiration.

I smiled so broadly I forced her to smile against her will. She gave me a mock-reproving look as if to say, You're a bad boy.

"And, Your Majesties," she said, quickly recovering her usual remarkable composure, "may I present you with many innovations of my own which I have developed since I came to the kingdom? Why, I have developed many potions, potions that can aid the most shy slaves to express their passion, and other potions to force sleep and rest at the appropriate times, and of course there are pastes and plasters for decorating slaves that I've developed that might well enhance female ponies, and the old tantalizing potions used to punish. Why, I have a great alchemist, Matthieu, working with me in the kingdom, and much can be done now that couldn't be done in the past because our late queen had no interest, but only if you would allow."

"We would allow," said Beauty. "Indeed this sounds most interesting, and precisely the kind of initiative we wish to encourage." She glanced at me brightly. "Now one thing further," she said turning to the group again, "that I should make clear. If many applicants come to us and are found worthy, we can greatly expand the use of slaves for different kinds of labor throughout the realm, with great incentives offered to slaves to work their way up the ladder of servitude from the most menial to the finer forms."

"Yes, this makes perfect sense," said Tristan. "As of now, after so many years of gradual decline, the kingdom contains only one very large village, and that is the Queen's Village. The small hamlets scattered throughout the forest and the few manor houses, except for mine, have had no slaves in years."

"There was a time when they did," said Alexi. "I remember noble slaves coming to Court to serve in those manor houses when I came. They were sons and daughters of lesser families."

"I remember talk of that," said Tristan. "I never saw them. But Nicholas told me years ago that there were no more noble slaves, only royal slaves. The kingdom had declined. It was declining up to the day we left it to come here. But surely with a new birth, many will return to the kingdom, and the manor houses and the little hamlets will take on a new life."

"But all citizens of the realm will treat all slaves with great care," I said firmly. "In my time there, slaves were well cared for, massaged, oiled, pampered, and well fed. And it did seem as if the roughest louts in the village knew the rules. No burning, no cutting, no breaking of the skin."

"Oh, most certainly," said Captain Gordon. "It is the same now. All slaves protected. All slaves are bathed, oiled, and massaged carefully, regardless of however lowly they might be. And we would be very vigilant with new citizens as to the rules. Slaves are costly. Slaves are precious." He was working himself up into a lather. I had apparently offended him. "Even of late, slaves are pampered and protected from neglect."

"I'm glad to hear it," I said. "And great care will be taken of course that all guests know the rules."

"Oh, most certainly, sire," said Tristan. "I never really knew when I was a slave how many guests did visit the kingdom simply to enjoy the slaves."

"There have always been hundreds in residence," said Lady Elvera. She regarded me with her usual cold stare, but her voice had an easy warmth to it, and her words came slowly and evenly. "And at times long ago, there were even thousands of guests for special festivals. But then the Queen grew weary, as we all know."

"And with a new and vital era beginning," said Tristan, "we will need our beautifully trained grooms and squires everywhere, always, keeping watch upon the kingdom's treasure: its slaves."

"We will need more grooms and squires," said Beauty. "And I am sure they will come."

"There are rooms in the castle in the north and east towers," said Lady Eva, "that have never been used. There is an entire wing of the castle that has been neglected. There must be fifty different rooms there, all waiting to be restored. And then Lord Gregory has the east tower all to himself. There are many rooms above his."

"Indeed there are manor houses that are now deserted," said Lady Elvera. "I have always lived at Court, but there are lords and ladies who would pay handsomely for an abandoned manor house which they might lovingly restore to the grandeur of the past—if they could keep their own slaves."

"And why not?" asked Beauty. "Oh, this is splendid. There is so much to be done, proclamations to be written, lists of rules to be drawn up, new buildings that must be designed."

"Yes, Your Majesty, it is all too astonishing," cried Lady Eva. "I will do anything and everything that I might to see your dreams realized."

"Well, then," I said. "You have our acceptance of your offer, and you have the main thrust of the changes we would make."

Prince Alexi rose to his feet. "Your Majesties, I salute you both." He appeared on the verge of tears. It didn't seem to me he'd been half so beautiful when he was younger, or perhaps my tastes had changed. He was a man of stunning face and form now, delicate, yes, like something made of dark glass that might break, but I liked him.

Of course I did not think of him now as I'd found him last night in my wife's bed, in my bed, and naked and childlike as he had hurried to get clear of me, to dress himself and leave the chamber. And I, I had so wickedly detained him, reaching inside his pants to feel his cock and balls before I let him go, and then kissing him myself as if to claim him. What a piquant and tasty man he was. Hmmm. Such lips, such kisses. But this was a new epoch for us all, wasn't it, including my precious queen who had not even waked last night to welcome me until I'd used my belt gently on her curvaceous little bottom. Well, suffice it to say that I understood why she'd chosen Alexi for her pleasure.

Tristan and Captain Gordon rose quickly, and Lady Eva rose and made a deep bow. "This is the happiest day of my recent life," she proclaimed.

"There is much to do," said Beauty. "And I am most interested in these pastes and plasters and potions you describe, Lady Eva, and some other ideas are coming to me, memories of things I have from the Sultan's realm."

"Yes, we are ready and willing with our whole hearts," said Tristan.

"You have fulfilled our dreams," said Lady Elvera as she rose slowly. "And I suspect this is as the old queen wished it to be. Bellavalten will be reborn."

"And in that matter of Lexius," I added. "You will write to him and invite him to return?" I looked at Lady Eva as if she were my personal scribe now.

"As you wish, Your Majesty," she answered. "I will do anything you command."

So it was decided.

So it was done.

I bid them all to be seated again, giddy and relieved as they were, and called for more wine for the entire company.

We had confided to no one the strange dreams we'd had of Titania of Mataquin, but then why should we? There was no necessity for that. Our past was ours, and not the possession of anyone but us. But this happiness belonged to all of us. Yet these moments would not have been so sweet to me had I not seen with my own eyes the splendid Titania of Mataquin, had I not heard it from her lips that I had always been the prince destined for my beloved Beauty.

The remainder of the day was spent in easy conversation and drinking, with Lady Eva and Prince Tristan both busy writing down much of what we had discussed. Soon my secretary Emlin was directed to call the royal scribes to me to assist with those letters that must be sent to Bellavalten and the whole world right away.

Supper was a veritable banquet, and by eight in the evening I was exhausted and ready once more to retire. Only one thing nagged at me and it was, of course, the matter of Lexius and "disgrace" involving Alexi and the mysterious Sonya, but there would be time to learn about all this. Alexi would not have so boldly admitted that he had written already to Lexius if there had been reasons not to pursue such a matter.

In fact, we made a long list of names, names of those slaves I remembered and those Beauty remembered, to which Captain Gordon added a number, and so did Lady Elvera, and Alexi—all of whom were to receive letters of invitation from us. And I could not keep track of the names of those already waiting for us in Bellavalten.

It would be four days at least before we set out for Bellavalten, and much work could be done during that time, and many letters would leave here before we did.

At last, the long and eventful day was done, and Beauty and I were alone—cozy once more in our private chambers, around our own most beloved hearth.

I had been enchanted with the manner in which she presented her ideas to the little assembly, and this made me all the more eager to hold her in my arms. Truly I did not care that she'd been with Alexi. I determined that I would not allow myself to care, and if I thought of it for one moment, I would relish the thought, allowing it to tantalize me, to stoke the fires in my heart, and never to dampen my spirits.

I was so hungry for Beauty, in fact, I all but tore her gown to pieces as I'd done with Lady Eva the night before, and I flung her down on the bed and ravaged her for the better part of an hour before I was finally worn out. She was hot and pliant, her kisses as heated as mine. She resisted nothing as I tormented her gently, playing with her nipples, punishing them, teasing her and holding her at bay, and then handling her with my usual affectionate abandon.

At last I lay there, deliciously exhausted, and I felt her cool hands touching all the little welts and bruises I had from Lady Eva's paddle and strap. Soon, Beauty was dabbing a soothing ointment here and there, and smoothing the sore muscles of my thighs and calves.

"You are such a wicked boy, Laurent," she said. "Such a wicked boy!"

"You don't know the half of it, Queen Beauty," I murmured into the pillow. My eyes were closed. Her fingers massaging my backside were arousing me again. She pinched and scratched at the welts playfully, then pressed the ointment deep into my sore flesh. Ripples of sweet sensation passed through me, and over all my skin.

"But my, how she whipped you," she said under her breath. "Wicked Lady Eva."

"Oh, yes, wicked Lady Eva." I sighed. "Inexhaustibly wicked Lady Eva."

There came a knock on our parlor door.

I put on my dressing gown and went to answer, expecting Emlin with some tiresome pesky message, but it was Tristan standing there.

"Well, come in," I said as I directed him to a chair by the fire. Beauty had retired into her little parlor adjoining the bedchamber. I took the chair opposite him.

"Just one thing more which I wanted to lay before you in private," he said confidentially, glancing anxiously at the bedroom door as if he did not want Beauty to hear.

"Continue," I said. "We are alone." I sat back, and rather enjoying his handsome looks as I had been enjoying them all day, but now especially that my desires were for the moment satisfied, and I did not want to mount him and make him bite the pillow under me as I had been wanting to do all afternoon. "And call me Laurent, now, please."

"Yes, sire, I mean, Laurent, yes," he said. "This is a delicate matter. But there is a great manor house in ruins way south of the castle, right near the border, that was in its time quite beautifully appointed and rich."

"You want this manor house?" I asked. "I thought you already had your own manor house."

"No, I don't want it, and yes, I do have my own, as a matter of fact," he replied. "But what I was wondering is . . . could this house not be restored by Your Majesties for a specific purpose, to wit, to become a place of luxurious accommodations for those lords and ladies of the kingdom, princes, princesses, dukes, duchesses, whatever, who might hunger for a night of being thoroughly mastered and punished in secret by those slaves who possess the gift?"

I laughed. "Of course," I said. I laughed again. This day would live forever in my memory! What else, I thought, might happen before the hour of midnight? "And who says it must be gifted slaves who do the mastering?"

"Well, no, it wouldn't have to be slaves necessarily, but there are some who are so singularly gifted. It could be a place where they are mastered by lords and ladies as well."

"So the old kingdom had no such accommodations?" I asked. "A courtier who longed for the lash wasn't allowed to feel it?"

"No."

"How absurd." I thought of the old queen. What an idiot! But I felt a bit foolish that I'd never even thought of this before. Not once during my years as a slave had I thought of it.

Yes, in the sultanate, I'd mastered Lexius, the Sultan's steward, right in his own splendid quarters. But Lexius had been no courtier. He had in my mind been a servant.

And Tristan surely remembered, too, how I'd mastered Prince Jerard, a handsome pony, when I caught him in the recreation yard of the stable. And Tristan remembered that I had mastered him, because I had done that too—in the ship returning from the sultanate, I'd whipped Tristan as often as I'd whipped Lexius. And sometimes Captain Gordon had watched, marveling at my skill at mastering as if it was something most slaves did not possess. It had not been a marvel to me. As I'd explained to Beauty, I had always relished the idea of both—being mastered, and mastering. But I'd never thought of mastering lords and ladies of the Court. Never.

But now I wondered keenly how many might have wanted such a thing.

"Then we shall establish such a place," I said, "replete with comfortably and richly outfitted chambers, where lords and ladies may go and no one will be the wiser as to who is master or mistress. We'll make the house a sumptuous, very private retreat."

"Marvelous!" he said with a sigh of relief. "It happens now, you see, that some are mastered by their slaves, but it is hidden, and secret."

"Ridiculous," I said.

Hmmm. *What if Beauty wanted to be mastered by someone other than me? What if Alexi had . . . No, that had not happened. I'd seen her fresh and innocent little bottom last night when I'd returned. Still, the thought of it . . .*

"It's something to be enjoyed like anything else," I said. "And to think that those of privilege would deny themselves such pleasures! What a waste."

But what if Beauty . . . ? No, I couldn't think of it. I could accept her taking Alexi into her bed, yes, of course, but— I wouldn't think anymore on that. Well, not for the moment. But then her voice in my memory saying she must have the very same prerogatives . . . the very same.

Alas, I had to grow into this new role as the King of Bellavalten.

"So it is with Lord Stefan," Tristan said. "You remember him, the Queen's cousin?"

"Yes. Of course. He'd been your lover before you were captured and brought to the kingdom. Of course I remember. He couldn't master you and so you rebelled."

"Yes," said Tristan, "and he has a fearsome yellow-haired slave named Becca of whom he is terrified, and it all takes place behind locked doors."

I couldn't help but laugh out loud. But this mention of Lord Stefan put me in mind of something.

"Wait," I said, putting up my hand as I tried to recollect this. "I heard something when I was a slave at the castle. I heard that every year on Midsummer Eve lords and ladies who wanted to be slaves, even princes or princesses of the Court, could come forward and ask to be sold in the village. I never knew for certain whether or not this was true but . . ."

"It had been a custom, yes," said Tristan. "My master, Nicholas the Chronicler, told me of it. But the Queen hated it. She had no respect for lords and ladies who voluntarily gave themselves up to slavery and she took no interest in such volunteers ever after. Also they had to go into it completely, banished from the castle. They were stripped and sold in the village. No turning back . . ."

"Of course. You're speaking now with the manor house of someone's choosing to be a slave for a few hours, a night perhaps."

"Yes," Tristan said. "That is what I am thinking of. Also the Queen abolished the custom that last year—the same year that you and I were sent to the village—because her very own cousin, Lord Stefan, of whom we've been speaking, wanted to be sold, and the Queen was furious that one of her own kinsmen would choose this." Tristan smiled and shook his head. "Ah, Stefan. He wanted it so desperately but was denied the opportunity forever."

"That's it. I remember now. Yes. Lord Stefan. I remember hearing that he might step forward . . ."

"Yes, well, she forbade Lord Stefan from being sold in the village and she abolished the custom. Now, she still allowed villagers to come forward on Midsummer Night and offer themselves for naked service. This was permissible to her, villagers, as they were not noble and not her kin. But that didn't always happen. Nicholas said few villagers had the courage for it."

"Yes, makes perfect sense."

I pondered for a long moment.

"I'll tell you something else," Tristan confided. "There were always slaves who were released if they showed absolutely no aptitude."

"There were?"

"Yes, those boys whose organs could not be aroused, those girls who dissolved in tears and paralysis. In sum, the ones who never found it stirring or pleasurable at all to serve. But no one was ever told about it. They only heard of rebels like Prince Alexi who, in spite of themselves, had hard cocks and fiercely beating hearts even when they would not obey, or little females who writhed like kittens when they were stroked and punished though they had to be bound most of the time."

I smiled. "Well, that makes sense too," I said.

"Queen Eleanor called those she sent away pallid little creatures, dimwits, and pitiable beings. Nicholas told me all this. But it was all secret."

I fell into deep thought for a long time. I remembered so many things. My cock had been hard even when I was on the Punishment Cross for public display as a runaway. I'd found it all so deeply and richly intoxicating. It had been spellbinding.

But Tristan was waiting on me.

"Put your worries aside," I said. "We'll establish this manor house. We shall have servants and naked slaves to run it; and it will be the place for such things. Oh, we have so much to do, don't we? I need maps of the kingdom. I intend to build walls around it entirely even if it takes years. And this manor house shall be a jewel when we are finished with it."

"Thank you, Laurent," he said. His voice was muted and there was a dark intensity to his eyes, to his expression. There was something very provocative about him suddenly, the way he lowered his eyes, the way he glanced up at me. He was daring me to master him now, I knew it. I wanted to do it. I found myself wondering what it would be like to master him now that he was a man, so self-possessed, so unlike the suffering pilgrim of passion he'd been in those days. I would do this, I knew I would. And I thought to myself, I shall do this when I wish, not when he wishes.

After I had seen him to the door, I found Beauty in her parlor at her dressing table, brushing her long hair. She was singing softly under her breath. I came up behind her, wrapped my arms around her, and began to kiss her tender little neck.

"Oh, Laurent, I am so tired," she said. "You have the spirit of a new king."

"Beauty! How are you going to be the queen of this new realm if you have so little stamina!" I said. I slipped my hand down between her legs, but the silk of her gown might as well have been a coat of mail.

"Doesn't a queen spend a great deal of her time presiding over and watching entertainments prepared for her?" she asked. "That doesn't take so much stamina, does it? Oh, I wish we were already at Bellavalten and in the gardens and that the gardens were filled with lanterns and that there were slave spectacles for us to enjoy this very night."

She turned and looked up at me.

"Do you remember when we were in the hold of the ship, sailing to the sultanate, and they took Tristan and me, and they rubbed us all over with gold? It was an oil they used, filled with gold pigment, and we were burnished like statues, and they painted our nails and our eyelids gold."

"I remember it vividly," I said. My cock was painfully hard. "We were kept in cages and all we could do was watch."

"Ah," she went on dreamily. "I would so love to have many slaves at the castle burnished in that way for evening festivals, like so many gold or silver statues. I must talk to Lady Eva about such things. Wouldn't that be lovely?"

"Lovely," I said. "You want to see a spectacle here now?" I knelt down beside her and, turning her towards me, I kissed her breasts through the pale blue silk of her gown.

"I wouldn't mind it," she whispered, kissing me tenderly. "Why, what do you have in mind?"

"I don't know. Maybe we need another night apart, visiting with our old friends, each of us . . ."

She nodded. I saw something quicken in her face. She didn't need my urging.

"Laurent, from now on every night for us should hold full promise, shouldn't it?"

"Yes, Beauty," I said. "It should. But I was wondering. Last night, when you and Alexi were alone here together . . ."

"My lord, why trouble yourself with such things? We coupled. That's what we did. We coupled, as we had long ago. But you are my king, my spouse, and my lord. You alone are my ruler."

How earnest she seemed, and how much wiser than I would ever be.

But what if he had mastered her, what if? Why did this matter to me? I knew that it should not matter, any more than it mattered to Beauty what I had suffered at the hands of Eva.

I kissed her again slowly, as if my lips were seeking her soul—as if my breath and her breath were one, as if our souls were linked with one vital fire.

"Queen of my heart," I said gravely. "I am yours and yours only."

"Yes, beloved sovereign," she whispered, throwing her arms tight around me, nuzzling into my neck. "I adore only you and no other."

7

PRINCESS BLANCHE: ISN'T SHE A DAINTY DISH TO SET BEFORE THE QUEEN?

Blanche lay naked on the floor of the dressing closet, her head on a pillow, the cruel golden chastity belt covering her tender sex with its little cage of mesh so that she could not hope to alleviate the burning desire that she felt.

All last night, she had languished in torment as her master Tristan had talked by the hour with Lady Elvera in the bedchamber beyond.

Only when Lady Eva came finally to tell them that "all was well with the King" did they stop their endless commiseration, but then Tristan had turned to his writing without so much as a word to her, and finally, she had cried herself to sleep.

This afternoon and this evening, they'd been in the great hall of the castle, feasting and talking all together, and she had again been left here in the shadows, alone and frightened and starved for her master's touch.

Galen had come more than once to see to her, to make certain that she had not left the dressing closet, and to spank her hard once or twice over his knee as he told her to behave herself and be patient, and not dare to touch the golden chastity belt that covered her private parts.

As if I knew how to unlock it, she thought bitterly. But Galen had not meant to be cruel. Not really. He was uneasy as was everyone else, waiting for the all-important decision of King Laurent and Queen Beauty, but Blanche's breasts and sex burned for Tristan, and these hours were a torment she could scarcely bear.

Nevertheless, in Blanche's mind, Galen left much to be desired in a groom.

At last, Galen had come rushing to tell her that it was decided: the King and Queen would take the thrones of Bellavalten, and were at this very minute giving forth their first all-important decrees. Galen had taken off the chastity belt long enough to bathe Blanche and rub her thoroughly with oil all over, and then to brush out her hair. But he'd been very strict that she must keep her legs apart as he tended to her. "Don't make me tell him that you haven't been a good girl." His slow firm hands had sent the chills ripping through her as they rubbed the oil into her breasts, into her underarms, and into the muscles of her arms and legs. Galen was always happy when he worked, whistling to himself, and he gave little random kisses to Blanche, on her mouth or on her forehead, and always whispered flattery into her ear.

"You're the most gorgeous slave I've ever groomed," he said. Or, "I can scarcely resist you. Someday, I'm going to beg the master just to let me lie with you once." This puzzled Blanche but she paid little attention. She'd been used in all ways by many grooms in the castle of the old kingdom. But then, her new master, Tristan, made his own rules.

Of course Blanche had been happy about the King's decision. How could she not be happy that the kingdom would continue, that she would not have to leave the life that had engulfed her now for two years. But all this excitement in the great hall meant more lying in wait on the floor of the dressing closet, her fingers prying vainly at the little cage that covered her, trying to touch just the edge of her nether lips but in vain. Now and then she pinched her own nipples but this only intensified her longing, and her frustration.

Finally she'd fallen asleep again, and she did not know how many hours passed before Galen again awakened her.

"Get up quickly," he said, snapping his fingers. "I mean it, now, hurry!" He was whispering. "Your master's had his late supper and he wants you."

She rose to her feet and stretched like a cat. He quickly unlocked the chastity belt and removed it. "Marks, it's left marks on your flesh," he said crossly.

She was tempted to say, Well, what did you expect?

He took the salve from the shelf and quickly rubbed it on the tender insides of her thighs, telling her as he always did to spread her legs wide.

"You know you are the sweetest darling," he crooned as he worked. "But I have to make these marks disappear."

Within minutes, he was working on her hair, brushing it free of tangles. She loved the heavy feel of it on her naked back.

"Now, down on all fours, little one, and eat those bits of apple," he said, putting the dish before her.

The apple was to sweeten her breath, of course, all lords and ladies and slaves of the kingdom ate bits of apple on awakening and several times during every day and night, and she enjoyed it, though it was a chore to nibble at it and chew it up without ever using her hands. Now and then Galen or some other efficient groom scrubbed her teeth with apple, and even her tongue. She rather liked it, though the first time had frightened her, her mouth open like that, and fingers prying into it.

Galen had Blanche on her feet again. He pinched her cheeks and rouged her lips. "Gorgeous," he said. How intent he looked, how thoroughly engaged with his work.

Then he thrust his hand between her legs.

"You're wet already," he said reprovingly. "I wonder what would happen if you were spanked for that, for getting wet."

Ah, it took all her patience to ignore him.

How could she not be moist there? Did he think this was something she could control?

Just the thought of Tristan brought the moisture flooding inside the secret cavity that only Tristan was allowed to fill or even touch. And no, it wouldn't do any good at all if she were spanked for it. It would make no difference whatsoever except that Galen would have an opportunity perhaps to deliver more of his excellent spankings of which he was justly proud.

And he did do it so very well. Each and every groom had a different manner, a different way of wielding the paddle or the strap. So did every master or mistress. With Galen, the blows came rapidly and smartly, while with his firm left hand he held tight to her neck. "Now, how do you like that, young lady!" he would say to her about halfway through. "You think that's enough?" She'd always known better than to answer one way or the other, pouring out her incoherent sobs instead. She loved nothing more than to be able to sob freely, her lips politely closed, of course, but her sobs nevertheless audible and unrestrained.

It was marvelous how good he was at it, the spanks coming so rapidly and with a kind of rhythm that she weakened all over as she ached under the paddle and let herself twist and dance without ever really struggling against Galen's firm grasp.

She said nothing now as Galen pushed her into the bedchamber and motioned for her to kneel down and remain quiet and still. It had been two full days since he'd last spanked her at her master's urging, and she knew her bottom would be fresh and pretty for Tristan if only Tristan cared to notice, which he very well might not.

The room was deliciously warm. The floor felt deliciously warm. Her beloved master sat at a table to the right of the fire. He was as always writing and he did not look up when Galen told him in a soft voice that Princess Blanche had been "prepared."

Though she knelt with her head bowed, she could see Tristan clearly and as always the very sight of him caused the desire in her to double and triple in intensity. In a daze, she watched his hand as he moved the quill so rapidly and with such quick little scratches over the parchment. And the other hand, which lay on his thigh, she could see even better gleaming in the light. It seemed to her she could feel that hand on her already. Feel its warmth, its strength. Tristan had such large and beautiful hands.

His soft curling golden hair was mussed and loose and half veiled his face. She longed to be able to touch it, lift it, move it back away from his eyes, but she had never been permitted to do such a thing, and she might never, she knew.

Without so much as looking up or away from the page before him, he said in a low voice, "On your hands and knees, come here."

At once she hurried to obey, and when she reached the table she at once kissed his feet. He had taken off his heavy boots and wore morocco-leather slippers now and she loved the feel of them under her lips. She dared not touch his ankle, his leg, or any part of him without permission. But she kissed him several times on each foot and then pressed her forehead to the floor. Again, the desire in her intensified. She was throbbing with it all over.

"You have no way of knowing what a momentous night this is," he said as he continued to move the pen. "The kingdom is saved, our future is saved, and you, little princess, are safe."

"Yes, my lord," she said softly.

"Kneel up," he said.

As she obeyed, glancing up furtively for a split second, he turned and smiled at her and it was as if a great bright light had washed over her warming her to her soul. How breathtakingly handsome he was. If only she could tell him, but that would never be allowed.

It was absolutely unreal to her that he, Prince Tristan, her master, had once been a slave. She knew the story of course. So did everyone. But she couldn't imagine it, her beloved Tristan naked and being whipped as she was so often whipped, even harnessed and tethered to a cart or a coach in the dreaded Queen's Village, where he'd served as a pony for years. Yet when she thought of it, it excited her, she had to admit, and pushed her closer to delirium as she let contrary thoughts collide in her mind now.

"Have you been a good little girl while I've been busy?" he asked. He stroked her hair back from her forehead. "Beautiful Blanche. You are so fair and sweet and inviting." He bent and kissed her lips. The passion inside her boiled upwards; it was all she could do not to rock her hips uncontrollably with it and let loose the orgasm that would humiliate her utterly and infuriate him with her loss of control.

She knelt still, very still, feeling the throbbing between her legs as his lips pressed hard against her mouth. Then his hand slid down to feel the telltale moisture, and he laughed under his breath. "Have you been obedient and chaste?"

"Yes, my lord," she said. Didn't he know that Galen had locked her in the chastity belt? Certainly he did.

He stood suddenly, and pulled her up on her feet.

"Darling, you don't know how happy I am," he said with a flood of uncommon warmth. He pressed her to his hard chest. "We are all safe once more, Bellavalten is safe!" He kissed her over and over again on her lips.

Tears sprang to her eyes. She went positively limp in his powerful arms.

"Master," she whispered.

"Yes, we are safe again, Princess. There is nothing to fear. I can't live anywhere else but Bellavalten, and now I will never have to contemplate such a thing."

His eyes were wet with rising tears. And his voice was roughened with emotion, with tenderness.

"Do you love me, Blanche?" he whispered as he kissed her ear. "I command you to lie to me if you do not, because I must hear it. I must hear it now."

"Master, I adore you, and that is not a lie," she said. The tears filled her eyes. He was trembling and now she felt herself shaking violently, tremors passing through her legs as he held her. "I have always adored you, from the very first moment I saw you. Master, you give my whole life meaning!"

"Ah, beautiful, lovely Blanche. I'll tell you a wicked secret," he said, still embracing her tightly, embracing the way people do on greeting or parting, his left hand cradling her bottom, holding her so securely that her feet were off the floor.

"It is safe with me forever, Master," she answered softly. "Put your secret in my heart."

He sat down, pulling her onto his lap. Holding her in his right arm, he squeezed her breasts tenderly with his left hand. She thought she would lose all control, but she fought the torment, fought it, gazing at him adoringly, wanting to kiss away the tears from his face.

"Years ago, Laurent, the King, he mastered me just like that. I mean it was so simple for him. One moment he'd been a slave beside me subject to the same punishments, and the next he'd picked up the belt of the Captain of the Guard and made me his trembling slave. How was he able to do that so easily, Blanche? How could he pass from one mode to the other? How could he find room in his heart for either role?"

He looked into her eyes.

"I don't know, my lord," she said. "I've never understood such things. I long to submit, to lose myself in submitting. I always have."

"He will make the greatest ruler Bellavalten ever had," said Tristan. "But it is the new queen who wants you tonight. Are you prepared to please her?"

"Master, how can you ask? I would do anything in this world you ordered me to do, for you, for Her Majesty, for anyone to whom you gave me. You know it."

"Yes, my darling," he said. "Well, first you're mine."

In a twinkling he was on his feet and so was she. He'd spun her around and his big firm right hand came down in a series of hard spanks.

"Fresh, sweet, beautiful," he said. "Now at once, over the end of the bed."

He drove her forward and bent her over the figured coverlet, and pushed her legs wide apart with his foot. The rough tapestried fabric made her nipples tingle. And she couldn't keep back a loud moan.

"You're barely blushing from my hand, little one," he said.

She felt his cock driving into her vagina, felt it fill her and split her open deliciously as her clitoris rubbed against the coverlet, yet not enough, not nearly enough. Oh, this was pain and pleasure mingling like smoke. Her hands were opening and closing vainly.

Again and again, he pounded her, lifting her now and holding her thighs in his powerful arms.

She came with loud uncontrollable gasps. His body spanked against her, and the pleasure flooded through her again and again.

This was the most precious of moments—when she thought nothing and saw nothing and likely heard nothing, when she was the pleasure she was feeling, when every sinew of her frame was taut with it, when she knew not where she lay or how long it would last.

Her body was limp, flopping like that of a doll.

At last, it was ebbing, leaving her. She rubbed her breasts against the tapestry, moaning, arching her back.

"Oh, my lord," she gasped. "My beautiful lord."

When he came it was with a muffled cry. That was always his way, that low, muffled, gentlemanly cry. The last few spasms of his cock reignited the orgasm. She thought she would cry out.

And then came the awful moment, the moment when the cock was pulled out, when she was emptied, but it was happening, it was over, over so quickly it seemed and so cruelly and she lay there, legs apart, feeling his hands on her hips, waiting, aching, hoping for what he might do or will next. The Queen . . . she could not quite imagine it, as she had only glimpsed the magnificent Beauty once since her arrival, and she had no sense of the woman's soul.

With a firm grip, he flung her over on her back, pulling her with his right hand to center her apparently on the bed.

She could still feel the carpeted floor with the balls of her feet.

"Wide apart!" he said.

And she struggled to open herself up totally and completely as he commanded, her eyes closed.

"Galen, come here," he said.

She didn't dare to look at him, but she knew he was right there, because she could feel his leggings against her own naked legs, and she could feel his fingers now touching her pubis, smoothing the hair.

"Now, I want this trimmed," he said. "Neatly. Not shaved, you understand. I don't care for that at all ever. But I want the hair neatly trimmed. And then wash her well inside and out. Oil her. Perfume her. And then bring her back to me to take to the Queen."

Within minutes, the rough cleansing and grooming were finished.

Galen had been anxious, fearful, and uncommonly clumsy, but she hadn't cared. Poor Galen. What did it matter to her?

The Queen's private chambers in the north tower were their destination, Tristan told her as he covered her with a heavy hooded purple cloak.

"Put on slippers. This castle is dusty," he said to her. And Galen fitted them to her feet.

She hated the touch of any fabric on her, anything that interfered with her pure nakedness, but they were not in Bellavalten now; that she well understood. The passion was building in her again, the telltale damp was returning. And then they hurried along the passage together, and up the stairway, Tristan deeply absorbed in his thoughts.

It was a well-appointed bedchamber, with costly tapestries and an inviting fire on the hearth. A grand bed stood back in the shadows. And in a high-backed well-carved chair by the fire sat the Queen.

There was another figure in the room as they entered, but Blanche could not see who this was.

At once, Tristan removed her cloak and told her to approach the Queen in the customary way.

Blanche quickly obeyed until she found herself kneeling before the Queen's golden slippers just peeping from beneath the gold embroidered hem of her dark blue gown.

Blanche kissed the soft gilded leather of each slipper appropriately, her heart melting at the smell of the Queen's exotic perfume. Crushed flowers and spice.

Then came the soft appealing sound of Prince Alexi's voice, deeper in timbre than Tristan's, the words running more slowly and evenly, suggesting patience, aloofness.

". . . simple thing to do what you want with her, if you want to do anything with her, that is."

"She's exquisite," said the Queen. "Like flower petals, this skin. Kneel up, Princess Blanche, and slip your hands to the back of your neck and look at me and then look down."

A shock passed through Blanche as she obeyed. The Queen's bright blue eyes were girlish and trusting, and her mouth appeared soft and guileless and naturally pink.

At once Blanche looked down and felt her face burn hot.

So this would be the new sovereign of Bellavalten, this comely and elegant young woman, so fresh, and so appealing and so seemingly without coldness. But faces could be deceiving, Blanche well knew. She'd been spanked hard many a time by the most innocent-looking young pages, cherubs with lilting voices who swung the paddle fiercely and laughed when Blanche moaned.

A deep delicious fear thrilled Blanche. Would this lovely creature punish her? It had been too long since she'd been punished by a woman.

Again her face burned.

"Why are you blushing, child?" asked the Queen.

Blanche felt the Queen's fingers under her chin. This touch, this gesture, always made Blanche feel doubly exposed and helpless. She knew the tears were springing into her eyes.

"Give me the paddle, Alexi," said the Queen. "Tristan, you may go or stay as you like. I thank you for this precious toy."

"The King's sent for me, Your Majesty," Tristan said.

And this too thrilled Blanche, but she did not know why. Could she more fully yield to these two, the Queen and dark-eyed Prince Alexi, if her master were gone?

"Well, then you must go, mustn't you?" said the Queen. "Don't keep the King waiting."

Blanche sighed inwardly and secretly when she heard the door of the chamber close.

To her left she could see the leather shoes of Prince Alexi, those soft slippers for house wear, wrinkled and curling at the toes. Dark green leggings and the hem of a long green tunic. She dared not look up for any more details.

With a shock she saw the Queen's sleeve in front of her and then she felt the Queen's warm fingers pressed in the tender part of her upper arm.

"You're softer than the petals of lilies," the Queen said thoughtfully. "Now stand up, and let me inspect you. Turn your back to me. And I am watching your demeanor. I am watching your smallest gestures."

Blanche obeyed, not daring to utter a word.

"Ah, yes, you are silent, because I haven't given you permission to speak," said the Queen. "Well, you may answer 'Yes, madam' or 'No, madam.' I like this simple form of address."

"Yes, madam," said Blanche. She was on her feet and felt painfully awkward, painfully desperate to please. Her eyes misted. She could see much of the rest of the chamber now, the dark solemn procession of fig-ures in the tapestries, and the sparkling jeweled red coverlet of the ele-gant bed. Red. Red seemed the dominant color everywhere—in the Turkish carpet on which Blanche stood, and even in the tapestries where the reds rang out from the somber background in which so many muted tones mingled around pale faces with sharp-edged eyes.

"How many years have you been a slave in the kingdom?" asked the Queen behind her.

"Five years, Your Highness," said Blanche anxiously. It should have been "madam." Oh, it certainly should have been "madam." Again the blood rushed to her face.

Prince Alexi had moved around in front of her, and she gazed now at his long tunic and his thick leather belt. Would he spank her soon with that belt? It had a thick silver buckle to it, intricate and beautifully worked.

"Five years," the Queen repeated. "And tell me whom and how you've served."

Blanche struggled for composure. She was crying. Why did women always bring tears to her eyes? Of course she wept with abandon when-ever she wanted, as all slaves were always encouraged to do. But with women it seemed her tears sprang quickly, and a little thrilling sadness gripped her at each syllable that Beauty spoke.

"I was sent to serve for a year, madam," she said, her back still to the Queen. "I served at the Court for the longest time. I was slave to Princess Lynette."

"Not the Princess Lynette of my time?" asked the Queen. "Turn around, girl, and face me and keep your eyes modestly lowered as they should be."

"Yes, madam." Turning, she found herself staring at the golden slippers, and the perfume rose in her nostrils again, delicious and bitingly sweet. And this queen had indeed been a slave herself long ago, Blanche thought. She had stood for others as I'm standing now.

"Yes, but Princess Lynette ran away, did she not?" asked the Queen. "I heard gossip of it in the village."

"Yes, madam, or so the old tales say," said Blanche. She bit her lip, struggling, unable suddenly to remember what she had heard and from whom. Suppose she revealed some gossip about her former and very strict mistress that she was not supposed to say.

But Prince Alexi came to the rescue, whether he knew it or not.

He came to the Queen's side, and placed his hand on the back of her chair.

"Lynette ran away, yes," he said, "and she lodged in King Lysius's kingdom for a long while. You remember, Your Majesty, he would not return escaped slaves, as he was skeptical of the Queen and her enjoyments. But then Princess Lynette returned on her own, confessing she'd only run to be captured, and she was quite bored with life at King Lysius's Court. She was sentenced to the village then and to the female pony stable and there she served for years. She was sent home a year before I was."

"Ah, I see. I remember your story of her, Alexi," said the Queen.

"Yes, madam, I told you quite a story there."

And Blanche too had heard the story of how Princess Lynette trained Prince Alexi for a delectable little performance before the whole Court.

"She came back some six years ago, as I understand it," said Alexi, "and the Queen received her kindly just as she later received me. I've dined with her many an evening since the Queen went away. She has marvelous tales to tell of having served in the Lord Mayor's stables. She would help you build the new stables for female ponies at the castle with all her heart."

"I shall rely on that," said the Queen. "And was she a strict mistress, Princess Blanche?"

"Yes, madam," said Blanche softly. "Very strict."

"And were you ever sent to the Queen's Village for punishment?"

"Yes, madam, I was sent there, but only for a summer, and for 'slight imperfections,' as my mistress called them, which she wanted to see cleaned away. I was there for three months in the hotter weather, and served in a shop that sold various trinkets. I was used there for display."

"I never saw such a shop. Explain this to me," said the Queen.

"Adornments, madam. Clips for nipples or earlobes, chastity belts of gold, leather cuffs, and chains and such." Blanche realized she was trembling. This was the last thing she'd expected, to have to speak so much. But the Queen made not a sound, and anxiously, Blanche continued, "I was adorned and stood near the door for the passersby to approve the wares." A vivid memory of it engulfed her, of the hot cobblestone village street, where she stood motionless by the door, just as she was standing now, only her nipples were painted and adorned with coiled wire, and from the wire had hung tiny golden bells. Men and women of the village passed her, some ignoring her completely, others stopping to pat her bottom, or pinch her, or tickle the golden bells. And then came the serious buyer who would inspect carefully, and order her inside as he asked for the golden bracelets she wore, or the jewel adorning her navel, or the tiny pearls strung through her pubic hair.

"Why is your face so red, Princess?" asked the Queen.

"I don't want to displease you, madam," Blanche said with a short muffled sob.

"Oh, nonsense, you are not displeasing me. I am only asking. I want to know what you feel."

"Helpless, madam," said Blanche. "I . . . I was remembering . . ."

"Was the shopkeeper rough or kind?"

"I cannot complain about my masters, can I, madam?"

"Ah, so rough. Did he beat you often?"

"He sent me to the Punishment Shop every morning," said Blanche, the tears sliding down her cheeks.

"Ah, now, I have heard of that, the Punishment Shop," said the Queen, "though I never saw it. It was where bad little boys and girls were spanked by a seated whipping master while the villagers gathered to gossip and drink."

"Yes, madam," said Blanche. "He always wore a big leather apron and he was . . . Forgive me, madam. Forgive me."

"Forgive you what? Was he harsh? I want the truth."

"Harsh, madam. He spanked with a wooden paddle. If the audience liked it, if they even took a little notice, well, he'd give extra smacks. And if anyone paid for another spanking, he was all too willing."

"And were you a favorite with the morning crowd?"

"Always, madam."

"Come now, girl. I'm going to spank you. And you are going to tell me whether or not I do it well."

Blanche shivered, and her eyes melted with thick tears. But the Queen had given her no command as to what to do.

"Come, over my knee," said the Queen, "with your head towards Prince Alexi. The simple and elegant way with your hands touching the floor."

Hurriedly, Blanche fell to her knees and stretched herself out over the Queen's lap, her sex pressed against the velvet of the Queen's gown, and the desire in her exploding soundlessly yet with a throb she felt in her ears.

Her shoulders were shaking with her sobs as she lowered her hands to touch the floor before Prince Alexi's boots.

She felt the Queen's right hand on her backside, just touching it, prodding the flesh.

"So soft, so fresh," said the Queen.

"She is lovely," said Prince Alexi. "But I should caution you. Her skin, pale as it is, is resilient and so it is tempting to spank her very hard, just to get the proper blush. I've seen her spanked along the Bridle Path at the castle and come out of it amazingly unblemished."

Blanche's sex was drenched with her own fluids. Surely the Queen would see this, see the moisture shining between her legs.

No sooner had this thought occurred to her than she felt the Queen prodding her anus, opening it, but not with her finger. "Tight little thing," she said. It was some sort of little rod which was now withdrawn and Blanche felt ever more utterly without will or dignity or purpose except to give pleasure to the Queen.

Suddenly the paddle caught her by surprise. With amazing force, it cracked down on her bottom, drawing a little cry from her undisciplined mouth. Blanche stiffened all over but the next blows came so quickly and so loudly that she was suddenly moaning aloud again. She pressed her lips together, and this only made her choke with sobs. Again and again, the Queen spanked her hard.

"Come on, little girl, arch your back for me," said the Queen, "that's it, I want your little bottom raised for the paddle." And on she spanked furiously until suddenly Blanche's bottom was a riot of tingling pain.

She felt utterly undone suddenly, without any composure, sobbing and biting down on the sobs, her fingers playing on the carpet, and her eyes seeing Prince Alexi's slippers in a blur.

His hand came down and gathered up her chin, and that was too much for her, the tender fingers lifting her face. She would have cried, No, please don't look at my face, if she could have, but this would have been unthinkable. And she sobbed bitterly, feeling her breasts shivering against the Queen's skirts.

She was spanked and spanked again, the paddle catching the underside of her bottom now, and slamming her hard on the right side and then the left.

The Queen's left hand rested suddenly on her back. "Arch your back. Must I tell you again?" said the Queen. "That's it. You want to make yourself as presentable as you can for me, don't you?"

"Yes, madam," she sobbed, horrified by the ragged and gasping sound of her own voice.

The Queen had apparently laid the paddle down and was now kneading her sore flesh. "You're right. Her skin is simply gorgeous. For fair skin it is remarkable."

"She's known for it," said Alexi. "But think now, Majesty, what is it you really want to do with her? Do you want to punish her more, break her down, or is there something else you prefer?"

The paddle was picked up again and this time the blows came down on her thighs. The Queen was displaying amazing strength. The stinging blows came in a flurry, and Blanche realized she was now sobbing softly, and with greater control. Not that the worst was over. Not by any means, but she had fallen through some barrier suddenly and felt prostrate in her pain. It was the new queen of Bellavalten who was punishing her and she had no idea whether she was pleasing the Queen or not.

Out of her mouth came the helpless cry, "My queen."

"Yes, kitten, what is it?" came the Queen's voice.

"I want to please you so," sobbed Blanche. Her backside and thighs were on fire. But the Queen still spanked her, moving back again to her bottom and lifting each side as she spanked the lower curve right where her bottom met her thigh. Blanche shook with her sobs. She had never been any more helpless with anyone, any more faint and weightless and without will. Her sex was wet and pulsing with desire, and her breasts were filled with tingling warmth as if it were moving up from her loins all through her, like a hot fluid more certainly part of her than her own blood.

Suddenly the Queen pulled her up by her shoulders and slammed her down on her knees. She took Blanche's wrists in both hands, and forced Blanche around to kneel right in front of her. "Look into my eyes," she said.

Slowly Blanche looked up as if into a blinding light.

"Your Majesty," she whispered imploringly.

Her breasts throbbed, and her sex was swelling as if it were something that could burst. The fluids ran down her inner thighs.

"Lift her up, Alexi," said the Queen.

Blanche was wrenched to her feet.

"Now present your hips to me," said the Queen. "That's it, thrust them towards me."

Blanche struggled to obey, careful to keep her legs apart. Always one was expected to keep one's legs apart. Her calves were trembling as she stood on the balls of her feet, and her thighs and bottom throbbed with pain, a delicious hot pulsing pain that was worse now than when she was being spanked.

The Queen was examining her sex, seeing the flood of moisture, the wetness as that dreadful Galen always called it, and she felt the Queen's thumbs suddenly inside her vagina.

Blanche gasped. She could not hold back. She would die before she let the pleasure crest, die before she disappointed the Queen and her beloved Tristan, but she couldn't hold back.

The orgasm broke loose and she felt her empty vagina gaping hungrily and desperately as the pleasure flooded up through her and the blood throbbed in her face.

They knew it, they saw it, they could not conceivably think it was anything but her spending and spending and her choking sobs became low hoarse cries.

"Take her," said the Queen.

Prince Alexi turned her.

"On the bed."

She was forced across the room and then down on the jeweled red coverlet. A thousand prickly jewels or bits of gold bit into her sore flesh. Prince Alexi pushed her up on the bed, and mounted her, without removing his clothes, only lifting his tunic to reveal his organ hard and ready, and then it plunged into her, into the hopeless aching emptiness, and she felt herself flooded with relief, riding yet another magnificent wave, spending yet again.

Her mouth was open and the cries were ripped out of her.

"Hush, little one," he said. "Hush." His lips covered hers and he took her cries into himself as he drove his cock harder and harder into her.

Unable to stop herself she wrapped her naked legs around him and rode up off the coverlet with him only to be wondrously slammed down once more.

She wanted to cry, Yes, and yes, and maybe she did. She didn't know. He sucked the breath out of her, his dark hair hanging down onto her face.

Finally, he came, and she came again with him, and they shuddered together until it was finally over, and she felt him rising, felt his soft wondrous weight taken away from her, and for a moment she felt cold, not because the room was cold, but because it was quiet and he was gone.

When she opened her eyes she saw the Queen standing at the window by the fireplace looking out into the night.

"Oh, my queen," Blanche cried, unable to restrain herself. And without thinking, she rushed off the bed and fell on her knees at the Queen's side. "I did so want to please you, truly I did. Oh, please forgive me if I've displeased you."

"Quiet, Blanche, quiet," said Alexi in a crooning voice as he approached. She felt his hands on her shoulders, gentle but firm. "Your Majesty, no one has ever been able to teach this little girl to restrain herself and her outbursts of devotion."

The Queen turned and looked down. The light of the fire was behind her so her face was dark, and the light played in her golden hair.

Blanched sobbed in defeat, her hands not behind her neck as they should have been but covering her face.

"You did please me, darling," said the Queen in the warmest sweetest voice.

Blanche felt the Queen's fingers gently moving her own hands away from her face. And now her face was lifted and she knew that the shadowy figure was smiling at her though she could hardly see the features of her face.

"You have pleased me very much, precious Blanche," she said. "I shall always love you, love you especially for this night. Now stand and come into my arms."

Blanche could not quite believe this was happening because her heart was filled with happiness such as she had seldom known. For Tristan to embrace her in this manner gave her the greatest pleasure, but this was the Queen, the new queen.

She embraced the Queen as tightly as she could, holding back nothing, covering the Queen's face in kisses as the Queen kissed her, her breasts pressing against the Queen's breasts, her pubis pressing against the Queen's skirts. The Queen's hands cupped Blanche's head, then moved to her shoulders, and her breasts, twisting her nipples, and the kisses became ever more ardent, ever more desperate. The Queen was moaning. Blanche felt the Queen's hand on her hand, pressing Blanche's fingers between her legs though the heavy fabric of the Queen's skirts protected her. Suddenly, madly, Blanche lifted the Queen's skirts and fell on her knees kissing the Queen's wet pubic lips, dipping her tongue into the Queen's hot salty vagina. She could hear the Queen sighing. Blanche clutched at the Queen's naked bottom and worked her with all her might, her tongue plunging ever deeper until the Queen came, came with loud sweet moans that caused the floodgates in Blanche to break again as she pressed against the Queen's legs.

Drowsily, contentedly, ready for whatever punishment she deserved for her boldness, Blanche felt herself being gently pushed away, petted, caressed, yet pushed away, and she sank down at the Queen's feet.

It seemed a long time passed. She crouched with her eyes shut tight, waiting.

"You will get better at it," said Prince Alexi to the Queen. "You will get better at everything."

"I know," said the Queen under her breath. "But if only, if only I could understand . . ."

"All will be revealed in time," said Alexi with even-greater gentleness. "You've only just begun."

Blanche felt the Queen's hands on her head. "Come, dearest, come into my arms again," said the Queen.

Blanche rose at once, and held the Queen as tightly as she dared. Oh, sweet, sweet beyond any caresses she'd ever enjoyed, ever known, this. Sweet and intoxicating.

"Oh, don't worry, Blanche," said the Queen in her ear. "Don't bother with our words. I am new to taking command in this way, in this secret and erotic way." The Queen's thumbs fondled Blanche's cheeks. "I do so love you, darling. You have been the best of teachers. Now kiss me again with all your heart."

II

WELCOME TO
BEAUTY'S
KINGDOM

8

PRINCE DMITRI:
THE NEW
KINGDOM
AT LAST

i

A full nine months had passed since King Laurent and Queen Beauty had been crowned at Bellavalten, and all the world, it seemed, knew of their proclamations. How many eager princes, princesses, lords and ladies, and eager would-be slaves had journeyed to Bellavalten—from all over the European lands, and from the lands to the south, and from those to the east, and from those to the north, and from the Hungarian lands and the Russian lands, and from the lands of exotic climes—part history and part legend?

Those seeking slaves in my own kingdom had met with many high-born applicants, and those proud and beautiful peasants who had dreams of being accepted.

One day, wrapped in a hooded cloak, I had stood about in the shadows and watched the eager neophytes as they hovered outside the inn where the emissaries of Bellavalten were receiving, wondering what fair hair and forms were concealed by the heavy garments that so well concealed face and rank. "Beauty's Kingdom," that is how they referred commonly to Bellavalten. "Beauty's Kingdom." And the legend of the Sleeping Beauty and her new realm was the talk of the land.

I would have left that very day for Beauty's Kingdom, had it been possible.

But perhaps the many tasks that had delayed me had been a blessing. For as I reached Bellavalten now riding ahead of the small caravan of wagons and mounted servants that had accompanied me, I realized that Laurent and Beauty, my old and beloved friends, had made great progress in reviving the kingdom and I would see it—not in its early days of resurrection and inevitable confusion—but now in full bloom, so to speak, as every innkeeper I'd encountered in the last fortnight had told me.

Whatever the case, I'd had little choice but to delay my return.

My older brother, the King now for some twenty years, was not eager to see me pursue my dreams, but he had finally accepted it murmuring that he'd always been against my being sent to Bellavalten in the first place. He'd served in Bellavalten long before me, it was true, but only for a year, whereas I had been there many years, when one included my time in the sultanate. Yes, it had been a strange and ecstatic pleasure, all that, he said, and much the fashion in those days. Yet why did I wish to go back? I couldn't explain. He had tasks for me to complete before I was allowed to depart—visits to make, bequests to bestow, cousins to be received, and attendance at conferences that went on forever—and I set out to satisfy him without argument, which had always been my way.

You might say I'd learned patience during my time as a naked slave. But in truth, I was patient before I ever knew what it meant to be the pampered plaything of alluring ladies and lords. I was not by nature controlled or disciplined, no. That I had learned over time.

Finally, my brother had given me his blessing, endowed me with abundant gifts and gold, and after a final week of weepy and riotous banqueting and endless farewells, I'd at last set out, confident that I might come back home if I didn't find the new realm to my liking.

Of course I brought my trusted servant Fabien with me—the only being in this world who had ever been allowed to see me naked since I'd left the far-off realm of my old friend Lexius, former steward to the Sultan and slave to Her Late Majesty Queen Eleanor.

There wasn't a chance that I wouldn't find the new realm to my liking!

Two long letters from King Laurent had come to me within the first month of the kingdom's rebirth, filled with amazing warmth and friendly words, just as if he were speaking to me, though no doubt some scribe had been taking his dictation, and I could almost hear and see my old friend whom I had known so briefly but with such pleasure. These letters had been brimming with his enthusiasm for all the new innovations and expansion of the old kingdom, and they had set my blood to simmering at once.

And I had received a letter as well from my beloved Prince Alexi, whose brother's kingdom bordered on our own, and he too had said only momentous things about Bellavalten where he now resided. He had also confided that very likely Lexius would be returning—Lexius whom I knew and loved above all others from the time of my service.

To think that I might see Lexius again was quite an inducement. But even if Lexius never did make the journey from his far-off home in India, I was bound to return to Bellavalten as soon as I heard of the new regime.

That Princesses Rosalynd and Elena had also written to me was an added inducement. They had served with me for years in the sultanate, and they too had returned to Bellavalten. In sum, I could not have turned away from all this.

It was a long and arduous journey, but of course the closer we came to the fabled kingdom, the warmer and sweeter the weather until we were in the blessed land itself. My last night at the nearby inn was torment. But I took the time to bathe, and be shaved, and to put on fresh garments for the morning ride to the kingdom's gates. In fact, I spent a long time with my mirror as I reflected on what might soon occur.

I'd been looking all too much in the mirror since news of the "new kingdom" had come.

When you are a naked pleasure slave, it seems to me, you learn not to be vain, but to reside completely in your physical being. You become aware of your gifts in a way that is lasting, and perhaps never quite understandable to those who have never been pleasure slaves. You hear yourself described, spoken about, unendingly by your masters and mistresses, and grooms. You learn what they notice, what interests them, what they value, what they like and don't like, and what ought to be enhanced.

Thick jet-black hair, rather pale blue eyes, a somewhat delicately modeled face, indeed a bit of a long face, and a large frame—these were my endowments in brief—and of course a cock that was easily as big as most others when standing at attention or in repose. But for the kingdom and the sultanate, these features were never the sum total of any slave's individual charm. The spirit of the slave was paramount—the slave's grace or polish, the timbre of the slave's voice and softest moan, and above all the expression on a slave's face.

I'd been known for hopeless spontaneity, openness, the inability to conceal my feelings or fears, and praised unendingly for appealing eyes.

I couldn't forget all this when I heard of the revival of Bellavalten. It mattered to me to be accepted in Bellavalten—not merely for sentiment's sake or because I'd once been a slave there but as a self-possessed and impressive courtier now.

So I had to make a careful and somewhat ruthless assessment of myself before this journey. Was I youthful still in any regard? Was I in my prime? Were there more tiny and delicate lines around my eyes than I cared to see in the glass? And it was useless of course to ask my mistress what she thought, as she would lie to me out of tenderness, and pointless to ask Fabien, as he adored me and was so blind to his own charms. He lacked a vocabulary for assessing beauty. Whatever Fabien gave me daily, he gave through the devotion in his face and doting voice.

Well, on the last night, I made the ruthless assessment once more. My hair was thick as ever and now down to my shoulders, lustrous, still very black, and that was good. Maybe I had kept some of my youthful beauty even if I had grown very tall during my time in the sultanate, and if anything I was fuller of chest now and better muscled than in those early years.

Whatever. Time would reveal the truth that I couldn't find for certain in any mirror. I wasn't turning back. I felt comfortable on the final morning. I wore my best dark puce-colored tunic, and trousers, though it was far too warm for them now, and my heavy Russian boots.

From a mile away, as we came out of the mountain pass, I saw the great castle on its cliff above the valley and marveled as I had that very first time so long ago at its immense size. It appeared to have a multitude of towers, and from its many crowded pinnacles and ramparts there streamed red and gold banners furling in the wind.

Before the walls and on either side of the great drawbridge, I saw gaily colored tents, and crowds of people about them, and there was an air of energy and business about the entire multitude milling as far as I could see. The road had been crowded, yes, but I was still surprised at the number of those congregating here. There were campgrounds and other tents off to the right and left near the heavy brooding thickets of oaks.

Fabien drew up beside me on his chestnut mare, anticipating my questions, and all I had to do was gesture for him to explain.

"So many are coming, applying as slaves, or grooms, or simply immigrants eager to live in the kingdom that the halls inside the walls can no longer contain them," he explained.

Of course he would know because while I'd rested at the various inns along the way, brooding, dreaming, looking in the mirror, and staring out the windows, he'd been gossiping in the kitchens and with the men in the yard.

Fabien was very excited about this venture. I had taken him with me to India when I'd gone there with Lexius, and he had been devoted to me since that time. Brown haired, big boned, with cold dark eyes and an amazing warm voice, he always looked splendid in his velvet livery, and went on to explain excitedly what he'd heard along the road.

"Many are being turned away for obvious reasons, but an amazing number are accepted," he went on. "Look there. That line. That's probably all slave postulants. You can tell even from here. Look, the guards are motioning some on, and sending others away. Of course those of royal or noble birth go through the gates. If the guards spot a postulant of exceptional quality, well, they spirit that one right inside."

Indeed I could see this happening to two lovely young peasant women as we watched, and one very comely boy.

But the majority were headed to the tents to be interviewed, it seemed, or tested in some way; and there were soldiers lounging about everywhere, to keep order, I suppose, though no one seemed to be breaking the peace. Wine and hot food were for sale from open stands here and there, and I saw a young girl, a very pretty young girl, seated on a bundle, weeping with her hands to her face.

We moved on steadily to the drawbridge and the soldiers greeted us with the predictable respect.

Fabien rattled off my many names and titles with appropriate dignity, and we were motioned to proceed through the courtyard gates.

Two messengers ran ahead to announce us, I presumed; and I felt my heart going wild inside me, as I strove to look cool and collected, my eyes moving over the tops of the walls.

There was an air of cleanliness and order everywhere that I looked.

And as we entered the first of the great courtyards before the doors of the castle proper, I saw on either side of us at a great distance the immense newly erected halls for arriving slaves and grooms. Applicants were giving up their mounts, their beasts of burden, and laying down their bundles and being escorted inside. There was so much easy and convivial commotion I couldn't make much of it, but I wondered at the tender feelings of these brave individuals who were hoping so desperately to be taken into Bellavalten's magnificent and engulfing world.

Liveried servants, in blue and gold, now poured through the yawning mouth of the inner courtyard to help out the members of our little caravan, and Fabien was on his feet to help me down from my mount.

I walked across the broad planks of the gaping passageway as if I hadn't a care in the world, and then there rose before me that vision of the great north façade of the castle with its endless arched windows rising higher and higher to the battlements far above.

I recalled, whether I wanted to or not, the first time I'd beheld it, a trembling naked slave thrown over the horse of the Captain of the Guard. It had been the custom in those days to strip slaves well before their arrival in Queen Eleanor's realm. She wanted her peasants and villagers to enjoy the spectacle of new arrivals. And I had walked a good deal of the way here, though the Captain, tiring of the slow pace, had thrown me over his horse for the final mile.

I'd been so fearful, so defenseless, so certain that I could never endure the things my older brother had so vaguely yet impishly described.

"You'll do well, Dmitri," he'd said. "Just as I did. Simply yield and obey." He had laughed. "Let me assure you, you'll know more good hot pleasure there than you'll ever know anywhere afterwards."

Within six months, the Queen had had enough of my clumsiness and uncontrollable tears and packed me off to the village for punishment. I'd wondered whether or not my disgrace was known to my family back home. In fact, it had never been communicated to them and they were never told that I'd been later kidnapped and taken to the sultanate where I served for so long.

I stood staring at the great doors before me, remembering how I had scarcely dared to look up on that first day. The Captain had smacked me hard with his leather belt, telling me to stand straight and bow my head, and take pride that I was about to serve the great queen.

He'd snapped his fingers for two of his soldiers, directing them towards me with silent gestures that I hadn't understood. In a moment, I understood all. They had stroked and teased my balls and cock until I was hard from it, pinching my nipples and spanking me with their hard calloused hands until I'd been "presentable" as they called it, and I'd been so confused by the intense desire I'd felt.

"The Queen will love you," the Captain had said with a wink as he rode off.

When I'd seen him next, six months later in the Queen's Village, he'd whipped me with his strap for what seemed an eternity, chiding me for having failed at Court and promising me the Place of Public Punishment would make me into a perfect prince for the Queen. That had been before I was auctioned in the Village Square and sold to one of the retired soldiers who kept a house on the outskirts of the little place.

"You let me take him right to the Place of Public Punishment," the Captain had told my new owner. "Let them have him for two or three days and nights there to curb all this trembling and weeping. Look at that dancing cock, he wants to please. Trust me, I know how to handle this one, truly, I do."

And so my new master had agreed. I was never to know him or meet him. The Sultan's men snatched me up from one of the many public pillories in the Place of Public Punishment within a couple of nights.

But the Captain's prediction had proved true. I had already learned a great deal there. A great deal. And as I walked slowly into the inner courtyard, it was that place . . . the Place of Punishment in the Queen's Village that I thought of, among other memories of the village as I had known it during my last year in the realm.

Then I woke to the inner courtyard and stood stock still, amazed. No horses or beasts were allowed this far, plainly, and the flat stone pavers were polished like glass. Great garlands of greenery and bright flowers decorated the lower portion of the walls, and a forest of potted fruit trees lined the façade on either side of the great doors.

Row after row of windows rising on all sides showed boxes of fresh flowers, and here and there a bit of curtain blowing in the breeze. Even high on the battlements I saw the luxuriant greenery, and the very stones themselves of every surface both near and far seemed smoothed and cleaned.

Out of the castle came a gaggle of shining naked slaves—radiant men and women—to greet us, to offer wine to us if we were immediately thirsty from our journey, and to direct our servants where they might take their master's parcels and trunks.

Ah, such a magnificent sight! How long had it been! Too long! I could tell Fabien was dazed as well, but not so dazed that he had not recovered the two caskets for me that contained my special gifts for the new king and queen.

It is tiresome to speak of women's breasts like melons, but that is precisely what I thought as the young nymphs approached us. Their breasts are like melons, so lush and so soft.

And yes, I took the goblet of cool sweetened and watered wine gratefully and drank it down in one gulp.

The slaves beamed at us, glancing up shyly, as they surrounded us.

"The King is coming to greet you, Prince Dmitri," said one remarkable vision of splendid black curling tresses and dark red nipples and glossy curly pubic hair. Her eyes were brimming with modest spirit. I'd always found this type of slave irresistible. I wanted to reach out and touch this pubic hair. But it did not seem polite to do such a thing until I'd been received. Any master or mistress of the kingdom could handle or examine any slave, but I was not yet part of the kingdom.

A tall naked young man with a cherub's mop of blond curls offered to take the precious caskets from Fabien but I shook my head, no. Fabien was devouring the stripling with his eyes. He couldn't help himself, and as the naked slaves surrounded us, Fabien seemed almost fearful, as though they were exotic beasts.

The little band urged us towards the open doors.

It was all I could do not to squeeze the little bottoms swaying before me, the high muscular backside of the boy or the soft swelling bottom of the succulent little girl.

Now I should say that none of these slaves were as young as we had been when we were sent here. And I knew from the many proclamations made by Beauty and Laurent that only those old enough to consent resolutely to their servitude were now accepted, but still these young men and women did seem to me in their freshness to be girls and boys.

Suddenly three familiar figures appeared in the great door at once.

My beloved Princess Rosalynd and darling Princess Elena and His Majesty, King Laurent.

The King opened his arms as we walked towards each other.

I was in tears.

Grand and handsome as I remembered, taller than any man I knew, and graced surely with one of the most appealing of beautiful faces I'd ever seen, Laurent smiled warmly as we came into each other's embrace.

"Beloved Dmitri, friend from the sultanate, how marvelous it is to see you." He looked so earnest and so cheerful.

"Your Majesty," I bowed from the waist but he bid me rise at once, and kissed me on the right and left cheeks.

"Don't stand on ceremony here, Dmitri. You come in and let us take you to the quarters waiting for you."

"Yes, I've been seeing to your chambers all day," said Rosalynd, as buxom and rosy cheeked as she had ever been, her dark hair daintily coiffed, her familiar voice bringing delicious chills to all my skin. "We'll take you up into the northeast tower. Coolest of the towers. Everything's ready for you."

"Beloved, we're so glad you've come," Princess Elena confided as she took my arm. If anything she was more beautiful. I could scarcely believe my eyes. "Tonight at supper, our king will introduce you to all the Court."

We were proceeding now into the great entrance hall.

Everywhere I looked I saw naked slaves with luxuriant well-groomed hair walking here and there with their heads bowed, and some positioned as in the old days along the walls, legs wide apart, heads bowed, hands behind their necks.

Why, there wasn't a space of bare wall in the entire immense hall.

Beside me, a gorgeous young satyr waited to take my gloves as I drew them off my hands. Doorways in every direction were flanked by naked slaves.

Even hugging my two beautiful companions warmly, and excited by Laurent's hand on my shoulder, I still felt the keen stab of memory of that long-ago day when I'd been brought here barefoot before so many staring eyes.

Why these thoughts when the spectacle was so dazzling? Had the old regime ever had such an abundance of delectable flesh?

Flashes of the Place of Public Punishment returned. How is one to ask about such a place when one is being received at Court with such generosity? And yet it was all I could think of suddenly, the Public Turntable— being brought up the ladder to it, and told to kneel over with my chin on the thick square wood post. The crowd had been hooting and cheering. I'd panicked, as always, and within seconds my hands had been placed in the small of my back, my wrists bound tight. The leather straps had gone over my calves binding me to the floor of the turntable, and the whipping master was laughing as he lifted the big wooden paddle in front of my face so I would see it.

"What do you think, young prince?" he'd roared for the benefit of the raucous crowd. "Is this fine enough for a spoilt little brat boy from the castle who spilled the Queen's wine and tried her patience?"

Laurent was leading me himself into one of the many parlors off the entrance hall, and I saw before me the lovely figure of Queen Beauty seated there in a high-backed chair.

There was a table piled with fancy cakes and silver goblets. Naked slaves stood ready with silver pitchers, and trays of steaming hot dainties. The scent of cinnamon and fresh-roasted apples filled the air.

"Come and sit here with me, dearest prince," said the Queen as I bowed and rose slowly to kiss her outstretched hand. Rosalynd and Elena stood beside her, beaming at me.

Fabien stood far back against the wall, anxious, yet excited, clutching the caskets to his chest. I could see the slaves smiling secretively to one another as they enjoyed his discomfort. He was red faced. Well, it had been a long time since the faraway land of Lexius's home across the seas.

"Your Majesties, I have gifts for you," I said. My voice sounded strained and raw. But I was seated now and the wine was welcome—yes, cool sweet wine. The young boy who poured it seemed as tentative and uncertain of himself as I did, not daring to steal the smallest glance at me, his hard chest well polished and buffed to a sheen. His nails were trimmed in gold.

"At Court this evening, of course, Prince, you are most gracious," said the lovely queen. "Don't bother with such things now. We are grateful for your presence here under our roof. And your man, there, let him take your things to your chambers." Such blue eyes. Of course I had blue eyes, and so did my lovely Rosalynd and Elena, but the Queen's were deeply blue and so big.

Princess Rosalynd was already leading Fabien away. I nodded to reassure him.

"Yes, we'll see to your room, make certain all is perfect," said Elena, who hurried after them.

"Well, I would have known you anywhere," said the King, seating himself near the hearth on the far right. "That black hair, thick and shining as ever. And your face. It's hardly changed at all."

A boy I hadn't seen before, a boy of incomparable dark brown skin and long black hair, filled the King's goblet.

The boy had gold earrings in his ears, and lashes so thick they cast a faint shadow on his smooth high cheeks. I stared at his pinkish cock, marveling at the color of it, the dark brown and pinkish tints blended into it. And such a nest of hair, curling hair. When he turned and put the pitcher on the sideboard I couldn't keep my eyes from his backside, wanting to see the pink anus between those firm buttocks. Yes.

Somehow I managed to speak.

"You're kind, sire," I said. "I wish I were a bard that I could sing of what I see when I look at you and your queen. Again, I'm so happy to be here at last, to be back in Bellavalten. I am so happy to be received."

And again in a jarring flash, I was on the turntable of the Place of Public Punishment and that wooden paddle came slamming down on my bottom, and I heard the excited roar of the crowd.

I tried to clear my vision, to hear what the Queen was saying—that they were so glad to receive me. I wanted to put my heated tumbling thoughts in order. Why, after all, when I'd been whipped there so often after my return from the sultanate, did my mind go back, right back, to that very first terrifying time?

"It will purify you," the Captain had said earnestly, almost tenderly, as I was forced up the ladder. "Believe me, it is the most effective punishment. That's why I want you to receive it now and often. You'll see. Now up you go!"

I felt the whipping master's left hand on my neck. Always. Left hand on the neck. My chin rested on the rough wood. And the crack over and over of the paddle, and the crowd screaming.

"Little piglet," said the whipping master, "you're giving the crowd a great show. You just keep struggling with all your might against those straps. But keep your chin on this post, or I'll let the crowd name the number of the blows."

Struggling. I felt it again, my toes hammering down on the wood, my thighs tensing, and my hands twisting and turning in the ropes. But the heavy hand on my neck kept my head firmly in place, my chin on the rough wooden post, and through my tears I saw the crowd in a haze before me, all around me, cheering and waving, and one lovely girl with a bright, round face smiling at me as she waved a blue scarf.

Strange to remember such a detail, but then after . . . yes, that scarf.

With a sudden shock, I realized the Captain, the very Captain who had taken me that day to the Public Turntable, was standing here beside the Queen.

"Prince Dmitri, of course you remember Captain Gordon," she was saying in her sweet, cordial voice.

I couldn't speak.

"Prince, you said in one of your letters you were eager to see the village," the King said casually. "Well, the Captain will escort you there whenever and however often you want to see it. Why, there's plenty of time before supper, if you're so inclined."

"Our guest might want to rest, my lord," said the Queen. "He has a world of time in which to see everything."

The village. Anytime.

"Yes, of course," said the King, "but I welcome Dmitri's estimation of the village. I really do. I'm pleased that Dmitri has asked about it, mentioned it."

"Yes, Your Majesty," said the Captain.

"I do so want to see it," I said, trying to steady my voice.

"But you are white, Prince, perfectly white with exhaustion," said the Queen. "You should sleep first."

"I am yours, my lord," said the Captain to me. "All afternoon, I'm at your service."

It was this man, this very man who stood at my service now, waiting, silent, waiting, who had brought me down the ladder and pushed me roughly towards the pillory, lifting the board, and forcing my hands and my head through the holes and then slapping the board down in place. The board had held me bent over from the waist, my bare feet in the dust. I could barely look up. But I did, and I saw the next victim on the distant turntable, a dainty red-haired princess blushing and gasping as the whipping master forced her to kneel down and bend over and place her chin on that post as he'd forced me to do. Her large lovely eyes were suddenly squeezed shut.

Then something blue filled my vision. Blue. It was that scarf, and a tender voice said in my ear:

"Let me wipe your tears. You are so handsome." It was that round-faced girl from the crowd, with skin like fresh cream. "There, there," she cooed, and another pair of hands appeared cupping a crude bowl of wine and I saw fingers dipped in it and I was given the fingers, dripping with wine, to suck.

"You know, Dmitri, we lack a guiding genius for the Place of Public Punishment," the King said. "Perhaps for many aspects of the village. You mentioned that place in your letter. I never really knew the place. . . ."

The words struck my heart. *A guiding genius.*

"It's going well, sire," said the Captain.

"Yes, Captain, I know," said the King. "And the Lady Mayor has the whole enterprise in hand. But it's huge now. And the opinions of our beloved returning princes and princesses provide much insight."

I saw the blue scarf in front of my eyes. Heard the sounds of the crowd. And it had only been the morning crowd.

The Captain had been scolding the villagers behind me as I lapped the wine from the girl's cupped hand. "That's it, dearest prince," she whispered. I was so thirsty! My tongue scraped the palm of her hand.

"No touching him there," said the Captain to the others, whom I couldn't see. "You may pinch and prod, but cocks starve in the Place of Public Punishment." It had been so warm there and so dusty. "Yes, with feathers you can tease him, that's fine, or whisk brooms, but that cock is to starve, and you know this."

The Captain's belt struck my backside, struck the flesh that was so sore and hot from the turntable. I knew it was the Captain.

"Now, you're going to spend the day here, little boy," he had said. "You'll be spanked again up there at noon and again at dusk. And by late evening, when you're brought up there for the last time, I want to see some composure, you understand me? I want to see an end to all that struggling. You're here to learn to be the perfect little boy the Queen desires." Crack of the strap.

"Prince, I think you should rest now," said the lovely new queen leaning towards me. "You are pale and trembling."

"I think you're right," I said. It was more of a stammer, a murmur. "And then later . . ."

Composure.

Well, I'd learned composure. But it was not there, not on that day, not with this man schooling me, though he had certainly given it his best. I'd learned it in the distant land of the Sultan, one of the last slaves privileged to know that strange exotic paradise before Lexius had come to warn all of its doom.

ii

My chambers were lavishly furnished. Two naked slaves were in attendance, and my befuddled servants and grooms were hustled off to a servants' wing to be fed and rested. Fabien remained, of course, with a bed in an ample closet adjacent to my bedchamber.

The cold stone walls had been paneled in finely polished dark wood, and draped here and there with heavily embroidered hangings, and even the floors which had always been damp in my time were covered by scattered exotic carpets.

The bed was quite impressive, draped in linen as well as richly dyed wool, and the writing table and chairs were exquisitely carved with the usual curlicues and tiny animals. Indeed there were more wood movables in the room than I'd ever seen, stools, tables, cushioned benches, whatever one might desire for sitting, or a goblet or a foot, and even the great fireplace itself had a coat of arms carved in the stone chimney piece, though whose coat of arms it was I didn't know.

The fire chased the damp, and the air outside was deliciously mild as it always was in Bellavalten. Perhaps the ancestors of the old queen would have never attempted naked pleasure slavery had not the kingdom existed in this sheltered valley, subject to warm breezes and a break in the mists that so often hover over coastlands.

I lay down on the bed and fell into a dead sleep for two hours.

It was only early afternoon when I waked, sat up, and looked about myself.

The two slaves knelt by the fireplace, facing me, sitting back on their heels, their heads bowed.

Immediately one rose, the girl slave, a beauty as were they all, but this one particularly was fair with the loveliest thick braids of blond hair and playful waves about her high smooth forehead. She came at once to the side of the bed with a goblet for me and a little plate of sliced apples.

"Master, what can I get for you?"

"Tell me if all the chambers in this new wing are so lavishly appointed," I asked. I devoured the apple hungrily. It was all the food I wanted just now. I drank the cool water.

"Yes, Master," she said. "Throughout the castle all the rooms have been restored. Merchants came day after day for months from Italy, Spain, and lands to the east, with cartloads of tapestries and carpets for the re-furnishing of the castle. Carts laden with beds and furnishings arrived every morning for so long, and even now the carpenters are at work in the Queen's Village, though now it's called the Royal Village."

She had pretty eyes, and plump cheeks, though her chin was small and delicate. Her breasts appeared slightly moist, dewy, and this time I didn't resist the urge to slip my hand between her legs, to feel the soft warm pubic hair, and the lips, so naked, so tender.

She held quite still as I did this, the goblet and plate in her hand, not daring to move.

"And have you been here since the King and Queen came?" I asked.

"I've been here for two years, Master," she said. "I was sent from a homeland that is gone now. I am at home here with the King's blessing."

Just the faintest blush flared in her white cheeks.

I examined her nipples idly, pinching them to make them nice and hard. How many times had that been done to me, how many times a day? I felt the old hands polishing my balls and cock with oil, oiling my anus, the old idle spanks, the pinching of my thighs.

She was incomparably lovely, but then so were they all.

"And your name, precious?" I asked.

"It is Kiera, Master. That's the new name that the King gave me when I was anointed in the Goddess Grove."

"Anointed? What in the world are you talking about?" I probed. I took the goblet again and drank the rest of the water.

"My lord, that is how it is done now with all new slaves, and of course those of us who had been here before had to renew our vow. We are taken to the Goddess Grove at night, by torchlight, and there we are confirmed in our given names or the new names we have chosen, and there we are received with kisses by King Laurent and Queen Beauty and blessed for two years' service. Of course the new ones are on probation for six months. But we are not, as we are well trained already."

It was difficult for her to keep her eyes down. She stole a lightning glance at me as she spoke.

"You may look at me, Kiera," I said, "though you must do it respectfully."

"Yes, my lord," she said.

I looked at the boy slave who knelt as before, waiting, it seemed, for my permission to rise.

"And your brother slave there," I asked. "His name? Come here, young man."

"Bertram is his name, my lord," said Kiera.

Bertram rose at once and came to the girl's side.

He was tall, very fair skinned with almost white hair, tousled and thick, yet trimmed just below his ears to unruly waves. Clearly he'd been sleeping as he knelt by the fire, and his big gray eyes were dreamy. His cock was coming awake. Motioning for the girl to move back I beckoned for him to come forward. Quite a cock. Not just long but thick.

"And you, Bertram?" I asked. "Have you been here long?"

"I was received a month ago, sire," he said. His voice was quaking. Indeed I could see now that he was very anxious. The muscles of his belly were tightening. He had good powerful arms, and elegant hands that hung at his sides.

The curling hair around his cock was dark, the color of ash or smoke, as so often happens with blond-haired boys.

"And anointed in the grove?" I asked.

"Yes, sir, and I will be confirmed in five months, if I please, my lord, and I hope to please you." He was as modest as the girl, gazing downward. His cock was now hard as a branch.

"Of course, you do," I said. "And are you of royal birth?"

"No, my lord." He blushed. "I was a clerk, a scribe. I heard of the new kingdom and came as quickly as I could."

"Go on," I said. I took another slice of the apple and munched on it.

"I rode night and day, my lord," he said. "I walked the last two days as I sold my mount for the last part of the journey. I wanted so to serve. I was accepted at once, and I'm grateful for that."

"Hmmm, impressive," I said. "You're as handsome as any prince I ever knew here. How many other magnificent flowers are there—beyond these walls, out there in the world—as fragrant and beautiful as the royal blooms that once adorned these halls? Turn around, both of you."

How many times had I been ordered to do that, and to stand silent for inspection of the most intimate sort?

My cock was getting hard looking at them, at their firm bottoms and straight backs, at their silky skin. The boy's bottom was lean and I could see his pink little anus plainly enough and his heavy balls. Very inviting.

But I wanted to go outdoors. I wanted to see the village. I wanted to use the daylight hours while they lasted.

"Very well, both of you, turn back around."

Fabien had wakened in his closet and come into the room, fully dressed as before, and he was holding my belt and tunic.

"Now, are you assigned to me, children?" I asked. "Or do you belong to this chamber or the hour of the day?"

I slipped off the bed and they stepped aside as Fabien put my tunic over my head and smoothed it down while I put my arms through the sleeves.

"We are yours, my lord, chosen for you by Prince Alexi and King Laurent, who hoped we would be pleasing to you, and will only retire when you dismiss us, at which time other slaves shall come, also chosen."

"Ah, the kingdom is rich," I said.

I took the girl's face in my hands and kissed her on the lips. She smelled of flowers and fresh air, and her little mouth quivered and stiffened against my lips.

It seemed a shock ran through her and then it passed into me.

I shifted uncomfortably, and stood back for Fabien to buckle my belt.

These were heavy Russian garments. I would change later to the lighter shorter belted tunic and swap these trousers for leggings. But now it didn't matter.

I took the boy's face and kissed him as well. He was my height. Utterly passive. When I was new, I'd trembled or shaken every time I was touched or kissed, and the old queen had been furious, but this lad was perfect.

And to think, if this boy does not please, he will not only be whipped for the next six months, harder and longer and more angrily than other slaves who do please, but sent away when the period of testing is over. Will he beg to remain? Will they make a groom of him perhaps?

I looked at both of them for a long moment.

"Fabien, go see if the Captain of the Guard is still prepared to take me down to the village." I eyed the boy and girl.

"Yes, my lord, he is and has come twice to ask after you," Fabien said. "I'll go tell him that you're ready."

"Bertram and Kiera," I said. "Tell me. How many of Queen Eleanor's slaves left when allowed to do so? The new king and queen did allow them the choice, did they not?"

"Yes, my lord," the girl answered. She was clearly the more confident, but the boy's voice was as cultured as hers. "They were allowed to make the choice. Two made the choice but only when the King allowed that they might return at some point in the future."

"Two out of the whole kingdom?"

"There were only a few hundred slaves, my lord," Kiera explained. "And most had been here a long time. The old queen, she was not—"

"I know, I've heard. She was tired, indifferent. Very well, I understand."

"Some of the great families, they insisted that they still be able to send their royal sons and daughters here," Kiera volunteered. "But the King and Queen were resolute. All slaves must be of age to decide for themselves. And so these kingdoms have been choosing from willing subjects of all rank and sending new offerings."

"I see. Well, I'm going out now, and you will remain here as you've no doubt been instructed."

"Yes, my lord," came from both of them more or less at the same moment, and they stood back, the girl still holding the two shining silver implements and the boy as submissive as before.

Oh, the hours of boredom. How I remembered that too, waiting, and the agony of my aching cock, and so longing for the slightest touch, even of the belt or the paddle, or fingers, living fingers.

I went to the window and looked out. I was on the top floor here, some five stories above the ground. The window was a great open arch, and the air was filled with the scent of orange blossoms or something just as sweet.

Below I saw gardens sprawling in all directions, with trees and neatly trimmed shrubbery running in courses and what seemed beaten pathways, those soft dusty pathways so silken to bare feet that I remembered from the old days, and figures, well-attired figures moving all over, and slaves, slaves everywhere. Countless courts and squares were visible and the sparkling dance of fountains.

I could make out the vast central garden of old surrounded by the Bridle Path and indeed I realized that slaves were being spanked along the rectangular courses of the Bridle Path now by mounted figures.

"Kiera, why is the Bridle Path in use at this hour?" I asked, beckoning for the girl to come to me. "In my time it was in the morning and the evening."

She came up near silently beside me. Again, that whiff of sweet perfume.

"My lord, it is always busy now, the Bridle Path," she said. "And the Hunt in the Maze and so many other games. There is always feasting outdoors. There are so many guests, so many slaves."

"I see. And were you both paddled on the path this morning? I saw no evidence of that."

"We were pardoned to attend you, my lord," she explained. "We are yours for as long as you want us. We are fresh for you."

"Indeed you are," I said, kissing her again. "Now back to your places by the fireplace, both of you."

They rushed to obey.

Fabien had returned. He held the door open for me.

iii

I had entered the great castle by its north gates. And the gardens I'd seen below lay to the east and the south as far as I could figure, something perhaps that I'd never thought about in years past. And I was led out now through a western gate to a vast paved courtyard.

There was a paved road leading out of it of the smoothest stones and right before us stood a great gilded chariot of sorts, in which three or four men might stand. Ample to hold me and Captain Gordon and, wonder of wonders, my beloved Prince Alexi, who came to join us.

But what astonished me more than anything, even more than the vibrant and welcoming smile on Alexi's face, was the great team of human ponies outfitted and ready to pull the chariot. I was stunned, speechless at the sheer spectacle of it. I noticed the handsome grooms in their ornate blue-and-gold livery, with long flat straps in their hands, or hooked to their belts, who stood back away from us and the team. There were four of them. Their clothes were richer than those of the servants I'd seen earlier at the castle, who wore the very same colors, but had no straps in hand or hanging from their belts.

Alexi wrapped his arms around me, and kissed me warmly. Ponies or no ponies, this was an exquisite moment.

"Dmitri, I'm so glad you're here," he said. Ah, such a beautiful deep voice, and the same delicate dark skin. "So very glad. You will allow me to go down to the village with you."

"Oh, most certainly," I said, holding him to my heart. "Alexi, you look as fit and happy as you were the day we rode out of here." Indeed he did. His auburn hair was long, curling, and beautifully groomed, and his face was fresh and rested and his dark eyes brilliantly clear. He was attired in burgundy velvet, a short tunic and leggings and boots, and he wore a great gold chain around his neck with a disk on it. There was writing on the disk. I knew there would be time for him to explain its significance to me.

"Come on, let's go. We can talk on the way," Alexi said. "You look positively dazed, my friend. This chariot was made specially by King Laurent in the fashion of olden times." He gestured to it, and indeed it was grand. "I believe it's called a quadriga."

The silent grooms were looking us over furtively, but their eyes were mainly fixed anxiously on the sixteen ponies.

"Perhaps you'd like to see the ponies first, Prince," said the Captain, but it was said in a cautious respectful voice, and once again, I heard the old voice behind it, the voice that had commanded me to the village stables when I'd returned from the sultanate. "The Queen wants all that exotic softness cleaned away," he'd said back then. So firm, so quick with the strap.

I forced myself to look into his blue eyes. "Yes, I do want to see them," I said. He was still a striking man, not the youthful golden god he'd seemed in those days, yet perhaps more powerful, more intriguing.

My stomach felt weak, but the desire in me was rising and when that happens I feel nothing in my head or stomach.

We walked slowly towards the team. It was four across and four rows in length, all strongly built men, gorgeous men with muscles oiled and gleaming, clearly matched for beauty and size, all of the same impressive height, and even their luxuriant hair was trimmed identically at the back of the neck and combed back out of their faces. Ah, a chariot for a team of four across, and now I understood the word "quadriga."

Never in all my time in the village, pulling wagons or carts, or even the occasional fancy coach, had I ever seen a team of men of this size or so lavishly ornamented. I was utterly dazzled. I saw gold and scarlet everywhere I looked, and jewels sparkling in the afternoon sunlight.

We'd been lowly beings, the work ponies of the village. These were ponies of a royal equipage. Maybe the pretty girls of the mayor's small stable had been so turned out, but never us, except in some meager fashion on race days.

Every male stood proud and tall, harnessed in bright gold-and-scarlet decorated leather, with gold blinders at the sides of his eyes, gold lacings covering his arms as they were folded behind his back, and a gleaming gold band around his forehead.

Even the anal plugs were gold with the long thick horse's-hair tail dyed red, and gold were the boots that ran halfway up the calf of each steed, with red jeweled buttons and loops. And added to that were bits of gold in each mouth, and the gilded reins that ran back to the chariot.

Countless adornments enhanced the harnessing and straps everywhere that I looked, tiny gold bells dripping everywhere, and gold and jeweled buckles and rosettes decorating all connective links, and the straps that ran over the shoulders and down between the legs, anchoring the butt-plug horse tails and binding them to the tight lacings that bound the erect cocks and shining oiled scrotum of each pony. How I remembered the feel of all this, the delicious snugness.

Even the hair of the ponies was dusted with gold, and their pubic hair as well. And the blinders, I saw now, were not solid gold at all, but stiff coverings of gold silk for the eyes, through which I could easily see the eyes staring forward, which meant that the ponies could see where they were going. And they could see me studying them, though they didn't dare to look at me.

Only the four at the very head of the team lacked these blinders. As I stood before them, I felt my own cock stirring in my trousers, and I wondered if my face was visibly burning. I was grateful to be well hidden under my loose Russian garb. There was something overwhelming about the sheer size of the team. Sixteen proud ponies tethered to one chariot, and how many ponies might there be in all?

"Now, this is the King's own team," said Alexi. "That's why you see the gold and scarlet everywhere, because these are the Court's colors."

"This is exquisite work," I said. "I've never even imagined anything like it." It was painted as well as carved leather, much of it. "But why the blinders for all except the first row?"

"These are the King's favorites," said the Captain as Prince Alexi deferred to him for the answer. "They don't need blinders to calm them down. This is Caspian, Bastian, Throck, and Carnell. They are always at the front of the King's team, and well experienced already and eager and frisky."

As I expected, the ponies gloried silently in this praise, tossing their heads, making tiny gold bells all along their harnesses jingle, and shifting in their harnesses, not struggling, no, but shifting and leaning on one horseshoed boot and then the other. I could hear the horseshoes striking the stones. There wasn't a tear on any of the faces of these four mounts and they stared straight forward. Only Throck, the darkest of all with his golden-brown hair, looked faintly bored, eyes roving the blue sky overhead, but he was essentially expressionless.

Slowly, unable to resist, I walked back and forth in front of them and studied them one by one. Their calf and thigh muscles were powerful. I remembered that, the sheer strength I developed as a pony.

The Captain had thought it such a crude debasement when he'd brought me to the stables. Yes, to have all the softness of the sultanate scrubbed away, as the Queen thought, but I had absolutely loved it. Obeying, submitting, that is what I'd found hard in my service under Queen Eleanor, and that is what I'd learned in the sultanate. But being harnessed, with one's arms bound tight to one's back, with a bit in my mouth? That had made everything profoundly simple. And if only I'd been allowed a set of gold silk blinders, covering my eyes, covering my gaze, covering my tears, that would have made it all even easier. I'd loved being a pony. One didn't have to think, one didn't have to submit. It was all done for me.

As I inspected these men now, I could see they loved it. Nipples were painted in gold, and even their lips stretched over the gold bits, and in their navels were bright red garnets—yes, red and gold—and never once, any more than soldiers at attention, did they acknowledge my inspecting gaze.

"Now, this is Caspian," said the Captain embracing the pony nearest him with his right arm, and there was the old affection he'd showed to us so often, embracing us, crude as we were. "The King never rides out with a team without Caspian or Bastian." And Caspian shivered all over as though he loved it, his blond hair gleaming with the dusted gold. Even his eyelashes were tinged with gold. Bastian was also fair, though his hair was darker and he had a thick fleece of chest hair as well, surrounding his gilded nipples and jeweled navel. He too seemed supremely happy and eager to run, pawing the ground in a stylized way that I'd learned so well long ago.

The Captain kissed Caspian's face and I could see Caspian smile in spite of the bit, and then the Captain's large hand, the hand that had struck me so many times, closed over Caspian's right buttock and squeezed it hard.

Only now did the waiting grooms, all young men, with those straps in their hands, look a little restless.

"And you'll notice that all have been well paddled to make their pretty hindquarters blush," said the Captain in a smooth slow voice. Tentative, gauging my reaction.

"Yes, I see that." I walked back slowly along the row.

They were all red indeed, and their thighs had been spanked as well.

"That's how the King demands it," said Alexi. "Ponies are under strict discipline. I believe all are strapped every morning and evening, regardless of how they perform."

"It keeps them in condition," said the Captain. Again, his voice was gentle, not that commanding voice of old, but I knew that voice still lived in him, like a lion ready to spring. I could feel it.

"Now this second set of four," said Alexi. "These too are dedicated ponies like Caspian and the others, are they not?"

"Yes, absolutely," said the Captain. "The King loves them. But when we get now to this third row, well, these are Punished Ponies, little boys who have been placed in the King's team to learn humility and dignity. And here you'll see the wet eyes and faces. This fourth row are very bad little boys, boys who've only just worked themselves up to the last row of the King's teams—the King has several teams—after having pulled refuse carts in the village."

Refuse carts. Yes, those I recalled very well.

The Captain's hand went out again, to squeeze the backside of one comely blond-haired boy who was obviously struggling to conceal his sobs. Why had I not seen this earlier? The Captain had a napkin out to blot the boy's cheeks. The soft sound of the muffled sobs ignited my blood.

"Now, that's enough of that, Henri," he said. "Stand up straight." The Captain lifted the short thick strap that dangled from his belt, unhooked it, and smacked the thighs of the pony hard several times, making him dance as if he knew what was good for him. Not to dance would have only incited more blows. You learn that fast when you're a pony. You can't speak, but you can respond, and that is what Henri did. But I could see the dignity in him. His cock was hopelessly hard in its lacings, held up straight with his scrotum laced close to it. He would go slack as he trotted. That couldn't be helped. But he'd be expected to be hard quick enough anytime the coach stopped.

My own cock was hopelessly hard, too. And I realized of course what this entire afternoon was going to be like for me, the pure torture of it. It would be like the torture of old, enduring for hours, even for those of us whose cocks were released three and four times a day.

I felt a low churning excitement inside me, something savage suddenly, something so familiar yet alien that I stood there in silent musing, allowing it to collect and to seek some definition for itself.

"Later on, perhaps, we'll go to see the stables," said Alexi. "They're quite beautiful now. I never saw the stables of the village until this year. I never knew the village." He didn't say this with pride or spite because I had known both. He said it simply.

"Yes, I would love to see them," I said.

We mounted the chariot, the Captain in the middle, Alexi on his far right and I on his left, and he started the team.

To my astonishment the grooms ran along two on each side of the team and began at once to whip the legs of the ponies.

It was a comfortable trot, nothing fast, but I could feel the smooth power of the immense team and the fine spoke wheels of the chariot moving over the stones.

I couldn't take my eyes off the men, how proudly they held themselves seeming not even to flinch as they were whipped, but then the whipping obviously wasn't hard and it was done with flat straps that made a noise. It would sting, yes, and I could feel that. Each of the four grooms had four ponies to drive, two in front, two behind, and now I could hear the groans and swallowed sobs of the Punished Ponies closest to us.

I felt the blood drain from my face.

This was the old road, I recognized it, that carts had once taken to the castle. It had been a dull and dreary road then, never used by the Queen or her courtiers. But now it was a great curving and gently sloping thoroughfare, lined on both sides by banks of flowers.

It must have been entirely rebuilt and regraded. Again, the sharp memory of the day I'd been taken down to the village came back, as if it were happening now, as if I weren't riding along beside the Captain, a guest of the Court, as if I were that naked slave in the cart with the other disgraced ones. And it had been that other captain, the Captain of the Castle Guard, who'd whipped us fiercely as the cart rolled on. I hadn't tried to hide in the crowd from his lash. I'd failed so miserably at the castle that I'd been almost glad to be going to the village. They wouldn't expect anything of me, I thought. They'd only punish me.

Wicked old Lord Gregory—in his fifties then—had told me over and over what the Queen might do to me if I didn't improve. And I'd been glad to get away from him.

As we rounded the bend I saw the great castle in all its breathtaking glory. It seemed its grim towers had been washed clean somehow and they shone in the sun as if cased in limestone. We were beyond the garden walls, descending very gradually towards the village. Somewhere up there, inside those towers and wings, old Lord Gregory still presided over trembling slaves, or so Alexi had written to me. Wicked Lord Gregory, always angry, always striking terror in the hearts of the most playful slaves.

"Prince, you see that all this has been replanted," said the Captain of the Guard, "as this is now a thoroughfare which the King and the Queen and courtiers travel all the time."

"It's very impressive, Captain," I said.

"That road there leads off south to Prince Tristan's manor house, and on to the other new manor houses."

"Oh, you must see them," said Alexi. "Tristan has his own little Court. He spends his days writing just as Lord Nicholas once did. He has become the new Court Chronicler."

At last I could see the walls of the Queen's Village up ahead or what was now called the Royal Village.

How we had all cried and moaned in the cart that awful morning. And how the sight of the battlements had terrified me, even though I'd been glad to be free of the angry queen and the angry Lord Gregory.

"I'll take you around the village," said the Captain. "It's quite large now. The walls have been extended and will be extended more in the future, and many live outside the walls, as it is quite as safe to live outside as it is to live within."

"Yes, I should like to see it," I said softly. My eyes fell on the ponies again, all the tossing heads, and the jingling bells and the jewels flashing.

I remembered the feel of the plug in my anus, the feel of the horse's tail brushing my naked legs, the feel of the harnesses holding me so firmly. It had been so simple! I'd wept only because it was expected that I weep, as bad little boys should when made into ponies, and I could still remember the anticipation I felt when the day was over that I'd be whipped hard and then some hot wet mouth would come to ease the torment of my cock, and I'd be able to sleep in my stall, standing up, bent over at the waist, my head on a pillow of straw.

My backside had been so toughened by then I could take the longest whippings or paddlings.

Suddenly we were on the flat plain before the gates of the village and then taking the road to the west around it. I could see soldiers up on top of the walls and many farmhouses now in the mown fields. The road was broad and well beaten and again there were flowers blossoming everywhere, and great shady copses of old trees.

And now I saw the old spectacle of naked slaves working in the fields, tossing seed from baskets they carried, and other slaves laboring along the road, some pulling little carts full of fresh goods, driven by a solitary master with a switch.

But I soon came to see that these weren't ordinary farm fields as they'd been in my time. No. Everywhere I looked I saw the crop was now flowers of various sorts and in the distance I could see the shining glint of glass hothouses no doubt for more tropical or delicate blooms. Slaves were doing the work as before, but I sensed even from the distance of the road that they seemed spirited and contented in what they were doing, tending the rosebushes, or the great patches of lilies, and I even saw two naked slaves obviously chatting with one another but then a busy master did appear with the inevitable strap.

Nevertheless much had changed indeed.

After my time as a village pony, I'd been sold off to a farmer who lived in the village, for more punitive service, and I remembered pulling a small plow through the fields. It wasn't backbreaking labor, not at all, and though I came to hate the tedium of it, and the mud and the inevitable sweat and my feet deep in the soft earth, I had loved the fresh breezes and the great open blue sky.

Once again a flood of memories came back to me, of being driven by the strap to work on the farm and then back to the village where I was often strapped outside the door of the farmer's narrow house, with my hands tied over my head to an iron bracket for the evening. I was turned facing out when the strapping was over. Barefoot, soiled, thirsty.

An old scholar often came by to chat with me, though why I never knew. He'd tease my cock as so many other passersby did, considering it their duty to keep the cocks up and down the street hard, and the old scholar, who was really no older than I am now, and rather elegant, told me that we naked slaves at the doorways were like the Herms of ancient cities.

"And what in the world, sir," I had asked one evening, "is a Herm?"

"In old Athens, they were pillars, young man, outside of houses, with the head of Hermes atop them, and cock and balls carved in relief. They were sacred. And they were for luck."

Then he had recounted an old story of how frightened the Athenians were when, the night before their fleet went out to fight a great war, all the Herms of the city had been vandalized. He thought the whole thing very interesting, and explained in depth to me how we naked slaves, almost all male, were exactly the same sort of sacred creatures, meant with our prominently displayed genitals to turn away harm.

Some Herms had the head of Athena, he told me, and from these old statues had come eventually the word "hermaphrodite." I'd been fascinated, uncomfortable as I was there, exposed and being teased idly by him, and helpless and listening as he took his time to tell me things of which I'd never dreamed.

I had no inkling then that this was something I would never forget. I remember only that my cock did jump at the thought of a pillar with the head of Athena and a cock and balls, and I had been quiet to encourage him to go on talking, which he likely would have done even if I'd gone to sleep.

I was shocked out of my reverie as there loomed into view one of the village pony teams, in their simple leather, pulling a large wagon full of people.

As it lumbered past us on the left I scarcely had a moment to drink in the spectacle of the struggling male ponies with their heads bowed, their boots dusty, and their black horsetails gleaming in the sunlight. Again the sight of the rippling muscles went to the root of my being. And only as the cart moved on did I realize the passengers were bowing to us.

I had served in the village two full years before Lexius was brought up on fearful charges, and, well, by then I don't think the Queen so much as remembered me, and when she let me go, a while after Lexius and Alexi, it had been with a careless wave of her hand. "Oh, that one, the clumsy boy, send him home too."

No wonder my brother's first words to me—after all the years—had been: "What are you doing here?"

There came other carts now laden with flowers, pots and baskets of flowers, and male slaves struggling as the farmer alongside swung his lash.

Did they envy our ponies in their splendid and glittering trappings?

I felt the Captain of the Guard's left hand on my shoulder suddenly. He was embracing me.

"Forgive me, Prince, you do look pale," he said.

iv

For an hour we walked around the village, the three of us, Alexi as fascinated as I. We were to meet Lady Eva at the Punishment Shop, he told me.

"Do you know what that is?"

I laughed. I couldn't help it. I glanced at Captain Gordon who had a remarkably serene smile on his face.

"Yes, Alexi, I was sentenced here for two years. I know what the Punishment Shop is." I didn't bother to add that my master, the farmer, hadn't wanted to spend the money to send me there, but had done so just to keep up appearances, now and then, and to please his wife.

She had been the anointed worrier of the household and felt I just wasn't whipped enough.

So we would sit there now as patrons of the establishment, would we? I couldn't quite wait.

But it was the Place of Public Punishment I wanted to see above all else.

As for the village itself, it was splendid now beyond imagining, with all façades freshly painted in shades of Roman red or olive green, or deep ochre—and brass doorknockers galore. The streets were so thronged with gentlefolk that I could scarce see the slaves adorning the open doorways, or working busily inside parlor and shops.

What astonished me was the new cleanliness, the lack of the old familiar smell, and the glitter of gold everywhere as people bought the rich wares on display at every turn.

We moved all too fast through the huge fountain court of the inns, as far as I was concerned. I'd never been inside any of those august establishments but Princess Beauty had told much of her time under the thumb of Mistress Loxley in one of them as we lay in our golden cages in the hold of the Sultan's ship. Captain Gordon had kept rooms at Mistress Loxley's inn and Beauty had first been given to him there.

"And where do you live now?" I asked, as if I'd been talking not thinking, and though my question startled him, he answered politely enough.

"I have a townhouse now, Prince, that His Majesty has given me. I'm grateful. It's more comfortable than any lodgings I've ever had."

As we walked on, finally, to the Place of Public Punishment, he pointed out the house, a narrow but grand three-story building, which had once been the house of Nicholas the Queen's Chronicler and his sister.

I remembered the Queen's Chronicler. He'd been a dreary miserable man during my years here, as he'd lost Prince Tristan, whom he loved with all his soul. He was held up to ridicule, but in whispers, as someone who had been foolish enough to ruin his heart on a slave.

I knew now that Tristan had eventually returned to the kingdom. Alexi's letters had mentioned this and so had the letters from the King. Tristan had his own fine manor house, and the King had indicated that I might want such a place of my own.

At last we came to the great fairgrounds that I'd been thinking about since news of the new kingdom had come to me.

I stood still as we left the paved street that had led us here so that I could take it all in.

It was the very same, yet utterly transformed. The old beaten earth was gone, and the stone paving went on forever, and once again it was swept and clean.

To the far right I saw three of the great maypoles, with the slaves tethered to long leather ribbons by their necks, forced to run in circles by those handsomely dressed grooms in special village livery, it seemed, who paddled them—and as before, the wheels to which slaves were strapped, spread-eagled, who might be turned upside down by a patron for a small coin. It was not the worst of punishment by any means, but it was frightening, and I had known it in my last six months, but I had been a very different slave by then from the one first brought here in terror and shame.

The slaves squealed and cried as the giant wheels turned, males as well as females, and of course the patrons teased them with little whisk brooms as they had in my time, but these now looked not so much like improvised or household tools, but like gaily beribboned trinkets sold here for the purpose and I soon saw that they were.

A slave forced to squat and walk behind a peddler carried two full baskets of such brooms for sale, on a long pole.

And all over, everywhere, were the bright striped tents—tents as I knew for having one's slave bathed, tents for having a slave male or female for a small payment, tents merely to look, or to watch or to spank.

But novelties had been added, or so it seemed. I saw a booth where female slaves were kneeling on a shelf, their hindquarters bared, of course, to the crowd, who bought three and four yellow balls at a time to hurl at them to see who might strike the heart of the target, which was, naturally, the anus of the slave. The backsides of these unfortunates were painted with brightly colored target stripes in what seemed like a thick adhesive paste, and I soon saw that some of the balls stuck to the targets in question, and the players argued spiritedly about who was better than whom in scoring at the game.

Seemed obvious enough to me.

As we walked about, we came to the rear of this tent, where I saw the heads of the bent-over slaves, fixed into a long yellow-painted wooden pillory, faces down, hands clenching and unclenching. I wondered did it hurt much when the ball struck one's backside. Likely not all that much. Again, it wasn't the worst punishment for a slave, but I knew those subjected to it would feel a thrilling shame nevertheless.

Variety was the spice of the kingdom.

"I heard this was a very dusty place and rather crude in the old days," said Alexi. "I only saw it once before the King and Queen came."

"Well, that was true," said Captain Gordon, "but truthfully, my lord, lots of the Court came down here just to see it from time to time, though they didn't let on to the old queen. It was supposed to be for the common people only, but look at the crowd now."

He was right. The area was milling with all manner of persons, from the finest and most ornately dressed to the simplest, but I could see that the gentry outnumbered the simple folk.

Yes, gaily dressed village boys and girls were lined up before the tents with their coins ready, but plenty of the richer men and women regarded this as a feast for the eyes. I saw dark-haired Prince Roger moving through the crowd—no mistake, it was he—whom I'd briefly known in my time in the village, but he did not see me, and I did not feel moved now to speak to him. That would occur naturally enough later on.

And it was larger, all of this. Much larger.

Only now as we moved through a field of high tents did I see the Public Turntable coming into view.

Like all else, it had been refurbished and ornamented. No more the crude wood ladder up which slaves had been driven to be paddled, but now there was a gilded stair. The great turntable itself was trimmed in dagged leather of many colors, and the great whipping master himself, who had always been a rotund and crude fellow with rolled-up sleeves and bulging arms, was now in a smart livery of gray and yellow—like all the grooms who paddled the maypole slaves, and pushed and directed other slaves all about.

But the whipping master was nevertheless a huge man, and I could hear the rumble of his deep, laughing voice from where I stood. He had a head of long flowing hair and enormous shoulders.

There was a row of unfortunates lined up to be paddled for the crowd on one side and on the other an endless row of gilded wooden pillories where slaves would be taken after their whippings to be displayed, bent over from the waist.

A huge burst of collective laughter erupted from the tents behind us. I turned, and only then realized that indeed I was near dizzy, my senses flooded with scents, sounds, and sights.

The Captain steadied me again, but very respectfully.

"Dmitri, we don't have to remain here," said Alexi.

"Oh, but I want to see it," I said.

"Well, you'll see it's changed," said the Captain softly and he kept his firm hand on my arm. I didn't mind it. I didn't care.

My cock was like a brick in my trousers. And I felt my nipples tingling and burning inside my shirt. Herms. Hermaphrodites. I heard the voice of the scholar.

". . . an ancient idea, of an ideal creature who combined the traits of male and female . . ."

"Here, my lord," said the Captain. "Drink this wine."

"The last thing I need in this sunshine," I said.

"It's weak, but it's very cold."

I did drink it.

In a daze, I saw a slave girl before us with a pitcher. And I knew that she had offered the cup. Hair the color of copper flowing over her shoulders; such a wealth of it, she seemed scarcely to be naked. If I'd been her master or mistress, I would have tied up her hair.

Her breasts were plump and delicious but pink as though they'd been gently spanked or whipped. I saw she had a phallus tucked into her with a large crest of flowers positioned right in front of her pubic lips, the whole held in place by thin straps leading to a belt that circled her waist.

How did I know there was a phallus there hidden inside of her? I could tell by the way she twitched and moved even as she stood still, her face flooded with a lovely blush and her eyes glazed.

She looked shyly at me as she refilled the cup.

"That is good," I said as I drank another deep gulp.

There came more laughter from the tents behind us.

"Oh, those games!" said Alexi.

I didn't want to see that now, though I knew I would want to see all of the tents later.

I wanted only to see the turntable, and the Captain, I realized suddenly, was blocking my view.

I stepped around him. The crowd was thickest near the turntable, possibly some fifteen or twenty deep before it thinned out.

There had been a break in the entertainment when we'd arrived, but the whipping master now motioned for a lovely princess or lady or "little girl" to come up the carpeted and gilded steps, and she did—sublimely flustered and blindingly succulent with rounded ivory limbs.

The whipping master, even with his gray-and-yellow livery, wore a great leather apron, but it was worked all over with gilding and yellow designs against a gray background.

The paddle in his hand was as I remembered, large and wooden, but it too was covered now in gold. And as he turned it this way and that for the roaring crowd, I saw that one side of the paddle was studded with what seemed tiny pearls.

The other side, thankfully for the shivering little girl, was smooth.

She had to kneel just as we had knelt—free, over from the waist with a small square pillar to support her chin. The pillar was carved and polished and had its share of gold worked into it, and there appeared to be a little cushion of some soft red stuff on the top. Not just the grainy wood.

I pressed closer, but not too close. I didn't want the men and women to block my view. I was back far enough where I might see all.

The little girl obeyed the whipping master submissively and almost gracefully, at once clasping her hands in the small of her beautifully arched back. Her little hindquarters were exquisitely displayed, and no one came to bind her calves to the floor.

Her little upturned face was very red, however, and her eyelids were fluttering. How I remembered my eyes being so tightly shut that first time, and yet they had kept opening, no matter what I did, no matter how many times I'd closed them, opening as if I had to see the crowds as well as hear them, the hundreds of people gathered there as they were gathered around now.

A liveried groom stepped up with a large bowl in his yellow-gloved hands. Out of the bowl, he scooped a thick cream which he now applied to the hindquarters of the quivering girl, vigorously rubbing it into her flawless skin.

The whipping master had wavy white hair and a florid complexion and he cried out something I couldn't catch that made the crowd roar. He placed his large meaty hand on the girl's neck, her soft long bronze curls spilling down in front of her on either side of the pillar where her chin rested.

Then down came his merciless paddle, with the smooth side towards the girl, and he spanked her thighs so hard that he lifted her knees off the wood. The crowd cheered and clapped.

One blow after another came at the girl in the same way, lifting her, forcing her up and off the wood, and letting her drop again, until finally she all but lost her balance and sank to the boards.

I could hear the dark rumble of the man's voice but not what he said.

The girl scrambled to regain her position.

And for the first time, by means of his foot pedal, the man spun the turntable to give the crowd to the far right a good look. Then back again, he turned her, as he was obviously right-handed, and down came the paddle again.

"Prince," the Captain whispered.

It was a shock hearing his voice.

I realized that I had put my hands to my lips.

"Quiet, please, Captain, not now," I said.

A woman's voice near me said, "Captain, he wishes to watch!"

On went the spanking on the turntable, the girl's tears flooding, but she did not break form. She couldn't keep her calves still, or her feet; she was dancing, as they call it. She couldn't help it. Dancing. But her little knees stayed in place.

The table was spun again and again.

The crowd was counting the blows aloud now and clapping loudly in time with each one.

It was a fierce paddling, and the whipping master was loving it, and I knew what the girl was feeling, I knew how time had stopped for her, how the very concept of time was now beyond her reach. But I was awestruck at her control and her form. Memories paled and vanished in the bright glare of her perfect ivory skin, her little fingers twisting, but her hands never breaking form, and her sweet delicate face awash with glistening tears.

I could scarcely breathe.

Suddenly the whipping master raised the paddle and turned it. Now the darling little bottom would get the prickly pearls.

The crowd cheered. The pearl-encrusted wood spanked her and she jumped helplessly and I thought I heard a high squeal come from her but in all the noise I couldn't be sure. The crowd loved it, and random clapping broke out all over.

Far off to my right I saw Prince Roger watching, with a handsome lady beside him.

"And how many of you," I whispered under my breath, "wish you were up there in her place?"

No one could hear that faint whisper or so I prayed. But in truth I didn't care.

My memories for the moment were not present. I saw only her— jumping, dancing, struggling, but never breaking form, her breasts shivering, such tender breasts shivering. The nipples of my chest felt like they'd explode with heat. My cock might have come if I'd dare to move and risk its rubbing against my clothes.

It was over. Now would come the part, I feared, that I truly loathed.

But it didn't happen.

As she knelt shivering and sobbing, the crowd threw only gold coins at her, pelting her with them from all sides. She was lost in a rain of glittering coins.

There was no refuse as there had been in my time, none of those rotten apples, and eggs or bits of potato or cabbage, pitched at her.

I felt myself weak suddenly with relief. I hadn't come, no, of course not, but my body had relinquished the heights and was settling down. My nipples throbbed and my legs were weak.

"They don't heave their garbage at the slave anymore," I blurted out.

"No, that's not done now," said the woman who was near me. "The King did away with that. He thought it vulgar and unnecessary and filthy as well. But anyone can buy little gilded wood tokens for a half penny to throw, and many do."

I glanced to my left to see her standing beside the Captain, one of those superb truly red-haired women who have clear blemish-free and creamy skin. She was very young and her fashionable gown revealed the fullness of her magnificent breasts exquisitely. Her green eyes were large and brilliant in the sun, and her lips were rouged. A peerless beauty, dressed in gaily printed silk and gold with glistening silk balloon sleeves. Even her slippers were gold, glinting in the sun.

"Let me present Lady Eva, Prince," said Alexi.

"Ah, yes, my pleasure, my lady," I said, but I kept glancing back to the turntable, and the incomparable Lady Eva gestured for me please to continue watching, and so I did.

The little doe on the turntable was lifted now by her wrists, the whipping master twisting and turning her as if she were on the auction block for all to see her punished bottom and legs. Her waist was small and her hips shapely, but then all of her was shapely, even her writhing fingers, and her breasts, though smaller than those of many slaves, were finely shaped.

The whipping master smacked her again forcing her hips forward, and she obviously cried out though I couldn't hear it. But she was as dainty and graceful as ever, her head almost demure as she bent it to one side, her shimmering hair tumbling beautifully down, her eyes modest and half closed.

How unlike in every conceivable way she was from the clumsy, struggling prince I'd been on the turntable long ago, time after time to the frustration of the Captain of the Guard. "You do realize you'll be paddled here four times a day if you don't stop struggling, don't you?" he'd whispered in my ear that last night.

A liveried groom, the very same who had prepared the girl's hindquarters for spanking, rushed around gathering up all the tokens and coins.

They were pushed into a little velvet sack and this was tied about her neck.

"You see, the King will not allow anything soiled to be forced into the slave's mouth," said the young woman at my elbow. "In the old days, they put the sack in the mouth, did they not?"

"They certainly did," I said. "Or in our backsides in the Punishment Shop."

"Well, that is not done now either," she said without hesitation. Her voice was warm, it seemed all the voices of this realm were warm, but she spoke with an easy serenity that was a marvel. Lady Eva. I was struggling to remember some context for her name from the letters that I'd received.

But a riot of memories was pressing in on me again.

It was all tangled. I felt myself, naked, sore, crying, being rushed to the pillory just as I watched the dainty accomplished little slave being rushed down the steps and thrust over and forward, her head and hands locked securely as mine had been locked. Gilded wood, of course. Wood decorated with curlicues and white flowers! And this a pillory in the village, one out of an endless number. But her little head was the finest flower.

Forgetting my manners, my friends, and the gracious lady beside me, I strode quickly through the loosening crowd and towards the distant pillory.

I came up before her.

Blue scarf. Wine. There it was again, those long-ago moments, as I was pilloried after each paddling. The Captain of the Guard had been so cross with me by sundown. "You are learning nothing, Prince."

I'd been so thirsty. And every time there had been the village girls with their cups of wine or cider or even milk, sweet white milk.

She sobbed uncontrollably.

Before I could turn and look for it, a tall slender male slave appeared beside me with a pitcher and cup.

"My lord, she can only lap it, from the cup or your fingers," he said as I shoved the coin into the leather purse he wore around his neck. Even his cock was half hard, his balls bound up tight to it, and the thin gold straps decorated with jeweled rosettes.

"Yes, I know that, little boy, believe me," I said.

I held the silver cup under her face, and dipping my fingers, I moistened her quivering lips. But she was far too distressed to drink. I reached into my tunic pocket for a handkerchief, and mercifully found one with which I wiped her face and her eyes and her nose. Blue scarf.

At sundown, after that third paddling, there had been the prettiest boy comforting me. "Prince, you'll learn," he'd confided in a shy halting voice.

And now the dish was silver and the wine was sweetened with honey. I could smell it.

This was wonderfully comforting to her. She glanced up fearfully and then down, then stared at the buckle of my belt, or at the cup I held in my right hand.

Now when I fed her the wine with my fingers, she lapped at it, and then I let her lap from the cup itself.

"What is your name, little blossom?" I said.

"Barbara, sire," she said through her sniffles and sobs.

"You were splendid on the turntable, Barbara," I said.

"But sire, I was so clumsy, I . . ."

"Ah, precious, never contradict your betters," I said. "That will never do. Thank me, if you like, but do not tell me I am wrong."

Her hair was almost golden in the sunlight but truly brown, a light shimmering brown.

"Yes, sire, forgive me!" She jumped suddenly and behind her, over the gilded pillory, I saw the boys and girls gathered there screaming with laughter. They'd been stroking her sex with those wicked little broom toys.

I put up my hand ominously and to my astonishment they backed away. Why did this surprise me?

"Listen, Barbara, you are very beautiful," I said. "I adore you. I have come many miles to revisit this place. I shall never forget you as the tender blossom I saw here during these moments."

"I'm so glad you're pleased, my lord," she cried. Crisp articulation. A well-spoken girl.

"Look up at me, go ahead."

Her eyes were dark blue and I could see her piquant nose and mouth. A ruddy finely shaped mouth.

I shifted the cup to my left hand and felt of her little chin, more flesh than bone. I pressed my thumb into the soft flesh—there was a dimple there, very pretty—beneath her lower lip.

One should not say eyes are intelligent but she had intelligent eyes.

"To whom do you belong, girl?" I asked.

"To the village, sire," she said, and her tears came again, thick and glassy and catching the sun. "I've only just . . ."

"Go on, little sparrow," I said.

"I've only just come to the kingdom." More tears. "I want so to please, my lord. I sold all I possessed to come here, my lord."

I turned.

The Captain was standing right behind me with Alexi and the lovely lady to whom I'd been unforgivably rude. But she seemed entirely patient and was smiling at me rather wistfully and said at once:

"What can I answer for you, Prince?"

"The girl, I want her!" I said.

"Arranged," said the Captain. "Whenever and wherever you like."

"I know what I want now, the sort of lodgings, if I'm to stay. I must talk to the King and Queen."

"And I will make certain of the details," said the lady eagerly. "Only tell me, Prince, and I'll see to it for you. I know full well that the King and Queen very much want you to stay."

"Yes, most definitely, they want you to stay," said Alexi. "No doubt of it at all."

"A townhouse, a townhouse here in the village," I said. "Is there a well-appointed townhouse that actually overlooks the Place of Public Punishment? That's what I want and, of course, will pay for it. And this girl as my slave."

I turned to offer the shuddering little damsel another drink. I knew she had heard every word.

Her pink tongue darted gracefully into the wine, lapping as swiftly and skillfully as that of a cat. Indeed there was something quite feline about her allure. This would certainly shape the manner in which I kept her, trained her, used her.

I was now hard and again on the verge of coming.

I looked around and I could see the distant windows and roofs surrounding the place. Surely those were the diamond-paned windows and gabled roofs of townhouses, had to be, all smartly painted, but they were some distance away.

"There is an available townhouse near, perhaps?" asked Lady Eva, looking up at the Captain.

"Oh, yes, several, though they are hardly the finest or the most popular," said the Captain. "Most people think the place too busy, too noisy. Prince, you do realize the place is almost never quiet now. There are so many coming and going . . ."

"Doesn't matter," I said. "It's precisely what I want."

"I'm thinking which one would be the best," said the Captain. He gestured to what appeared the broadest of the distant townhouses, the last one in the row that partially enclosed the far side of the square. "I think that one is indeed available, used now for guests who come and go."

"We can have it appointed beautifully for you, my lord," said lovely Lady Eva.

"Yes, that one," I said. "It looks down here on the turntable and the pillory."

"I'm sure I can arrange all of this immediately," said the Captain. "The visitors in that house left early this morning for their native land." He turned to gesture for someone behind him.

Lady Eva volunteered that she would oversee all the amenities herself.

"Dmitri, are you certain?" asked Alexi. "You don't want to be in the castle with us?"

"Alexi, darling," said the lady. "I think our beloved king might be quite pleased with all this. He's eager to hear Dmitri's views of the village and this very place."

"He feels it lacks innovation and expansive ideas," said the Captain in a low voice.

"Yes, but not to live at Court—" Alexi persisted.

"But of course Prince Dmitri would be living at Court, able to ride up at any time."

"I never actually lived at Court when I was here," I said to Alexi. I could hear the poorly suppressed emotion in my voice. And I knew that these words were foolish. They offered no real explanation for my choice.

I laughed suddenly, inexplicably.

I held the cup in my left hand while I smoothed Barbara's hair with my right. I leaned over and spoke into her ear.

"You're going to find me a very demanding master," I said. "But fear not, when I'm finished with you, you'll be perfection, and I may just keep you for a very long time, ever driving you to greater heights."

"Master!" she whispered.

"I am Prince Dmitri. Remember that name," I confided to her. "I'll be back for you. Perhaps not tonight, perhaps not tomorrow, but very soon." I turned to the Captain. "There's no chance of my losing her, with all of these people, all of these slaves!"

"None," said the Captain. I saw now that there were two grooms beside him, and they were eyeing the girl. "All slaves are carefully watched. No slave is left to slip from vigilance. And actually, Prince, that was always true even when the kingdom was one-third of what it is now."

Had I insulted him? Of course. He'd certainly stood over me on that first day here so many years ago, hadn't he? And we'd all known then that we were watched, accounted for, protected to be punished only in the approved ways. Again, I almost laughed, but why I didn't know.

The noise of the place rose around me, as if stirred by a latent breeze, and the sun felt a bit warm to me suddenly. Ah, it was these Russian clothes. I imagined myself naked, completely naked in this balmy air.

Barbara had almost finished the wine, clever little creature.

I took the last few droplets on my right fingers and I pushed these against her tongue. Then I pushed my thumb into her mouth, opening it, feeling the hot wet inside of her mouth. I wished I could see all of her and not this gilded pillory. Well, I would soon enough.

"Say it, girl."

"Prince Dmitri, my lord and master," she said, her bright dark blue eyes flashing on me again.

v

We were in the Punishment Shop and what a grand tavern that turned out to be. In old times, said the Captain to Lady Eva, these little places had been crowded and noisy with straw-strewn floors and cheap cider and ale.

I knew this. I remembered. I remembered the farmer's wife sending me here on foot, alone, to be punished. We wore tags around our necks. The choice of tag suggested the punishment. A small black tag on a thin thong meant "Spank." A red tag meant "Spank Severely," or so I'd been told. I'd always been sent with the red tag dangling between my nipples, hands clamped to the back of my neck, as that was the only way we'd ever been allowed to walk through the village on our own. And woe to the slave who wandered without a tag, a purpose, some emblem of intent from his master or mistress in sending him or her on an errand.

The place had been narrow then, with a bare stage four feet off the floor, and crowded little tables where villagers drank their cider or ale, gossiped, and with some of the women knitting or embroidering with their little rings.

Now it was vast, the beams of the ceiling painted with bright green vines and yellow flowers against a plaster blue sky.

We had a polished table and carved chairs, and so did the other patrons, rich and poor, and the stage directly just in front of us, some four feet off the ground still, was painted and polished and draped in sumptuous wool hangings and lighted with great multibranching iron candelabra.

The whipping master was caparisoned in yellow and gray with the same ornate apron worn by his fellow on the Public Turntable, and if anything this one was a more impressive figure in his high-backed armless chair.

In the kingdom, always beware of armless chairs.

He was a giant of a man with a mane of long flowing gray hair and a broad beard, with rosy cheeks and big shining gold boots.

He crooned to the slave bent over his apron now, tousling his hair, and stroking his back, and patting his upturned backside gently. The spanking had apparently just ended as we came in. He appeared to be comforting the victim and taking his time.

"He thinks he's a loving grandfather," said Lady Eva confidentially to me as he might easily hear us, we were so close.

But the din was considerable. Everywhere patrons drank their cider or ale and chatted with spirit, as if nothing, absolutely nothing, were happening on the stage.

"It's really too amusing," Lady Eva said to me with a brilliant smile. "That's why I've seated us so close. You must hear and see this kindly father of paddlings for yourself."

Alexi laughed as he lifted his mug of mulled wine. "I love the man!" he said. "I come down here for this more than anything else."

More patrons pressed into the Punishment Shop now, and beyond the tiny diamond-paned windows others were lined up to get in. There were villagers here, ordinary people, yes, but it did seem to me the gentry was now the majority, so unlike the old times.

The floor of the stage was carpeted in dark blue, and the whipping master's thronelike chair was placed on a carpeted platform elevated above it by one foot. He had taken a little break for himself, it seemed, and drank from a flagon offered him by his liveried attendant. Yellow gloves. So many of the grooms and attendants wore yellow gloves. I saw the stool beside him, fancy and carved as was every movable, and the pot of cream there and a pile of what appeared to be more yellow leather gloves.

The slaves were lined up on their hands and knees on a long easily sloping ramp to the far side from us, which brought them from a pen inside the front door to the stage.

I remembered that ramp very well, making my way up it slowly, as it sometimes took an hour before my turn to be "Spanked Severely" and hoping that the crowd would take no interest, which was often the case. After all, I'd known this place after my return from the sultanate, and I had become a master of control.

I didn't give them a good performance. I was far too resigned, and polished. And even when told to "wag my little tail," I did it too gracefully to interest the commoners who used to congregate here more to see one another than to bother with us.

I was eager for the show to begin, and felt oddly detached even from Alexi, though the courtesy and sweetness of Lady Eva touched me. The Captain had gone off to see to my townhouse and to the delivery of Barbara along with all the furnishings and goods. I felt his absence, but I didn't know whether I was grateful for it. It seemed I missed him.

I looked around the shop slowly, noting a multitude of changes, the dark blue painted walls, the polished floor. Ah, such polished floors. The ramp for the waiting slaves had its blue carpet, same as the stage. Tables were set with small silver lamplets or candles. Goblets, flagons, or cups were of silver or enameled earthenware. And the smell of the place was sweet from the honey and spices in the heated drinks.

"I came here many times," I murmured under my breath, principally to convince my companions that I was not altogether ignoring them, though in fact I was.

A young gentleman had caught my eyes, a figure and face I thought I might know. He was my age, I had come to realize, though on first sight he'd seemed much younger, with an oval face and long red hair. It was slightly darker than Lady Eva's voluminous hair, and his eyes, though green, were paler than hers, but he was handsome in the extreme—and dressed fussily and finely in a long peach-colored embroidered tunic and soft ornate morocco-leather boots.

He wore the same heavy gold chain and medallion that Alexi wore, and I wondered at it. Then it hit me: "Prince Richard," I said aloud.

Alexi leaned forward, and quickly I explained. Richard had been in the village when I'd returned from the land of the Sultan, a prince who'd displeased the Queen as much as I had, sent down to punishment, just as I had been, and he'd served the hard demanding Mistress Jennifer Loxley at the inn. He'd left before I had, and now I could see he was back.

"Oh, yes," said Lady Eva. "That is Prince Richard indeed. He returned two years ago and the Queen was glad to receive him. He languished at Court until the new king and queen arrived. He's the guiding genius of this place, so to speak. The King relies upon him to oversee this and all the Punishment Shops, and he enjoys this very much. He lodges at the inn now where once he was a slave. But no one would recognize the inn now, for it's become a place of luxury for moneyed guests and even nobility. He's devoted to our new monarchs. He especially adores the Queen and takes the noon meal with her almost daily. He has lodgings at the castle as well."

"Guiding genius." These were the words that the King had used in referring to the Place of Public Punishment.

"And you, Alexi," I said, turning to him and pointing to his chain and medallion. "Does this have to do with being the guiding genius of something? Is it permitted for me to ask?"

"Naturally, and I'm glad to tell you," he said. "I'm in charge of evening Court entertainments along with Rosalynd and Elena. The ladies wear a medallion linked to their belts, and often hidden in their pockets. I'm happy to wear this, as you see."

"And Prince Richard's medallion indicates his responsibilities," said Lady Eva. "The villagers and guests know by these medallions that they might approach him and ask questions, that he is ever ready to help. Prince Richard is the master of His Majesty's Punishment Shops."

I understood. I understood more than I could put into words. I understood everything! Of course. Prince Richard had been punished innumerable times over the years here. He knew the ways of the place intimately. He was the perfect person to refine and perfect it in the rush of conflicting forces that characterized any new kingdom, any new regime. *Guiding Genius.*

"Dmitri," said Alexi gently and confidentially. "You need accept no such position, you know. You are entirely free to enjoy the kingdom. Prince Roger is back, do you remember him? He has no task as yet and may never seek for one. Tonight, you and other returnees will be presented officially and that means welcomed, welcomed as guests to Court."

"I know, I understand that, Alexi," I said, my eyes fixed on the stately almost prim figure of Prince Richard. His arms were folded. He sat with his back to the ramp of waiting slaves. He was studying the patrons of the place, not the slaves, watching the naked serving boys and girls, watching the great red-cheeked whipping master laugh with his groom as he drank his ale.

"Listen, Prince," said Lady Eva suddenly. "I know you want to be alone with your thoughts here. I'll go on to see to your house. When you're ready to return to Court, I'll have the King's chariot waiting for you at the village gates. Alexi, you can handle the team, can you not? Now I'll leave you."

We rose to bid her goodbye and she took me boldly in her arms.

"Lady, you read my mind and my heart," I said.

"I understand, my lord," she said. "You have only just returned. I cannot know what it is like for you, but I have seen what it has been like for others."

She kissed me on both cheeks and made her way out of the place, quite independently though I caught sight now of a groom who followed her, a groom in castle livery, who'd been waiting quietly on her all along.

"She knows much," I said to Alexi.

"That's why she is in charge of all slaves in this kingdom," said Alexi. "That's why the King and Queen completely depend on her. As she admitted, she does not know what we know. She is very young and has never been anyone's naked slave. But her comprehension of this world we share is unsurpassed. Do you want me to go?"

"No!" I took his hand almost desperately. "Not at all."

A naked serving girl refilled my goblet. And a boy appeared with a fresh mug of mulled wine for Alexi.

The whipping master drew himself up, wiped his heavy gray mustache with his enormous hand, and a little sprinkling of applause broke out here and there. His face shone bright in the candlelight. No doubt dusk was coming down in the crowded street beyond.

"Come now, poor little piglet," he said to the slave boy who had been waiting his turn all this while—first on the ramp.

Oh, is there no end to beauty here, I thought.

"Piglet" was the word often used in the village for a male slave, just as "partridge" was for a female, and this young man was a plump pink piglet indeed, with deliciously shaped hindquarters and an exquisite face. He made his way on hands and knees with a very straight back and graceful fingers up onto the platform and then knelt up for the whipping master to take the dreaded red leather tag from his neck, which was tossed in a gilded basket to the man's far right.

"Such an expression," said Alexi. "What is he, do you think, twenty?"

"Maybe," I said, "and like a young god."

The boy had a marvelously well-proportioned face with a narrow nose and large sensuous inviting lips. His chin was strong, and so were his shoulders, and his hair fell down on his shoulders, rather like that of Prince Richard, but it was pale yellow, perhaps much bleached by the summer sun.

He glanced timidly at the whipping master with gray eyes, but there was no cowardice in him.

"Now, what have you done, young Valentine," said the whipping master, affectionately smoothing the boy's hair. "Come now, youngling, tell the truth, why has your master sent you here again today?"

Suddenly tears sprang to the boy's eyes. He kept his hands beneath his hair and clamped on his neck but his chest heaved.

"He is put out with me, sir," he said under his breath, but I could easily hear him. "No matter what I do my hands shake. I spilt his ink. I dropped the bottle."

"Well, you'll get over that, poor little brat," said the whipping master, smiling. "You'll soon learn not to fumble at all." He patted the boy again gently, first on his head and then on his backside. He kissed the boy's cheek. "Now you know I'm going to give you a sound spanking, don't you?" he said. "And that's going to help you to be a good boy. Spanking softens the soul."

He hugged and kissed the boy again and then with his left hand pulled him forward by the hair until the boy lay over his lap.

"Now you keep the cock well behaved, little fellow," he said, "or I'll be spanking you all evening, you know that, don't you?"

"Yes, sir," the boy said. And only now were the tears gathering. The "over the knee" position almost always brought tears, tears even from the most proud and mocking.

The whipping master drew on a yellow leather glove and picked up a glob of fresh cream and worked this into the boy's hindquarters, lovingly massaging his thighs.

"Such pretty plump legs, muscular yet soft," he crooned to the boy. "I have to confess, Valentine, paddling you is always a pleasure. Oh, I know you're going to be bawling in a minute, but you're such a little pork pie, so ripe, so pretty. Now you be a good boy, and you think on your faults with every smack!"

"Yes, sir," said the boy again.

I glanced at Prince Richard, so far away, sitting against the ramp. His eyes were fixed on the boy. Ink. The matter of ink put me in mind of that scholar who used to chat with me when I was a Herm against the wall.

"Now, you pick up those balls of yours," said the whipping master, "and you hold them up to your cock and you keep that cock up off my apron, little fellow, understand?"

"Yes, sir," said the boy yet again.

"You see what I mean?" said Alex. "You hear how he talks to them?"

"Well, the guiding genius over there must approve of it," I said. It was igniting my blood, the tone of his voice, its appeal to utter dependency in the slave.

"Oh, yes, or he would be replaced!" said Alexi. "And he and Eva are developing names for these types of whipping masters and all masters and mistresses and grooms—scolding mistresses, angry masters, comforting masters, cross mistresses, and so on—and by the way, the smallest of the Punishment Shops has whipping mistresses only and some of them are a spectacle indeed."

The whipping master patted the boy tenderly all over his gleaming bottom and thighs, then stripped off the glove and picked up the inevitable gold paddle which had a pair of pretty blue ribbons streaming from its tooled handle.

"Now who's going to be the best possible little boy for me, hmm?" he asked.

"I am, sir," said Valentine.

"And who's going to go back to his master and try very hard to please?"

"I am, sir," came the inevitable reply.

Down came the paddle with such a riff of blows I was amazed. I drew back, glancing in surprise at Alexi.

The boy got fifteen to twenty spanks within seconds and they were hard. And they didn't stop. The whipping master raised his eyebrows and appeared to be singing as he spanked away, and Valentine's head was bowed and he was soon dancing on his knees and crying completely, indeed reduced to the deepest and most complete vulnerability before our eyes. But his hands held fast to his gathered scrotum and hard cock and though he bounced on his knees—he couldn't help it—his organ never once touched the master's apron.

The rumble of voices in the place grew louder, more spirited, though no one actually turned to look—that I could see—at the poor boy.

I could feel the current of excitement passing through the room, as if the paddle were a drum beating a lusty cadence.

Now the boy was squirming desperately in that hopeless effort to escape the paddle, the body unable to accept what the mind knew. The loud hard spanks came slower, but the boy was woefully red.

The whipping master snapped the fingers of his left hand for his groom and made a gesture I did not know.

At once the groom came round and reached down for the boy's ankles and then effortlessly hiked them high into the air, the boy's twisting and turning body pulled back and lifted off the apron so only his chest and shoulders rested on it, and the whipping master pounded the elevated backside, whistling or singing to himself as before. How he seemed to love it. I'd never thought before about these men who did nothing day in and day out but paddle and spank. He seemed a paragon of his profession. His blue eyes positively twinkled beneath his heavy gray brows.

At last he drew a breath and sat back. The boy's sobs were loud though his lips were shut.

"Now, do I give the best spanking in this village, or do I not?" asked the whipping master, rubbing the boy's pretty hair with his hand. "Come on, speak up, Valentine, I'm not hearing anything. I'm going to spank you again, if you don't speak up."

"Yes, sir," sobbed the boy but his voice was low and restrained and had dignity to it. "The best, sir, and please, sir, spank me as you please, sir."

More paddling on the bottom now swinging in the air. The powerful groom had no problem holding the boy's ankles, and the boy's hands never left his genitals nor tried to cover them up. His cock was red and gleaming. I could see the tip of it lathering. Oh, how I knew that desperation.

I knew it now.

And as if Alexi were reading my mind as surely as Lady Eva had, he said:

"Are you nearly coming under those fancy Russian clothes?"

"How about you?" I asked.

"Just about!"

We must have been there an hour.

Finally it was full dark and I'd seen five slaves, three boys and two girls, very efficiently and effectively spanked.

One of the girls, a precious nymph with black curls, had obviously come while being spanked, but it didn't seem the great cheerful Lord of the Paddle knew it. The groom certainly knew it as he saw her red face and her stuttering spasms. I saw him smile.

The patrons had seen it and they began to scold and point and shake their heads and wag their fingers.

And so she was forced to make the round of the Punishment Shop on her knees after—the groom holding her wrists high—touching her tender little moist pelt to each boot in so far as she could squat that low, and begging pardon for her indulgence of those who scarcely took the time to wiggle her chin or tousle her curls. Many gentlemen and even ladies extended their boots or shoes for her to touch them with her moist sex, and patted her on the head forgivingly.

I'd never been made to do this. I'd never come while being paddled in this shop.

Patrons filled a little pouch hanging around her neck for another spanking.

When she'd come round to us, having made a circuit of the place from left to right, I felt her succulent wet sex and kissed her upturned mouth.

"Bad girl!" I said. "Take it from a bad boy. I know." I put two coins in her pouch.

"My lord," she whispered with perfect manners.

I felt of the sweet firm flesh under her arms, and then pinched both her nipples.

Alexi, who'd been watching all with very detached eyes, beckoned for her to be brought round to him. "Lift her," he said. The groom did this so that her hips were right in front of him. "Now offer me your ripe little plum, girl," he said.

She pushed her pelvis forward as best as she could, fresh tears springing to her eyes. He spanked her pubis hard with his flat fingers over and over. "Bad, bad, bad girl!" he said in a low scornful voice. "Do you know the meaning of the word 'perfection'?"

"I'm so sorry, my lord," she said, her lips quivering, her wet cheeks glistening in the candlelight.

I observed all this with a little surprise. But I said nothing.

He slipped coins into her little purse for more spanking.

"You tell the whipping master to spank her until she exhibits complete control," he told the handler.

And off she was taken to be put in the line and spanked once more. Maybe only once more.

It was then that Prince Richard saw us and joined us and he chatted with Alexi as though he could afford to have a little relief from his vigilance. He remembered me.

"Prince Dmitri," he said. "You don't know how I envied you, that you knew the sultanate before it was destroyed."

"Yes, that was an education, Prince," I said, "but this is our world, and frankly, I find it now infinitely superior. I suspect whatever we learned in the sultanate will blossom in this realm under a brighter more loving sun than ever we knew there." I thought of Lexius; I thought of many things.

He smiled at me. "Dmitri, you are as I remembered you," he said. "Always so filled with philosophy."

"I'd call it poetry," said Alexi with a little grin.

"Ah, it's all talk," I confessed. "We learned things in the sultanate, true, but in a way, everything that truly shaped my soul had occurred here."

"Yes, I know what you mean," Richard answered. "Well, you have chosen the most glorious time for your return."

"That is undoubtedly true," I said.

It was full dark when the three of us went out, as Prince Richard wanted to be at Court tonight and lived at the castle besides, and Alexi invited him to return with us.

We walked through the village together. It was filled with light—torches, lighted windows, candlelighted shops open for late visitors, and lanterns hung outside doors. Lots of gaily painted paddles and straps for sale, along with myriad other toys.

Lots of slaves on display, Herms indeed. I saw one splendid damsel with a silver phallus rising between her legs. Alexi pointed out it was a new fashion, the double phallus—one-half well anchored in the girl, the other half displayed in manly fashion. There were many such new toys for sale in the shop behind her. "It can be strapped on tight if she's meant to use it to penetrate a young piglet in the rear," said Prince Richard. "Lady Eva designed it."

Prince Alexi said that Eva was brilliant.

"I'll come down later, after all the festivities," Richard explained to me. "Should you want to join me, you're welcome. The crowd's a bit more rowdy and the late-night whipping mistress is a marvel. She's a different story from the loving old father you just witnessed."

This set my cock to stirring again. But then so had the double phallus.

"Thin, pointed features, but hands made of living marble," Richard continued describing the late-night whipping mistress. "She wears an old-fashioned wimple over her hair, and is immaculate and severe in attire."

"A child's nurse from the Underworld," said Alexi breezily, "where Sisyphus struggles forever to move his boulder up the hill."

Richard laughed. "She is a great believer in her own dour methods," he said scornfully.

"She puts me in mind of old Lord Gregory," said Alexi. "He is still with us, Dmitri, and the same. Always angry, always in a state of indignation, always believing that a slave is beyond hope!"

"Yes," said Richard. "She's cut from that very cloth. She offers vicious indignation and horror to each little piglet and partridge at their disobedience, and even those sent merely for their weekly maintenance hear her imprecations and ominous warnings against being lazy and disrespectful and utterly lost."

I'd never known a whipping mistress in the village in my time. Oh, the women of the village whipped their slaves hard enough, but women had not worked in these places then.

When we reached the gate, I expected to see all the King's ponies refreshed, but this was an entire new team except for Caspian and Bastian in the lead and a tall magnificent pony tethered to their far right. It was all as blindingly impressive as it had been before.

I went up to have a look at that splendid new pony.

"That's César, Prince," said a groom. "The King's favorite of the moment."

The pony was too tall to be well matched with the others, but likely there weren't many with whom he could be matched.

He stood staring straight ahead, his back respectfully arched, and his chin high as I looked at him. He had a great mane of white-blond hair, but with some of it tied back and braided to keep it out of his face.

And this pony had an extraordinary face—a high and broad and serene forehead and beautifully etched dark eyebrows that were high placed to show off his huge blue eyes. His cheekbones were beautiful. His mouth, even with the bit in it, was clearly magnificent.

I reached out tentatively towards his mouth.

"Oh, do examine him," said Alexi softly to me.

I felt of the man's lower lip. I could see him sigh and lift his shoulders and then straighten himself, all but shivering under my touch. His gilded nipples were enormous and had been wound with adhesive paste and fine wire, and from the wire hung teardrop weights against his chest.

In his navel was a gold medallion with a lion's head on it.

He was one of the more nearly perfect humans I'd ever beheld.

"He pulls the King's small chariot, my lord," said the enthusiastic and helpful groom. He drew up and smoothed back César's hair. "He's the 'king of the stable,' if you will. Aren't you, César?"

The pony smiled, his eyes crinkling, his cheeks plumping, and I heard a low secretive laugh come from him.

The groom smacked his backside and he jumped, but only a little. His legs were like marble.

"He's been kept idle all day," said the groom, "in case His Majesty should want to ride out, so we're to work him hard tonight."

"And does this mean he is a paragon?" I asked.

"He had better be," said Alexi in a droll voice. "If he weren't, well, let's just say his backside and legs would be the color of burgundy wine, and his face would be so wet you would think it freshly enameled."

The groom thought that was wondrously clever. And something quickened in César's face as if he too were amused, but he stood firm as if on principle.

All the while Richard observed these things with vague amusement.

We returned to the chariot, the ponies straining at their harnesses and shifting their weight from foot to foot as if eager to run.

"Tell me, Richard, if you can—there was an old scholar in my time," I said. "Well, no older then than we are now. A very cheerful and learned man. Do you remember him? Is he still in the village? He used to stroll by my old master's house . . ."

"Why, of course, I recall the man. He's the bookseller, and quite the connoisseur of ancient texts as well. His shop is the only one of its kind in the kingdom and it's a bit of a library, with everyone borrowing from it now and then, and with the King sending down for books, and even donating new ones. Seems the King is as partial to books as to gold when visitors come."

"Ah, of course. A bookseller!"

"Yes, and the scribe for the most demanding documents or letters, you know, as he knows all the official greetings and even some of the law. Roland is his name."

"Ah, that's it," I said. "I remember now, Roland. I recalled him when that poor boy, Valentine, said that he spilt the ink."

"Did he say that?" asked Richard. "Well, Valentine belongs to Roland, and Roland is hardly the strictest of masters. Likely he must write himself notes to remember to send Valentine to the Punishment Shop, but it's demanding work in that bookshop, and Roland makes a pretty footstool of Valentine for hours when he's writing. He paid a lot at the public sale for Valentine, as Valentine is highly educated and can read and write. Our lady mayor bid against him for Valentine, but lost."

I smiled. Often the slaves with the most serene faces were those who knew how to read and write, why I had no idea.

But it was time to mount the chariot and be off. The festivities would begin late and I was tired and needed the warmth and comfort and cleansing of the bath.

The long winding way back up the hill was lined with torches. And at several points I marveled to see brightly illuminated shrines in which highly polished slaves were posed and bound in what seemed rather beautiful positions. The lanterns surrounding these niches and their human artifacts were large and glittered with multiple candle flames.

"It's not as taxing as it looks," said Alexi, following my eyes. "They are mounted in those niches for no more than three hours each evening. They'll be relieved later on by others and then by the stroke of midnight they'll be packed off to bed. The King and Lady Eva are ever vigilant that every slave be well treated. And Queen Beauty would be shocked were they not."

The castle and the castle gardens were splendidly illuminated as we drove up. I could hear a great gentle buzz of voices everywhere, and the high crenellated walls of the castle were ablaze with torches as well.

I kissed my companions goodbye, hurried up to my room, and fell down on the bed in a dead faint. My cock pulsed and demanded things of me. I told it to be still, and fresh for the night.

vi

The great red-and-gold-canopied pavilion of the King and Queen dominated an immense garden that I didn't recognize from before, so huge was it, and filled with other smaller pavilions, fountains, and potted and natural trees.

The King and Queen were feasting at a long banquet table when at last I was summoned, along with several other royal returnees, and told I might be introduced and present my gifts now.

I'd dressed carefully for this in a lighter silken European tunic and leggings and slippers, and felt much more comfortable now in the warm delightful breeze.

The air was filled with the music of harps and horns and drums.

On great polished platforms laid down on the grass, lords and ladies danced with stately precision, and a long carpet ran up to the platform before the King and Queen.

King Laurent looked larger than life in his brilliant scarlet velvet and gold tunic and long full bordered sleeves, and the Queen was a vision of delicacy and enticing loveliness, suggestive of lilies, with her pale skin, golden hair, and girlish eyes.

To either side well-dressed members of the Court dined with them, the tables seeming to go forever out of sight. I knew some of these faces, even from a distance, and thought I glimpsed old Lord Gregory there, bending over his plate rather moodily with heavy brows. And if I wasn't mistaken the severe cold-eyed woman looking back at me sharply from the Queen's left was Lady Elvera who had once been the harsh, merciless mistress of the King.

There were others far too numerous for me to note. Everywhere I beheld costly attire, jewels on throats and fingers and wrists, and shimmering veils of the sheerest silk, and the glitter of silver and gold plate. The many tables all around me and before me were strewn with fresh flowers.

The scent of gardenias and lilies was intoxicating. Potted rose trees bloomed everywhere I looked, it seemed, and pathways had been made through the maze of the garden by fine India carpets, trodden under foot now as carelessly as the grass.

Naked slaves, exquisitely coiffed and groomed, and some even decorated with leafy chains of little flowers laid over their hips, served wine and steaming hot platters of food to the royal guests and to a wilderness of other banqueting nobility and gentlefolk in pavilions or at open tables everywhere I looked.

Behind the King and Queen, naked slaves stood on a low wall, still as statues, legs wide apart, oiled genitals gleaming, garlanded heads bowed. Man, woman, man, woman. Arms raised, hands clasped behind the neck.

To the far right as I approached I saw slaves running on the familiar Bridle Path where I'd been such a failure in my time, falling down and then crawling away from the mounted lord who sought to drive me with his paddle—such a disgrace.

The slaves I glimpsed ran fast and with grace, knees high, booted feet striking the earth gracefully, but I realized quite suddenly that the "mounted figures" driving them were not mounted on horses at all. Each was in a small light chariot, like an ancient battle chariot, pulled by a male pony!

I wanted to see more of this and knew that later I would.

I could see companion slaves everywhere at the feet of those they served, sitting back on their heels waiting for the slightest command, and some being made to play "fetch" with a flowering branch or a bright golden ball.

There were fountains surrounded by naked slaves on their knees facing out with their arms bound to the rim of the fountain, and in the center of these busy sparkling pools of water stood other slaves about the high pillar that held the smaller second basin with its splashing spout.

Now all this took me back to the sultanate where every night it seemed I'd been in a lighted garden, playing at games of fetch, or adorning some fountain, superbly taught by my dark-faced and delicate-fingered masters, none of whom spoke our tongue, but managed to convey their wishes to us effortlessly with their firm hands. Only Lexius had spoken our tongue and he'd been taken away by Laurent and the Captain shortly after we'd been brought there.

Surely the Sultan's influence was alive here in this endless paradise of sweetly illuminated trees with its countless guests.

I saw slaves as footstools, and kneeling as pets beside their masters and mistresses. And then the spectacle of X crosses, to which spread-eagled slaves were bound with shining silver and gold cuffs at ankles and uplifted wrists, heads held in place with stately collars, and often crowned with flowers, genitals decorated in gold.

Here and there leashed slaves were being driven as puppies through the festive crowds, their necks collared, their heads bowed. Inevitably some were prodded about by a phallus driven into the anus at the end of a handsome tooled leather rod. How I recalled the feel of that phallus and the way one was prodded forward by the rod or wand.

I saw a stately young noblewoman standing idly beneath a tree strung with flickering lanterns, making her little boy kneel up and beg for the sweets she dangled over his head, with his hands bound behind his back.

Slave cocks were everywhere erect, bottoms red, faces modest and submissive. The serving slaves with the pretty fluttering flower chains around their hips looked more naked than all the rest.

I found myself in a short line of others waiting for my audience. Fabien stood beside me with my gifts. I think he had become more used to things by this time, perhaps with memories of India and Lexius returning to him, but he was devouring what he saw.

I'd added to my gifts since my visit to the village—several antique volumes of history in Greek and in Latin, and a book of old Roman poetry especially for my lord, the King. These I'd brought with me for my own sometime pleasure, but was now delighted to offer them to Laurent.

At last my name was announced.

I stepped forward before the long banquet table and bowed.

"Prince Dmitri, we welcome you to the kingdom," said the sweet-faced and generous queen as if we hadn't met earlier that day. She was outfitted entirely in blue, blue that matched her peerless eyes, and her thin white veil barely concealed her magnificent hair.

The King stood and put out his arms to me, his face filled with warmth and good cheer, and we embraced over the litter of meats and fruits and platters of sweets and then I stepped back smiling at both of them, and telling them from my heart how happy I was to be here and how I hoped to remain. This is usually where I dip my long full sleeves into a plate of sauce and despise myself for it, but this time I did not.

Fabien stepped forward at my summons and I opened the first casket and presented my gracious hosts with the gold and silver vessels I'd brought from the Russian lands.

"These came from old Constantinople in my grandfather's time," I said with muted pride. "For Your Majesties, with all my heart."

Then came the casket of gold, equivalent to the collective dowries of all my sisters and female cousins, and the King nodded gratefully with the seemingly very sincere words that I was "too kind."

Other gifts followed—candlesticks and plate, a necklace of Indian diamonds for the Queen, emerald brooches, and finally the books and the book of poetry which I gave to the King with my own hands.

"The Latin poem of Propertius, my lord," I said.

"Ah, but I shall treasure this, Prince," he said. "And will you remain with us? We are so hoping that you have made your decision to stay."

"My lord," said the Queen. "Prince Dmitri will be living in a fine townhouse adjacent to the Place of Public Punishment. Lady Eva has arranged it all."

The Queen nodded to her left and for the first time I saw Lady Eva there, her hair pinned up and back and studded with pearls and diamonds and ivory combs. How grand she looked, how truly regal, and I had treated her so casually. I was ashamed. After I kissed the Queen's hand, I took Lady Eva's hand.

"Ah, Prince, I do hope you'll be pleased," she said to me. "Your house is ready for you tonight, if you so choose, though it's our hope you'll feast late with us and go tomorrow at your leisure. It's your choice."

She was indeed high in favor here, and had a self-possession well beyond her years.

A sweet-faced naked boy stood behind her chair, arms pulled back as if they were folded against his back. I could see his cock was about half hard, which is the usual thing during long banquets, but his pubic hair was decorated with small flowers, and so was the full blond hair of his head. His nipples had been gilded, but apparently with a paste of gold, because small bells hung from them on delicate shimmering threads. I could feel this when I looked at it, feel the paste on my own nipples, feel the bells against my chest. Soon I realized that was true of almost all the slaves. Nipples were tinted with paste and many decorated with flowers and bells. And this fine stripling dared not raise his eyes to me as the lady spoke.

"What's your pleasure now, Prince," asked another voice. It was Alexi at my elbow, in fresh garments with an exotic Eastern embroidery. "I'm here," he said, "to take you wherever you might like to go." His hair was clean and lustrous and in his deep gray velvet he looked more impressive.

"Might I have some wine near to the Bridle Path, Your Majesties," I asked, "and watch the slaves being run there?"

Of course, anything I wished, said a clamor of voices, and soon, tired and dazed as I was, I found myself seated at a small table right at the edge of the Bridle Path, beneath the limbs of a great old tree that was strung with lanterns, and with torches on both sides of the path burning brightly to illuminate the figures flying by. There were guests on raised platforms on the far side of the Bridle Path and they seemed to go on forever. The scope of this was weakening me all over and lulling me into a gorgeous sense of safety and peace.

Never in the days of Queen Eleanor had I seen such scope and grandeur. The kingdom seemed invincible in its splendor as if it had always been what it was on this night.

Fabien rested against the bark of the tree. He looked as amazed as I was. He couldn't keep his eyes off the voluptuous slaves who drifted past, setting sweets out for me, and refilling my goblet, or the twitching and undulating slave bound to the X cross nearby.

Whether this was special punishment or mere adornment, I didn't know, but I saw this slave had been rubbed and burnished with gold-pigmented oil. He was a powerfully built male. In fact he put me in mind of Laurent, he was so sturdy, and he dozed on the X cross, his head held upright by a beautifully embossed collar of blue and silver and gold, but he never stopped his subtle twisting movements. His hair was strewn with flower petals and tiny flowers like those that grow wild in the grass. Flowers were bound up with his scrotum and balls as well.

There came one of those moments when I could do no more than absorb all that I was seeing and had seen. My mind was empty of words.

But the Bridle Path I had not even begun to observe! I drank another gulp of wine. It was tart but delicious. I looked at the goblet. It was fitted with jewels the size of those I wore on my fingers. I smiled to think I was part of the spectacle in my finest dress and with rings on my hands, and emeralds studding the border of my tunic—as much a part of it as the bound slaves.

I turned my full attention to one slave after another running past on the Bridle Path trying to keep pace with the lord or lady in the pony chariot beside him—or her—who whacked away hard with the great paddle, laughing and urging the slave on. Soon several girls in a row came running by, seeming as fast as men, though they never were really as fast as the men at all, and again came the flashing pageant of the masters and mistresses in their little enameled chariots, and the ponies, male all, in delicate but gleaming red-and-gold harnesses, bells jingling, running as fast, apparently, as they could. It seemed to me the laboring ponies were not really ornamented for the occasion but merely hard at work, though each wore a streaming horse tail out of his anus, and some even had flowers fixed to these tails.

But it was the enameled and embossed chariots, the lords and ladies, and the helpless running slaves who were the magnet of attention.

How terrified many of them appeared. I wondered if for any it was their first time, fitted into the boots with wrists laced tight behind their necks, told to run as fast as they could.

The ponies certainly had the advantage over the poor slaves being spanked along, as the ponies had muscular legs and no doubt strong lungs.

And these poor beauties were being driven, quite literally, to distraction to keep up.

I'd never made it even once around the old circuit before I'd fallen down and tried to get away. I'd ended every attempt hung upside down by my ankles for half an hour while being whipped hard by a stinging leather thrash. And then there had been so many other punishments—crawling on my belly with back arched, so that my balls and cock were off the ground, behind the strolling queen, with the bit in my mouth tethered to her heel, and the red X painted on my back which meant "Bad Boy." Oh, the scorn. That I could bear.

A hot memory came back to me of those long crawling journeys when my anus was stuffed with a plug of flowers, which the Queen thought so amusing, and my mouth sometimes was distorted by thick metal bits with bells on the ends. I could feel the plug in my anus now. I could positively feel the grass beneath me. And the Queen's cold voice, "Come along, Dmitri, don't make me any angrier than I already am."

I studied the moving figures before me. I wondered how Barbara and Valentine had been chosen for the village rather than the Court, now that slaves were given duties suited to them. And I did not see slaves here any more beautiful than either Valentine or Barbara, or the little black-haired "bad girl" from the Punishment Shop. Just thinking of any one of them was too much.

I sat back, sleepy, and almost in a dream. When would I have time and privacy to enjoy a slave of my very own? I had no thought of ever leaving here.

I could see to my right and left gentlemen coarsely enjoying their slaves at their tables, though ladies did not indulge themselves in the same crude way.

A proud young lord had forced his slave to stand bent over for mounting with the slave's forehead and hands on the ground. That was common enough. He pounded away at the slave with complete abandon, ripping his cock out of the slave's backside when he was finished and shoving it back in his clothes. With a pat or two he dismissed the slave who scampered on his hands and knees, though to where I did not know.

Grooms were everywhere, it was true. No doubt they did keep watch on each and every naked little personage. And now I saw a groom approach the magnificent male tethered to the cross and give him a few sips of wine. With his head up, the poor boy couldn't lap it, so he was allowed to sip it. Then the groom tormented his immense cock to make it stand up in its lacings, and then he moved on.

Though noblewomen would not make spectacles of themselves as the lords here with their ever-ready cocks, obviously many were slipping away. And I realized there were handsome little tents scattered about with fringed roofs and billowing flags. Perhaps in those noblewomen coupled with the slaves of their choice or offered their privy parts for pleasuring.

The whole garden was busy.

Bands of musicians clad in pied garments were strolling through the sea of tables and gaily dressed people. I heard the low nasal melody of horns, the soft throb of flutes, and heard the soft crash of cymbals. Now and then a sprightly drummer appeared, beating the two little drums affixed to his belt as he danced and turned artful circles.

My cock was hard, but I was so tired. It had a life the rest of me did not possess. My brain was warring with my cock.

All day I had maintained myself in a state of torture.

I looked about and saw none other than beautiful Princess Rosalynd coming towards me, such a welcome sight. All those years we'd been together in the Sultan's land. She was buxom as she'd been then, with glowing skin and huge breasts, and the most noble of faces. Her gown was a deep rose color and her slippers were silver.

I stood to greet her.

"You are tired, Dmitri. Truly tired! Tired from your journey and all you've seen."

Behind me the slaves struggled on, pounding the beaten earth of the Bridle Path. I could hear the eager cries of the mistresses driving them.

"Your raven hair is as thick as ever, darling," I said. I crushed Rosalynd to me. My chest was burning, my nipples pulsing, and when I felt the crush of her breasts I felt my cock take over. "Precious one," I said, drawing back carefully and looking into her large always-mournful blue eyes. "Would the King and Queen take it amiss if I slipped away now to my rooms?"

"Not at all, Dmitri," she said. "I've been sent to tell you so expressly. The Queen is worried. You are white as those flowers there. Let me take you back myself."

Before we ever reached the castle, we were kissing and fondling one another coyly, and I was licking at her ears. I had always loved her small ears. Ears always make me think of seashells. In the sultanate my ears had been fitted with gold rings, like many other slaves', and sometimes stuffed with fresh flowers. When that was done the world became a blur of sounds as if my sight had somehow been affected as well as my hearing.

We stopped more than once to observe the activities going on in the garden. On a large grassy court we found an eager crowd surrounding girl slaves playing at a ball game with knees and elbows, their hands bound behind their backs. The girls were delightfully adorned, one team burnished with gold pigment and the other with silver, hair pinned up to reveal tender necks.

"Don't ask what happens to the losing team," Rosalynd said, laughing gaily. "But then, don't ask what happens to the winning team, either."

The Hunt in the Maze was taking place as we passed by, and I could see the torches flickering through the shrubbery and hear the excited voices.

"I failed at that one always," I confided.

"I'm surprised," said Rosalynd, stroking my hair tenderly. "I rather enjoyed it. They really had a challenge hunting me down. I knew just where to hide, and how to outsmart them. I emerged the victor more than once." Victors were celebrated and then rewarded by being chosen for more hunts.

I shook my head. All I could remember was the blast of the trumpet telling me to flee, and then crawling desperately through one long corridor of shrubbery after another, until they found me and forced me up with loud cries to be punished with all the other quarry who hadn't provided good sport. It was held in the afternoons then mostly, not by torchlight, and the Queen had scolded me endlessly for being such an utter disappointment.

Again, the sheer size of the garden was astonishing to me. The torches and lanterns were dazzling me as we moved along. And many different threads of music blended in a low rushing noise rather like the sound of the fountains we passed.

Truly, the festivities seemed to go on forever. And all the courtiers I observed seemed utterly at home in it, familiar with its pastimes, and busy and not dazed as I was at all.

"And this is every night?" I asked.

"For now," said Rosalynd, "with so many guests and so many returning. Remember Prince Jerard, the blond one, not the dark-haired one, the blond pony who was in the village stables with you, the one always mourning back then for Laurent? Well, he's just returned. The King was so glad to see him. And Gareth, one of the old grooms adored by the King during his time in the stables, has just returned also to help with the King's steeds. Have you seen the Royal Stables? I must take you around tomorrow."

"Yes, there's so much to see, but I want—" I didn't have to finish. She kissed me full on the mouth and guided me through the castle doors.

We went up the stairs, stopping briefly on each landing to embrace. I reached up under her heavy skirts and felt her ripe warm sex, always such a delightful shock under all the silk and velvet.

At last, we were in my quarters.

Maybe the two obedient night slaves were disappointed when called to unlace Princess Rosalynd's gown. I hardly cared. They obeyed at once, releasing her from her bindings and lacings, and now I could clutch her immense breasts the way I wanted to do it, and bury my face in them as I nestled them together.

We fell under the covers, like people of the great world beyond might do, and she crouched above me as I suckled her nipples hungrily. I loved the sight of them dangling over my face like delicious fruit from a bough.

"You don't want to take off your shirt?" she asked. "It's so heavy."

"No," I said. "I prefer it this way, if you'll forgive me." Of course my leggings and tunic were gone and my sex was poking at her greedily.

But she wanted to tease me just a little more. She turned suddenly to the slaves who had retreated to the fireplace.

"Good little girl, bring me a blindfold," she said. "Silk, see-through, now."
I laughed.

"Hush, Prince," she said teasingly. "Each cock is a story unto itself, and yours is gorgeous. Oh, how I hungered for it in the sultanate. And they were always so strict with us, so cruel in never allowing us to touch one another or ourselves."

"Seems we managed now and then," I said.

The blindfold was a pretty gold thing and she tied it around my eyes. Indeed I could see through it, but it made the world a dreamlike magical place and my excitement grew even more painful and sharp. I'd worn such blindfolds many a time. I marveled at the sense of release that accompanied the wearing of them, the new level of abandon. But the story my cock was telling me was one of agony.

"Stand up, Prince," she said in my ear, jumping off the bed suddenly and stretching her long legs and arms. This I could make out in the golden haze that had become the room. Then she pulled her dark hair down out of its combs and let it fall behind her like a great shadow.

"Lovely," I whispered. I reached for her voluptuous arms.

"Now I'm going to mount you and ride you," she said.

"I'll come and fall to the floor!"

"We shall see."

She jumped up and onto my cock, my cock slipping into her, and her sex clamping down on it with the tenacity of the most eager pleasure slave. At last. I almost wept as I stabbed her in a series of jerking spasms.

"Not so fast, beautiful prince," she said. "Now walk, walk around the bed carrying me." She wrapped her legs around my hips and her arms around my neck. She was kissing me.

I didn't make it five steps.

After that, it was a bit slower. Her hips and bottom were so voluptuous, and even her calves were soft and tender to the touch. I spread her apart like a peach sliced in half and gazed at the dark pit of her sex for the longest time, the dark purplish lips, the gleaming clitoris.

For the third time, we were on the carpet. She begged me to remove my shirt but I wouldn't. I forced her over and up on her hands and knees, and rode her now, my cock inside her, forcing her forward on her path. When she started to come, my hands found the little slippery clitoris and I pinched it and stroked it as I spent into her from the rear and felt her spend as she cried out.

All the day's torment and agonies and delicious surprises and tantalizing memories had heated everything I felt for her, and then there was the familiarity of her, after all those years together—this succulent wench whom I'd never been allowed to touch.

An hour later I woke to the stillness of the room. The night slaves were still as statues in their positions by the hearth. Rosalynd was gone. Fabien had gone to his closet a long time back.

But at some point he had set out my writing things, as he knew I would want. A lamp burned on the table. Dim sounds came to me as if from throughout the castle, dim vibrations and hints of scraping music, and even bits and pieces of song.

I got up, and turning my back to the night slaves who were dozing anyway, stripped off my tunic and shirt and put on my dressing gown, lacing it at the neck and tying the sash. I was pleasantly exhausted, but my mind was as feverish as it had been all the long day.

At the table I sat down, smelled the black ink, and then dipped my quill pen.

There was a fresh little bound book before me—the kind I had made for my private thoughts. It was thick, but not too thick, the parchment good quality, and covers made of soft leather engraved with the letter *D*.

I began to write. But I found I'd seen and felt and thought so much that I could only list things, list items and people and moments, and places, and so finally, this was all that I did.

When next I fell on the pillow, I slept like the dead.

vii

By noon I was in my townhouse and what a pleasant affair it was.

Like all village townhouses it was more a work of wood than stone, and its buffed and gleaming floors and stairs and railings were its glory, along with its soft painted plaster walls. The tones of peach and yellow and occasional blue were fine for me, the heavy oak furnishings fit for a castle, and by afternoon, I had positioned my chair by the high fourth-story window to look down on the open square.

No Barbara as yet, but I had been promised she would be delivered soon.

By evening, I'd sent my letter to His Majesty begging to speak with him about the Place of Public Punishment and asking to offer my services if they should be wanted as "guiding genius," to use his well-chosen words.

That night, he came himself to bring me my gold chain and medallion. A messenger came first to say he would shortly arrive.

I was again at the window, and the square below was wondrously illuminated, nothing like the shadowy place it had been before.

Slaves were being spanked on the turntable, of course, and I could see the maypoles were busy and people were going in and out of the tents. I thought of many things, many innovations. The ball game with the bent-over painted slaves was fun, but what if the balls were driven at the targets by paddles? I could think of several other variations. Slaves on hands and knees with heads straight to receive the circular garlands tossed from a distance by competing lords and ladies.

I had been watching it all for hours, and picturing to myself the King coming down from the castle—did he drive his own chariot with his finest ponies four abreast—when, suddenly, I saw him with his retinue below in the square. What a grand figure he was, with his streaming red-and-gold cloak, striding through the crowds as they broke for him and bowed on all sides.

And how he nodded and reached out to clasp hands here and there, and how buoyant and gladsome he looked.

I could see it all even from this distance, the fine figure he cut, and I thought, Yes, he has the greatness to rule Bellavalten, with his gracious queen at his side. She was not with him, no, but her devotion to him had been obvious when I'd seen them last night. She had a shyness about her, a shrinking quality. She'd had that when she was a slave.

But he was immense—immense in stature and also in spirit. I had never had such a strong sense of it as I did now watching him receive the admiration of so many eyes and the humble respect of so many hands as he made his way right towards my house.

He didn't remain with me for long.

I received him in my new parlor which must have looked quaint and small and confining to him. Had he ever resided or even stayed in such a place?

He stood the whole while with his secretary, Emlin, and his attendants behind him, a giant beneath the low ceiling.

He put the chain about my neck.

"You are now the master of the Place of Public Punishment," he said.

He embraced me, and kissed me. He was perhaps the tallest man I knew.

"I'm glad you've returned, Dmitri," he said. "Now I'm told that Lexius will return soon. I am so curious to see him."

"Is this truly so, sire?" I asked. Lexius here. Lexius coming all the way from India, from his own realm.

"A letter arrived from him late today," said the King. "He's on the continent. He's not far away."

I felt my heart beating. I wondered if the King could sense it. It seemed loud enough for all the world to hear.

"Alexi has promised to tell me what happened between Lexius and the late queen," said Laurent. "I don't mean to press for unpleasant stories, and I will make no judgments, of course, but I do so want to know."

I felt the blood rush to my face, though this shouldn't have been happening. That old tale was simple enough. It was the mysteries of— But then I didn't let myself think on it again, only telling myself, I will soon see Lexius. Lexius has actually been lured by the new Bellavalten. What can this mean?

"Come dine with us, Dmitri," said the King as he left the room, "whenever you like. And now, I have gifts for you."

He snapped his fingers, and through the front door, three naked slaves were delivered by two of the predictably comely grooms in Court livery.

There stood Barbara, trembling magnificently, of course, and lovely Kiera of the blond braids who'd been provided for me in my chambers, and handsome fetching Bertram.

At once the trio fell on their knees and rushed to kiss my slippers. A delicious perfume filled the air.

"Sire, thank you," I said at once. "I'm speechless. Truly."

"Enjoy them, Prince," said Laurent. "And remember, here in the village you can pack them off to the Slaves' Hall at any time for their bath, oiling, and sleep, and send for them at your leisure. No need to service them here under your roof unless you prefer it." His voice was easy and casual. "These grooms are two of the best, and they'll be with you until you dismiss them. They're artists at working slaves, putting them through their paces, if you're of a mind to watch, and will obey your every command. And, Prince, your grooms may all wear the Court's livery if you like, as you are a member of the Court, not the village livery."

"Thank you, sire," I said.

"And there's the Place of Public Punishment right outside your door of course. Now I cannot vouch for the particular virtues of this delectable little sweetheart, Barbara, but I can assure you that Kiera and Bertram have met my most exacting standards for performance."

Once more, we embraced and then he left me.

It seemed a great brilliant light had gone out of the little parlor once he was gone. I stood stranded on the polished floor, staring back into the past, into the dark narrow face of Lexius, into his black eyes. I smelled the hot air of another place. I heard the songs of the jungle in my ears. Saw ancient walls covered with dancing naked figures. Gods and goddesses of another land.

The grooms stood waiting and the three slaves knelt at my feet. At my mercy. Ah, such breasts, such luscious breasts, and the cock on Bertram.

"What would you like to do now, my lord?" asked Fabien.

For a long moment, I said nothing.

Then I heard myself speaking.

"Welcome to my house, lovelies. I shall take my time enjoying you one by one as suits my pace. And you, gentlemen," I said to the grooms. "One of you is to spank Kiera and Bertram over the knee now and put them beside this little fireplace as I saw them positioned in the great castle until I send for them. The other attend on me."

Without further explanation, I bid Barbara to rise.

Then I picked her up with both hands and pitched her over my right shoulder. I caught her ankles firmly as she cried out and I carried her up the staircase in this way until I reached the bedchamber.

I laid her down on the bed. She shivered and dared not look at me, glancing up at the polished mahogany of the ceiling of the bed and then closing her eyes. Quickly, desperately, she put her hands behind her neck.

I pushed her naked legs wide apart.

I inspected her delicate little gaping sex—the dark wrinkled pink lips peeping through the glistening black hair, and the curve of her little bottom making me think of a fruit cut in half with its core exposed—as women's upturned privates often did—dark, mysterious, the kernel of so many secrets. I had thought of a peach last night when inspecting Rosalynd in this same way.

Barbara let out a little scream as I buried my face in her pubic hair.

I pressed my tongue into her, tasting her delicious smoking and fragrant juices. I lapped at her juices. Her hips rode up and down helplessly under me. With my mouth over her clitoris, over her gasping sex, I knew she had no control, no control whatsoever, and I stabbed at her clitoris with my tongue until she came without stinting. On and on she came, abandoned to the pleasure, helpless in the grip of it.

Delirious torture for me but that's what I wanted.

I seated myself on the bed and brought her hips up onto my lap, again studying her sex, smoothing the hair with my hand, parting her legs and prying open the lips.

She shuddered and wept, but her hips rocked. She couldn't control them.

I pondered the mystery of her gleaming wet sex, the mystery of these little lips and this curious opening, this secret little chamber in which pleasure raged as surely as it raged in my cock.

"You have so much to learn," I said. "But you're beautiful to me, precious to me, and you're my first acquisition, my first slave, my first chosen one."

"My lord." She wept softly. "Deliver me to your pleasure. Only show me what it is you want of me."

I flipped her over on her face on the coverlet.

Her skin was petal perfect and so smooth to the touch, so sweet.

Her little bottom was made up of the most shapely little mounds.

"Is there anyone there?" I called out.

"Yes, Prince," came a voice. "Kenan, Prince, here to serve you."

"Her little anus is too tender for my cock," I said to Kenan. "What toys do we have under this roof, if any? What emollients?"

"Right here, Prince," he said. He stepped to the side of the bed with a large shallow casket, holding open the lid. "These are wax, Prince, these little plugs and phalluses. The Queen designed these, and Lady Eva has them made. After you use them they will be melted down for new ones."

"Excellent," I said gazing over the selection. "This is exactly what I wanted." I selected a small butt plug with a gentle head, flared at the bottom and with a place in the base to insert flowers or feathers of which the casket had a little heap. "That one and fit it with the red feathers."

At once, Kenan prepared it for me. He held open the jar of rich rose-colored cream. Lovely scent.

I smoothed the cream over the plug and then slipping my left hand under Barbara's tender belly, I lifted her. She moaned.

I slipped the well-lubricated butt plug into her.

She looked so fetching with the little feathers coming out of her hind end, and so helpless as she lay against the palm of my left hand.

"Now I think you'll ride me about the room the way a certain lady did last night," I said.

I climbed to my feet and brought her up to stand on hers, and then I lifted her and pushed her down on my hard cock.

I went weak with the shock of it, of her hot slippery sex enclosing me.

Without being told she wrapped her legs about me as Rosalynd had done and her arms too because she had to. I felt her little head tumble onto my shoulder and smelled the lovely perfume of her hair.

I walked to the window, with her firmly clasped to my cock, and looked down on the Place of Public Punishment. I saw the row of pillories where I had found her.

Then I turned and thrust into her hard and felt her bounce on me wildly with an abandon that dimmed the memory of my sweet Rosalynd.

When I spent, she went rigid, gasping, and then coming, carrying me past the peak, until I could bear it no more.

I lifted her off, and held her in my arms, a bundle of the softest warmest limbs against me.

"You are the tastiest of repasts, my sweet," I crooned in her ear. "And just look at your shining little bottom, all white and fresh, healed from the turntable. So tender."

"Yes, my lord," she whispered.

I smoothed her hair back and told her to look at me. These were the eyes I'd remembered. No disappointment there. The intelligence of these eyes.

"What do you fear the most now, little partridge?" I asked.

"Whatever pleases you, my lord," she said calmly. She didn't smile. But I did.

"Very clever," I said.

I turned and told the groom to lay out a paddle and strap for me.

I flung her over the side of the bed facedown and told her to spread her arms out and spread her legs wide, wide until she couldn't spread them any further.

She obeyed until both legs were wobbling, shaking wildly. The little red feathers coming out of her anus would be easy to avoid.

I took the belt in my hands—very smooth gilded leather, and doubled on a hook, perhaps three feet wide. It wouldn't cut her. No. And it would not bruise her easily either.

And then in a fury, I began to spank her with it, spank her hard and fast, careful not to strike the feathered butt plug, until she screamed and sought to muffle her scream in the covers.

I kept on spanking her, harder and faster until she was undulating madly under the blows, twisting and turning feverishly, her little feet rising, then falling back down to the carpet. I didn't let up.

I spanked her over and over and over again.

I loved the sound of it, the sight of the broad leather smacking her reddening skin, her sweet tender skin. I smacked the tender underside of her bottom until it was too red and I had to spread the blows.

A great exhilaration came over me, and on and on I worked on her tender high calves, and her soft pale thighs and then back again on the top of her little bottom, spanking her till she was all the color of a red rose garden.

Finally I stopped. My arm was tired. I was in a daze, but it was a different daze from all those through which I'd passed earlier.

I saw my left hand play with her tender red flesh. How hot it was, how delectably hot. I didn't want the butt plug now. I pulled it out of her and threw it to the side.

Yes, just her red little backside, and her red legs.

For a long moment I stood there looking at her. I could hear the sounds from the square below, the rise and fall of a mass of voices as if they were water. And there came to my ears, Barbara's soft sobbing cries, so eloquent of total surrender.

The groom made no sound.

I went to her and, gathering up her long brown curls, I lifted her gently off the bed by them, catching her chin with my right hand to make her stand upright. She was limp, utterly without any resistance.

"My first slave," I whispered. And so she was. She was my very first, and this the very first time I'd possessed a slave utterly. And she could not grasp perhaps what it meant to me.

I covered her face with wet eager kisses. I think I was crying. Our tears were mingling.

"Barbara," I whispered. "I adore you." I wanted to say *I am you,* but I didn't, because she would not have wanted it. "Barbara." I sighed against her ear. I caught the heated perfume of her sex, her sweet little sex.

Then she had her trusting arms around my neck again, her silken arms, and I was sliding my cock into her fragrant little cloister and from the square below came a great roar as if of applause or triumph.

9

BRENN:
TO SERVE IN
THE REALM OF
THE PADDLE
AND THE
STRAP

i

I would have gone to Bellavalten without Sybil. I had determined to go from the day I'd copied out the Proclamation and read it in the town square. The whole country was talking of King Laurent and Queen Beauty—and that slaves of the new kingdom would be accepted from all ranks, and allowed to offer their vow of allegiance for two or more years to enjoy the pleasures of naked slavery.

My father was secretary to the old duke, and I'd been educated to take his place since I was a small child, to keep the libraries and the archives and to write letters for the family as was required.

Lady Sybil grew up the fifth daughter of the old duke's eldest son and, with four daughters ahead of her, had little hope of a dowry or even the chance to meet a fine man.

She and I ran in the fields together, and played in the castle gardens and read books together, because nobody much paid attention, with Lady Sybil's mother dead and my mother busy with three more sons. I taught Sybil to read, and then her father obtained a tutor for her and soon she surpassed me in my Latin.

We remained friends even when her duties as a woman put a great divide between us, with Sybil often coming to the library or archives simply to visit with me. She wouldn't hear of formal addresses. "I am your Sybil, Brenn," she whispered to me whenever I bowed or offered her titles.

It was a month after the Proclamation had been posted, and the emissaries of Bellavalten had already left our land with the postulants for pleasure slavery whom they had accepted. I'd seen some of those lovelies with my own eyes as they congregated around the caravan on the edges of town, and they were beautiful creatures indeed and certainly from the lower ranks, as highborn applicants came to the emissaries by night in secret.

I could not get away in time. But soon I was packed and ready to go with everything I possessed—a few changes of clothes, my savings, and my books—in a small bundle that I could carry over my shoulder as I made the long walk to the kingdom.

I was determined to give my life to pleasure slavery. I'd heard all about it years ago from an aunt of Lady Sybil or a cousin, I don't recall which, who'd told us amazing stories of the kingdom.

"Imagine living naked for three years," the lady had said without so much as a blush, "and enjoying pleasure every day of one's life, and sometimes three and four times a day—the sort of pleasure that makes fools of men and women as they pursue it in vain in the shadowy corners of the wide world. Well, there are no shadowy corners in the land of Queen Eleanor."

Of course the lady had rebelled at first. That was expected of one, she'd admitted with much laughter. "But those were the most vibrant days of my life," she'd told us.

Over the years I'd heard plenty from others, tales sometimes second- and thirdhand, but all on the same theme.

I knew I was going. And in truth I had little interest in thinking it over. I'd been teased, as soon as the emissaries had arrived to receive slaves, that I was beautiful enough. My older brother had said, "Why don't you go, Brenn, and then we'd never have to listen to your poetry at dinner again ever!" to which my uncle had added, "As a matter of fact, pretty as you are, you might pass for a boy or a girl slave—a girl slave with a beard, that is!" Roaring laughter.

I'd said nothing.

I left a letter that would be found only after I was well on my way, in an account book that would not be opened for a fortnight.

And on the first morning, Lady Sybil found me walking, already miles from home, my bundle over my back, my face and body pretty much covered by the dark hooded cloak I wore, ignoring her as she rode up, as I had every other rider on the road so far, and she called out:

"Brenn, how could you leave without me?"

I knew her voice instantly, though what I saw on the horse's back appeared to be a young man under a bright green hooded cloak as concealing as my own, with only some of her curling dark hair revealed by it.

But this was Sybil all right, and I rushed up to her when I realized it.

"Precious, what are you doing here?" I demanded.

"I'm riding to Bellavalten, same as you, to see if I will be accepted."

"But Sybil—"

"But Sybil what? Get on behind me. How long do you think it will take you to walk the entire way?"

She was right and I was too excited to argue with her, protect her, offer her inducements not to be reckless, all that nonsense. Besides, I knew why I wanted to be a naked slave. Should I insult her with reasons why she shouldn't?

She was riding a big old horse, a strong mount who could easily carry both of us, and our baggage.

"Brenn, to tell you the truth, I was hoping I would find you. I don't relish the dangers of the road on my own, though I don't have a particle of fear when it comes to Beauty's Kingdom."

That's what they were calling it now, more often than Bellavalten. I'd heard that more than once.

"I know, darling. Well, we're together now and I can handle our arrangements at the inns and pass you off as my servant. No one needs to have a good look at you."

"I went searching for you to tell you early this morning. And that's when I was told you'd been seen slipping out while it was still dark with a bundle over your shoulder. I thought to myself: Could this be true? I was ecstatic. I knew where you were headed, and now I've no guilt for luring you away with me."

We laughed together, because we were of the same mind on all of this. Beauty's Kingdom.

It was said that Bellavalten meant "beautiful woods" or "beautiful land." But it was the legend of the Sleeping Beauty that fired the thoughts of those who heard the Proclamation of the new king and queen. All knew she'd been waked by Queen Eleanor's son from her legendary sleep, and brought to Bellavalten as a naked slave decades ago. If she, the fabled princess of the old tale, would dare to revive the ways of Queen Eleanor and take them to greater heights of renown, well, people were in awe of that. As for King Laurent, he was the most feared monarch in all the world, as far as I knew. And that such a mighty conqueror had claimed the scepter of Bellavalten drew only utterances of awe and admiration.

At the first inn, Sybil's gold bought far finer accommodations than I'd ever have arranged for myself, and we fell on each other in the big bed with its crackling straw mattress. We'd been sometime lovers all these years, always fearful of discovery. And it was a great treat to us to moan and cry out as we wished now without worry, and I drank too much, and Sybil ate too much, and we finally slept, tumbled against each other like puppies.

We slept that night under her green cloak with its soft lining of miniver. But after that, we chose to save ourselves for Bellavalten.

The day before we reached the gates, we encountered many a traveler headed in the same direction, and many another returning, blaming his rejection on the fact that the kingdom "must not need any more slaves," but we went on hoping desperately that when we were seen and examined, we'd be accepted.

My main worry was that I was not the pretty boy my uncles always teased me about being. I was a strange combination of a pretty girlish face and overmuscular arms and legs, and though I was tall enough, I was not a giant like the great King Laurent, or even Prince Tristan and other legends of the kingdom.

My mother had said once I had a double dose of the magic juice for a girl and for a boy—with pretty hair and eyelashes and girlish skin, and the limbs of a farm boy. And then there was my beard, which I had to shave twice a day; how did that look on a baby-faced young man? Well, I would know soon enough, I brooded.

Sybil had no such doubts. She was a celebrated beauty, regardless of her poor prospects for a dowry.

We both had the curly black hair common in our land, and blue eyes, and she had voluptuous breasts which drew teasing from girls who envied her. Sybil had a high beautiful forehead and a kissable red mouth, and a long graceful neck and hands that were long and pretty too. I always notice women's hands. I loved Sybil's fingers.

As we neared the great walls of Bellavalten and its gates, we saw something of a makeshift fairground all about with tents and booths, and serving boys came up to offer us a drink, but we pressed on to the guards who looked at us expectantly.

"They know already," said Sybil, leaning forward as I was the one with the reins at present. "See? They know."

But what did they know?

She had let down her hood a while back and now I did the same and it did seem that the guards liked what they saw because one of them, waving the serving boys away, came up to us.

"We're here because we want to serve the King and Queen," I said at once.

"Ah, yes, and in what capacity?" asked the guard.

I think we both blushed, and Sybil laughed.

"What do you think, soldier?" said Sybil. "Do I look like a cook or a maid to you? Does my companion look like a footman?"

"No, my lady," he said at once, and he bowed. "Ride ahead, please, to the great white tent on the left. And there you'll find the questioner."

As we approached the tent, it seemed there was no one before us, and glancing back before dismounting, I saw the soldiers already turning away other travelers.

"Come on, hurry," said Sybil as I lifted her down. "But first you kiss me and kiss me hard. And promise you'll wait to see if I'm accepted and I'll wait to see if you are."

"No, darling, I won't have you do that for me," I said. We walked towards the tent together. "You're very likely to be accepted and you must go ahead."

She didn't reply, but squeezed my hand, and though the guard at the door of the tent tried to stop us, we insisted that we must go in together.

The questioner was polite to a fault, an elderly gentleman with thin white hair and gray eyes who rose at once to greet us. Then he seated himself and began his questions.

"No, we are not brother and sister, no kin at all," explained Sybil, "but we've come together and want to stay together as long as we can. But we're prepared for what may come. Only give us a chance for a kiss farewell, if it comes to that, that's all we're asking."

"Well, it will certainly come to that, my lady," said the questioner, his voice polite and gentle, "because you cannot be admitted and trained together. That has never been done, not as far as I know, but let's see what you can answer now for me and we'll leave the separating to others."

We were asked to put off our cloaks, and lay our bundles down which we did. And I realized that two other finely clad gentlemen who stood nearby were taking our measure carefully. Now Sybil looked enticing to me in her boyish leggings and little tunic, and I'm sure they saw the same and this was hardly the first woman who'd come here disguised as a man for obvious reasons.

The questioner began to recite from memory what we knew—that we'd be carefully inspected and tested for service before we would be admitted. That if we were not found fit to be "anointed" slaves for the King and Queen, we might be invited to serve in the kingdom in some other capacity. If we were accepted, we would take the oath for six months, and then, at the end of that period, for two years, and then again perhaps after that for however long we were found to be fit and pleasing . . .

We knew all this. It had been in the Proclamation.

"Yes, I would welcome that chance, for honest employment," I volunteered. "Though that is not why I've come. I am a good scholar, and scribe."

But Sybil of course stood silent.

"And the paddle and the strap," said the questioner, "are the emblems of this kingdom, and the discipline of slaves is strict and relentless. You are aware of this?"

We were. It had all been in the Proclamation.

We divulged much else, that we were educated, that we were of age to make the decision to come to Bellavalten on our own, that no one had coerced us, and we gave our first names, and were told no other names were needed.

Then the questioner recited the protections we would enjoy, but we knew all that as well.

Soon two small chests or caskets were brought, and our cloaks and bundles were put into these respectfully and then we were taken through a side flap in the tent, and towards a small gate in the wall where a guard beckoned to us.

"Kiss goodbye now, children," called out the old questioner. "And don't dare to inquire after one another."

And so we did, standing on the beaten green grass under the blue sky, the great wall of Bellavalten seeming to reach above us to the heavens.

ii

In a small chamber, rather well furnished for a gatehouse, it seemed, I was told to sit on a bench and wait, and Sybil went on without me.

I felt a terrible convulsion of fear as I saw the door close behind her. Why had I ever come with her? I mean, why had I not come strictly alone so that only my fate was a burden to my soul now?

An hour dragged by until I was summoned.

I found myself in a spacious but shadowy room, and when the door was shut I was the only one present. I stood on a carpet and there was a small carved table there and no chairs, and a heavy wooden screen before me.

From behind the screen, a masculine voice spoke to me:

"Young man, your deportment is of the utmost importance from this moment forward, do you hear me?"

"Yes, Master," I said.

"You wish to be a pleasure slave in this kingdom, is that true?"

"Yes, Master."

"Then remove your clothes, all of them, and your shoes and put them on that table. And do not ask to keep any article of clothing about you."

I did this immediately, and only as I felt the soothing air on my naked skin did it hit me that at last, at last, I was here and this was truly happening to me. I felt weak suddenly, and my hands trembled. But I was soon completely naked, and very much ashamed of the dust of the road that seemed to cling to my hair and my hands, and I was staring at the floor and struggling to appear collected.

A very long moment passed.

Any spoken word might have been a mercy.

None came, and then a door in the side wall opened and a lovely young woman in a servant's livery of apron and wimple beckoned for me to come to her. She smiled.

"Don't worry about your clothes, little boy," she said in the most cheerful voice. "They'll be put in your chest with everything else."

Surely I blushed violently. It certainly felt like it, this pretty girl speaking to me and me being utterly naked. I went into the room and found it was smaller than the other but very warm with a big bronze tub there of steaming water, and a little fire roaring on the hearth and buckets set all around it.

"Into the bath, little boy," said the girl.

I stepped in and sank down into the water, and she commenced to scrub me all over. She washed my hair thoroughly, rinsing it with buckets of warm water, and then, telling me to stand, started to wash between my legs with the same thoroughness she'd used all along.

"Well, I can tell you, that you're gorgeous enough all right, but I don't make the decisions. And look at that cock, standing up already."

She turned me around and scrubbed my bottom in the same efficient way.

"Now you answer me as 'madam' and you answer all men as 'sir,' do you hear, though you may say 'master' or 'mistress' if you like, but I wouldn't bother. Your lips are sealed, you understand, unless you're directly questioned. And you never make an openmouthed sound—never an openmouthed moan or a sob or a cry, do you hear? Lips tight at all times. Now, go stand by the fire."

I said, "Yes, madam."

She rubbed me hard all over with the towel, and then oiled me with a delicious perfumed oil, and then dried and brushed my hair till she said it was "shining."

None of this took very long as she was very good at what she did.

I was desperate to ask about the girl who'd come before me, but I didn't dare.

"Well, if they don't accept you, little boy, then I don't know anything," she said when she was finished. "So! From now on you walk with your eyes down and your hands on the back of your neck. Go through that door, and I wish you luck."

She gave me a peck on the cheek. "Little boy," she said as I was almost to the door. "If they don't accept you, they'll hire you for some service,

I'm sure of it. You're not just pretty. You're a precious little knave if ever I saw one."

The door opened before she finished, as though someone had been watching through a chink in the wall, and I headed into a larger room on a red carpet.

I realized there were at least four people around me, and from the sound of voices and other noise that I was in a large space.

At once a woman appeared before me, clamped her soft hands on the side of my head, and told me to look at her.

In a blur I saw the others were all men in long rich tunics, and that she was a goddess with red hair, or so one might think.

Her green eyes were beyond anything I'd ever beheld and so were her smiling lips.

"And you're known by?"

"Brenn, madam," I said. I almost stammered. I feared suddenly I'd faint! That was absurd, but the weakness I felt in my belly and the hardness of my cock were paralyzing me.

"That's a pretty name," said a tall blond-haired man beside her. He had a long sheet of parchment against a writing board and was scratching on it with a quill pen. The board had an ink well in it. He was remarkably handsome, with curling golden hair, and his own eyes were almost as exceptional as the lady's eyes. "Brenn, is this the name you wish to be known by in the kingdom if you are accepted?"

"Yes, sir," I replied.

"You look down now, little Brenn," said the woman, "and you must not raise your eyes again. Remember, you are being tested in all things and have been for some time now. You must do your best to be obedient and perfect, but dignity is also highly desirable—only you must remember that your masters and mistresses ultimately define what is dignified."

"Yes, madam," I said.

My head swam. It was all too real! It was beyond anything I might have imagined, because I had never been able to imagine just how it would play out in detail here.

"And know that when I call you 'little boy' or 'little Brenn,'" said the lady, "this is customary with all slaves to refer to them with such pet names and diminutives." Her voice was kindly and sweet.

"Yes, madam."

The tall blond man stepped forward and putting his hand on my shoulder he directed me to turn around.

"You are in fact a splendid big boy in every sense, Brenn," he said. "And sometimes you'll be called a 'big boy' with just as much affection as anything else." His voice was more tender than the lady's voice, deeper naturally and ever so more melodious. I found it disconcertingly beautiful. Somehow the way he said his words, the resonance, it made me feel more naked. But that seemed ridiculous.

I was now facing two other persons I could not clearly see.

"He's too muscular for my taste," said one, and it was a quavering elderly voice and full of anger. It was as if he'd slapped me.

"Now, Lord Gregory," came a much-younger male voice, "I find this a most appealing sort—"

"Oh, yes, of course, Prince, you would," said the elderly Lord Gregory. "And I'm sure His Majesty is likely to agree with you!" This was said with nothing short of disgust and rage. But the lady behind me was laughing.

I stared at the carpet, stared at the slippers of the men, stared at the ornate hems of their robes . . . at golden bees and curling vines, and pointed leaves embroidered on velvet. My face was flaming.

All at once, there were hands all over me, touching me, squeezing my arms and my legs, and my backside. Again, I thought I might go down in a faint like a coward! But I held steady. Even the long white hand of the elderly gentleman came out and touched my right nipple. Then he pinched it hard. I bit down not to cry out. He did the very same thing to my left nipple.

Then he slapped my cock so hard he almost knocked me off balance. I couldn't help but make a little sound but my lips were sealed, as the pretty girl had told me they must be.

Meanwhile the others continued to examine to their heart's content. The lady removed my right hand from the back of my neck and examined my fingers. And to my utter amazement I felt tears spring into my eyes, tears of utter helplessness. As she gently stroked my left hand I realized my legs were wobbling.

And to think this had all been done to Sybil, but then they'd likely said the nicest things about Sybil. Oh, what had made me think I'd be acceptable! Double dose of the potion that makes for a man or a woman!

The elderly man rubbed my shaven beard and made a sound of revulsion. "And look at his pubic hair, well, that will have to be groomed."

"Oh, nonsense, my lord," said the lady behind me. "It's gorgeous. Black and thick. The King will love it. And I suspect the Queen will love it. Indeed, there is something about this one which suggests to me that the Queen might adore him. Now if the King likes him, well, the problem will be finding any other slave to match him if the King wants him for a team to pull his chariot."

Pull his chariot!

"Steady, little boy," said the Prince behind me with the wicked Lord Gregory. "I think you're beautiful, simply beautiful. What do you think, Tristan?"

"Tristan" answered that he thought so too. "He's what I would call quite wondrous. Unique certainly. He is near to six feet, near enough, and his thighs and calves are like a Roman statue's! And look at his feet. They're large but high arched with short thick toes. I like that. I like his shoulders, and well, his backside is perfect. The thing about his backside is, that for all his muscularity, he's softly padded there. The Queen will love these details. Anyone would love these gifts."

Keep steady, just keep steady, I thought to myself. Just as the Prince said to do. Keep steady. They are accepting you! Yet a sweet terror was threatening me.

I felt a hand for the first time on my balls. My cock was bobbing and I couldn't control it. It was the hand of the Prince behind me. I felt something prod at my backside, prod at my anus.

Well, if I was actually going to faint it would be now. I knew this. But I didn't. I felt a peak of excitement it seemed I'd never known before. A gloved finger was exploring my anus, and fingers were pushing at my bottom. The gloved finger had been oiled, and it went deep into me.

"I say not only is he acceptable," said the lady, "but that he should be sent directly to the King and Queen as soon as he's properly prepared." As always her voice was almost gay and cheerful.

"Agreed," said the one named Tristan. "All the details are perfect."

And was it possible that he was the famous Tristan, friend of the King and Queen, who had helped to revive the kingdom?

The elderly man grumbled; indeed, he positively growled.

"Lord Gregory, look at his little backside," said the lady, and I was turned around now to face her, so that I saw her slippers and the pretty ribbons sewn to her skirts. "Don't you see how charmingly he's made? The Queen will take an interest, I assure you. Indeed, I have an idea for the Queen with this one."

I realized my eyes had glassed over. Never in all my life had I experienced anything like this moment. It was at such a pitch of intensity that I couldn't measure it.

"He has aptitude," said Tristan. "That's plain enough and I like his nipples. The area around them—"

"The aureole," said the lady.

"The aureoles are dark and large and beautiful. The King will love that. And I'd be amazed if the Queen didn't love it too. Yes, the pubic hair is thick and unkempt. Look, it crawls up to his navel and down his thighs, but again, look at his face, his eyes . . . he's like a . . ."

"He has a highly unusual combination of endowments," said the Prince behind me. There was something faintly amused and mocking in his tone, but I think it might have been meant for the elderly gentleman. "I like him myself very much, and if neither the King nor the Queen chooses him, I'll choose him. That's quite enough for me right there."

The garrulous old lord snorted. Then his wicked hand was on my bottom squeezing it painfully. Had to be his fingers doing this.

"You overrule me as you always do," he muttered behind me.

"Well, not always, my lord, that is not fair," said the Prince beside me. "And more often than not we all agree as we did with the last young lady."

This might mean Sybil. Desperately, I had to believe that it meant Sybil.

"Now that was an appropriate applicant," said the old man. "And proud and spoilt and deserving of punishment. But decent, nevertheless, promising."

The tears were now flowing from my eyes, but I held steady, swallowing, trying not to work my lips. They had all agreed on Sybil! Think of that. Now I *must* be accepted.

"Look at me again, little boy," said the lady lifting my face. Punishment. The word echoed in my ears. And real punishment had not even begun.

It was a shock to see her face, to see anyone's face, because this meant that others had been seeing my face all along. When you look into a person's eyes you feel that they are looking at you.

"Now stop trembling so much, little satyr," she said. "You've been well brought up, haven't you? You've dined with nobility."

"Yes, my lady, clerk to a duke," I said and then bit my lip.

"Ah, excellent. And you have lovely hands. And you keep them on the back of your neck as you've been told."

"Yes, madam."

"With these muscles and that beard," said the elderly lord, "he ought to be at the lowest work in the village. In the fields in fact."

I stared expressionless at the lady but she smiled warmly.

"Well, now, that will be the decision of the King or the Queen," she replied. She turned and requested from someone that her strap and paddle should be brought.

Now, likely, my blushing stopped and I drained of all color. I was suddenly terrified. What if I couldn't endure it, couldn't endure standing still for it, couldn't possibly— I felt a sudden urge to drop to my knees and ask them to give me a moment to prepare, but that was absurd, and absolutely unacceptable.

"You don't want to send him on to be spanked?" asked Prince Tristan.

"No, I want to see it settled here and now," said the lady. "I like this one."

"Well, then you'll allow me to put him to the test," said the elderly man.

He reached past me and took a long black leather strap from someone who had just brought it for the lady.

It was a thick strap.

There was a noise behind me, a soft sound, and as the lady turned me around now, or I should say as she turned me to the side, I saw a low stool there.

"Up on this, you crude little brat," said the elderly man. "Move now. I'll see what you're made of! You want to serve in Bellavalten, do you?"

I climbed on the stool—it was only a foot off the ground—and the two princes stood in front of me. The lord's voice stung me to the quick. But I was determined to endure. Indeed I was so determined that it seemed I had no choice. I felt elated.

"Reach up over your head," said Prince Tristan. "Yes, that ring. Grasp it with both hands. And keep your eyes fixed downward, as is proper."

The tears were splashing down my face. But the elation grew ever more intense. It was as if I were floating.

As I took the round leather-clad ring firmly in my hands, Prince Tristan stepped up closer.

"Now be brave, Brenn, you want to serve, remember?" said Tristan. "Your lips are to remain closed—sealed, as we say in the kingdom. You may cry, of course. Your masters and mistresses fancy the pretty sparkle of tears. But sobbing, moaning, whatever you cannot suppress, all this must be done with lips tightly shut." His voice was so gentle it was like being comforted, stroked. "I'm going to hold your chin firmly while you're beaten. And please know that Prince Alexi here and I both know how hard this is for you."

I pressed my lips together, vowing not to make a sound.

Though I was looking down I could see them both through my tears. And the voice, the tenderness in the voice, was as piercing and paralyzing as the anger of the old Lord Gregory. I couldn't quite understand why, but it made me cry all the more freely.

"Keep your legs closed," said the elderly gentleman. "Those balls of yours are enormous. I don't want to hit them. And if you dare move your feet from the wood or your hands from that ring, I'll beat you over every inch of your body before I send you back where you came from!"

He drew up close, his garments touching me all over in a feathery way, and he said in my ear: "If you dare to waste my time, you'll be sorry for it!" Then he moved back.

The strap almost knocked me to the side. He must have doubled it because the blows came so fast, one after another, cutting me from below and then slicing across my thighs.

Tristan's fingers tightened on my chin, and another hand, the hand of Prince Alexi, reached out and began to gently squeeze the tip of my cock.

"That's it," he said softly. Same loving tenderness as Tristan. "Stand firm, Brenn. You are doing very well."

I barely heard him over the loud smacking blows, coming so fast I'd lost all count. My bottom felt as if it had doubled in size and was ablaze with the sweetest pain, a strange delicious pain, a throbbing pain, and I was afraid suddenly that if Prince Alexi didn't stop I would come in his hand. Maybe he wanted me to do this!

I was so confused, so helpless, being pushed this way and that by the strap, struggling to stand firm and not to come, that the tears just flooded my eyes and I could hear, hear as if it were someone else, my own sobs behind my clenched teeth.

I realized I was struggling, but I hadn't moved either my hands or my feet, and I closed my eyes shut, I couldn't help it and tried with all my will not to wriggle or squirm when the strap hit me.

"Stand up straight!" said the angry lord. He whacked away at my thighs now, back and forth, back and forth, and worked down now to my calves, jumping past the tender underside of my knees.

The blows stung in a different way on my calves, but all my backside was aflame from the strap. The strap whipped at my ankles, hard, and then suddenly it was back up again on my bottom.

"See, it is a very shapely and lovely bottom," said the lady.

The lord paused in his work. I shook violently all over. A surge of electric sensation passed through me. I felt I was floating again.

Prince Alexi, thankfully, let go of my cock.

I felt his fingers cup my balls. He was using both hands.

"Priceless," he said. "Their Majesties will love this equipment." There was that dark slightly mocking tone again. But he wasn't mocking me. I knew it.

I couldn't stop the tears, hadn't been able to stop them from the start, so I stopped trying and just stood there feet together, hands grasping the hook and cried.

"Keep your eyes down now, Brenn," said the lady. She moved around until she stood between the two princes who made way for her.

I thought, If she touches my cock, I'll spend. Nobody could ask otherwise!

"Now, Lord Gregory, perhaps you should beat the young man a little more. I want to see this cock perform."

The strap struck hard. The intense hot pain felt gorgeously sweet again and agonizing at the same time. I felt weightless, as if I were rising when I wasn't, and the blows filled my senses, my ears with the sound, my flesh with the vibrating smack, and even my eyes as the darkness into which I gazed seemed to throb and brighten.

I turned my head towards my left arm, but Prince Tristan said no very clearly to this and held my chin firm.

Again and again the strap crisscrossed my backside, and the pain seemed to flood my entire body, to move through my legs and even my arms, and to gather in my cock.

The lady's hand closed over it and began to stroke it, stroke it hard and fast and tight. Her hand had been greased and the greasing made it slip very fast back and forth.

I came with a loud irrepressible groan.

On and on she stroked until the spasm stopped.

I hung there, the strap slowing, the leather almost caressing me.

"You're adorable!" said the lady. "Just adorable. And I think the King and the Queen will eat you up with a golden spoon."

"Yes, madam," I said. I might have fallen then on the floor.

"I vote to send him on now to sign his documents," she said.

The Princes agreed. The elderly old man said nothing.

Then I heard him clear his throat.

"Well, that makes two for this morning, and what was her name?"

"Sybil, my lord," said the lady. "Let go of the ring, Brenn, and step down."

Sybil. They had spoken her name. They had confirmed it. Two, and they had accepted her and accepted me.

I stepped off the stool though my legs were positively vibrating like harp strings.

The lady turned me around to face where she had stood before. And once again, she held my face in her hands.

I'd dropped my hands to the back of my neck. I hoped this was right, hoped I had done it gracefully and properly.

My backside throbbed with the most penetrating and exquisite sensation.

"Now walk quietly to that door," she said. "You'll sign your documents and then you'll be groomed and oiled, you understand? But think hard in these next few minutes on all you've endured here. I'm recommending you to the Court itself, to the very highest level of the kingdom. And yes, I know that you are eager for news of your friend, Sybil, and she has been sent on for the Court, for the King and Queen, as well."

"Thank you, most gracious madam," I whispered, though it seemed impossible that I had formed words at all.

I was weak with relief, weak to hear her speak these kind words, these merciful words on Sybil, but the old lord was mumbling that I was not fit to kiss Sybil's toes, that she was the very kind of Naiad that the old queen had cherished, but I was a crude hairy satyr fit only to be hunted through the forest by the King for sport, if anything. . . .

"Come, darling," said the lady guiding me to the door. To the guard, she whispered, "Take him to sign his documents and tell the groom that Lady Eva said she has taken a special interest in Brenn as she has with Sybil. I want them rested and ready for me by dusk. Shave this one's face, of course, closely and trim the hair of his head but only a little—and trim absolutely nothing else!"

iii

The office of the clerk was down a long carpeted corridor. And what I'd imagined as a gatehouse was revealing itself to be a large stone compound. Bright summer light burned through the narrow arched window at the far end, but we never got that far.

The handsome attendant guided me firmly with a warm tight-gloved hand on my upper arm. He was as tall as I was.

"Well, quite the whipping, young man," he said evenly. "And you must have taken it very well if Lady Eva is passing you through without a full 'over the knee' paddling and other tests. Be assured, your groom will get her message. Go in here, and try to think straight about what you're doing, as there is no undoing it. And I'm supposed to remind you of that."

As he forced me into the clerk's chamber, he gave me a hard squeeze with his gloved hand right on the sorest of my sore flesh. And I winced, but didn't break form or respond except to murmur, "Yes, sir."

It seemed I could hear a strap or paddle going somewhere working hard, and there flashed into my mind the image of Sybil being paddled over the knee and I felt my cock stiffen again. She's been accepted, I told myself, now leave the matter.

The clerk's office was cluttered, and I found myself before a high desk littered with parchment and ink stands and feather pens while a wall of fat bulging books rose to the ceiling behind the man.

I didn't look him in the face naturally. But I could see in a blur that he was older with dark gray hair.

The door shut behind me.

"Look to the right, Brendon of Arcolot," said the clerk. "In that open chest there, are those your belongings?"

"Yes, sir," I replied at once because they were. My bundle had been emptied, and my books and papers and clothes and shoes were all neatly arranged, with the sack itself in which I'd carried them folded. It even appeared to have been washed, but there seemed scarcely time for that.

He was busy scribbling for a while, as I stood waiting, the pain simmering warmly all through my bottom and my legs. My calf muscles twitched. And I realized my cock was hard again.

It didn't seem to matter at all to him.

"Very well, and is that all you possess? Do you wish to look through it?"

"No, sir, that's all. I can see it."

"Very well, and you can read this document, can you?"

"Yes, sir."

He turned the long page to me.

I saw it had been written out in advance in wonderful script and my name had been filled in by a careful but less-fluent hand.

"I, Brendon of Arcolot, hereafter to be known as Brenn, do of my own free will . . ." And on it went, affirming that in six months' time, if I failed to please, I'd be sent from the kingdom, but that I might at that juncture choose to go of my own free will, and would be released without question if I so wished it. But I was being received now for no less than two years' service, and once that probationary period was past, I would continue in that service, not to be released on any account ever unless the King and the Queen chose to find me unfit and exile me.

All the protections were spelled out—no cutting, burning, harming the skin, the organs, the health of a slave, and so forth—and the promises that I would be well fed, well groomed, and allowed plenty of sleep and so forth and so on.

It was easy to wrest the sense from the ornate and official language, and I marveled even in my trembling state at the beauty of the hand and the phrasing.

As I took the quill and signed my full name, I acknowledged as the document said that my body was now the property of King Laurent and Queen Beauty of Bellavalten, to do with as they wished within the constraints assured to me. I would never be sold outside the kingdom nor given to anyone who did not abide by its laws.

There was a lot more there, all about how incorrigibles might be exiled, and what it meant to be incorrigible. But I knew all this.

I wasn't going to be incorrigible.

As the clerk seemed so utterly indifferent to my physical state, my nakedness, the redness of my limbs, or the manner in which I stood there, I almost ventured the question of whether or not Sybil had signed her document.

But at that very moment, I saw Sybil's green wool mantle, the one she'd worn all the way from our home, and that it was folded in an open chest that stood beside my chest. I saw the lining of gray miniver. And in that chest there was also a long parchment document. Daring to turn my head in full I read the huge and familiar signature of Sybil of Arcolot on it plainly.

The clerk never noticed. He was making some notes in a great book.

Then he lifted a brass bell with a wooden handle and rang it.

"This one is ready for you," he said without looking up to another well-dressed man who appeared. Like the other attendant earlier, he was comely, obviously chosen for his grace and his looks.

"Ah, so this is the second one directed for the royal table or stable," said the attendant.

Table or stable! He's spoken these words without a touch of humor. It startled me.

I felt his gloved fingers closing on my left arm and he pulled me out the door.

Then came the weary murmuring voice of the clerk.

"I wish you good fortune, Brendan of Arcolot," he said, "you and your sweet Lady Sybil. When the King comes tonight to inspect as he so often does, and ask whether this has been a good day, I shall tell him that it has been splendid."

iv

This seemed to be a vast garden. I couldn't tell. The quality of the light was bright yet not outdoor light, and only gradually did I realize as I was led through the potted trees that this was a tented enclosure that filtered the sun through white cloth.

I saw stone flooring beneath me strewn with mats and felt the mats under my naked feet and caught the scent of oranges. The air was sweet with other mingled scents, jasmine and mint, and slightly damp.

It seemed we'd walked forever until we came to a great bathing area where naked slaves were being bathed by liveried attendants in bronze or pewter tubs.

Water in tin buckets simmered on smoking braziers and the scent of cedar and incense thickened.

With my eyes down I could only catch furtive glimpses of the naked bodies standing or kneeling all around me for this bathing, and the glossy green leaves of potted shrubs brushed my legs softly as we moved on.

"Ah, there," said the attendant, "and a great and good groom, Fane, who is beckoning for us. You're blessed."

He pushed me roughly forward until I was staring down into the warm water swirling with flower petals.

I heard him say to the groom named Fane that Lady Eva would likely be presenting me at Court this very night, and that I was to be thoroughly prepared, my face shaved but none of my body hair touched.

"Hmm, the chest hair is becoming enough," said Fane, a young man in a light white short-sleeved tunic with what appeared a big scrubbing brush in his hand. "But the pubic hair, it's so thick and so long."

"Lady Eva was explicit," said the attendant. "Goodbye, Brenn, and good luck to you." He gave my backside a fierce smack.

I was ordered into the water by the groom who went to work as fiercely as the pretty female before.

"Quite a physique, young boy," he said. "My name is Fane, by the way, and when you answer me, you may address me as 'sir' or as 'Fane.' That's the way with all grooms or pages or handlers—the name or the respectful 'sir' or 'madam.'"

"Yes, Fane," I murmured.

"Oh, you don't have to speak unless asked a question," he said, correcting me.

I didn't know what to do but nod.

He had me kneel up, then on all fours, then sit in the warm water as he worked, and spared no part of my body with the big, and thankfully soft, brush.

I couldn't stop glancing about me—seeing flashes of other slaves being lathered and scrubbed and rubbed with foaming oils, the many grooms all quite similar in build and beauty, young men with powerful arms and sturdy backs and legs.

Beyond this ring of baths, I glimpsed a wilderness of what seemed high narrow beds on which naked flesh was being pounded and kneaded and rubbed with oil.

That part of the preparation came for me as soon as Fane had closely shaved my face and dried my hair.

He began to talk now as he stretched me out on the table and told me to slip my cock through the open hole provided for this before he pressed me down flat.

"Now, listen, Brenn, remembering my name's not important, as you'll likely not see me again if you behave yourself, but you'll soon have regular grooms, grooms you'll come to know and depend on," he said.

He rubbed oil into my sore abraded bottom first and then my aching legs. The oil felt wondrously good and so did his powerful hands.

"Grooms are always willing to answer any questions you might have," he went on. "And to make certain that you're fearing all the proper things." He laughed. "By that I mean, we're to reassure you of what is in store for you and reassure you as to what is not."

He turned my head to one side and let me rest on the left side of my face and now as he worked on my hair, brushing it strongly, obviously to bring up the natural luster of it, I could see beyond this area, and what appeared an entire wall of niches where naked slaves slept. So many! It seemed I could see thirty or forty, though I didn't try to count.

"So you have nothing to ask me, Brenn?" he coaxed. "As long as you address me properly as 'sir,' and ask nothing importunate or willful, I'm here to tell you what I can."

"May I ask about the woman who came here with me, who went in before me?"

"No, that you may not do," he said. "Never ask about another slave, and always address me as 'sir' when you speak." He slapped me hard on my backside as he said this. "It's not for me to discipline you or punish you," he explained. "Unless I'm told to do so. You're for your masters and mistresses, but I'm to whip you hard if you show the slightest disrespect."

"I'm sorry, sir," I said. It feel so strange to say it, and yet so simple at the same time.

"That's better," he said. His powerful fingers were rubbing my scalp. Ripples of sensation traveled my head and my back and the backs of my arms. I felt drowsy suddenly. And there came a flash of dream as though sleep were suddenly reaching for me.

I was awakened suddenly by his fingers oiling my anus, though it seemed now that he wore a glove. He was not rough but he wasn't gentle either.

"Nice and tight," he said in a matter-of-fact voice. "The King will love that."

"Do you think I'll be taken directly to the King, sir?" I asked.

"Now that you shouldn't ask either."

He smacked me hard several times. I kept my lips tightly closed but I groaned. I couldn't help it.

"Brenn, don't you understand what types of questions are not permitted?"

"I'm trying, sir," I said under my breath.

"Well, since I said I'd answer what I could, I will," he said. "Yes, Lady Eva is taking you to see the King and the Queen. But that doesn't mean you'll ever see either of them again. Many new piglets like you are presented to Their Majesties, all those whom Lady Eva selects, but they may send you off at once to some other part of the Court or the kingdom. So spend your precious time with them wisely. You do not bow to them as if you were a free man. You wait to be commanded as to whether you kneel down or up or stand. But you may kiss their feet when you're presented. A slave may always drop down and kiss the feet of a master or mistress, including the King and Queen, but don't do it clumsily or awkwardly. Be completely submissive. You know what that word means? And don't dare look at your masters or mistresses the way you were glancing at me from that tub. Don't dare look at anyone that way!"

"I'm sorry, sir," I said. I hadn't realized that he had noticed.

"Now turn completely over and keep your eyes half shut," he said. He set to work on my chest with the same vigor he'd used on my back, rubbing the oil into me as if I were carved of wood.

"You do have the prettiest face," he said. "Such baby cheeks and lips, like a Cupid."

I closed my eyes to avoid looking at him because I didn't know what else to do, and he didn't reprove me for this, but went to work positively polishing my balls and cock as he'd polished everything else.

I was hard, hopelessly hard, and he was maddeningly careful not to touch the tip of my cock.

"Behave yourself," he said in a low voice. "You dare come, and I'll have to report that to Lady Eva. And I can't say what will happen to you then. That cock belongs to the King and Queen and the Court now, and all the noble and gentlefolk of this kingdom, and even to the common people and the peasants, you understand?"

"Yes, sir, I understand."

"To even the lowliest people of the kingdom, it belongs, you understand? No longer to you. Your entire body, your eyes, your voice, all belong to the kingdom."

"Yes, sir."

His ministrations continued and lulled me again to the edge of a dreamy erotic sleep, my cock being the only substantial thing in my mind as I drifted off.

When he finally pulled me up by my wrists, I woke up from this half slumber with a shiver, and once again he smacked my backside very hard with his hand.

Suddenly, as if he couldn't stop himself, he put his foot up on a stool and pulled me over his thigh and spanked my backside over and over, hard, in the same way, his naked fingers hard as wood.

I found myself groaning again. I couldn't help it. But to the walloping with the strap, this was like spice compared to supper. To say that my cock loved it would be an understatement.

I saw the whole room in a bright flash. I saw slaves being very roughly bathed and others soothed, it seemed, and some being smacked over and over by their grooms, in one stage or another of their toilet. I saw some over the knee as I was.

He didn't spank me all that long, but my cock felt like it was made of stone.

He brought me up straight.

"You're a good boy," he said approvingly. "A very good boy. I have this feeling, ah, but what do I know? If the Queen or the King don't take you, you'll still be at Court at table or stable."

There it was again, that phrase. But I was weeping at his praise and reassurance. Then realizing I'd said nothing I answered frantically under my breath:

"Yes, sir."

"Not required." He laughed. "I didn't ask you a question." Another hard squeeze on my sore bottom. "But you'll learn. You might be gagged for a while, but that's to be avoided. Your betters can't see your pretty mouth when you're gagged. And the Queen especially does not care for gags on her slaves unless they're being corrected for impertinence. See that you're not corrected for impertinence."

We passed many others as we moved towards the far wall. I scanned the countless niches in vain for my precious Sybil. But she might have been one of many sleeping dark-haired beauties, with her head turned away.

There were small stools and stepladders by the wall of beds.

Suddenly, I was being lifted by Fane and another groom to a niche just above my head. I was slipped into it and onto the softest silken mattress I ever felt.

"Over on your back," said Fane, mounting a little ladder. He reached in and tethered my hands by means of leather thongs to a hook just above my head. My arms weren't pulled tight, and it wasn't painful, but there was no way I could touch my cock.

"Now, you go to sleep, Brenn," he said. "Of course you'll twist your neck trying to see all that's going on here. Well, do that and be done with it, and then let sleep come. You'll be surprised how easy it will be for you to sleep. And don't dare to try to turn over, or get your hands free, or pleasure yourself, or you'll be punished in ways you haven't foreseen. Never touch your own cock or your privates, Brenn. Never. They don't belong to you. Remember."

Then he was gone.

I was in the soft silken-lined niche and I was staring up at the low painted ceiling, and at my own hands tethered to the hook.

Of course I turned my head and looked out on the vast room. So much to see, but then sleep came down over me like a veil.

Sometime much later, I was turned over and my hands were tethered loosely at my sides. My cock and balls had been placed on an opening so that they got no friction. I dozed off again with a groom rubbing unguents into my skin all over. There came the prickling delicious pain when his hands found the raw abraded skin but the sensations melted into sleep.

V

It was dusk when I awoke. A soft golden light filled the tented room, and a young naked slave was lighting the candles in the many standing candelabra.

I blinked. The figure of a tall, slender elegant lady was coming towards me, and gradually I realized it was the red-haired Lady Eva.

Two young men walked beside her and she directed them towards me.

I was taken out of the niche carefully and gently and planted on my feet, then turned around so that she might inspect me.

Her cool hands prodded and felt of me all over. I wondered if this would be worse, more shaming, if she were not so beautiful.

"Excellent skin. Very fine skin," she said. "Feed him the apples."

One of the grooms put a small slice of apple into my mouth and told me to chew it up thoroughly.

"You'll always be given apples when you waken, and several times a day, to clean your teeth and freshen your mouth," Lady Eva said. "Never go before your masters and mistresses without this little ritual, Brenn. Do wake up and answer me."

"Yes, my lady. I mean, yes, madam," I said.

"You may use that form of address if you like. I'm taking you to the Queen."

The two attendants were rubbing me down with oil again, and one blotting the excess with a clean linen towel. As I stood there, one did a skilled job of again shaving my beard very close.

"Ah, your cock is sensitive, attentive, and beautiful," Lady Eva said.

With a shock, I felt her fingers on my balls. She fondled them and patted them very lightly.

"Now, you may address the Queen as 'my queen' or 'Your Majesty.' Same for the King of course, 'my king,' and so forth."

"Yes, madam," I said.

Another man approached. He was taller than the two grooms, and very powerfully built. I had no idea why he was there.

My hair was brushed, my fingernails inspected, my toenails, my pubic hair combed, which amazed me, and then the lady pinched my nipples and said they were bright pink, which she liked.

Then she told the man we were going to the Queen's parlor.

He heaved me over his shoulder as if I were no more than a child to him, and holding my ankles firmly in his hands, he headed off behind her, with me dangling down his back, my hands clasped to my neck and my eyes fixed on Lady Eva's rose-colored silk skirts as she walked before me.

The blood was rushing to my head, but that was the least of my concerns. I felt more feeble and powerless than ever before. The man walked very fast and so did Lady Eva.

Through a garden we were moving and I could hear music around us and the hum of voices, but I could see almost nothing. With a shock it came to me that we were in a vast place and lots of people were passing us without so much as a word as to my being carried like this in their midst.

Indeed the noise grew thicker and thicker and the ground beneath us was layered with overlapping carpets of red and blue with intricate Eastern patterns. Torches flickered brightly all around us, and I could hear the sound of fountains.

This was utterly unnerving. To have been examined as I'd been by a few people and in an enclosed place was one thing, but this was like being carried naked through a marketplace or a fairground.

My face was down, hidden, however, and I was very grateful for that. But I peeped from left to right to see what I could, and suddenly saw with a shock a gorgeous noble lady seated at a marble table who smiled at me.

The shock was too much and I shut my eyes.

Then someone else passed and patted my head saying, "Lovely boy, Lady Eva."

"Nothing too good for the King and Queen," Lady Eva replied airily.

Again shock. I was exposed, my backside, legs, likely my genitals were visible, and there was nothing I could do about it even if I wanted to do something. The powerful man held my ankles firmly.

We entered a stone passage, and moved through a vast echoing hall, filled with voices and the soft tread of shoes, and then up a staircase.

The lady climbed the steps in front of me effortlessly, I could hear her, and now I could not see her, and again I closed my eyes because something about the stairs, climbing higher and higher, alarmed me.

We must have gone quite high up in the castle, before we entered a broad passage and proceeded down it.

I saw a floor of polished pavers carpeted again with a multitude of patterned carpets. All the merchants of Italy and the Orient must have come with these wares, I thought.

Doors here and there opened and closed and lords and ladies passed. I glimpsed brocade and tooled slippers.

We came to a stop and a man's voice announced:

"Lady Eva to see Her Majesty."

We advanced and the door was closed behind us.

The silence of the room suddenly enclosed us.

The man pulled down my ankles and flipped me back into his left arm, then turned me around and planted me on my feet and held my bottom firmly as I found my balance.

I clamped my hands tightly on the back of my neck. And I stared at the thick burgundy wool carpet.

Silence.

The low crackling of a fire, and its dim flashing light on the walls and in the corner of my eyes; the sound of breathing. And perhaps a caged bird singing.

"Well, you did not exaggerate," said a woman's soft melodious voice.

The Sleeping Beauty!

Could it be? I had been told over and over I would be brought here, yet my heart beat wildly inside me and I trembled.

"Yes, I think this is quite remarkable," said Lady Eva. "Now down on your knees, Brenn. Yes, like that. Your Majesty, I haven't trained this lovely porklet at all, I've brought him straight from the Hall of Postulants but I thought you should see him."

"You did right, absolutely right, and little piglet, your posture and demeanor are perfect." The voice was kindly, generous. "Now come here to me, that's it, slowly, and though you are on your hands and knees you must be graceful. At all times, graceful. Do you know how beautiful you are, little boy?"

How could I answer that!

I moved forward, the carpet thick and soft under my hands and knees, forward, hoping that soon I'd know if I was going in the right direction. I was of course heading towards the source of the voice.

Then I saw the legs of a heavily carved oak chair, and I saw great full skirts of sky-blue silk and delicate gold tracery, and slippers, beautifully shaped slippers with pointed toes.

And the voice of Fane still in my mind, I kept moving until I could kiss the slippers of the woman and I did so.

"Ah, that is so touching," she said kindly. "What an excellent boy. You are a gem. Now kneel up so I can see your endowments and your handsome strong chest and your face."

I obeyed, hands to the regular position, and I felt my face burning hot. I knew I was blinking and trying to blink back tears. Why were the tears coming so quickly? My cock had never been harder in my life.

Staring down, I could see it, bloodred, with a shining wet tip. I bit my lip and waited in agony. Nothing that had gone before was quite like this.

"Well, you are a faun!" said the Queen. "I expect to find hooves on those feet, but no, they're beautiful. Eva, he has the body of a satyr and the face of a Cupid."

"Yes, Your Majesty."

"And look at all this luxuriant hair."

I saw a slender graceful hand move towards me, the fingers tugging at the dark hair of my chest, and moving down my belly, pulling at the hair gently, sending tingling sensations through me. The fingers plunged into my pubic hair and the Queen laughed and laughed. As before, I thought I might lose consciousness, or at least conscious control of my body.

"This is truly a magnificent young faun!" she said. "And your name is Brenn, precious one?"

"Yes, my queen," I said. My throat was so dry the words came out scratchy and low. My mouth was quivering.

"Ah, what a little banquet you are for your mistress!" The long tapering fingers touched my cock but very lightly. I bit down on a gasp. "Now stand up and turn around, young faun," she said, "without moving your hands . . . that's it. Good boy. Oh, what a splendid backside."

"It's tightly muscled," said Lady Eva. "Yet nicely padded. And if you could have seen the spanking with a belt that Lord Gregory gave him just hours ago, well, you wouldn't believe it."

"No, he's barely pink," said the Queen. "Pink as a rabbit's ear or a kitten's tongue. Turn around towards me again, Brenn."

I obeyed.

I swallowed. My legs were vibrating but I don't think they were visibly shaking.

I heard the sound of a door open.

"Laurent, I'm so glad you've come. Look at this little satyr who arrived today."

A heavy tread approached, and even with my eyes down I could see the enormous figure of King Laurent beside me. The blood drained from my face. The tears hovered in my eyes.

A low laugh of amazement came from the King.

"Well, Eva, darling, this is beyond all imagining. Young man, I expect to find pointed ears here." His hand clasped my chin and lifted it. "And this beard, ah, what a thick beard."

The Queen laughed. "I said very nearly the same thing myself," she confessed. "But he's all little boy, every morsel of him."

"This face was just shaved for the second time today, sire," said Lady Eva. "That's going to take attending, and of course the hair, all of it can be trimmed, or shaved."

"Oh, no, I wouldn't hear of it," said the Queen. "I love it. Why even his backside has a nice thin covering of fleecy dark hair. This is sublime. Turn around again, Brenn."

I obeyed.

"But you must speak up when I give you an order, darling," said the Queen behind me. "You must acknowledge that your queen has spoken to you."

I swallowed hard, and said, "Yes, my queen" immediately. I didn't dare protest I'd been taught the opposite.

"I like his voice too," said the King.

"He's educated," said Lady Eva, "clerk to a duke."

"Ah, very good," said the King. "Well, young Brenn——" He lifted my chin again. "Recite a line to me from Propertius."

"In Latin, sire, or in the translation?" I asked.

The King roared with laugher. "You know Propertius's elegies?" he asked.

"Yes, sire. 'Amor takes no little happiness in a sprinkling of tears . . .

there is joy in a new slavery as well . . .'" I broke off, after combining two lines.

"And where did you discover the translation?" the King asked.

"I translated it from the Latin, sire, when I was bored and had nothing else to do," I answered. Was this too bold, too proud? Instantly I regretted it.

"Ooh no, no!" cried the Queen. "You can't make of him a poet here, Laurent. He's mine. I declare it."

"Of course, my darling, my love," said the King. "Don't be so suspicious of me, but this is a fine scholar, and who says his duties can't include the recitation of poetry now and then?"

"In time, perhaps, my lord," said the Queen. "Right now, I want him. I don't know quite what I shall do with him."

"I have an idea, Your Majesty," said Lady Eva.

"Well, then speak," said the Queen.

"My queen, your lady ponies are lovely, but it takes two or more to pull even the lightest chariot for you. What about a male pony, a male pony so strong and striking that he can pull your little chariot and you all by himself? I think this would make a magnificent picture!"

"That would be quite tasty," said the Queen. "Who's to say I cannot have a male for such a thing?"

"No one," said the King. "But I do want to play with this boy for a while. Can we take the matter slowly?"

"Of course," said the Queen. "But couldn't we have him trained in your stables?"

"Your Majesty, I can, of course," said Lady Eva, "but why not in your very own stable, right with the girl ponies? Bring the few males, as you select them, into your stable to be trained. Every groom you have knows how to train both male and female ponies."

"I don't see why not," said the Queen. "But he is a very sturdy and strong boy, and I thought the boy ponies had harsher training."

"Share him with me," said the King. "Put him in with the males for now. Male ponies have a special camaraderie. Let him train with my men, with César and Bastian and Caspian. I'm thinking this boy is strong enough to pull even my solitary chariot. I'll have him trained and then sent to you ready for your equipage. After he's learned with my men, been worked with my men, he can handle your little chariot beautifully."

"Very well," said the Queen, "that's fine, but tonight at supper in the garden, he will be my footstool. And Brenn, this is a simple task for a young man who is inherently well behaved. You'll kneel before my chair, and I assure you, my feet are not heavy."

The King laughed. "He'll do well. But first I think I'll drain the cup so that he doesn't spill over."

Suddenly his powerful arm swung round in front of me and he hoisted me in the air as easily as the strong attendant had done it, flung me over his shoulder and carried me from the room, leaving the women laughing together.

I was only dangling that way for a split second. He slammed a door behind him and lifted me and put me on a broad oak sideboard facing him.

"Look at me, little Pan," he said.

I did. I looked at a face I'd heard described a thousand times, and none of those paeans touched it. He had huge glittering brown eyes, crinkled at the corners, and a brilliant generous smile. His skin was dark and lustrous and his hair a tangled raiment of brown waves.

"Oh, you are so pretty!" he said.

"Yes, sire," I whispered. There was a lump in my throat.

He laughed.

"Spread your legs wide. I want that cock for my supper!"

He grabbed at my nipples with both his hands pushing me back against the wall and then he descended on my cock as I gasped and shut my eyes.

His tight lips worked it hard, stroking it back and forth, back and forth, his tongue licking at the tip. I thought I would cry out in ecstasy. His fingers ground at my nipples.

I felt nothing, knew nothing, but this searing, blinding pleasure.

Surely he would turn away when I had to come. I sought respectfully as I could to pull loose, to warn him, moaning frantically, but he clutched my backside, lifting it off the wood, and held me fast to his mouth. *It is the King!*

When I came I let out a series of choking sobs. I couldn't stop myself.

I felt myself dropped down again on the wood, and a large hand steadying my chest.

"Cupid's nectar," he said. Then he moved away.

In a blur, I saw the ceiling, the burning candles of the room, and then his figure again looming before me. He was drinking from a goblet thirstily, and I could smell the wine.

A low laugh came out of him. He seemed enormous, larger than any man I'd ever beheld, and I felt small, deliciously weak! Of course I myself was a big man and he was tall though not a giant. But in my mind he appeared to grow and I to shrink immeasurably.

I melted. I dissolved. I wasn't there. Yet I had never been more present anywhere else in all my existence, seated naked on this broad sideboard, my sore bottom aching on the wood and my cock limp and my soul sunk down into some deep stratum of quiet beyond language.

I dared not look at his face. I closed my eyes again.

The kingdom. Bellavalten!

Oh, Sybil, I pray your hours have been as eventful and as glorious as mine have been!

"Tell you what, you tasty little sausage, you may be headed to the stables all right, but not for a few nights, not till Queen Beauty and I have had some fun with you."

He stared at my cock. It was already hard again.

vi

It was full night but the gardens were as brightly lighted as if it were day. The roar of voices was all around me, with music rising in waves above it.

The Queen led me on a scarlet leather leash by a scarlet collar around my neck. She'd combed my hair herself with the gentlest fingers, and she pulled me along on my hands and knees beside her skirts. I was not to lift my head on any account, or a wider collar would be used for me that didn't allow me to lift my head, and she didn't want for that to happen.

On and on we walked over the great floor of carpets and soft grass and carpets once more. I glimpsed figures dancing, heard the quick rhythm of drums or tambourines. And everywhere great shining explosions of laughter and excited conversation.

Again and again, people to the right and left bowed to the Queen: "Your Majesty!" The hushed and reverent voices hurled their whispers at her feet.

I couldn't bear to think of what they saw if they looked at me, if they even noticed me at all, but then my heart would swell with pride. She had chosen me for this, for her pet, to be led like her favored puppy alongside of her. She had chosen me and on my very first night in the kingdom!

Now and then a paddle smacked my bottom hard. But it was not the Queen who did this, but Lady Eva. "Straight back now, Brenn," she said. "That's it. Now, look up just a little, as you must climb this step onto the dais and you must do it gracefully. The entire Court is watching you, young man."

I obeyed.

"Under the table now, that's it," said Lady Eva. "And you're to kneel there."

"Ah yes, and now you may crouch down, and rest back on your heels and lower your shoulders and rest on your forearms," said the Queen. "And put your head down, yes, that's very nice. And don't move and don't speak. You might want to sleep now. You can be a good little footstool and still sleep. But when I prod that pretty cock with my slipper, I want to feel it wake."

I obeyed. The carpet under my feet was soft, and the light poured gently through the thin linen and silk that draped the table, making a long golden corridor here in which I knelt.

Right in front of me, I saw another slave being put into place in the very same manner, but he was large boned and had balls even bigger than mine. He settled down just as I had done, and I saw a man's fancy boot plant itself on his back.

A gush of silent tears came out of me. I had never been more devoid of tension, more limp, except for my cock of course.

The voices of the party were muted, but I could hear the Queen above me chatting with Lady Eva. Her slippered foot suddenly rested, small and light, on my back.

I lay still, my heart thudding in my ears, my cock, which had been hard all this while, was softening a little, and I became sleepy, wondering if I could hold my position perfectly while I dozed.

Then a delicate hand appeared before me with a bit of fruit, and I heard the Queen speak. "Here, precious Brenn, here."

I hadn't eaten since morning, and I licked the bits of fruit from her beautiful and graceful fingers.

I was dozing when a dish with more fruit was given to me to eat. It contained a thick sweet meat sauce and bits of meat that were savory and delicious.

"No hands, darling," she said. "You eat like a good little slave, like a good little puppy dog."

I would have done anything she said, any way she said to do it. I had obeyed all the others to be admitted, to be received. I obeyed her because I loved her, because every word from her thrilled me. And when I heard the King's deep voice above, when I heard him talking to her and laughing in that natural spontaneous way of his, I knew I loved him too. And to think I would become their pony, a pony for Her Majesty and a pony for His Majesty. I had no real idea what it meant to be a pony, but only that I would be theirs, their very own, and I would do all in my power to please them forever.

Ah, Beauty's Kingdom. I have made it so far. I am at home. I am the pet of the Sleeping Beauty herself. I am here. And nothing beyond this kingdom any longer matters at all.

Hours passed. I slept. The dish was gone. Now and then both the Queen's feet rested on my back, sometimes only one.

Then I was waked and pulled by my leash, and once again walking as I had before only now the garden seemed livelier than ever.

I felt my cock stirring again, getting hard.

I heard Lady Eva say, "Yes, perfect." And something feathery touched my cock, and I jumped. "He's a natural," she said. "Perfect attitude, perfect responses."

This seemed a dream of uncommonly vivid intensity, something too palpably exciting to be mere real life.

It was not easy to move up the stone stairs on hands and knees and Lady Eva corrected me several times on grace.

In the Queen's parlor again, I was led to the side of Lady Eva's chair.

"Now, spank that luscious little bottom," said the Queen. "I want to see it bright red."

What had I done! But then I realized I'd done nothing! I was being enjoyed, not punished.

"Up over my knee, little faun," said Lady Eva. "And put that pretty chin in my left hand. The Queen wants to see your face. And don't try to hide it." A pause. I could feel and hear the paddle in my mind, but in fact all was silence.

I lay across her skirts, over her knee, hands pressing into my neck with feverish pressure, and waited. Her skirts tickled my cock, tortured it.

"Your Majesty, don't you want to enjoy this little repast yourself?" Lady Eva said.

"I do, but I'll enjoy it even more," said the Queen, "if you do it. You do it better than I do, Eva."

"Your Majesty!"

"No, truly you do."

"Well, this precious little porkling hasn't been spanked over the knee yet," said Lady Eva, as though reflecting. "And I do so love doing it. Brenn, I want perfection now, little boy, do you hear me? Lips sealed, hands clamped to your neck as if they were bound."

"Yes, madam," I said, and this unleashed a sob in my throat but my lips didn't release it. The tears rose in my eyes. This was infinitely more humiliating than standing for a beating with a belt, more humiliating somehow even than being walked on a leash, puppy-style, in the gardens. When my groom, Fane, had done it earlier, it had not registered with me so intensely. It had been abrupt, simple, brief. But now in this perfumed parlor with the Queen herself to watch what was happening, it seemed the greatest test of submission I had yet to endure. Yet it never occurred to me to beg, plead, or try to move away, or to protest in any way. I was delivered utterly to the moment, helpless as if I were bound hand and foot.

Though my eyes were half closed I looked at the fire and wished with all my heart I could see the Queen, at least see her slippers.

It was a paddle, not a belt as I expected it would be.

"Count the spanks, little goatling," sang Lady Eva.

"Yes, madam, three, four, five, six . . ."

The delicious simmering pain spread through the skin and then deep into my backside, or so it seemed.

"Ten, eleven, twelve, thirteen . . ."

Soon with all my might, I was struggling to lie still, my arms tensing, my fingers rigid as I struggled not to move, not to reach back like a helpless child to shield myself, and I knew my legs and bottom were moving.

At last, Lady Eva stopped. She gave a great sigh.

I lay waiting, my backside so hot surely it must glow in the shadows, my thighs blazing. I had counted some thirty spanks. I was coughing and shivering with sobs. And lips closed or not, I couldn't keep quiet. It was impossible. My body was spasming with my sobs.

I heard the fire crackling loudly. Suddenly the pain in my sore hind-quarters increased. Then softened and spread out all through me in a warm, delicious way. And my tears flowed even more freely.

I belong to you, my queen, I was thinking. If only I could say it, and to you, Lady Eva, who lifted me from the new applicants and brought me here. I only want to please.

"Kneel up now, Brenn, over here, before me," said the Queen.

At once I obeyed, struggling to withdraw from Lady Eva's lap without touching her in any disrespectful way. The sensation in my cock doubled and kicked, and throbbed.

I moved forward towards the Queen's skirts on my hands and knees.

"Closer," said the Queen. There was the long delicate hand again, with its shining nails, and a lovely perfume rose from her skirts as though they'd been washed in rosewater.

I struggled closer. I was almost touching her.

Her fingers examined my erect cock, and my pubic hair again.

"I'd love to see this all brushed with gold," she said. "Yet I like the blackness of it, so very black." She felt of my thigh, inside, and pulled gently at the hair. "Brenn, my precious faun," she said. "My little satyr."

She rose suddenly, her skirts sweeping over my face and form, blinding me, and then I watched furtively as she walked to the far wall. She stood against it beside a sideboard with silver candles on it. How shapely and young she appeared with her small waist and her bright yellow hair.

"Come here, on your hands and knees," she said.

I obeyed, and as I came up before her, she lifted her skirts gracefully to reveal her long wonderfully curved white legs and the golden triangle of her pubic hair. Such a delicate sex, such a sweet tender-looking sex.

"Stand up and take me, little faun!" she said.

I rose up at once. If I had stopped to think, I would have lost my nerve in disbelief.

"Put your arms around my neck and your lips on mine," she said.

I did as she told me, her high round breasts warm against my chest through the fabric of her gown, her face against mine, soft and tender as a fresh peach. Her mouth tasted of honey.

My cock rammed clumsily at her little cleft, but then I felt her fingers there, parting her lips, guiding me. Such a girlish sex. So shy.

"Bad little boy!" she said. Then the hot sheath had descended on me, wet and small like the sex of a girl.

Her hand clenched my sore backside. I could feel her little crypt throbbing against the whole length of my shaft.

"Kiss me and take me hard, hard as if you'd found me in the street of a besieged town," she said.

I thrust into her blindly and madly, as hard and as fast as I could, while my lips closed over her, tasting her sweetness, my eyes looking down at her closed eyelids. "Yes," she said. "Yes, harder, my little woodland god. Come and carry me away with you."

I rammed her against the wall. I bucked and rode her hard until I suddenly spent, unable to keep back a loud moan, and then she rode the wave with me.

At last I stood, still holding her.

"All right, little boy," said Lady Eva. "Down on your hands and knees. You're going to eat your supper now from the little bowl on the hearth. Come."

The Queen smiled at me. I looked full at her, into her enchanting blue eyes, such pure blue eyes, so trusting, so loving, and then I looked down, bashfully. She kissed me.

I dropped to the floor to obey.

I was so delightfully tired, my head swam. I could smell the food suddenly, beef and gravy.

I crawled towards the steaming dish.

"With your mouth only, piglet," said Lady Eva. "Every morsel."

I wrestled with the first few bites and then thought, Why am I holding back, and for whom, and then I began to eat faster.

"That's it, Brenn. I tell you, Your Majesty, this is the finest little postulant to come through the gates."

"Yes," said the Queen, "but I think His Majesty is quite delighted as well with the girl who came with him."

So the King was with Sybil? I went on eating until I was licking the empty dish. My face was smeared with gravy. But my heart leapt at the thought of Sybil pleasing, Sybil being with the King, Sybil being accepted as I'd been.

Lady Eva pulled me up and wiped at my mouth and chin a little roughly with a napkin. "You will learn to do all this just a little bit better," she said holding me by a lock of my hair on the top of my head. "But you are a nonpareil."

vii

I lay in a small bedchamber with no furnishings. A great brawny attendant had carried me back to the Postulants' Hall, and there a sleepy groom I did not know had bathed me and oiled me with amazing tenderness. He'd stopped to kiss me many times, rubbing oil into my fingers and my toes, and spreading some thick healing compound over my sore backside.

He was so gentle he seemed some sort of spirit in the drowsy quiet night in which all slept.

Then I was placed in this bedroom.

No restraints, no holes in the bed, just Chinese cushions and incense, and a tiny silver lamp with a little shivering flame sending shadows leaping along the low ceiling.

Of course I didn't dare to touch myself, to try to relive what had happened and use my own hand to relive the pleasure I felt.

When the door opened, I woke with a start, realizing that somehow I must have been sleeping.

Sybil stood in the door. Naked.

Her long black hair hung down covering her breasts. Her pubic hair was a perfect little heart, it seemed, and her face was glowing. She beamed at me.

"You can't be here. This isn't real," I said.

"Oh, I'm here all right," she said. She dropped down on her hands and knees and crawled into the bed next to me. A sweet fragrance came from her skin and her hair. "Queen Beauty has sent me. She says we're to have our recreation together until tomorrow."

"You mean it?" I sat up. "But I thought they would never allow such a thing."

"Well, in the old days the kingdom did not," said Sybil. She turned to me, resting on her elbow, and ran her fingers through my hair. She had a glow to her. "Brenn, she adores you."

I didn't know what to say.

Her face was animated and flushed and she spoke excitedly, as though she'd traveled to distant lands of the mind since I'd last seen her, as if time itself was meaningless here.

"She says slaves must have time to be with their fellows, as she puts it. She says in the old days they stole such time but she will not have such deceitfulness. She grants many slaves a respite with others. And as we came together, she says we may take our recreation together."

She went on, her eyes wide, and her lips glistening.

"The Queen says we may do as we like during this time together, that village ponies had that privilege even in their punishment, recreation together, and we're to have it. She says when it's time for us to rest up for our duties, they'll come and they'll separate us."

"I never expected it."

Sybil started kissing me. Her mouth was sweet and fresh, and her hair tickled me as it fell down around me.

"My dear," I said. "Countless times tonight I've been called a little faun, a satyr, a god. But I'm not. I'm only human."

"Oh, come now, Brenn," she said.

And sure enough, I was rising to the occasion. I bore down on her, driving my cock into her, my hands holding her arms high above her head, my tongue lapping at her mouth, forcing it open. Not a thought came to my mind, not a flash of memory, only Sybil, as it had been only the Queen and before that only the King, and all fantasies of the past were gone like thin bits of silk caught in a wind and carried heavenward.

Before morning, I held her close and wept as I told her some of what had happened. I couldn't possibly recount all. She was much calmer recounting her own adventures. She wiped my tears, and she did now and then become dewy eyed and a little soft with feeling, but she spoke more with distant amazement.

Sybil's introduction to the kingdom had been much the same as mine, though obviously they'd bathed her in compliments since the beginning as to her irresistible attributes, and I didn't see any reason to go on about the insults I'd received.

The infamous Lord Gregory had also paddled her to test her, and so had another prince whose name she'd never known, and also a "great lady" who had made her perform many servile tasks.

"I never found it so pleasurable before in my life to gather discarded garments from the floor of a room, or arrange slippers in a closet primarily with the use of my teeth." She laughed. "And Brenn, the lady's voice was so gentle with me, and loving and comforting all the while. And then do you know what happened, Brenn? I discovered that this 'great lady' was none other than the Queen! She put me in her bed and toyed with me as if I were a doll."

In the great gardens, Sybil had been tethered to a huge X cross for exhibition, along with other new slaves, for the approval of the King.

"Brenn, it was liberating, being bound like that, my wrists up and far apart, my ankles near the base of the arms of the cross! I thought they'd blindfold me as some of the slaves were blindfolded, but they were crying frantically, and I was not. I'd been polished with silver pigment and oil beforehand, and they decorated me with all manner of pretty blossoms. I was there for hours in a swoon. I tell you, it was a positive swoon. Passing lords and ladies touched me, examined me, played with me. It never stopped for very long. I'd fall asleep and then waken to hands stroking me between my legs, soft voices talking of the smallest details of my body, praising my 'little juices' and my nipples, making me blush. But I was so sublimely helpless, Brenn. So free. I could twist and struggle and it didn't matter. Indeed, they seemed to be amused by it. My groom told me to put on a good show for my masters and mistresses, and then laughed and said he needn't bother to teach me a thing."

She lay on her arm gazing into my eyes.

"Then this great lord came, the Grand Duke. He was most refined and spoke with such courtesy. I was told later he was the late queen's uncle. He wanted me taken down for him to play with. He was most insistent in a gentlemanly way. He liked my eyes, my mouth. He wanted to see my bottom. He said he loved the texture of my skin.

"The groom told him he must walk behind the 'scaffold' and there he could see my bottom plainly enough. Brenn, when the Grand Duke spanked my bottom it nearly brought me to climax. All the while he had his left hand against the collar around my neck and he was speaking to me in the most cultured voice. 'Darling, darling,' he said, 'you're the finest of the new stock that I've seen. Some slaves are infinitely better than others.' Brenn, his voice could have brought me to the pinnacle, without the sharp spanks."

"I understand."

"But my groom said the Grand Duke would have to wait to have me to himself. The Grand Duke didn't give up easily, but he was never really rude."

"Lovely," I said.

"Brenn, it's over, all our struggles, our hopes, our dreams. It's over. We're here!"

"For six months, Sybil," I said. "We can be rejected in six months."

"But they won't reject us, Brenn. I know they won't. I faced my worst moment with the Queen, obeying her instructions to straighten her quarters, and when she paddled me I only wanted to please her more! That is the key, Brenn. I love her and want to please her and I do not care precisely why."

"What do you mean, 'why'?"

"Do I want to please her because she is beautiful and sweet? Or does she seem beautiful and sweet to me because she is strict and demanding? I don't know and I don't care. We were all alone, the Queen and I. No one was there, and the Queen said that I had taught her things. I couldn't imagine what. It didn't matter what she said, it was the tone of her voice, her air of easy command, the way she felt of my breasts, cuddled me, kissed me, and punished me. I was so sore by then, and yet I was utterly pliant."

She paused.

She kissed me lovingly, her tongue playing on my teeth.

"Brenn, you know how big the King is, what a tall man!"

"He's larger than life in all ways," I said.

"Yes, well, after the banquet, when I was given to him, I knew a kind of exalted fear. The sound of his deep voice produced a great dreamy and lofty abandon in me. He plunged his cock into me, Brenn, his cock, and it filled me as I've never been filled, worked me as I've never been worked. Oh, you do not mind my confessing this, do you?"

"Certainly not," I murmured. "Go on."

"He never stripped off his clothes or went near the bed, but simply took me as if I were a light, diminutive thing that he could taste effortlessly, pumping into me as he remained standing. And when he was finished with me, he had the groom slip a jeweled red glove over his right hand, and he plunged his fingers into me and touched secret places I hadn't known existed, as if my most private parts were known to him, like a valley in which he'd wandered many a time. Brenn, I was gasping, groaning, out of my mind. I have never been so thoroughly worked, drained."

"Yes . . . ," I said.

"This was after the evening supper in the gardens, as I said, and I hoped and prayed he'd let me sleep somewhere in his chamber, anywhere, but he kissed me goodbye tenderly, and gave me over to Lady Eva and said to her that I must be trained in the Queen's Stables, Brenn! That I was to be a pony girl for the Queen.

"Lady Eva said this was a great honor and that I'd be taken there very soon. Brenn, what can this mean? I know what the words signify, but what will it be like to become a filly in harness pulling a coach or a chariot!"

"I don't know, Sybil," I confessed. "But I'm to find out what it means to be a steed myself."

"I hope it's like the X cross in the garden," she said with a deep sigh. She smiled sleepily and dreamily. "I love being bound! I love the feel of the straps on my wrists and my ankles. I love the fragrance of the leather and gilding. I love the grooms who have firm hands. They don't all have firm hands."

"No."

"It was late, very late, when the King sent me off. The whole castle was quiet. Yet who should come down the passage but the Grand Duke? And Lady Eva allowed him some minutes with me in his chamber! I had not even been bathed since I was with the King, but when Lady Eva told the Grand Duke, he thought it amusing that she even cared.

"I was brought on hands and knees by a leash into his quarters. Why, it had the grandeur of an audience hall, his immense parlor, and he examined me all over, kissing me and squeezing my flesh, and burying his face in my hair. Such an elegant man. He said he was honored to share my little secret bower with the King. When he took me, it was with hard slow thrusts. He's older, of course. But he was incomparable in his grace, his deliberation, his slow rhythm. He brought out of me all I had left to give when I'd thought I had nothing. And like the King, he was standing while he took me. He called me his sweet little parcel, and his finchling, and he teased me about being a plump little bird with a very red tail. It might have sounded vulgar coming from someone else, 'tail.' I mean such a common word! But from him it sounded affectionate and tantalizing to me.

"He did spank me a little, but then Lady Eva was standing by, and the great clock in his parlor struck the hour and he let me go."

"Hmmm, I wish I had seen him," I said, "known who he was. Sybil, you do realize the nature of this paradise, don't you, that there are all kinds of strength, all flavors of mastery."

"Yes, darling, and he was such a distinguished man!"

"Yes, an older distinguished man."

"And then the King and the Queen and . . ." She sighed.

"Yes, all of them."

"What do I want, Brenn?" she asked. "Do I want to be the Queen's filly or do I want to be the Grand Duke's little finchling with a very red tail?"

"Maybe you'll come to be both, Sybil," I said. I snuggled against her, felt her hot breasts pulsing against my chest, her hand playing idly on my back.

"Brenn, do you think anyone will come looking for us?" she asked.

I laughed. It woke me out of my drowsiness to laugh. "I don't care if someone comes looking for me," I said.

"Nor do I, but I asked Lady Eva about it before she gave me over to be bathed. She said the King and Queen would never hear such requests. No one looking for us would get past the gates. I was so glad to hear this."

"They'll simply disown us, perhaps," I said. "Again, I don't care. I've cared about a multitude of things in the last twenty-four hours, but about that I do not care."

She was silent. I opened my eyes. She had finally dozed off, and slept peacefully and deeply. I touched her lips carefully with my fingers. Sweet Sybil.

viii

The following evening we were anointed in the Goddess Grove. We'd spent the day being measured, tested in many ways, and trained in simple deportment, how to answer any and all questions with modesty and respect, and how to eat and fetch with our teeth and not our hands. We were together some of the time and at other times not. We were given potions to drink and studied for our behavior afterwards. One potion enflamed me so miserably that I wept. Another potion made me sleep at once. In a yard, we were made to trot in a circle around a central pillar and spanked hard as we did it, and then we were groomed meticulously, our nails being trimmed. And I was shaved more than once by the gentlest barbers. But not my pubic hair or any body hair. My pubic hair was carefully groomed, fluffed, even curled a bit here and there, though it was curly enough already.

At last at dark, we were assembled with ten other new slaves to be anointed.

The Goddess Grove was venerable, ancient, we were told. It had fallen into ruin in the old kingdom, but our new monarchs had restored it.

Our procession moved silently through the great gardens and then out and down a broad path towards it with lighted torches. Many lords and ladies watched.

It was a place of thick soft grass and abundant flowers.

A great half circle of arches in the grove held some twelve antique statues—some broken, some whole—of gods and goddesses. Flickering lamps illuminated each of these figures or groupings. I knew Aphrodite spanking her disobedient Cupid with a sandal, and Dionysius and the great god Pan. I knew Apollo as he tried to capture Daphne. And Priapus, yes. Others I could not identify. The grass was cool and torches were flaring everywhere, but the light was shadowy and an air of mystery enveloped us.

The King and Queen came into the grove and received each of us by name, for kisses and embraces, and we were prompted to repeat our vows to serve in our own words. Sybil was positioned some distance from me, but I got a good glimpse of her and she looked glorious, her hair never more lustrous and beautifully groomed with flowers and jewels.

Then as the Lord High Chamberlain held the oils for the King, we were anointed as slaves of the realm, by the King's thumbprint on our foreheads, and the Queen decorated our heads with green garlands. Lady Eva came forward to anoint our private parts and claim them for the pleasure of the realm as indeed our entire persons were claimed. There was the strong sweet smell of gardenias and lilies everywhere. And we were made to kneel down before our sovereigns to receive their final blessing.

The King wished us a long life in the kingdom and reminded us of our protections and promises. His voice was natural and sincere as if he trusted completely to the words themselves. There was no cloying artificiality.

"Tomorrow," said my groom as he led me away, "you'll be a plaything of the King. And mark you scramble to obey his slightest command. To be the King's pet is a great honor."

10

BEAUTY:
THE AGONY OF
LORD STEFAN

i

He was a man of good height, clean limbed and well built, with a gentle, appealing face and eyes of near-perfect cobalt blue that made Beauty think of fine glazed porcelain. He had a youthful manner, not becoming of necessity in a man of his age, but not off-putting either. Beauty liked it.

And in his narrow face and almond-shaped eyes, Beauty could see something of the late Queen Eleanor, his first cousin.

But his real charm lay in his fine manners and his vibrant and tender voice, coupled with a thoughtful reticence. That one so handsome should seem so unaware of it, well, that too had its appeal and perhaps united all of the other seductive traits he possessed in the eyes of Beauty.

"Lord Stefan, please, be at your ease," Beauty said. She sat opposite him at the table, the morning sun spilling down into her private parlor from the high-arched windows. "You need hold nothing back from me, my lord. I am your queen. I am listening."

It was plain he wanted to open his soul. Tears hovered in his eyes suddenly, and Tristan who sat beside him, Tristan who was taller, stronger, and so much more imposing, reached out for Lord Stefan as he might to a younger brother.

Long years ago, when Beauty and Tristan had been slaves together on their return voyage from the sultanate, Tristan had told her all of his love for this diffident and sweet lord who had failed to be Tristan's master. And Beauty had forgotten none of the story. Lord Stefan and Tristan had known each other and loved each other before Tristan was brought as a bound and naked slave to the feet of Queen Eleanor. What a disaster that she'd given Tristan over to the fearful and anxious Lord Stefan to master.

Lord Stefan's hair was a golden brown, exquisitely highlighted by the sun, and that he wore it very long and very full gave him a slight suggestion of the feminine. But his shaven beard and mustache were thick and had left a dark shadow on his face, attesting to his virility. And then there was the touch of hair on the backs of his wrists and even on his long fingers. And the depth of his voice, so like a smooth thick syrup when he spoke. But then what about the exquisite character of his dress, his lace shirt studded with tiny pearls and the heavy slashed balloon sleeves that covered it with the lining of violet silk? It was all rather confusing. Virility, femininity—for Beauty they had more to do with the subtle presentation of self than any physical attributes.

And in Lord Stefan's eyes, Beauty saw timidity and anguish that might belong to any soul, regardless of gender.

As for his slave Becca, what an icy and merciless gaze she cast on him from her place in the corner, where, naked and still, she rested back on her heels gazing at him. Her breasts were almost too big to be beautiful, but not quite. And her mouth was not cruel but coldly perfect. Her flaxen hair, parted in the middle, made Beauty think of her own hair. She had an oval face not unlike Beauty's face as well and large well-shaped hands. She sat there utterly still as if she controlled every fiber of her physical being. Her eyes were paler than those of her master, an ice blue as vivid as the coral tint of her lips and her nipples.

She put Beauty in mind of a white panther if such a thing existed—a sleek white cat the size of a human.

"Your Majesty," said Lord Stefan. "I cannot bear it anymore. I am unable to pretend any longer. In the last years of the old kingdom, I died on the vine like everyone else. No, Tristan, don't protest. I did. You know I did. I might as well have lived in any kingdom or no kingdom at all. I kept to my chambers with Becca. And it was a farce, I tell you, whenever we appeared together before others."

Beauty understood. Of course. But she didn't say so. I am living my own farce, she thought, pretending that I love wielding the paddle and the strap, pretending that I delight in the submission of others. I admire it, and I envy it, but I don't delight in it. I delight in the glory of the Court, the realm, the well-run kingdom of Bellavalten, the kingdom they now call Beauty's Kingdom, but I don't delight in anyone's submission. It does not send my blood rising. But this Beauty had confessed to no one and she did not confess it now.

Of course Laurent knew. Laurent knew Beauty as he knew himself, and he had always known how to handle her, take her, thrill her, and leave her satisfied. But they had never really spoken of it, not in the old days before the gates of the kingdom came crashing shut behind them.

And now in the midst of the great revival of the immense Court that swirled around them, Laurent assured Beauty that she must in all things please herself.

"If it does not come naturally to you to enjoy disciplining slaves," he'd said, "then don't do it, my darling. Leave it to Lady Eva. Leave it to me. Leave it to your grooms. Who says that you must enjoy wielding the paddle? You are queen here, Beauty. Not Eleanor. Eleanor is gone. All those around you long only to make you happy day and night."

But Beauty had not been entirely comforted by Laurent's words. She wanted a deeper immersion in the thrilling complexities of the kingdom, and held herself to be too timid and unsure.

She struggled now to clear her mind and look at Lord Stefan, who was in such need of her.

"And how so is it all a farce, my lord?" she asked him. Uppermost in her thoughts was the resolve to listen, to be attentive, to comfort, and to solve the problem of this soul who depended so upon her.

"I long to serve," said Lord Stefan in a tremulous voice. He looked directly into her eyes. That was hardly difficult for her or anyone, thought Beauty. For what did her eyes say, but that she wanted so to help him? "My queen, I long to serve with all my heart! I always have. My cousin the late queen despised me utterly for it, forbade me ever to speak of it to her or to others, excoriated me for my unseemly weakness."

Beauty said nothing. Tristan leaned closer to his friend, the fingers of his left hand gently cradling Lord Stefan's shoulder.

Nothing quivered at all in the alabaster face of the feline Becca. Indifferent as a cat. As secretive and aloof.

"Go on, my lord, tell me all," said Beauty. Her heart went out to Stefan.

"You know there was an old custom in the kingdom, that on Midsummer Eve, those of the Court who wanted to be slaves could become slaves—but only to be sent to the village. And the Queen forbade me from ever disgracing the royal family by such a step, threatening me with banishment if I were even to suggest it. And so I kept my peace and I lived as one condemned to burn with passion forever without respite, and did what I could, sought what I could in secret." His eyes shifted, lighted upon Becca, and then veered away as if he had been slapped. He looked to Beauty. "Your Majesty, now that the new kingdom blossoms like a magic garden planted and watered by the wise women of legend, I am in ever-increasing agony!"

"My lord, what would you like me to do?" asked Beauty. "Hasn't my lord, the King, set up a manor house where you might go to seek the discipline you so crave, without judgment?" *Oh, how I should like to go there myself!*

"Yes, my queen, and it was very generous of the King to allow this," Stefan replied.

"Nonsense, my lord, the King was happy to allow it. And I am happy that it is allowed. We do not conform to the ideas of the late Queen Eleanor."

"My queen," Tristan said. He spoke softly, haltingly, waiting for Beauty's permission to continue. She nodded at once. And he went on, "What Stefan wants is to come to live with me permanently in my household."

"Ah, well why not?" said Beauty. "I can see no reason to prohibit it."

"But as my naked slave," said Tristan, "entirely subject to my authority and bound to me for six months like any postulant to the kingdom, and thereafter for years of his own free will and mine."

"Ah. Well, I see no objection to it whatsoever," said the Queen. "And my lord, the King, has entrusted this matter entirely to me, and won't question my decision. Why not, Lord Stefan? Why not?"

Lord Stefan sat back and closed his eyes. A long shudder passed through him. Obviously he was overcome with gratitude. Yet he was afraid. He was tense. He was still anxious.

"But you do realize, my lord," said Beauty. "That this may be far more difficult for you than you now realize."

"I have explained the terms on which I will accept this," said Tristan gently, gesturing with his open palm. "I have told Stefan that there will be no special rules for him, or special allowances."

"And you are right. There cannot be any special allowances," said Beauty. "For the discipline of the kingdom is the citadel of all slaves and their masters or mistresses."

"I understand, my queen," said Lord Stefan. "I have every confidence that Tristan, my new master, will allow no half measures." A deep blush came over Stefan's face. He glanced at Tristan, then lowered his eyes. Such pain. Such fear.

"And Stefan understands as well," said Beauty, "that he will not be shielded from the eyes of others in any certain safety in your house, does he not, Tristan? He cannot be closeted away there with any guarantee of perfect privacy. Once he becomes a slave of the kingdom, inevitably this will be known, and someone sooner or later, someone of his former kith or kindred, will see him in his new state. From that he cannot be protected. It is a practical fact as well as a matter of propriety. No slave is given special concealment."

Tristan glanced at Stefan.

"I do understand," said Stefan under his breath, gazing at the Queen. But she could see the timidity, the uncertainty.

He is taller than me, Beauty thought, yet he tilts his head so that he is looking up at me. That is his manner, always to be looking up even at those who are shorter, smaller than he is. Very pretty and in a slave irresistibly charming.

"Frankly, it terrifies me," said Lord Stefan. "I cannot but think of being seen by those at Court, I cannot bear to think of ever being brought into the gardens and displayed, I cannot bear to think of those who'd supped with me and talked with me, and hunted with me and lived with me suddenly having me naked and at their feet. But I have no choice but to pursue this path, and I have no hope except that Tristan will bring me along with gentleness and indulgence and some mercy on me for my fears. I cannot—" He broke off helplessly.

Tristan nodded silently at Beauty. There was a trace of a smile on his full lips. His blue eyes were filled with patience and understanding, and when he embraced Stefan again it was tenderly.

"Well, my lord," said Beauty, "no man in the kingdom knows more of what it means to master and to serve—no man except the King—than Prince Tristan."

"Yes, my queen," said Lord Stefan. His eyes were thick with tears. "I am so grateful to you."

Then why are you still so miserable, thought Beauty. And why am I so afraid for you?

"And may I then take my Lord Stefan with me now?" asked Tristan. "My servants may pack up all that belongs to him and store this safely in my house? And then we need trouble you no more with this."

"Ah, not quite so simple," said the Queen. She was thinking, pondering, thinking of all the great ways of Bellavalten and the principles that lay behind them. She looked at the cold and comely Becca who was staring forward as before, as if she heard nothing when in fact she heard everything.

"I shall tell you how it will be," Beauty said. "In that you have come to me for an innovation, I shall set the terms of it."

Her eyes moved idly over the distant window, and over the many objects of the room waked by morning sun, as she continued speaking.

"Given that you are who you are, I shall arrange it for you. Now, tonight, or tomorrow night, or the night after—Tristan, you decide—the King and I, before the usual grand feast, will come down to your manor house, and there in a garden grove or fountain court of your choosing, you will present your new and naked slave to us for anointing. We will hear his vows—to serve with his whole heart for six months—and then we shall leave him to you. And then it is in your hands, Prince, as to when, if ever, you bring him into the great gardens of the castle with you, or what you do with him on all accounts."

No one spoke. But the casual lift of Beauty's right hand held them in abeyance.

"In three nights," said Tristan earnestly. "Please, my queen. Give me three nights to work with him before he's to be anointed. I can turn him out beautifully in three nights, surely."

Looking around the room as before, Beauty continued:

"Very well, three nights it shall be. But he must be anointed."

"Yes, my queen."

"And I give you now the benefit of my experience." She lowered her voice as if to underscore the importance of her words. "Be strict, very strict, and don't wait too long, Tristan, to bring your obedient slave to Court, and whip your charge yourself along the castle Bridle Path."

Lord Stefan flinched. He stared forward, his lips quivering. Beauty caught this though she was not looking directly at him.

"Choose a late hour if you like," said Beauty, looking at the distant window. "When not many are about, for the first time. It doesn't matter. But don't wait too long. And at the end of six months, I trust to your judgment that this must be a perfect novice to take his vows for another two years. Do not present him for that moment if he is truly unworthy."

Silence.

Slowly Beauty turned and looked at Lord Stefan. The color had drained from his face and he was staring at her. His mouth, so tender and boyish, so vulnerable, was still quivering. But there was a wild gleam in his eyes that was more than his tears sparkling in the sunlight.

"I understand," said Tristan. "I understand completely. And if I cannot put Stefan forward as a worthy slave at the end of six months?"

"Well, then that will require extraordinary measures," said Beauty. "A period of retirement perhaps from the kingdom or a year of gentle imprisonment in Lord Stefan's old quarters. I do not know which. I cannot say. But I say only that Lord Stefan will not be permitted to serve if he cannot serve, any more than any other slave who fails at it. And we shall have no hybrids here, no creatures who are half slave and half master. We shall have no breakdown of ritual or discipline which could spell ruin for all. What I allow, I will allow. But it shall be enshrined for all to know, and shall have its consistency and its principles." She sighed. "I owe this," she said, "to every single slave in the realm. I owe this to every single master as well."

"I understand," Tristan hastened to say again.

"Lord Stefan?" Beauty looked at him expectantly.

"Yes, my queen," Lord Stefan said. His voice was low. He swallowed. "I am your grateful servant."

"Be certain you do understand."

"Yes, my queen." His voice was barely audible. But she would settle for it. "My queen, I've had years to think on this, years to suffer over it, years to dream of a moment such as this."

Beauty nodded. She smiled.

"You may go, my lords," she said. "On the third night, at dusk, Prince, have your slave ready for us. The Lord Chamberlain will appear with us bearing the sacred oils for the anointing."

They were on their feet, both of them, bowing to Beauty.

"And what of this grave Egyptian cat here?" asked Beauty pointing to Becca.

"I shall give her over to Lord Gregory, my queen," said Stefan without so much as a glance at Becca. No affection there obviously. "Unless Your Majesty wishes me to do something else to make future arrangements for her. She's served faithfully and well for two years." He clearly didn't want to say more or reveal more and he was not going to look at Becca.

"I shall see to her then. Leave me."

Beauty turned again towards the window. She loved the play of the sun on the furnishings of the room—on the ornate silver vessels on the sideboard, on the mirrors in their gilded frames, on the polished wood of the bed, the chairs, the table.

Slowly her eyes fixed on Becca, who at once glanced down, though it was plainly obvious she'd been studying Beauty.

How cool and unruffled she appeared, her breasts heaving just a little.

Then slowly Becca looked up, and unbidden spoke in a deep cold voice, her eyes burning as she stared at Beauty.

"And now shall I be your harsh and secret mistress as well!" She sneered.

Beauty was silently stunned. She marveled. But she held the girl's gaze effortlessly.

"Don't be a fool, my girl," said Beauty calmly.

At once Becca looked down and the fingers of her right hand began to tremble.

So that is all it takes, thought Beauty, just that little show of strength and dominance and she is undone, is she?

"I know your game," said Beauty in the same calm voice. "I know what your service to Lord Stefan has been like. You were given a chance when we took the twin crowns to declare whether you chose to remain. And choose to remain you did. But you were your master's secret mistress then, his secret tormentor. And obviously for all the latitude allowed you by your lord, you didn't teach him to love you or to need you."

The girl made not a sound, but her face changed completely. Her eyes grew bright and then narrowed and her lips moved and then she bit her lower lip but nothing else about her changed.

"Yes, my queen," she whispered. It was a low fearful whisper. A terrible sadness came over her face as she stared at the floor, or perhaps at Beauty's slippers.

"Well, now that the unique conditions of your life have changed," said Beauty, "I give you another chance to leave the kingdom. Is that what you want? I'll see that you're dressed, paid out, and gone before dusk. Or would you have another night or so to contemplate your decision?"

Silence. The sun was moving high in the sky and the entire chamber was filled now with light. The mirrors were sheets of reflected gold. And a great starburst of light emanated from one of the jeweled goblets set out on the sideboard.

"No, my queen," said Becca. "I need no further time to decide. Forgive me."

"You're in my hands as you were before?" asked Beauty. She drew her eyes away from the sparkling goblet and looked at the girl.

"Yes, my queen, inalterably, forever."

"Ah, now that is a tone I like," said Beauty. She made it a point to be polite. She took no exultation in the girl's miscalculation. "Ring the bell there for my attendant."

The girl obeyed, quickly pulling the long embroidered sash that hung beside the bed, and then she returned to her former position. There was a bloom to her cheeks. And a small blue vein throbbed in her temple. Her hands were definitely trembling.

"My queen," she whispered, her head bowed, her dark smoky eyebrows drawn together in obvious distress. "May I speak?"

"Yes, you may, but be wise when you do," said Beauty.

"I am so sorry that I have offended you."

Well, I know precisely why you did and what you thought, Beauty mused to herself. But she said nothing.

"I beg to be restored to your good graces."

The young attendant Tereus appeared, who had become Beauty's favorite of late, the boy who knew just how to make all things pleasant for her, and how to fulfill her wishes. A freckled boy with tousled strawberry-blond hair, he did not possess great beauty, but was profoundly appealing with his sweet smile, ruddy cheeks, and his natural tendency to protect and support the Queen in all matters great and small. And others did speak of him all the time as "delectable."

"Tereus, send a messenger to the village and to Prince Dmitri. Ask the Prince to come to my chambers here. Tell him when he arrives that he is to take this girl under his authority."

She wondered if the girl understood the implications of this summons.

Only two nights ago, she'd seen Prince Dmitri, resplendent in his glistening tunic of Baudekyn, attending to his duties as the minister of the Place of Public Punishment. She'd seen his fierce scowling face and swift gestures as he spanked a quivering slave boy furiously towards the Public Turntable. She'd heard his strict and menacing voice as he'd pulled the boy up to look into his flinching eyes. "Play games with me? I'll see that every ounce of rebellion is purged from you!"

The Captain of the Guard, on the sidelines, had been the picture of admiration. "He's a terror," he confided to Beauty. "He's perfect. He descends on them like a windstorm!"

"Yes," Laurent had said as he stood idly by with Alexi and Lady Eva. "A windstorm of blows and carefully chosen words. And words do mean so very much in the proper training of slaves."

"Everyone, from the whipping masters to the lowliest grooms," Alexi had said, "to the humblest villager and the greatest lord, is in his thrall. He's made of mundane punishments a nightly pageant."

Becca, though her hands trembled and her eyes were glazed, gave no indication that she knew what awaited her. But then, thought Beauty, she is very clever, clever enough to know I share Lord Stefan's inclinations. She knows. And therefore likely she had heard and seen much. And perhaps she is resigned to it.

"I'm giving you to Prince Dmitri," Beauty said. "And only when he tells me that you are chastened and tuned to a new song, will I summon you back to Court."

"Yes, my queen," the girl whispered. She started to say something else but stopped.

"Pray, continue," Beauty said. "Say what you will while you have the chance with me."

"My fault is one of bitterness," the girl said. Her voice was thick now, quite a change from her iron tone earlier. "I am guilty of resenting my former master." This was a shocking admission yet it came easily to her as if some faith in the truth of her words guided her. Her forehead was creased with an anguished frown.

"I know," said Beauty. "I understand quite completely. And that's why I gave you an opportunity to reaffirm your decision for the kingdom. Trust in me that the kingdom will not fail you."

Tears. The girl could hold them back no longer. But this reply had taken her aback. She was unsettled.

"Come here to me, Becca," said Beauty.

Becca approached on her hands and knees and Beauty received her with tender gestures, pressing the girl's face gently into her lap. She stroked the girl's thick fair hair—so like her own—and her flawless naked back. "Come," she said softly. "Kiss me."

At once Becca obeyed, rising up on her knees and offering her mouth to Beauty. Her kiss was firm, not yielding, an unhurried offering of intense fervor. And Becca's long hair mingled with Beauty's hair.

"Such a reservoir of devotion to be drunk from this precious cup," said Beauty. She smoothed Becca's hair back from her forehead, and the girl's eyes fixed on her, as if deliberately inviting reprimand.

"Yes," the girl whispered. "Oh, yes, my beloved queen, and he never wanted it! Never asked for it, never—" She stopped, ashamed, and broke into silent sobs. She closed her eyes and waited, it seemed, for what might come.

Such anguish.

"I know, my darling. I understand."

There was an air to Becca of utter silent submission—submission to the moment, submission to Beauty, submission to the kingdom, but, more significant, submission to her own nature, her own soul.

Gradually, she opened her eyes. A deeply probing expression came over Becca, and she searched Beauty's face.

"If only I might take my time myself with you," said Beauty. "But there are others now waiting on me, more decisions to be made, audiences to be given. Don't take lightly your time in Prince Dmitri's hands. Don't be so foolish as to waste what he offers you. I deliver you to him with love of you, my dear, as certainly as I have delivered your master to Prince Tristan. You understand?"

"My queen," the girl said. The words came out like a deep sigh. Without permission, she inclined towards Beauty, and carefully lay her head on Beauty's shoulder.

Beauty found her huge breasts irresistible. She lifted Becca and moved her back so that she might kiss her breasts slowly, savoring the texture and fragrance of the skin. The coral nipples were like raisins.

Vaguely, it occurred to her that Becca might have gotten from Beauty precisely what Becca wanted. Of course. She smiled. How could Beauty have confused or surprised one so experienced? The girl's limpid grace and thoughtful expression intrigued her. She longed to lay bare the complexities locked within the girl, the subtle entangled secrets that Lord Stefan likely had never found compelling.

"No," said Beauty, "you won't waste Prince Dmitri's precious heat, will you, because you yourself know what it means to have been wasted."

The softest bitter laugh came from the girl's lips, not a challenge but an affirmation. She smiled, and her eyes closed, and tears welled from under her long lids, and she said again, "My queen," as Beauty kissed her.

The mysteries of her own heart troubled Beauty.

But she knew that, whatever the case, she had done right this morning by this girl, and by Lord Stefan, and by her beloved Tristan. And if that was so, then she had done right by herself, her troubled and tremulous self.

Slowly, she extricated herself from Becca's embrace and gestured for her to kneel in the customary place beside the hearth. It was an agony to let her go, to see her drawing away, to lose the warmth and fragrance of her.

A most important conference had been called this morning. Beauty must dress for this, and for the audiences in the great hall after it. So many demands. But then such was her life and she was eager for it.

She rose and moved past the girl indifferently and into her small parlor. There on her writing desk were her sheets of parchment and her ink and quills trimmed and prepared by Tereus.

Beauty sat down in the small carved chair and began to write:

Prince Dmitri,
  This is a proud and haughty girl, thoroughly spoiled but capable of reformation. The harshest and most effective instruments of the village

are recommended. I commit her to your authority and your judgment for as long as you think best. And she is not to be returned until she has completely surrendered to your utmost satisfaction.

To this Beauty signed her name quickly, and then blotted the note carefully. She rolled the stiff page into a small tight scroll, binding it with one of the many scarlet ribbons laid out for the purpose. Then into a small silver cylinder, she placed the note. And with a bit of wax and the impress of her ring she sealed the cap of the cylinder.

She approached the girl who had not moved an inch from her former position. Something about the girl from the back made her think of herself. It was not only the flaxen hair. It was the girl's size and proportions. They were made from the same physical mold, it seemed, Beauty and this girl, though how different was Becca in temperament.

"Kneel up and open your mouth," she said.

At once Becca did as she was commanded. Beauty slipped the silver cylinder sideways into her mouth, like a bit. The girl was shocked. Clearly no one had put a gag or a bit into her mouth in a very long time. But she held the cylinder between her teeth obediently. She began to shiver.

Tereus had only just returned.

"The message has been sent, my queen."

"Give the little parcel here to the Prince when he comes," she said. "My instructions are there." She pointed to the cylinder.

Becca's eyes were squeezed shut and she was crying. Yes, she is so like me, thought Beauty suddenly. This girl tugged at her heart, but Beauty only smiled. I know what she needs, she thought. I shall not fail her any more than I have failed Lord Stefan.

ii

Outside the council chamber, Beauty paused. She could hear the busy voices of those within. She knew that she was late. So many decisions had to be made. There was so much business every day. But she waited. She stood quiet, her attendants waiting unquestioningly behind her, and her beloved pet, Brenn, kneeling on all fours at her side.

Why had she not punished Becca for impertinence herself? It would have been easy enough to do. She knew how to wield the paddle. Why had it not given her pleasure to think of disciplining the girl into submission the way she herself had once been schooled in submission—through pain and pleasure? Beauty had surrendered utterly and sublimely to her punishments, glorying in them, grateful for cold implacable authority as much as for affection, grateful for severity as for ardor, hungering for engulfing discipline as much as love.

She had been tempted, yes, for just a moment. But the girl for all her anxiety and confusion had not really captured Beauty's keen interest. If Beauty were ever to wield the paddle and the strap with passion it would be for a slave more like this one, Brenn, whose stout soul bewitched her, a slave she could break in the name of perfection rather than mere correction, a slave whose lust for discipline was his lure. And who knew, perhaps someday, someday she could do this. She did not know.

As she looked down at Brenn, at his soft curly black hair, and straight shoulders, a shadow fell over her, and she woke from her thoughts to see the King standing there.

"What is it, dearest?" Laurent whispered. "We're all waiting. Just the usual matters, nothing more."

When she did not answer, Laurent spoke to the slave beside her.

"Brenn, you go in now and kneel by the Queen's chair." He motioned to the attendants to leave them as well.

At once Brenn moved to obey, and the King and Queen, outside the doors to the council chamber, were alone.

"Beauty, what is it?" Laurent asked. "You're not still troubled by self-doubts, are you, my lovely one?"

Beauty wished she could find words to answer, to explain.

"Forgive me, my lord," she said. "I'm coming better to understand myself every day."

"I have always understood you," said Laurent. "You cannot be all things to all subjects, Beauty. You can only love them in your own way."

She smiled. "My own way," she said. "Yes, my own way."

"Did Eleanor ever offer her slaves understanding or comfort?" Laurent pressed. "Did Eleanor ever grasp the power of loving discipline rather than severity and disdain?"

Beauty smiled. "No, you're right. She never did understand the subtleties."

"Beauty," he said as he bent to kiss her. "Be the Queen of Bellavalten in your own way."

It was enough for now, wasn't it? She nodded. She put her hand into Laurent's hand.

No sooner had they stepped into the council chamber, and no sooner had those gathered there risen to bow and to greet them, than she was the confident and smiling queen once more. Bellavalten, she thought, how deeply I do love you.

And how very odd, wasn't it, that she had no doubt that Bellavalten loved her in return.

II

BEAUTY:
A STORY
OF THE
OLD KINGDOM

The enigmatic Lexius, tall, slender, dark skinned, and dark eyed—the silken and seductive steward of the Sultan whom Laurent had brought back to Bellavalten as a slave, was indeed coming. Two letters reached the kingdom before he did. And it was the opinion of Alexi that Lexius might arrive at any moment.

"Of course I want to hear the whole story," said Laurent. "What did he do? What do you mean he broke the old queen's heart?"

Beauty walked down the long corridor with Laurent, her left hand on his right hand, both of them sumptuously dressed for yet another day of official decisions, but headed now to a small hall where they could meet only with the inner circle, so to speak—Alexi, Dmitri, Rosalynd, Elena, and the indispensable Lady Eva. No important meeting took place without the attendance of Lady Eva, busy as she might be with the postulant slaves and the novices.

"If some scandal surrounds this man, we should know of it," Beauty affirmed. "And I know, my lord, how he's always fascinated you."

"And you mean to say, lovely one, that he didn't fascinate you?" asked Laurent. He was cheerful, in good spirits as always. He woke each single morning with a new enthusiasm for life, fully embracing his priapic duties with a stamina that amazed Beauty. But then Laurent's stamina, in all forms, had always amazed Beauty, she had to admit, so why was she surprised at this?

"Yes, he fascinates me," said Beauty. "But I was never drawn to him once you made him your plaything. But as I said, we must find out what actually happened."

It was a lovely day of balmy breezes and blue skies, with only a thin mist streaking the sky over the valley here and there, and likely to burn off by noon.

All was well with the realm, but yesterday had been an exhausting day for the monarchs, with many audiences and decisions to be made. Three returning grooms—dismissed by the late queen—had asked for an audience, and the Court had heard their plea, along with the petitions of others, for hours on end. Two beautiful dark-skinned African eunuchs had come to the kingdom, begging for sanctuary, so to speak, and a strange and mighty northern lord appeared with two naked slaves trained by him in a remote castle whom he wanted to sell to the kingdom "for their own good." Artists and merchants petitioned to be admitted to the villages and hamlets. So many different matters to consider.

Beauty was happy today to be meeting only with the small council, and she greeted those standing about the table with genuine warmth.

"Well, be seated all," Laurent said. "Let's have some cider, if you will, and perhaps some sweetmeats, and get to talking straightaway about Lexius."

Laurent took the head of the table and Beauty the chair to his right. Alexi sat down opposite Beauty, with Dmitri beside him, and the ladies across from one another after that. Lady Eva settled at the foot of the table with her quill and ink, and bound book for note taking.

"So what is all the mystery?" asked Beauty.

At once the others looked to Alexi, and he, seeing this, made a small graceful gesture of acceptance with both hands. He looked most beautiful this morning to Beauty, with his auburn hair now considerably longer than it had been at their first meeting, a prince from a tapestry, in her mind, and as always he was impeccably turned out in the finest patterned silk tunic, and adornments that suggested the treasures of Byzantium.

No one devoted to the new kingdom had given any more passion and devotion than Alexi. Not even Dmitri, who worked tirelessly every day to refine the Place of Public Punishment, or Lady Eva herself, or even

Rosalynd and Elena, who were in charge of the nightly spectacles in the castle gardens.

Beauty had a special love for these two sisters who'd shared captivity in the sultanate, and she found them most appealing. Rosalynd in her mind had attained the pinnacle of buxom voluptuousness, whereas the smaller, more delicate Elena was a clever-tongued tasty sylph with high pointed breasts and a low purring voice that delighted Beauty.

"I shall be spokesman, then, why not?" said Alexi, raising his eyebrows and settling against the carved back of the chair. "I'll tell what I know. But some things I do not know, and perhaps others here will be inspired by my candor."

"What the hell happened?" asked Laurent with a little wink and smile. "Get to it! We were bound together night after night in the hold of the ship that brought us back here, he and I, bound, bound by our delicious desires. I probably did more to train him than anyone who came after."

That produced a low respectful bit of laughter from everyone.

"Well, I think you did," said Alexi. "As you know he was brought before the Queen, accepted reluctantly because the Queen would not have anyone choose slavery of his own will, and then packed off to the kitchen. But the report soon came upstairs that he was wilting like a lily under the coarse treatment of the servants and ought to be tended with more care. So she sent for him."

He paused and shrugged. "I was her favorite as everyone knew," he said, his voice philosophical rather than mocking, "and I can't say I was delighted to see him absorb so much of her attention."

"Of course not," said Laurent, with a gesture for Alexi to continue.

"Well, she had time enough for both of us," said Alexi. "And Lexius was as abject and servile as any naked slave who ever kissed the Queen's slippers. He was graceful by instinct, and knew subtleties of service that no one can teach. He had a lissome charm and an eloquence in ignominy that was breathtaking. Of course I did with him what I had done before with others—I seduced him while the Queen slept and proved a harsher master than she was a mistress."

"Ah, so that's how it was with you two," said Laurent.

"Yes," said Alexi. "Lexius taught me how to master him in his submission. We had to be careful, of course. The old queen forbade all such trysts among her slaves, though they happened throughout the castle nightly. And he and I were never caught. Meanwhile the Queen delighted in talking about how Lexius had once been a powerful steward of slaves under his former master, the Sultan, and constantly demanded he offer up to her refinements and innovations in the ways slaves should be displayed and used at Court. And he was more than willing to do it.

"Then at night he became my adoring attendant! Well, all this might have gone on for years and years, but the Captain of the Guard came up and informed the Queen that the sultanate was in grave danger, and almost certain to be destroyed. Soldiers had heard the rumors from the sailors putting in. And soon the Queen confirmed the worst: a powerful army was gathering to invade the sultanate and other realms like it.

"The Captain of the Guard was adamant that if he were to rescue Dmitri, Rosalynd, and Elena, he had to have Lexius with him. Lexius knew the sultanate after his years there. He could find a way for the Captain to accomplish the rescue speedily, and speed was of the utmost importance.

"So the Queen had Lexius groomed and dressed from head to toe, and armed for battle. Lexius was well acquainted with weapons, and swore to assist the Captain in every possible way. And off they went at once to the docks to board the ship for the secretive mission.

"Well, you can imagine what this must have been like for Lexius who for two years at least had been a naked plaything. Here he was once again possessed of the implements of power.

"He and the Captain accomplished the mission, with only a few nights to spare, and before they even returned the sultanate was destroyed utterly. Lexius and the Captain had both warned the Sultan of what was to come, by letters left for him which he would not receive until they were safely away with their charges. But whether that was of any help at all no one ever knew. The sultanate was obliterated. And the custom of pleasure slavery was stamped out in that land forever, though not by persons who had the slightest interest in it. It simply fell out that way."

"And so you were all brought back at that time," Beauty said. She paused and looked at Dmitri.

"Yes, my queen," Dmitri said. "It was all quite sudden. To be immersed in the village again was quite sudden."

Rosalynd and Elena laughed knowingly, and Elena shook her head.

"Go on, Alexi," said Beauty.

"Well, I did not before this time think the old queen had loved

Lexius, but I should have known that she did. And when he returned, when he brought these slaves back to her feet, I should have observed more carefully the way that she looked at him. Picture it, if you will. Here, this languid, sinewy, and feline man who'd been her naked doll, and suddenly there he was before her in a long black velvet tunic, purloined from the fallen sultanate, trimmed with magnificent designs, his fingers covered in massive rings, his jeweled sword belt girdling his waist and his weapon now not the broadsword he'd taken with him but a gleaming scimitar. He brought the slaves to her in golden collars and chains and, making her a magnificent bow, assured her that they had offered complete compliance in their rescue."

"How fortunate for them," said Laurent with a laugh.

"Yes, well, I should have seen her black eyes devouring him, devouring all the delicious aspects of his person, his seductive Eastern dignity. But I didn't see it.

"Well, she said that having such pampered and spoiled slaves returned to Court wouldn't do, and that Lexius was to take them down to the village and see they were appropriately worked and punished there so that all the cloying softness was removed from them. Lexius was to remain in the village at Jennifer Loxley's inn and watch over them daily. She said a month or two would be sufficient for Lexius to ensure that things were being done properly, and then he was to return to her. But in the meantime he might make himself entirely comfortable in the inn and do whatever he liked."

"Ah," said Beauty. "What a stunning idea. So he would enjoy this freedom, this privilege, and then come back to her naked and abject."

"Yes, that is it, exactly," said Alexi. "But how much Her Majesty understood of what she was doing here is not clear. She wanted total obedience and that seemed her emphasis. And maybe she thought this time in the village was some sort of reward to Lexius for his bravery in journeying to the sultanate on the eve of war. I mean she wanted to reward him in some way."

Alexi shifted in his chair. He was speaking almost entirely to Beauty now but didn't seem to realize it, but Beauty realized it, and as always she loved to watch the shifting expressions of his face, and she loved the tone of his voice.

"Anyway, down to the village Lexius went with plenty of her gold," Alexi said, "and so went Dmitri and Elena and Rosalynd to be punished there. And all were sent initially to the stables. But Lexius had leave to take them out of harness at any time and subject them to the Public Turntable, the Punishment Shop, or whatever he thought appropriate.

"Now, the mayor at that time was the only keeper of female ponies in the village, and his stable was much smaller and infinitely more elegant than the public stable. But you know all this, of course. Well, it was a new sight for Lexius. And he fell in love with the high style of the harnesses, the plumes, the golden bits, and shapely boots worn by the female ponies. And so did Elena and Rosalynd." Alexi paused and looked to them for confirmation.

"Oh, absolutely," said Rosalynd. "It was superb, all of it, and the stable, small as it was, all polished and shining, more like a great, how shall I say, stage setting perhaps than a real place, and the grooms were magnificent— big powerful boys with huge hands and loving voices. We had such fun with them. But then, Your Majesty, you see what we have done with your own stables. And it all began there."

Elena blushed and nodded. She glanced sideways at the Queen. "The old stable there is nothing compared with your own stables today. But please understand, we'd never seen anything like it."

"Well, the genius behind it," said Alexi, "was Sonya, and Sonya, a niece of the mayor, was one of the fairest women in the village. She had mountains of wavy black hair and bewitching eyes, not to mention a lovely voice, and she was madly devoted to her fillies.

"A single look passed between Sonya and Lexius and both were undone. But more of that shortly.

"Lexius returned to the castle after two months as the Queen demanded, and knelt at her feet and accepted her pronouncement. He should be stripped of his finery and once more serve her in her private chambers.

"I was very glad to see him come back as I missed our secret meetings. And the Queen again thought nothing of this except that he was to prove his undying devotion.

"Well, Lexius very respectfully and with his Eastern polish made a proposal to Her Majesty. Let him go every month for at least two nights to the inn, once more clothed and with gold in his pockets, so that he might check on his charges. And would not this back and forth, he asked, serve to make him even more keenly aware than ever of his devotion to his queen?"

Beauty smiled. "And no one had ever thought of such a thing before?"

she asked. "Of a slave dressed and given privileges and then broken down to servitude for the greater appreciation of his own helplessness?"

Laurent smiled at her. "I don't remember anyone ever doing it," he said.

"No, no one had ever proposed it," said Alexi. "But the Queen with a toss of her head, said, 'Oh, do go, yes.'

"And Lexius was stripped right there at Court, all his accoutrements of authority taken away, and put back into the lowliest service.

"And that night, when the Queen slept, I had him to myself again."

"And that was when, let me guess," said Laurent, "he confessed to you that he was mad for Sonya."

"Exactly!" said Alexi. "He dissolved into tears in my arms. He could not live without Sonya. Sonya had mastered him in such ways that the Queen had paled in his heart. He was living now for the two nights when he might go to the inn only to sneak off from it to Sonya's cottage behind the mayor's little manor house.

"I told him this was a dangerous game. He'd be caught, and if the Queen discovered this, that he in clothes of rank and privilege had stripped himself for a village woman to whip, she'd be furious. It would offend every principle she maintained. Yet even then I did not guess how much the Queen actually loved him.

"He told me he knew it was dangerous, and more than for himself he feared for Sonya. But he carried out his plan, and for months on end he accomplished his secret and heated rituals with the merciless Sonya."

"And you and Lexius, during this time," asked Beauty. "Did you continue with your embraces?"

"Yes, but they became more loving, more tender. I didn't seek to make him my little puppy anymore. I merely loved him. And frankly, I was so afraid for him, I was hoping we'd be caught before he and Sonya would be caught, thinking that would be more tolerable for him, and the Queen in punishing him would extinguish his passion for sneaking off with Sonya.

"As the months passed, he fell deeper into the thrall of Sonya, and at last he was in perpetual agony. I could no longer really comfort him. Finally I resorted to trying to frighten him, reminding him what the Queen might do, that he was not highborn, that she might strap him to a wall naked for the next ten years if she chose, only taking him down for feeding and grooming a few hours out of every day. Did he not realize her power?

"And then he confessed to who he really was. Not royal? No. I was mistaken. Indeed, he said, he was from a great and noble family in India, and he had never been the Sultan's servant. On the contrary, he'd been sent by his family as a guest to the Sultan to learn the ways of the Sultan's type of pleasure slavery. He'd assumed the role of steward for the Sultan to perfect his learning. His family was rich, powerful, and could ransom him anytime he fell into difficulty. He had only to get a letter to them, and this he could do easily from the inn. He also told me he had gold aplenty hidden in the woods near the village. This he had taken from the doomed sultanate, but it was no more than he'd possessed when he had arrived there.

"'But Lexius,' I'd said to him. 'What if you have no opportunity to defend yourself, to say who you are, to write a letter, to get to your gold?'

"He paid no attention to me. He went on with his 'two lives,' serving the Queen and loving Sonya.

"At that time, my family sent for me. My brother had died, and my nephew needed my guidance for a few years before he would ascend the throne. My clothes were brought to me, and because I'd served the Queen for so long and so well, I was given a luxurious apartment in the castle to rest before my long journey.

"Of course, ingrate that I am by nature, I smuggled Lexius in to see me. But I had to do it. I had to hold him in my arms before leaving him forever.

"And so we wept and talked together and went over all the many aspects of his dilemma. He told me he was from the city of Arikamandu, a port city in the southern part of India. And though he would not tell me his family's name, he spoke of their dedication to a cruel goddess of love to whom they'd pledged eternal service.

"'Perhaps I am ready now to return,' he told me, 'if only I can take my beloved Sonya with me. Alexi, will you help me? Your father's soldiers are here. You are free. You are leaving. If I can get down to the village now and retrieve my gold and persuade Sonya to leave with me, will you help us go? Will you explain to the Queen who I am and that she cannot hold me?'

"I was horrified, but more to the point, I thought his plan was doomed to failure of another sort. 'How will you and Sonya live and love without this kingdom?' I asked him. 'Don't you see, your devotion to Sonya flourishes here in this atmosphere but likely will wither in no time outside of this unique realm.'"

Beauty smiled. How well she understood. The sanctuary of the bedroom, no matter how opulent and protected, was not the great engulfing world of the kingdom. The great world had a way of working itself into any bedchamber outside this kingdom, as she and Laurent had always accepted and always known. She'd loved Laurent with her whole soul since the day they married, but the heated embraces and rituals of mastery and submission they enjoyed in their bedroom were not really the glorious and luminous ways of the kingdom. And a conjugal love had been their everlasting defense.

Alexi had come to a stop.

"Well?" Beauty prodded.

Alexi swallowed and looked up. "Lexius said something strange in answer to this, that Bellavalten was not the only kingdom of its sort, even with the sultanate obliterated. He said he would handle the matter of where to go, where to take his cruel mistress, Sonya, and how his love for Sonya would flourish.

"And before I could answer him, or learn more, we were undone. The Queen appeared. She had been listening to everything we had said to one another from a small antechamber behind a curtain."

There was an audible gasp from Lady Eva. But Beauty could see that none of this was news to Dmitri or Rosalynd or Elena, and the King merely waited attentively for the rest of the story. He had turned a little in his chair and rested his chin on his fist, studying Alexi, but plainly not seeing what was before him, but rather what might have happened long ago.

"We were confronted with our disobedience of course. I was denounced in the most vile terms and told to turn my back on the kingdom in the morning. But over Lexius's deception, his failure to tell her who he really was, and his devotion to Sonya, she went mad with rage and grief. I had never seen her shed such tears. She smashed the mirrors of the room. She sent pitchers and goblets and plates crashing. She tore the necklaces from her throat, she rent her clothes like someone in mourning."

He stopped. He shook his head. He looked stricken.

Beauty realized that Rosalynd and Elena had tears in their eyes, but Laurent and Lady Eva were merely fascinated. Had they really loved the old queen? It didn't seem possible to her. No, they had loved Lexius.

"Well, what happened?" asked Lady Eva. She was bright and curious as always, fresh as if she'd stepped from a mountain waterfall, her quick green eyes filled with the usual optimism—that things could be known and understood and made better. How Beauty loved her.

"I had no choice but to appeal to her," said Alexi. "I was no longer a naked slave. I was wearing the clothing brought to me from my father's house. I was the regent of my own land, and wore the ring of regent brought to me by my father's soldiers. I had not even undressed for bed. I wore my full attire, such as it was. Of course one doesn't really emerge from naked pleasure slavery in a matter of hours, or days, or even perhaps months. But the point is, I was a royal guest in Queen Eleanor's castle now, not a naked sacrifice on the altar of her desire. And I had to speak for Lexius. I had to. I loved Lexius. I would have spoken even if I had not been lately restored to my old status. But of course I knew as a guest that I'd wronged the Queen in her house. Of that I was painfully aware. I remember feeling a certain shame that I had deceived her, even as a guest, as I had done as a slave. Whatever the case, I drew myself up and spoke to her as a mighty prince might speak.

"'I love you, Queen Eleanor,' I said to her, and this was true. It was. 'I existed here for you. My cock existed for you. My body existed for you to use and punish. And I have deceived you and I am ashamed. But we cannot be commanded to love. And we cannot command ourselves to love either. I love you, but Lexius loves Sonya!'"

Beauty nodded silently. No, we most certainly cannot be commanded to love. Beauty gazed at him fearfully, wanting him desperately to continue yet afraid of what he might reveal.

"Well, she answered me in unvarnished words," said Alexi. "'My heart is broken,' she said. 'I lose you, Alexi, you who were to me the sun and the moon, and I lose him, this dark bewitching god of love who makes a fire in my blood that nothing can cool, all in the same night! I cannot bear it.' She began to wail like a woman at a funeral pyre. And she sent for Sonya.

"It was daylight by the time Sonya was brought into these chambers. Lexius was on his knees, nude, with his head bowed, saying nothing. And never had he looked more like a god, in fact, with his slender face and downcast eyes and strange patient submission. As for Sonya, this was the first time I'd ever beheld her and she had a humbling magnificence to her, that's the only way I can describe it—a statuesque beauty who was clearly frightening. For one thing, she was exceptionally large for a woman, all over, large of bone, with facial features that were large, but the entire sculpture was that of exquisite and extreme femininity without doubt. She'd dressed hastily yet the impression was one of village opulence, I suppose, with the shorter hem required of villagers, yes, but beautiful sleeves and skirts and finely made boots. Her raven hair she had not done up, nor had time to brush, and as a consequence she looked as if she'd been pulled from bed, mussed with her cheeks burning, and her eyes aflame with a kind of raw indignation that can't be suppressed.

"I could see in a flash why Lexius had succumbed to her. Sonya, of course, had never been anyone's slave, and was in fact a terror of a mistress except to those who adored her. And when she began to speak to the Queen, she spoke much too much and she was not wise.

"'Your Majesty,' she cried, 'I would never have left the kingdom with him and gone anywhere. I only took him into my private rooms because he needed so badly to be instructed, trained, broken. He had never really surrendered to anyone.' Of course this infuriated Queen Eleanor as she thought she had already instructed, trained, and broken Lexius long ago, and that he'd surrendered to her completely.

"She banished all of us from the kingdom. Sonya, sobbing and crying, was not even allowed to see her uncle the mayor or say farewell to her beloved fillies, as she called them. Lexius was allowed his fine clothes, his sword, and his gold from its hiding place in the woods, as it was indeed his, and we were all put out of the kingdom.

"The Queen in those last hours was as a flower withered overnight, a flower that had been past its prime already for some time but as lovely still as other blooms—only to wither all at once, and drop its petals in a silent downpour. She was a ghost of herself as she stood accepting our parting bows. She gave gold aplenty to me as was the custom, but not her kiss, her forgiveness, or her blessing. And it was then—as I learned later on—that she began her turning away from the kingdom.

"I journeyed with Lexius and Sonya to a port from which they sailed for India. We spent many nights together in the inn there talking to one another as we waited for the right ship. Sonya and Lexius, well, they had begun to quarrel before they sailed.

"A year later, maybe a little more, I received a letter from Lexius that Sonya had disappeared. She had not found the climate of Arikamandu and its surrounding country congenial to her. She had gone away. Lexius had bestowed great wealth on her. But she was never coming back, this he knew. He was bereft. About that time, Dmitri had long been free and was visiting with me. . . . Dmitri wanted to visit Lexius—" He stopped.

"I went on to Arikamandu," said Dmitri carefully. "I wanted to see Lexius. A bond had been forged between me and Lexius when he brought us back from the sultanate. I visited for some time with Lexius in India. We were bound together by many things. And then I returned, and now Lexius is returning as well."

Beauty was amazed. What had the distant city of Arikamandu been like? And what of Lexius's powerful family? There was so much she wanted to know. She did not yearn for foreign places or new adventures beyond Bellavalten, but she did long for knowledge, knowledge of all sorts, and she always had.

She tried to picture Lexius as she remembered him. There came back to her a seductive memory of him as the Sultan's exacting steward, examining her body as he had received her into the Sultan's service. There had been something melancholy and languid about him always. And when Laurent had made a slave of him, he'd enjoyed a sweet terror that she well understood.

"But what of his strange remarks?" asked Laurent. "What did he mean when he said that this was not the only such kingdom?" He waited and then gestured for Dmitri to speak. "How long precisely did you stay in Arikamandu?"

Alexi looked up shyly at Dmitri, and Dmitri looked at Alexi in silence for a protracted moment that almost threatened disrespect for the King, but then Dmitri came to some inner resolve, and he looked towards Laurent.

"Sire, if you will forgive me, I must say that that is Lexius's story to tell," he said softly and pleadingly. "Please, I beg you, ask me not about those things. For that is another country, and another people."

Laurent was obviously reflecting on this. Of course Beauty understood. Dmitri had been a guest in that other country, with those other people, and he did not want to violate his honor in any way.

Since he'd taken over the Place of Public Punishment, Dmitri had grown strong and resolute, losing entirely the tentative movements and speech that had marked him on the day of his return.

"I returned to my own country," said Dmitri. "And it is this kingdom to which I belong now. Please let me say no more of Lexius than what I've said so far."

"And Lexius will be here soon enough to tell his story," Beauty said. "He's made a long journey to come here. He must want to offer us more than his greetings and his good wishes. Those he might have given us by letter. Surely he has a purpose in coming himself."

And that purpose had to be the very same purpose that brought all of them back, she thought, that he wanted to be part of the kingdom again.

A moment of silence fell. They were all pondering. Lady Eva was the first to speak.

"And was it this, you think, Alexi, this treachery of Lexius that started the decline of the old kingdom?"

"Yes, I suppose that it was, Lady Eva," said Alexi. "But forgive me, Your Majesties, for saying so, because I must say so: the Queen did not understand things! I mean the undoing of the kingdom lay within the Queen for she had such strong ideas and was, well, blind to so much that was plain to others."

"I agree," said Laurent. "You don't offend me when you speak of her in that way. I have spoken of her in that way, and so has my queen. All one has to do is listen to the grumblings and rantings of old Lord Gregory to understand what the Queen never understood."

"Ah, but Lord Gregory has his uses," said Lady Eva, rolling her eyes. She smiled and the King smiled at her in a secretive confiding way.

Beauty never minded when that happened. She'd grown accustomed to the King's devotion to Lady Eva. She tended the King's bruises and welts when Lady Eva had left his chambers. And Laurent came to her hot and hungry for her embraces on those nights as if Lady Eva had fed him one of her potions when in fact her potion had consisted only of her great gift for command.

"We have taken our building blocks from Queen Eleanor here," said Beauty, "but we have laid a new foundation. We have built new and wondrous edifices of our own."

"Yes, Your Majesty, that is so true," said Lady Eva, and now she flashed the smile she always reserved for Beauty, one of admiration and trust. "Well, maybe Lexius will have things to teach us, tricks and rituals from the Sultan's kingdom for which the old queen had no taste."

"Oh, he knows many," said Rosalynd with a soft laugh. Elena nodded in agreement. "But then we know them too, don't we?"

"You have been indispensable, Rosalynd and Elena, to the splendor in the gardens," said Beauty. And this was a simple statement of truth. And then there were the slaves tethered in niches throughout the castle and on the road down to the village, works of art in bondage. These singular figures and clever tableaux were Beauty's delight. "But then all of you here are indispensable. Yet there is room for more."

"I will gladly receive Lexius," said Laurent, with an air of finality. "Without hesitation, I will welcome him. It was I who brought him here years ago. I would have welcomed him had he come to me after he was banished. I'm glad he found friendship with you, Alexi and Dmitri."

"Thank you, sire," said Alexi. "I can't claim to have done anything much but follow my heart."

"And you are right," Beauty said softly, gazing up at Alexi. "One cannot command oneself to love. How blessed we are those of us who do not have to try to do this. And we cannot command ourselves to love one form of loving over another." She looked down, down at her hands folded in her lap, and her thoughts were suddenly confused and frightening to her. She wanted to speak of many things, but this was not the time or the place, and she feared she had revealed too much of her soul already.

"So true," said Laurent. He turned and looked at her for a long moment.

"And Lexius should be here within days," said Lady Eva.

"Alexi," Beauty said, gesturing for a moment's patience. "We are pressed to leave here for other matters. But I would know several things first. Was Sonya truly indifferent to Lexius?"

"Oh, no, Your Majesty," said Alexi. "She lied unwisely but desperately when she spoke to the Queen, and more to the point Lexius had a special destiny for her—" He broke off looking helplessly towards Dmitri.

Dmitri shot him a dark glance and shook his head.

It was subtle, quick, but Beauty caught the exchange, and she caught the look of regret in Alexi's face. She also knew that Laurent had seen this, but Laurent would be in no great rush to acknowledge it. He would wait until it suited him, which might not be just now.

"I never knew exactly what he meant by that," said Alexi quickly, obviously trying to repair the breech. "But Lexius said it, something, that is, about a special destiny." He shrugged. "And she was quite enthralled with him when they sailed away together. They were quarreling, yes. But they were tired and facing a long journey. I don't know that she would ever have agreed to leave Bellavalten with him, but once banished, she clung to him, was devoted to him, and linked her destiny with his. At least as far as I ever saw."

"I'm sure," Dmitri said softly, "that Lexius will answer many questions when he comes. Why ever would he come if he did not intend to answer any questions that our beloved king and queen might have? Surely he knows that he will be asked."

Laurent drew himself up and laughed. "So he was rich, of noble birth, and might have called on his family anytime for his release." He shook his head, marveling. "What a man!" He laughed again. "What a remarkable man."

Beauty almost laughed too, simply because Laurent's good spirits were always infectious, but she had to admit that the silken Lexius who seemed to glide rather than walk as other mortals walked was quite a tantalizing figure on the horizon. Again, she saw him in those moments when he'd first examined her as the Sultan's slave, when he'd studied her all over without ever speaking a word to her, when he'd felt her teeth and her tongue, her naked sex. He'd seemed a giant of a man at that time, and his smile had been blinding. Yet she'd felt delicious menace emanating from him; she remembered that acutely, though only the thrilling menace of a master with a treasured naked pleasure slave.

"He does know we'll be asking him many questions," said Lady Eva. "In his letters to me he has spoken of dispelling the mysteries that surround him, of cutting the knots of so many tangled misunderstandings. He's eager to see the new kingdom. Indeed, if he does know of any other kingdom in all the world like Bellavalten it is not enough for him to keep him from returning here. He speaks warmly of you, my king, and you, my queen. He remembers others. He has a multitude of questions of his own."

"Very well then," said Laurent. "This is quite enough on the matter of our beloved dark-eyed magician Lexius." He rose, reaching for Beauty's hand, and the entire company rose.

"And now we must go," Beauty said. "The day-to-day cares of Bellavalten are calling us."

12

SYBIL: EVERY LITTLE SLAVE GIRL'S DREAM: THE QUEEN'S STABLES

i

Sybil was awakened before dawn. By now, she was used to the quick toilet, the scrubbing, polishing, cleaning of her teeth and her tongue, and the brushing of her hair. It felt good to her, and she luxuriated in the firm handling of her now-familiar grooms.

But this was the day she was going to the stables, so her bottom and legs were given even more oiling than usual, and Neshi, her handsome golden-skinned groom, warned her that if she was accepted into the Queen's Stables, she would likely sleep there and he would not see her again.

Princess Lucinda, the mistress of the Queen's Stables, had approved of Sybil but only conditionally. Today, Sybil would have to prove herself.

"You be a ripe little confection, Sybil," Neshi said, kissing her tenderly. "Don't be sent back to the Hall of Postulants. This is an immense privilege! But remember the Queen for all her strictness is very understanding and takes great pains to effectively correct her slaves."

"Yes, sir," Sybil answered, and said no more. She had no doubt of it. She'd been the Queen's pet kitten in the great gardens last night, and so revered was Queen Beauty that slaves and courtiers alike fell over themselves to bow to her wherever she went, not with the icy formality of a weary Court such as those Sybil had known, but with an enthusiasm that bordered on worship.

The gardens had dazzled Sybil even more the second time she saw them than the first—what with the many gold-burnished slaves everywhere bound in artistic positions as so many magnificent sculptures and the busy games and the spectacle of naked slaves attending to all the needs of the immense Court.

The Queen had ordered Sybil exquisitely decorated for the evening with tiny jewels threaded into her pubic hair, her nipples rouged, and her ears pierced and hung with teardrop agates. Sybil's hair had been tied up on the back of her head to fall down in long ringlets all around as she crawled beside the Queen. She'd been fitted with a silver collar of agates, and a matching leash.

The elegant and ever-charming Grand Duke André had once again pressed his suit for Sybil, as the Queen had called it, but the Queen was adamant that her "precious one," a mere postulant, was not ready for service in the lord's private chambers. The Queen had had no objections whatsoever to the Grand Duke handling and studying her "little kitten" Sybil, however, and Sybil had been pulled up and ordered to display herself as his gentle fingers had probed Sybil's privates with impressive politeness. Sybil could not think of the Grand Duke's cheerful eyes and agreeable smile without feeling weak all over. He revered her as he might an exotic cat or bird, or an artfully worked silver statuette.

Another brief experience last night had weakened her too. At one point as she accompanied the Queen on her hands and knees, she'd seen her beloved Brenn bound to a gaily decorated cross beside a table at which the King played cards with one of his friends, a Russian prince.

Brenn had been rubbed and polished with gold all over, and his arms had been bent back over the beam of the cross, his legs wide apart at the knees and bound at the ankles. His eyes had been closed as a lord or prince in impressive apparel sucked Brenn's cock. A group of highborn spectators surrounded the cross watching the little ritual with obvious glaze-eyed fascination. The King was only a few feet away insisting the Prince pull back and make Brenn thrust his hips forward, but Sybil could see the Prince was lustily at work on his own game. The Prince's hands had been clutching at Brenn's backside as he sucked.

The Queen had taken the time to remark that she "adored" Brenn. And the King had said that well she ought, as Brenn was a perfect fount of elixir for those who clamored for it, as the Queen could well see. How lovingly the Queen had stroked Brenn's hair as she stood for a moment beside him. Then she and her pet kitten had moved on.

The ashen-haired Lady Lucinda had been there, and that is when she'd seen Sybil and remarked what a fine pony Sybil would make.

Lady Lucinda was a delicate, fine-boned woman with pretty hazel eyes. It was she—with the help of the famous princesses Rosalynd and Elena— who had designed the Queen's Stables and saw to them every day. But Sybil had been so taken with the Queen she'd hardly noticed Lady Lucinda. Oh, surely sooner or later, I shall be a pony for the Queen, she had thought.

"It is impossible to exaggerate the will of the Queen and her hand in everything," said Neshi, his dark eyes flashing as he lectured Sybil. "So never mistake her kindness for indulgence."

"Yes, sir," said Sybil quietly, savoring the strokes of the brush moving through her perfumed hair, bringing up the luster that she would never see for herself in a looking glass.

"Indeed the talk of the kingdom this morning," said Neshi, "is that Queen Beauty only yesterday at a Court audience readmitted to the kingdom three remarkable grooms who'd been banished under Queen Eleanor, accepting them back with such kindness and consideration that all were amazed. But that's the Queen's will, don't you see, and the King never questions her. The King leaves many matters in her hands entirely. It's said the King feels the Queen has a greater wisdom in refinements than he has."

Sybil didn't dare to ask Neshi to continue, knowing full well he would continue anyway. Neshi was the most talkative of her grooms so far, a thin, feline creature whose skin looked all the more deeply golden for the thin silver bracelets he wore. Of course it was entirely permissible to put questions to one's groom, she'd been taught that again yesterday during her general lessons in slave etiquette, but she knew full well that idle curiosity was not tolerated.

"Georgette, Charlotte, and Samantha, those are their names!" said Neshi. "Only no one ever knew them by those names when they served as grooms under the late queen." He shook his head. He was applying rouge to Sybil's lips and a touch to her nipples. "No, we certainly did not. In those days, they were George, Charles and Samuel!"

"Truly?" asked Sybil, losing her reserve. "But what do you mean?"

"That they passed as men here, as grooms, dressing as men, living as men, right here in our midst, until the late queen discovered them!"

Sybil was fascinated.

"They were caught in the woods one day outside the village. They'd gone together to bathe in a little creek there and thought they were all alone, when a soldier stumbled on them. When Lord Gregory heard, he had them dragged before the Queen. He was furious at their fraudulent behavior; their bold deceit."

Neshi again shook his head. "I tell you, what a shock. I'd lived, dined, worked with all three of them. And they turned out to be women! And I never even guessed! Yes, they had beautiful skin, and yes, their voices weren't all that deep, but still, there are plenty of young grooms around here with sweet faces. The kingdom likes sweet faces. But all grooms are men. Men. That is how it's always been. Well, to give the Captain of the Guard credit, he pleaded for mercy, saying they'd never harmed anyone, and that they'd been excellent grooms in the Lord Mayor's female pony stable. They were as strong as any other groom, said the Captain. Well, that's hard to believe!"

"What happened to them?"

"The old queen listened to Lord Gregory. She had them stripped of their male clothes and dressed in ragged dirty cast-off women's clothing and then exiled from the kingdom. Well, they've come back, and dressed as men! Same as before. Same bobbed hair. Dressed as men, and begging the new queen to allow them to serve once more. And the new queen has allowed it. 'Why not?' she said. 'Why should they not live as men if they choose?' Lord Gregory was steaming. But the Court thought it amusing. So did the King. The Queen said the same thing the Captain had said years ago. What harm had they done? So let them do as they like. Besides, they were skilled grooms of remarkable accomplishment. And off the Queen sent them—to be liveried for her service. It's said she's taken Charlotte into her own quarters."

Sybil gasped. "Why, I saw her last night! Charles, that's what the Queen called her. It was Charlotte who turned me out as a pet kitten last night. I thought she was a tall youth. I had no idea. Why, she was my groom last night in the garden! She was quite strong, quite dexterous."

"There, you see what I mean about the Queen's will? So please the Queen! Never take her kindness for lack of will. And Sybil, I don't want to see you here again."

"Yes, Neshi," said Sybil. "I want only to please."

"Yes, well, to be a pony is one of the most demanding forms of slavery," said Neshi, "but I can assure you that once you've been perfected in the stables, you'll be perfect for anything."

Was that really true? Sybil didn't think so.

"Goodbye, little dearest," said Neshi as he helped her up off the table. A husky attendant had arrived to take her to the stables. At once he pitched her up over his shoulder, and started off at a brisk walk.

"Wait, now," said Neshi. "Not so fast." He gathered Sybil's hair up and placed her hands on top of it on the back of her neck. "There now, that's how that's done!" he said. "When you carry a slave with long hair, he or she is to hold it to the back of the neck. Oh, so many new ones to train." He gave Sybil's bottom two hard spanks. "Do well, my girl," he said. "You can't imagine how many other little sugar babies wish they had the chance you've been given."

ii

It was as all else, thought Sybil. The stables were infinitely larger than she had ever imagined, and the full trappings of the place enthralled her. Never in the world beyond the realm had she seen such a stable whose doors, rafters, and stalls were all built of high-polished wood with gleaming brass fittings, and in which the harnesses were gilded or painted crimson.

But the most breathtaking sight was of the ponies themselves in the stalls, a long row on either side of the stable, of shapely posteriors and long legs—each girl bent over a beam from the waist, her wrists strapped tight to the small of her back.

Into a vacant stall, Sybil was rushed at once by an able-bodied and boyish groom with huge muscles, and a round handsome face sprinkled with freckles.

"Ah, little Sybil, the Queen's new pet," said the groom. "Well, my name's Oweyn, dearest, and you'll be in good strong hands with me, never fear it. I've been training little girl ponies for years. And Lady Lucinda has told me to pay special attention to you. Now, in you go, and bend over the beam. It's smooth enough, lacquered and polished, there, that's it, see? Your breasts hang quite free and your little chin can rest on the pillow there. Now plant your feet firmly on the ground. That's it. You're going to be booted immediately."

Sybil was forced over the beam, and her toes barely touched the hay-strewn floor, but to her amazement, the beam was suddenly adjusted in height for her by means of a crank. Oweyn's hand forced her face down on the pillow, and she felt the nudge of his boot forcing her legs apart.

A panic rose in her along with a sudden heat between her legs, and the feeling of her vagina thrumming and almost gasping. I can't escape now, she thought as she had countless times. I've given up my will entirely, and what if, what if I can't bear it all, what if? But her mind went blank.

"Now, let's understand pony behavior from the beginning," said Oweyn in his rapid cheerful voice. "No talking of any kind ever from a pony unless I say speak. When I ask you a direct question, you're to nod. Now, nod for me, Sybil."

Why did nodding to this simple command bring the tears to her eyes? She felt a sob in her throat but her sex was burning. Oweyn was strapping her wrists together, and that too made her feel more utterly defenseless. That all power over her fate was gone from her took her breath away.

Then with a shock, she felt his hand under her sex, lifting her pubis, stroking it and fondling it as if he were weighing it. "Nice little pelt!" he said. "Needs no trimming at all. Pretty black curling hair, and pretty red pubic lips, very visible, very plump. I like that."

Sybil blushed hot and the tears washed down her cheeks. But she thought desperately that she must be happy the anticipation was over. She was here now, plunged into it, as Brenn might have said, a part of it all, and she had surrendered the right to do or say anything.

A great languid ease came over her. She lay on the beam and on the pillow, and she did not jump as Oweyn felt of her breasts, patted them, and pinched her nipples. All she could see before her was the curve of the pillow and the polished back wall of the stall.

"Fine little filly," he said. "Now, stop shivering and crying. Do you want to be a good filly, or end up a dreary little pack horse pulling a cart?"

Sybil nodded. What else could she do?

"That's not a nod. I want a real nod," said Oweyn. "I want to see all these ringlets shake!"

She nodded more vigorously.

"Now, here's Georgette with the boots."

Sybil felt the left boot going on, and well fitted it was for her foot. Now someone, Georgette, presumably, was lacing it up tight to her calf. The boot was heavy and she realized with another blush and flood of tears that it was fitted with a heavy horseshoe. On came the second boot. The leather of the boots felt delicious over her ankles.

Hands lifted Sybil's head and she felt the soft titillating tug of a hairbrush, and a voice in her ear.

"Now, I'm Georgette, little Sybil," said the voice. "And I'm grooming your hair to match the hair of all the other young pony ladies. Two combs to hold it back from your face and jeweled clips to see it's gathered to hang down the back of your neck. And you do have the loveliest raven hair. So curly. So bouncy. So full. This will keep it out of your face when you're in harness."

Sybil nodded as vigorously as she could.

"Good girl," said Georgette. Surely this was the Georgette that Neshi had described. Her voice was a low purring alto, and her hands were as quick and deft as those of Oweyn. She didn't know which one stirred the desire in her the most.

"Now you're going to live in this stall, sugarplum," said Georgette. "You'll sleep in it and eat in it and rest in it when you're not tethered or harnessed, and if the Queen approves you, your name will be above on the beam, for the Queen likes to see names, and has them made of brass letters. She frequently selects her teams herself, and whenever you're under the Queen's eye, you stamp your little feet to show your willingness, your eagerness to serve, you understand me?"

Again, Sybil nodded, but the tears were flowing helplessly. She sobbed deeply in her throat. And her sex was so plumped with desire and wetness that she could scarcely endure it. Panic seized her and she tensed all over suddenly and felt her leg muscles quivering as though she would suddenly try to run, to escape.

Hands pressed down on her—Oweyn's hands which she knew, and then the hands of Georgette who spoke.

"Nothing is going to settle this lady down but a good spanking," said Georgette.

"But the Queen might want her fresh—" Oweyn started.

"The Queen wants her in harness and trained," said Georgette. "Oweyn, you're too soft. You always were. Now you wouldn't hesitate to spank any experienced little pony who was sobbing like this."

"You're right," said Oweyn. "Now, Sybil, you behave. Georgette's going to wear you out with her paddle and you need it and deserve it."

Sybil sobbed into the pillow, barely able to keep her lips shut, and suddenly with all her might she struggled. She couldn't help it. It just happened. She struggled wildly, though never really trying to stand up or run. But Georgette's paddle came down hard on her backside.

As soon as she felt the next spank, she went limp, and as a whole series of smart spanks came down upon her, she found herself utterly subdued and moaning softly, utterly delivered up by her own soul to the chastening pain. The pain was warm and tingling and she felt herself undulating under the paddle, and deep moans came from her chest. Oh, how right they were that she needed this, this thudding assault that reminded her of her nakedness, of her hopelessness, and of her great desire to please.

Suddenly Georgette's cool fingers kneaded her bottom, and squeezed each cheek. Then the paddle came again with one fierce resounding blow after another.

"Keep those feet on the ground, young lady," said Georgette. "We're not anywhere near finished with this. Prop her chin, Oweyn, so I can see her face. Excellent."

Sybil shut her eyes as Oweyn lifted her face, smoothing her hair back. She could feel the tears dripping from her face.

The spanking resumed. This time she caught it on the thighs as well, hot sizzling spanks that caused her to gasp. But all resistance had left her. Only the paddle moved her, pushing her slightly this way or that with the force of the spank, or making her backside jump reflexively. She had become her body in a wordless way, become her private parts, her hindquarters, her bouncing bottom, and her quivering hungry sex.

"That's better now, much better," said Georgette. "Oweyn, I can tell you with this one a spanking every morning and every night is absolutely required, no matter what else the Queen wishes. This is a high-spirited and delicate girl."

"Georgette, it's good to have you back," said Oweyn, "but I always spank them all. Every single one of them. Always have. No matter how tired I am, I make sure they're all well spanked every night, and in the morning, they get the worst spanking, I can assure you. Now you know me, George."

"Now Sybil, I'm going to bit you and harness you," said Georgette. "Up on your feet, now."

"Well, a little cream first," said Oweyn. At once his hands went to work on Sybil's backside.

She struggled to stand up straight, Georgette's firm left hand cradling her chin, and Oweyn holding her by the hip as he rubbed the cream into her.

"Nice and hot," said Oweyn. "And a becoming shade of pink. Sybil, your skin is precisely the kind the Queen fancies."

"You must tell me what else she likes," said Georgette.

"Well, I will as we go along. This little bird the Queen's been taming on her own, she and a little buck who came in with her, and that sturdy little god you won't believe. Both have very black hair, and lily-white skin. But the Queen likes quite a few other combinations as well."

With every word, Sybil's sex throbbed. When Georgette's fingers again stroked her pubic hair, she winced. She had never dreamed how long she might endure in an exalted state of torment.

"Open your eyes, young lady," said Oweyn. "Take a look around yourself, and then eyes down."

Sybil was shaking with suppressed sobs. She opened her eyes and in a blur she saw the magnificently tall figure of Georgette—with soft curly reddish-brown hair cut very short, short as an old Greek god, and long bright gray eyes. Taller than Oweyn, she was quite slim and her hands were long and tapering as they passed before Sybil's dazed face, reaching to smooth Sybil's hair back from her temples. There was something terrifying about her, about the blending of masculine and feminine in her, about her naked neck above her manly collar, and the obvious strength of her hand.

And there was the muscular Oweyn, with his happy smiling face as his fingers cradled Sybil's backside and rubbed it and he whispered how pretty she was.

"Legs apart, young filly," said Georgette. "That's it. You never press your legs together, do you hear, not with a plump red little sex like that. Haven't they taught you this already? If Her Majesty wants you to squeal with pleasure for her, that will be her choice. For me, you behave yourself."

Georgette gave a firm slap to Sybil's pubis and then another.

"No, stand still, no twisting away when you're spanked or slapped ever," said Georgette, but the voice was patient.

"Now I'm going to let you go," said Oweyn, "and I want you to stand firmly on your own two feet, and then stamp one foot and then the other."

Sybil began to weep all over again. It seemed impossible that she was standing. Why had she not collapsed? It was just as Brenn had described it so well, this feeling of melting, of delicious and engulfing shame. She had nothing to lose now, nothing, no dignity, no secrets, nothing held back. She stood still because she was commanded to do it.

A soft cloth wiped at her cheeks and her nose.

Georgette had slipped behind her but Oweyn stood in front, inspecting her obviously, feeling of her thighs with hard pinches.

"She's a good strong little girl," he said. "Highborn, well bred, small hands and feet, but strong, strong as lilies are strong with strong stems."

Suddenly something hard was forced into Sybil's mouth.

"That's it, between your teeth," said Georgette. "Bite down. It's soft leather, and it's been rubbed with a nice sweet taste, that's it. Open wide and bite down." And suddenly Sybil had been bitted and the bit had long reins and she felt them lying over her shoulders.

"Now, this is just for your mistress or driver to get you to lift your head, and to jerk you to attention. But the leads that guide you to turn will be fitted to these straps on your shoulders."

The harness came down around her, its straps being fitted around her arms, across her breasts but above them, and then buckled tight in back.

"When you feel the tug on your shoulder, you turn to left or right, accordingly. You don't think. You turn."

Sybil nodded but the spill of sobs from behind the bit sounded all too shamefully like a complaint. The paddle cracked her backside hard again.

"You want another spanking right here and now?" asked Georgette.

"I'll be glad to provide it. I love to spank bad little fillies. I have a nice strong strap I can use, if that works better. And I can hold you upside down by one ankle, too, if you force me to do it."

Sybil didn't dare shake her head yes or no. She'd been taught in etiquette class never, never to make that mistake. All she could do was shiver and quiet her sobs.

More straps were being fitted to her head, running from under her chin over the top and then around her forehead. The reins attached to the ends of the bit were run through loops on these straps. She could feel all this, but not see it. All she could see was the ground right before her, and the legs of Oweyn and Georgette as they went about their work.

Then there came the firm prod of a phallus against her anus, something smooth and very well creamed or oiled, prying open her tiny secret nether mouth and then being inserted into her.

"Now this is made of wax, girl," said Georgette, "and a good size. In the old kingdom they were all the same size and often too big. But Lady Eva has these molded and made every day. And all must pass Lady Lucinda's approval. And this one's perfect for you. And it's got metal loops embedded in it for the harnessing."

Sybil jumped but caught herself. The soft swishing horse tail moved against her thighs. It was streaming out of that little phallus and the phallus was being anchored tight inside her by the straps that ran between her legs and then up across her belly to be hooked to a broad girdle being fitted to her waist. With a few tugs she was firmly wound up in these leather straps, but could feel the pull of reins running through a hook in the phallus.

Another agonizing wave of desire passed through her, heating her breasts, hardening her nipples, and her sex throbbed again with hungry spasms. She could feel it in her ears, this pounding pull that seemed to originate not in her heart but in her loins. The straps running from the phallus were against her pubic lips, and pressed them together, but not enough to alleviate the desire that burned through her, burned even her face and made her face go soft suddenly, her tongue playing on the bit, her eyes closing.

"Now that looks lovely," said Georgette. "Blindfold, Oweyn."

"Yes, ma'am," said Oweyn.

Oh, but I can't run with a blindfold, thought Sybil desperately. How could she tell them? She'd lose her balance. It had always been so. But there was no need. The blindfold was over her eyes, and she could see through it, see the world in a soft golden light, and there was no need to look down away from the indistinct figures who adjusted her straps and petted her comfortingly.

A new sense of powerlessness came over her, something deeper and more languid than before. No one can see my eyes, she thought, and I can't cry out, the bit is a gag. And she was tempted to struggle again just to feel the restraint of the harnessing, but that would be very bad etiquette and she knew it.

"Now, I want you to keep that chin up for me," said Georgette, "without a collar, you understand? If I have to put a collar on you, it will be high and it will really force your chin uncomfortably."

"And the Queen does not like collars," said Oweyn. "Nor elaborate corsets. She wants her beautiful fillies as naked as possible."

Sybil nodded frantically.

"Good girl," said Georgette. "Now all day I'm going to be watching you. That chin is to stay up!"

Suddenly Sybil's wrists were unbound, only so that her arms could be folded behind her, folded just the way one might fold them in front, and she felt the straps tightening to hold them together. The straps around her shoulders were tightened and connected to the straps holding her arms. It was marvelously comforting, all of it, and there came over her that thought again—no more anticipation or fear. It is happening!

"Now this is called arm harnessing," said Georgette, "and it's for training and forces your breasts out in marvelous display. Now march forward!"

Sybil was swiftly spanked.

"Lift those knees, lift them higher," came Georgette's voice. "And you do it briskly."

Georgette walked beside her, wielding the paddle, and it woke up Sybil's burning backside with its blows as she scurried to obey. Now it was Oweyn telling her sharply to lift her knees. Georgette and Oweyn flanked her as she marched slowly on through the long stable and out the double doors into a bright yard.

The blindfold shielded Sybil's eyes from the glare of the warm sun, and the breeze played sweetly with her hair and on her hot face. And she could see more clearly now than in the shadowy stable. There was a huge oval track here and ponies were pulling small chariots around it. Each chariot had a rider, and some were pulled by two ponies, some by four, and some by only one.

I can't do it, I can't, thought Sybil desperately, I can't be made to pull a chariot like that, I can't, but this was a lie, and she knew it. Escape was impossible and rebellion useless.

She could see, some distance away, a pony girl, fitted in harnesses, who was being soundly spanked over a groom's knee as he rested his boot on the lower rail of the fence that surrounded the yard. And to her right were two harnessed fillies bound to the fence being soundly paddled also.

On a raised platform many yards away on the far side of the track stood a grand lady in blue velvet whom Sybil recognized as Lady Lucinda, with two grooms beside her surveying the yard.

Oh, I must be approved, I must, Sybil thought.

Suddenly a chariot appeared out of the corner of her eyes, a high graceful chariot decorated all over in gold and embossed-gold figures, with great delicate sparkling wheels. There was a red-haired filly between the shafts but her hands weren't bound behind her back. They were resting on a crossbar by which she was pulling the chariot. She appeared very straight and proud, and her horse tail matched the red hair of her head and was further decorated with flowers. But the long gilded shafts went on past the red-haired pony, and it was to the front, where the shafts ended, that Sybil was brought and planted between them.

Straps were being fitted to her thighs and these were being harnessed to the shafts. Also her shoulder straps were harnessed to them. Again, Sybil couldn't see quite how, but she was suddenly firmly anchored in place. The reins connected to her shoulders and to her bit were pulled taut behind her.

"Now, Cressida is going to push the bar and pull the chariot," said Georgette. "And Oweyn tells us she's quite strong and good at it. And you are going to be the lead pony, Sybil, do you see, but you'll pull the chariot too. Your girdle has been tethered to the bar that Cressida is pushing."

Suddenly the straps were jerked and the girdle pulled hard so that Sybil understood. But so were the shoulder straps tethered to the shafts, and also the straps around her thighs and around her waist.

Helpless, desperately, completely helpless, thought Sybil, sublimely helpless. A fresh flood of tears poured from her eyes, and the blindfold was suddenly soaked but still effective to shield her from the eyes of others because hers were covered. What an absurd idea. Surely anyone could see her naked, displayed, bound, her pubis mercilessly exposed, her hindquarters exposed. She had become her naked body utterly once again.

She felt the chariot moving, felt the shudder through all the straps, felt the pull on the bit.

"Now trot, young ladies, and trot smartly! Not fast, but smartly. Knees high. Right, into the track."

All will had left Sybil. She was suddenly trotting as she'd been commanded, lapsing into the pace of the filly behind her, and with the harnesses tugging on her shoulders, her waist, her thighs, her bit as she moved forward. Other faster chariots moved past her on the track, the sight of them jarring her and confusing her, but she was trotting, thinking only of keeping her chin up and her knees up, and how she might be punished if she failed, but the thought of failing was too bitter, too dreadful. She couldn't fail. If all these other beautiful girls could do this, so could she, and for the Queen, yes, for the Queen, she had to do it.

The reins tugged her to the left as if she had not seen the track turn to the left, and she followed the curve of it.

"Now, faster, young ladies, faster, into a run, that's it!" sang out the voice of Georgette. "Head up, Cressida!"

Sybil's sobs were mingled with her gasping breaths. A dreadful ache came into her thighs and her calves, but after a few minutes it was gone and she ran with a new exhilaration.

"Slower, Sybil," Georgette cried out. "That's it. That's it. You want to feel the weight of the chariot but not pull it loose from Cressida."

When at last the reins pulled her to a halt, Sybil stood panting behind the gag, her breasts heaving. They were at the opposite end of the track from the stables. They had passed under Lady Lucinda's platform without Sybil even realizing it. The yard was now very busy, filled with harnessed ponies and grooms.

"You're good enough for the team," said Georgette, coming up to her and running a leather-gloved hand back through her hair. "And look at this sex, positively dripping! Spread your legs. This little honey pouch is so wet. Always at rest, spread your legs."

Georgette's hand patted and stroked Sybil's pubis. She tugged at the curls. Sybil shuddered. The pleasure was agonizing, and suddenly she felt all of her body singing in its harnesses, her bottom stinging from the paddling, her anus throbbing against the phallus, even the swishing hair of the tail tickling her inner thighs as the breeze stirred it and moved it. Sybil didn't dare to turn her head to try to see Georgette more clearly.

Georgette squeezed Sybil's breast and opened her mouth on it and sucked at her nipple. Her tongue teased Sybil's nipple. Sybil sighed uncontrollably. She couldn't keep her hips still. It seemed a shuddering cord within her connected her nipple to her vagina, to the hard little kernel of her clitoris! A paralyzing sense of utter surrender washed through her but she ached for satisfaction. Even with the greased phallus tucked into her anus, she had never felt so empty.

"We'll be training for another hour," said Georgette. She moved away, back towards Cressida. "Then you'll be fed and rested and scrubbed down. And we'll see what we can do to soothe these little hungry honey cups here. I mean we have two of them. Such apt little slaves. Such dainty honey cups for the Queen. And when the Queen comes you'll be harnessed with her favorites for the drive down to Prince Tristan's manor."

The hour seemed a full morning, though Sybil knew it was not. Again and again, Sybil caught glances of Lady Lucinda inspecting this or that pony, or merely walking past.

Again and again, Sybil's agonizing desire had subsided only to build again, and as she excelled at lesson after lesson, her calves ached and her nipples throbbed until all sensations were mingled in her and she knew only she was more fully a feeling being than ever before.

In the gloom of the stable, her harnesses and other accoutrements pulled off, she was held up by Oweyn, who cradled her in his right arm as he offered her to Georgette. "Lie back, close those eyes," he said. His left hand held her thigh as he pulled it to the side.

"It's been a while since I had anything as sweet as this," said Georgette.

She plunged her face into Sybil's hot pubis, lifting Sybil higher, and it was all Sybil could do not to cry out.

She felt Georgette's tongue exploring her vagina, lapping strongly at it, and then the lips tight on her clitoris, sucking it, and Sybil let out a long raw moan she scarcely recognized as her own.

It seemed she'd reached the pinnacle and it was over and she ought to be glad of it, but the hunger went on and on, and again Georgette brought her to climax and then again.

"All right, dear boy," said Georgette, "I think you may have her now."

Sybil was turned around, her arms falling over Oweyn's shoulders and her head lolling there as she felt herself brought down over his cock.

And it was beginning all over again, her hands suddenly clutching at the air, her body spanked against Oweyn's pelvis and the cock filling her over and over, slippery, huge, and sublimely hard. Oweyn grunted as he came, and she could feel the sound emanating from his chest, passing into her breasts. Don't stop, she wanted to wait, but then she went over the peak once more.

"Now let's see to our precious little Cressida," said Georgette. "Put this one down for her rest."

iii

Full dress harness. Sybil dozed on the pillow. They'd given her a potion that had brought sleep to her immediately, a sweet syrup that had been poured into her wine bowl for lapping. Then the bowl had been taken away and the pillow laid down for her. She'd gone into a blank and dreamless sleep as hands still scrubbed and oiled her.

When she opened her eyes, she heard the words, "Full dress harness." Her body shimmered and thrummed with sensation.

A great after echo of the pleasure washed through her.

As they stood her on her feet, a fresh silk blindfold fitted over her eyes, she saw the other ponies in the paddock being painted, decorated, harnessed.

Soon her own nipples were gilded with thick gold paste, and little chains were strung to connect them. How she loved this particular ornament. Emeralds were being hung from her earlobes, and a large emerald was pressed into the adhesive in her navel.

But the wax phallus pushed up into her vagina caught her off guard. It was well oiled and not too large, and her body sang in response to it. But a handful of golden bells hung from it on thin chains, and these gave off their high tinkling music with every breath she took. Then came the anal plug, made she knew now of the same wax, all these little instruments supplied fresh every day from Lady Eva's stores of such things, and this anal plug not only contained the root of the shining black horse tail but more delicate gold chains with their little bells.

The boots she wore this time were painted gold, and fitted just as snugly to her ankles and calves, laced up by the busy fingers of two grooms who hastened to outfit her completely with every finishing touch. Gold combs for her hair, a touch of kohl to her lashes, gold for her lips.

Georgette and Oweyn moved up and down the paddock, inspecting, giving an order here or there, telling this or that filly to stand straight, their paddles ready.

Through the blindfold, Sybil could see Cressida opposite being similarly outfitted and she wondered what Cressida's thoughts were. She had seemed so perfect during their training.

The Queen appeared. Princess Lucinda walked beside her.

No one had expected the Queen so soon.

At once the grooms fell to their knees but all ponies remained as before, many tethered to hooks at the foot of their stalls, others merely knowing what was expected, that a slave does nothing unless told, and Sybil, trembling all over at the sight of the Queen, bowed her head and prayed it was proper to stand still and wait for an order. Cressida was doing the same.

Even through the gauzy silk of the blindfold, Sybil could see the Queen was magnificently attired in a great shimmering gown of silver weave, her breasts barely covered by the ruby-red border of her bodice, her skirts flowing from a high waist in great graceful gores to the tips of her silver slippers. Her glossy yellow hair was piled on her head with only a few flaxen locks falling down to her shoulders. Diamond-studded combs decorated her hair. And her fingernails had been painted silver.

To the right and the left she looked as she made her way slowly through the stable, calling her fillies by name and asking as to their progress.

Her words to Princess Lucinda were too low and confidential for Sybil to catch more than the tone. But she had come to Sybil and she drew in close, the scent of roses rising from her garments.

"Ah, and this is my little one, Sybil, my new postulant, my precious new pony," she said in her soft, affectionate voice. Her fine white hand with its glittering silver nails reached for the end of the phallus in Sybil's vagina, and lifted it apparently by the loop that would soon be threaded with a harness.

Sybil struggled to keep her balance as she stood, hands clasped behind her back, feeling herself lifted slightly and then tugged forward by the phallus.

"Have you behaved, Sybil?" the Queen asked.

Without permission to speak, all Sybil could do was nod her head. Her heart was bursting. It seemed forever since she'd felt the Queen's eyes on her, felt the touch of the Queen's hand. She swallowed hard on her sobs. However, Georgette had stepped up to answer.

"She's doing very well, my queen. I worked with her all morning. She learns quickly. She's a promising little filly. She needs hard spanking to settle her down, but that's not unusual with frisky ponies."

Tears of gratitude spilled down from under Sybil's blindfold.

"Turn her around," said the Queen. "I want to see how hard she's been spanked."

At once Georgette's firm hands turned Sybil by her shoulders. Sybil felt keenly the indignity of the phallus with the horse tail in her rear, saw in her mind how it must look, the cheeks of her backside pushed apart by the big glossy black tail with its myriad bells. Her face burned. The Queen had demanded many things of her, but never this, and she hoped with all her soul the Queen would be pleased.

"Oh, but Georgette, this will never do," said the Queen. Her tone was gentle as always. "Oweyn, I've spoken to you about this. These girls are pink, but they are not red."

"Yes, my queen," said Georgette. "At once, my queen."

"I'm so sorry," said Princess Lucinda. "I shall see that you're never disappointed again." Her voice was as mellow and polite as that of the Queen, just the way Sybil remembered it.

"Spank all of them soundly," said Princess Lucinda, "until they are red, until I can feel the heat coming off their backsides without touching them. Do this now, and then put back their tails, and finish with the harnessing."

The Queen then gave a list of nine names of those she'd chosen for her evening drive. "And Sybil, of course, but I want to see a red backside there."

Why did Sybil feel such gratitude, gratitude for the gentle words, that the dissatisfaction was not with her? There came into her mind the moment last night when the Queen had given her a saucer of milk to lap at her feet. How helplessly Sybil had lapped it and how she'd loved the feel of the Queen's fingers playing with her curls, stroking her naked back.

Sybil waited on her knees in one of two lines to be spanked. Georgette, seated on a three-legged stool, put her girls over her lap to paddle them. Oweyn merely held them by the chin standing in front of him, swinging his paddle wide and hard. Somewhere else in the paddock other paddles were busy, but Sybil didn't dare to try to see.

Princess Lucinda stood watching all, her arms folded. Her gray velvet dress was beautiful with her smoky ashen hair.

A girl might be taken from either line by Georgette or Oweyn, and Sybil found herself wondering which of them would give her the punishment the Queen had ordered.

Sybil glanced up fearfully as she drew closer and closer. What demeanor the ponies had, their bodies utterly pliant as they were prepared by the paddle for the Queen's approval. Sybil wasn't at all sure she could master herself in the same way.

Then she felt Oweyn's big warm hand lifting her by her chin. "Stand up, Sybil, and turn to the side. I want to see a pretty little dance as I paddle you, but nothing else. And that's what Princess Lucinda is watching for as well."

The paddle came down hard on her bottom. When she squirmed and struggled not to cry out, she felt Oweyn's fingers tighten on her chin.

"Good girl!" he said, walloping her again and again and again.

Before her, even with her eyes down she had a clear view of Cressida thrown over Georgette's lap, and Georgette's gilded paddle slamming her again and again. Georgette appeared as strong as a man. It seemed Cressida was bouncing on Georgette's lap. She marveled at the beauty of Cressida's bottom and her long perfectly shaped legs. Was she herself that well made? She had no idea. And she could see Cressida's pubic lips and the way her bottom flexed and contracted with each spank.

Sybil's senses were flooded with the thudding pain, yet she couldn't take her eyes off Cressida's comely backside. Oh, surely it is enough, she cried in her mind, pressing her lips tight. Her bottom was on fire and certainly Cressida must be feeling the same unbearable heat. Then at last, the paddle stopped and Oweyn's left fingers caressed and cupped Sybil's breasts as he kissed her wet face. Georgette's paddle continued working on Cressida.

"Now, get back to that stall, young lady," said Oweyn, "with knees high as you march. Your dressers are waiting for you. And so is the Queen."

Princess Lucinda was suddenly beside her. "Lovely," she said in her gentle ladylike voice. "I've never seen a little filly in my life who didn't improve with every single spanking."

As Sybil marched as smartly as she could, Cressida caught up with her. She couldn't resist a sideways glance, and sure enough Cressida was glancing at her too and giving her a little confidential smile. A hot wave of desire nearly caused Sybil to buckle. But the dressers reached out to catch her.

iv

It was a magnificent open coach, plated in embossed silver, with two facing seats, and an elevated place for the driver. Nine ponies, three across in three rows, were being harnessed to pull it.

Samuel, or Samantha, the Queen's new female groom, would be that driver. Seems different voices called her different names, including Sammy and Sam. In her black velvet male garb, she looked smart and beautiful like a very tall boy of tender age with her black hair as long as many a page. She had high cheekbones and sensuous lips. She certainly carried herself like a man.

Harnessed and decorated, Sybil was ushered to the last row of the team, the countless little bells ringing between her legs and in the horse's tail, the chains that connected her breasts shivering and flashing in the light as she looked down at them.

Like all the other ponies, she'd been fitted with gold plumes attached to her head harness. Gold rosettes adorned her many buckles and hooks. And her breasts had been more lavishly decorated for the royal team. Large gold rings had been pasted around each breast, forcing the breast itself a little higher on her chest. And the gold rings around each nipple were affixed with a stronger paste so that they more securely held the strands of gold chain that connected each breast. Sybil had never been so aware of all the parts of her body as she was now with the phallus in her anus and in her vagina, and the many straps binding her. Even the boots caressing her ankles, like fingers squeezing her ankles, and the leather halfway up her calves made her thighs feel naked and visible to her in her own mind.

When her hands were gloved in very tight leather she was astonished at how this added to the racing sensations she felt. The gloves covered the underside of her fingers and palms but on top they were artfully cut open to reveal the skin on the back of her fingers and hands.

Pushed firmly into place by Georgette she was told to put her gloved hands on the smooth bar in front of her. She and all the nine ponies, three abreast, would push the coach by means of the bars. And her wrists were firmly manacled to them. Cressida was right beside her.

"Obey your reins," said Georgette. "Sammy tolerates nothing! When she jerks the reins, you lift your head and you turn as she directs you. The entire team will be turning. The lead fillies are the Queen's favorites. They know what they are doing. They know the way too. You won't find it hard. But don't you think for a minute Sammy won't see you individually as well as each one of all the others! You're on trial with this run, Sybil. Cressida, you too. Look sharp. Disappoint the Queen and I shudder to think."

Smack came the paddle on her thighs over and over until Sybil was gasping, sobbing behind the inevitable bit, and jumping in place. Then reaching past her, Georgette went to work on Cressida. "Chin up, girl!"

It seemed to Sybil that all the team was aglitter with their lovely decorations sparkling in the light of the torches that lined the yard and the road. The sky was still light—a lovely shade of violet sprinkled with faint stars—and indeed a great sunset lay across the west in fading ribbons of crimson and purple.

How beautiful it seemed, as if Sybil had never noticed it before. And Princess Lucinda appeared so distinctive and pretty as she slowly inspected the entire team, her gray velvet shimmering in the light, her quick hazel eyes passing over all straps, buckles, upturned faces, nipples, boots.

And it is happening, Sybil thought. It is real. I am here. How many times in my dreams did I imagine such things as I lay in Brenn's arms, but it was never the same, those imaginings, no never enough, no, the pale shadow of what is real. Now I am in the kingdom, I am part of it, part of the things I imagined! A great swelling pride rose in her mingling with the tormenting pleasure between her legs. She felt safe among the other ponies. She felt utterly cradled by the entire equipage, and hearing the crack of a whip over her head, she lifted her chin and stamped her horseshoed feet.

"Remember your lessons of this afternoon, little ones!" cried Georgette and the team was off.

If only I could see the Queen in the carriage behind me, thought Sybil, but she could not, though quite suddenly she realized she could hear the King's ringing laughter and a mingling of others laughing too. Yes, an open coach with two bench seats and nine girls to pull it. The King was there too.

Run, little ponies run, she thought, and they were indeed running and she was with them, the cool air moving over her sizzling skin. The phalluses ground into her with every jogging movement, every marching or trotting step. She loved it. Loved the straps pulling, and the jerk of the reins reminding her to keep her head high.

The grand equipage moved towards the great gleaming battlements of the castle and she looked up to see the banners streaming in the wind! My kingdom, she thought, Beauty's Kingdom and I am part of it.

But when she saw the crowds all along both sides of the road—as they moved past the castle and out into the country—a hot shame flooded her. I can't be seen like this by all these people, she thought, but then she was being seen, that was the great wonder of it—as it had been in the gardens last night—and there was nothing she could do to escape the sublime coercion to which she'd committed herself, nothing whatsoever, and she strained with all her might to raise her knees as high as Cressida beside her or the girl ahead with the swaying mass of blond hair. She strained to arch her back and display her breasts, the chains and their tiny bells jangling sweetly, and she pushed at the bar eagerly with both hands.

The whip cracked above again and again.

As they moved well clear of the castle, the crowd changed from high-born lords and ladies out for an evening stroll perhaps to the villagers and the many guests prowling the kingdom, and again the shame brought a flood of tears from beneath her blindfold to see simple peasant men watching with folded arms, women in aprons, and even naked slaves made to kneel beside them like puppies on leash.

Sybil's throat began to burn. She was panting. But then mercifully the team slowed and Sammy's voice rang out: "Team, slow trot."

At once she was able to breathe more freely and a lovely relaxation coursed through her. The road was soft earth now. The horseshoes made no clatter but rather a dull thumping. Massive forests rose to meet the luminous lavender sky on either side.

But the flickering roadside torches—and the eager spectators—never seemed to go away.

What a spectacle we must be, Sybil thought, and again her pride surged. Her nipples throbbed, and indeed it seemed her breasts were actually swelling with the desire that tormented her.

The team was allowed to walk slowly for a long while, and those who'd come to admire it now enjoyed quite a careful and close look. Never had she felt so deliciously exposed, so completely delivered of all will and resistance. It was a grand sensation to strain against the harnesses in vain as she moved on. She did not know what tantalized her the most, the bit, or her arms strapped behind her back, or the boots so tight around her ankles and calves.

The voices of the Queen and the King mingled in Sybil's ears, but she could not make out the words, or the words of those laughing and murmuring along the sides of the road. People were bowing now to the royal majesties and more than one man or woman shouted out, "Long live our king and queen!"

At one point the spectators not only bowed but broke into applause, apparently for the beauty of the coach and its fillies. Sybil could only imagine how the King and Queen must be waving to all.

Full darkness descended soundlessly on the woods, but the torches illuminated the road up ahead, and at last the great hulk of a handsome manor house came into view. Its many windows blazed with light.

Sybil was ready for a rest as the ponies slowly brought the coach to the entrance. She struggled to see those who had come out to greet the arriving royal guests. There was the mighty golden-haired Prince Tristan, lovingly arrayed in green silk, and the alluring Prince Alexi, always in burgundy, it seemed, both of whom she knew well on sight from her induction. Was that Lady Eva?

They were gone from her sight now as the coach behind her stopped.

Over her own panting breaths and those of the other slaves, she heard the eager greetings—the Queen's sweet and affectionate voice, and the King's obvious good humor, and that other voice, Lady Eva, of course.

Then the whip cracked again and the team was off at a brisk trot, circling the gray stone walls to move towards the brightly lighted stables against the backdrop of the black forest.

All ponies were ushered into stalls, but no harnesses were really undone. What grooming came now to attend without disturbing all the elaborate adornments and Sybil tried feverishly to press her legs together before anyone caught her. The phallus inside her felt deliciously large and hard, but she could not crush hard enough against it to satisfy herself. A groom was upon her, buckling her gloved hands on her back. A bowl of wine was given her to lap, and her face was wiped clean and patted gently even as she drank.

When the pillow was put before her she lay her head down carefully not to dislodge the bit or to push or pull the many straps. In the gloom of the stable she could scarcely make out the polished wooden side of her stall.

Her body ached for pleasure, for satisfaction, oh, for anything to alleviate the hunger in her loins, even to be spanked, but this was not to be.

As the grooms massaged her naked bottom and legs, she realized they were talking about a special spectacle, as they called it, "the King's little puppy," who had been in the coach and taken into the manor.

"Brenn, that's his name," one of the grooms said. "Yes, he's all the rage of the Court."

"I heard they can't get enough of that Cupid's milk from between his legs!" said another. "Have you ever seen a slave like that, with so much hair, and such powerful arms and legs and such a lovely face?"

Ah, so my beloved Brenn is the King's puppy, Sybil thought. She was laughing with delight silently behind the bit. Good for Brenn! She remembered him straining on the cross in the garden as the Prince had drained that "Cupid's milk" from his cock, as the King had called it. I know what that tastes like, she thought, chuckling to herself. I've had plenty of it! It was so amusing! And how many times had Brenn imagined this world, as she had, when they were in one another's arms. Was he feeling now what she felt—helplessness and wonder that he'd been delivered up to his fantasies and carried beyond them? Terror that he could not escape this overpowering world at will?

Deft fingers pulled the bit out of Sybil's mouth. She realized she'd been dozing. A grape covered with syrup was put on her tongue—such a sweet taste!

"Sleep, little filly," said the groom. "They'll be visiting in the great house for hours. Keep those legs apart."

Yes, yes, keep those legs apart. But he didn't wait for her to obey. He kicked her boots this way and that and a block was put there, a heavy beam on the ground perhaps, so that she couldn't close her legs. Her sex thrummed and throbbed with wave after wave of desire. But the groom only spanked her casually with his open hand. "That's it," he said. "Now you can wriggle this pretty little rump all you like, little girl. But sleep."

And this is all you have to do now, Sybil, she thought, feel this, feel this desire. This is what's required of you—not hiding it behind closed doors, seeking out desperate embraces with Brenn—no. You are to feel it, you are naked and all decisions are now gone from you, all burdens, all choice—and this is your sublime lot.

13

DMITRI:
A NEW
CHALLENGE
WITH THE
MASKED
ONE

i

The arrival of the royal coach was a sensation. Never since my return had I seen female ponies so exquisite. I'd come down to the manor house with a village team hired for the little journey, who would be back to pick me up at the eleventh hour. And frankly, I hadn't paid too much attention to ponies since I'd arrived. I'd been far too busy, directing and refining the Place of Public Punishment.

When I got the message from Eva to come to Tristan's house this evening, I had been glad of a respite.

Earlier, upon my arrival, Eva had brought me into a private chamber with her heartfelt thanks. I saw a comely slave kneeling there with a finely painted mask over his eyes and most of his nose. As masks always do, this made his mouth look especially succulent and beautiful. He had fine brown hair, full of blond streaks, to his shoulders, and he knelt with his hands clasped behind his back. He was crying and trying to keep quiet.

"What do you see?" Eva asked.

"Well, he's beautiful. Glorious hair, good-sized cock and balls, and nipples that look tender, almost virginal."

"Stand up, little boy, and show yourself to Prince Dmitri," she said. Her voice was almost angry and this was not Eva's way. Eva almost always spoke gently to slaves. We'd discussed this matter any number of times since I'd returned. Eva believed in courtesy to slaves even as she demanded the utmost from them. She could whip a slave raw while carrying on a very pleasant conversation with him.

My style had developed quite differently. I had become a disdainful scolding master, a perfectionist, following an instinct to do what gave me the highest pleasure and do what produced the finest effects in the slaves. Of course I wasn't relentlessly scolding with my pets, Kiera, Bertram, and Barbara. Far from it. But my abrupt demanding voice wrought unfailing submission from them.

My style of fierce expectations and ruthless punishment was known throughout the village and set the tone for the Place of Public Punishment. Slaves trembled at my approach. And so did grooms, squires, handlers, and whipping masters.

The slave was on his feet but wobbling badly. Tall. That was good. Well-formed legs, excellent. A fine and slender build, suggestive of the Court not the farm or the village. As he drew closer I could see that his cock was nice and long and thick. Not exceptional, no, but a goodly size and hard, hard and red.

But his chest was quivering and shaking with his moans and sobs, and he was trembling visibly. His small nipples were erect. And his tight flat belly was quivering.

I drew close. The room was already quite dark though the sunset was not finished, and I lifted my candle the better to see what I could of his face. Blue eyes shining through the mask. No point in telling him to lower them.

Only now did I see he was an older man. His body was fine, pampered, strong. But I could see tiny lines on his upper lip now, very faint, but clear, and I could see other tiny indications of age. A bit of wrinkled flesh at his underarms, and something altogether that told me he was no boy, but a man who would always be a boy in many respects, with a boy's needs and a man's shame.

This excited me powerfully and I felt my own cock harden between my legs. There were many older slaves in the village, but I had not had my chance with many. It was a seductive thought to have this man perhaps at my mercy.

I felt of his shimmering brown hair. Silk. Just silk. Remarkably fine. I was shocked by a little memory of the only time I'd ever felt Queen Eleanor's hair.

I'd been whipped and paddled for days by her, failing in everything, and she'd ordered me to brush her hair—to do it gently with the brush in my hand, not my teeth, as I had no skill for holding anything let alone a hairbrush with my teeth, and I'd stood behind her chair, brushing her hair, terrified lest I pull it, shivering at the thought of her inevitable rage.

I'd felt how silky it was, her hair, and of course it was lustrous as pampered hair so often is.

Well, he had hair like that, this slave, rich and curling and something to be enhanced whenever he was groomed.

"Turn around at once, young man," said Eva. The same harsh voice.

He obeyed. He'd been well spanked, I could see that, and I suspected it was the strap that had been used for his legs. His backside had a fine curve to it, though it was more muscular than soft, and it quivered now as though he couldn't control it. The longer he stood there, the more he trembled.

Eva put her hand on his shoulders.

"Be still," she said, but he was quite incapable of responding to this in any way. Finally she said:

"You're dismissed. Now go into your closet and remain there, until I send for you. And if I or the grooms catch you rubbing that hungry cock against anything, you know what will happen."

He nodded. "Yes, madam," he said. His head was bowed and I saw the nape of his neck where his hair parted, and I liked the look of it, the tender nape of his neck. How nice it would be to force him down, take him, and bite gently at the back of his neck.

Eva led me out of the room. We heard noises from the hall below. The King and the Queen were approaching.

"Do you think you can make something out of him?" she asked. "Does he appeal to you, a likely applicant for your special attentions?"

"Eva, I'll discipline anyone you send to me," I said. "That's the purpose of the Place of Public Punishment. Today I had a powerful male field slave of forty years whipped raw three times on the turntable, and after that my delicate castle beauty named Becca strapped through the streets of the village behind a pair of running ponies before her second trip up the ladder for the inevitable paddling. I cherish them all, ponder them all, and work them all. You know this."

She nodded.

We went down the wooden staircase together. I saw the table laid for a huge supper and the fire going as usual, and I could smell the mulled wine.

The doors were open to the drive before the hall.

"But does he appeal to you, specially?" she asked. We stopped on the landing.

"Yes, he does. I feel sorry for him. He wants to obey, but he's lost. I'd love a chance to send him back to you perfected. He's older, isn't he? I like that. I've come to love working with older slaves."

"Why?"

"Why not?" I shrugged. "I find them as interesting in their own way as the young ones. They have a different rhythm. How old is this slave?"

"Your age, and he's spoiled and proud," she said. "Come, we must greet the King and Queen."

It was then that I saw the equipage—the huge silver coach with its fixed lanterns and the nine gorgeous female ponies turned out in spectacular harness and plumes. What a display. And now I understood why female ponies had taken the Court by storm. Of course the King's teams were a triumph. And male pony race days were never missed by anyone. Even I came up from the village for race days. But the females arrayed in all their glory were bewitching. They seemed as exotic as peacocks. Indeed, I wondered how they might look if decorated with peacock feathers.

I made a mental note: send bushels of peacock feathers to Court as a present for the King and Queen. When Lexius arrived, well, Lexius would know how to obtain peacock feathers in abundance.

After greeting the royal couple I watched the team driven off to the stables, and marveled at how natural and exquisite they were.

The King embraced me as always and asked how things were going in the village and apologized for being too busy of late to come down.

"Sire, I'm there so that you do not have to come down," I said. "Isn't that my purpose? To oversee the Place of Public Punishment so that you need worry about nothing at all?"

He had the most interesting puppy boy with him I'd ever beheld. I knew I was glancing at him over and over, though I was trying to pay heed to the King. Finally the King said, "Oh, I'm quite thrilled that you're admiring him. Have a look. Brenn, up for inspection on your knees."

The boy obeyed immediately with perfect submission and grace.

He had thick unruly black hair and a face like an angel in an Italian painting, with ruddy lips and immense blue eyes. His skin was creamy and flawless, but the marvel was the thick shadow of his shaved beard and the dark fleecy hair on his chest, his arms and legs, and the thick boiling pubic hair that surrounded his swollen cock. And what a cock. I wasn't going to say so, but it was like the King's cock. Not as big, no, but then this man was not as big a man as the King. He was of moderate size, very well proportioned with powerful shoulders.

"May I see his back?" I asked.

"Of course," said the King. "Brenn!" He snapped his fingers easily, and with a louder crisper snap than I could ever produce.

The boy turned on his knees, and I saw what I wanted to see—the loveliest backside perhaps I'd ever beheld. Tight, muscular, yet protruding just enough to be utterly inviting. Best combination of hard and soft I'd ever observed.

I let out a low whistle and shook my head running my tongue over my lips.

"I know," said King Laurent. "You don't have to say it, and he's another natural! I tell you, the old kingdom never had such quality in such numbers."

"Yes, sire," I responded. "When you sent out the Proclamation you waked the gods and goddesses of old from their sensuous sleep. And they have sent their minions. How many more can the kingdom receive?"

And the boy *was* a natural.

As we sat down to meat and drink, he knelt silently and motionlessly by the King and ate quickly any tidbits thrown on his little silver plate.

I was seated to the King's left and had a clear view of him at the King's left side, a perfect pup if ever I saw one.

But the matter of the shivering suffering slave in the chamber above never left my mind. I was wondering if I would be allowed to take him out of here with me. I had a deep raging desire to whip him angrily all the way to the village on foot. I'd been doing this of late with those committed for public punishment.

Two days ago, when the Queen had handed over to me the proud flaxen-haired slave Becca, I'd strapped her fiercely on foot all the way down from the castle to the village, stopping over and over to scold her and berate her and whack her till she was squealing behind her lips. It took half an hour. I hadn't minded the walk in the fresh air and the exercise of swinging the strap. And it was well worth every minute, to drive her dusty and sobbing into the village, walloping her furiously every step of the way. "Move, march, faster!" She'd blossomed under my raging commands like a flower that had never known rainwater.

By the time she was flung on her knees on the Public Turntable for the first time she was no more a haughty vixen but a whimpering partridge with a quivering little backside grateful for the cream smoothed on her by the whipping master's groom. The crowd had screamed as she held her position perfectly, tears flooding down her face, chin on the post, for her sound paddling, her breasts shivering and her backside swaying with each blow.

Scampering down the carpeted steps, she hadn't just kissed my feet, she'd licked them over and over, moaning in abject misery. She'd pressed her nipples to my slippers. Throughout it all she was a picture of remarkable loveliness, with fine clean limbs and that shining hair, such hair.

I'd gone down twice in that first night to check on her at the pillory. Even very late, there were always some around tickling and teasing the pilloried slaves and she sobbed in gratitude when she saw me and licked my hand over and over with her pink tongue to show her complete adoration. I'd rewarded her with a harsh, angry spanking. She'd been dripping with sweet juices when I'd finished with her. And though I'd planned to starve her, I hadn't been able to resist her little plum-colored pubic lips, turned up to me as they were with her bent over at the pillory, and when I'd buried my cock in her, she had spent again and again, unable to muffle her cries.

Tonight, before I turned in, I'd be sure to march her up and down the main street of the village yet again, whacking her till she was hopping on the balls of her feet. She'd become used to that, my driving her before me on my late-night inspections. And if there were Herms out that late, good hard erect Herms, I'd mount her on any one I chose, spanking her as she struggled up and down on those cocks—pulling her hair back so I could see her face as she came. I knew that she lived now for the sound of my voice, or the sound of my boots approaching her. I kept her bound and starved when I was not working her. My voice and my voice alone meant good sound discipline for her spoiled backside and pleasure for her sweet hungry little cleft.

Just thinking of her on all fours, her little hind end turned up to me and her hot little strawberry tart opening to me, made me shift in my chair.

Now the whimpering male slave upstairs would present his own brand of challenge, but a furious flogging through the countryside, with my strap cracking him forward with every jump and staggering step, would soften him up wonderfully for whatever else might need to be done.

He wouldn't see that grand kindly whipping master at the Punishment Shop, not with that shivering little posterior, until he was licking my hand the way Becca had licked it.

Becca grew more beautiful and self-confident in her service every day.

I waited, knowing Lady Eva would enlighten me soon as to what she wanted of me.

The Queen, as soon as all the usual pleasantries had been exchanged, and the first morsels of food devoured, asked Tristan tenderly what had "gone wrong."

I was immediately intrigued.

"He is not ready, I understand, but why not, do you think, Tristan?"

"Ah, Your Majesty," Tristan said. "He wants with all his heart to please but he can't. He is not ready to be anointed. Not at all. Believe me, I want him to be anointed. But I feel something more drastic is required to prepare him."

"Is the fault with you, Tristan?" asked the King, but it was asked in his usual kindly manner. "I don't blame you if you can't master him, but this should be considered. Perhaps it's pointless for you to try, as pointless as it was for him to try to master you years ago."

Ah, could this slave possibly be Lord Stefan? I didn't believe it. Not Queen Eleanor's young cousin, the tender male flower of the old royal family! The thought excited me completely.

"Well, I have considered it, my lord," Tristan answered. "This is why I invited Lady Eva to come down earlier today."

"And you've seen him, Eva?" asked the King. "So what do you think? Can you break him? I'd be surprised if you couldn't. I've yet to see a slave you couldn't break."

"I thank you, sire," she said. "He's as fit to be a slave as any man I've ever whipped. He wants it with his whole heart, but he's going to require great severity and I suspect that severity must come from a man."

"But shouldn't he be taught to obey both men and women?" asked Tristan. "Who is he to choose one over the other?"

"Once he's broken and trained, Prince," said Eva, "he will submit to either with good manners. But he's a long way from being broken."

"What do you suggest?" asked the Queen.

"Well, I have asked Prince Dmitri to join us because I think that he may well be the one to break and train this sort of slave in the village."

The King laughed. I'm sure that he already suspected that I'd been summoned for this purpose, but he laughed when it was said aloud. "The village for the late queen's cousin. And to think years ago he so wanted to be sent there!" He took a deep drink of his wine and then bent to pour out a little of it in the puppy boy's plate.

I couldn't prevent myself from watching as the boy lapped up the wine, tongue darting like that of a puppy all right and licking his lips in the same way. Quite a puppy boy, and quite a slave—secretly bristling with humiliation and shame, as far as I could tell, yet obeying so unreservedly.

"Prince Dmitri," asked the Queen. "What do you have to say?"

"I am more than willing to take him in hand, Your Majesty," I answered. "I find him very appealing. I remember . . . I remember when I first came to the kingdom, how I failed everyone for months on end. I am rather excited by the challenge. I'll gladly whip him back to the village tonight."

The Queen raised her eyebrows. "Lady Eva, this is what you have in mind?"

Tristan looked forlorn. He was resting his elbows, staring at the glistening joint of meat before him, which he had hardly touched. His eyes were dreamy and sad.

"Tristan, you are unhappy?" asked the Queen. "Please speak completely. I must know your heart. And more to the point, I must know what you think of his."

Tristan started to answer but then fell silent as if he needed to gather his thoughts.

I spoke up softly. "You have not told me this slave's name, but I think I know exactly who he is. May I ask—are there some special circumstances surrounding his training of which I'm not aware? I noticed he was wearing a handsome painted mask. It covered not just his eyes but the upper part of his cheeks and most of his nose. I'm not sure anyone would know him with this mask. Has he asked for this mask?"

"No, Prince," said Tristan. "I was the one who put him in the mask. I thought it would go easier for him if he were masked. And if he goes to the village, if that is the decision here, might he not be masked for the first week?"

Tristan looked miserable.

"I mean if it all goes wrong," said Tristan. "Can he be spared the gossip and the shame? A week perhaps with the mask lest someone from the Court see him and cry out 'There goes Lord Stefan!'"

"You're imagining the worst," said Beauty. "He is quite beautiful and sensitive and I suspect he has aptitude, as we say."

"Well, he does, without question," I replied. "I saw that myself. His cock couldn't have been any harder when I'd seen him. And it never flagged as I inspected him."

Tristan was too downcast to speak. He shook his head.

"Tristan, Lord Stefan has lived in this kingdom all his life," said Queen Beauty. "He's never lived anywhere else. It is unspeakable to live in misery in such a kingdom as this and never be able to give vent to your deepest feelings, to be denied what you truly want." A blush flared in her cheeks as she said this. "I say give him to Prince Dmitri and let him be plunged mercilessly into what he wants! Has he begged you to let him go, to return him to his old station?"

"No, he hasn't," said Tristan in a murmur. "But he suffers."

"He suffers because he isn't broken," said Lady Eva, "and the mask, the mask is a way of bringing him along slowly. He's a colt. But he can certainly grow into a stallion."

Tristan gestured that he would speak. He looked imploringly at Beauty. His large blue eyes were filled with the glint of the nearby fire, and his hair looked golden. I secretly thought this fine and philosophical man was hardly the right person to master any unbroken slave, but I waited.

"I think this," said Tristan. "Stefan cannot return to Court and be as he was. He cannot. He will go out of his mind with grief for his failures, and over his longings, and he will end up eventually wandering away from the kingdom and he will be lost."

The Queen nodded. "I agree with you."

"He has never once begged to return," Tristan said. "He has not begged me and he has not begged Lady Eva, but he weeps uncontrollably for hours, and my precious Blanche and Galen her groom are miserable in trying to console him. I don't know if he can survive the village without running away, running away from his own desires, from the shame of living in the old way, from the rigors he's forced to embrace. I just don't know."

"Give him to me," I said. "I used to be just like him."

"But you were young then," said Tristan. "So was I."

"He's young," said Eva, "in his heart he's young. And besides, age does not matter. We have older slaves coming to us now daily. Dmitri likes older slaves. He was just explaining this to me earlier. Surely you've all seen César, the King's favorite pony. César is forty."

"Yes, but he's been a pony in the village for twenty years," said Tristan, "and now he's been elevated to the Royal Stables."

Silence.

"Clearly you are as torn as he is," said Eva to Tristan. "Tristan, it is you. You are the problem here. You cannot train him. And the King is right. It goes back to your early love as boys, and to his failure to master you. You're pleading with him to be your obedient slave, as he once pleaded with you."

I knew this was true. I remembered.

I had seen Lord Stefan with Tristan at Court before I'd been exiled to the village. Lord Stefan couldn't master anyone.

No one spoke.

"Give him to me," I said.

Tristan turned to me and our eyes met.

"If I think he's going mad, I will send for you," I said.

Silence.

"Tristan," said Beauty. She looked across the table, her blue eyes as soft and earnest as they had always been. "Dmitri is right and perfect for this. I shall take the decision out of your hands. I do this for both you and Stefan. Stefan will go with Dmitri tonight. And yes, he will be masked for seven days at least, and for however long after that Dmitri feels is right. And you, my lord, must put your old lover out of your mind till he's broken, trained, and perfected."

ii

It was a clear night. I stood on the old road, the winding road that ran through the woods to the village. It was rocky in places and overgrown, but it was perfect. I'd walked it only a week ago alone, in my roaming of the kingdom.

I'd sent word to the village that I did not need a coach tonight. Here, beyond the torches of the manor house, I could see the stars clearly above in the wide margin of glowing sky between the banks of the high oak forest. The air was warm and sweet with the scent of pine and oak and all the lively green things of the wood. No wild beasts prowled the great thick forests of Bellavalten.

Slowly three figures approached. Two big hulking guards with bright torches who would lead the way, and the pale, naked, and trembling masked slave between them.

A thin leather strap had been bound around Stefan's chest and arms, and his hands, behind his back, had been tethered to it.

The first guard came up to me and gave me the handle of the leash.

The slave was booted and gloved as I'd requested. I inspected him carefully. He stood before me shaking more violently perhaps than any slave I'd ever beheld. His golden mask glinted in the torchlight. It was impossible to see into his soul through the dark eyeholes. But the artful work of the mask made him look handsome. And his mouth was wet and shuddering. His cock was hard.

I looked at the leash.

"Unhook it," I said. "He's going to walk for me of his own will quite well. Unbind him. Gather up the straps. Roll up the leash and keep all this in your belt."

The guard obeyed without the slightest argument. I knew him well, one of the Captain's finest. What did he care if a slave was going to be beaten through the forest?

The other guard came forward with the long thick leather strap I'd requested. I took it and felt of it and weighed it. A fine thong for whipping.

Not too wide or heavy for my hand to hold it easily, but broad enough and heavy enough to make a good spanking sound. It was three feet long and dark, almost black, the natural color of the leather.

"Walk ahead, just a little way," I said to the two guards. "That's it. Now keep that distance in front of us so we are in the light of your torches."

They acknowledged and waited.

Stefan suddenly sank to his knees, his hands flung out before him. He cried bitterly.

"No, my lord, that will never do!" I said. I pulled him up hard by his left arm until he found his footing. "Now get those hands on the back of your neck!"

At once he obeyed, though he cried as bitterly as ever.

"Lips sealed!" I said in a sharp impatient voice. I ran a finger over his mouth. Certainly he was trying to obey. "I mean keep them firmly pressed shut! You can sob your heart out, but not out loud!"

I whacked him hard with the belt three, four, five times, but he stood firm, though he was choked with sobs.

"Now start walking!"

I began to whip him hard as he obeyed.

"Faster," I said. "I mean it. Pick up the pace!"

At once he struggled forward and I continued to pile on the blows, and of course the guards picked up their pace too.

"Onward, pick up those feet!" I whipped him again and again.

Finally I was driving him as fast as he could go, with the guards striding ahead, and smacking him harder and harder.

As I had hoped, he had forgotten about everything else in the world but moving at my command, and his sobs had died to groans.

I now chased him handily with the belt, smacking his legs, making him jump, but he scurried to keep ahead of me.

"Move those feet. Move them faster. Guards, set a brisker pace."

I drew up alongside of him and spanked his posterior as hard as I could, driving him into a frantic trot. I was still quite comfortable walking but this was perfect, his trotting, and I pounded him all the harder. His cock never wavered, but remained hard as stone. And so did mine.

On and on through the dark forest we moved, the only sound the crackling of the torches, the thwack of the strap, and his high-pitched moans, and occasional bursts of muted sobbing.

He was breathing harder and harder, so I slowed down, commanding him to walk again and not to trot, and spanking his backside with even harder blows when he failed to immediately obey.

He was getting out of breath. I could hear it and see it.

"Stop," I commanded. With a deep shudder he stood still. "Back straight," I said. "Head up. And don't you dare unclasp those hands!" I gave him four or five very hard whacks. He was bending with each blow, almost dancing, as we say, and this was precisely what I wanted.

"Guards, come here." They obeyed at once, flanking us. "Now you, my lord, put your gloved hands down on the ground and spread your legs."

He began to go down on his knees.

"No, hands down, legs straight and wide!" I commanded. I lifted him under his belly, jerking him up, and soundly punished him for his clumsiness. His hands were now on the earth but his legs were wobbling. His cock jumped.

"Now guards, each carry one ankle. Our postulant is going to walk on his hands for a while. And I am going to walk beside him and school his pretty posterior in obedience."

A wail went up from him as if this were positively anguishing to him, but the guards speedily obeyed, each clasping one ankle and carrying the torch with the other hand.

"Now walk fast. We're going to teach our little pupil what it means to please his master!" I said.

And off he went on his hands desperately because he couldn't do anything else as the guards forced him to a brisk pace.

His beautiful backside was turned up towards me, open to me, and I wanted so to sink my aching cock into it, but this was not the time and I whacked him over and over as we walked on, moving as fast as I could move.

He cried with more abandon and more softly and exhaustedly, but his cock never flagged.

When we'd gone a good ways in this way with him scrabbling desperately to keep up the pace with his hands, I told the guards to set him on his feet again.

"Stand up straight and on both feet!" I shouted. "And now you're going to run for me! Hands to the back of your neck. And you know what I want to see. I want to see those knees high and that head back. You've seen a thousand slaves run in that way, and you are going to do it for me perfectly."

Desperately he struggled to obey. His sobs came evenly and brokenly but on he ran and I drove him faster and faster and faster till he began to wail again.

And so it went—walking, running, stopping, him dancing on his hands, and then running again—until we approached the gates of the village.

I saw the Captain of the Guard had come out to meet me.

I greeted him but was far too busy just now to chat, and I kept whacking my charge and forcing him to march as we passed through the gates.

Stefan was now drenched in sweat and utterly worn down and thoroughly exhausted. I wished I could see beneath the mask, but I couldn't. His cock told the story if his face could not.

"Now, carry him," I said to the guard I knew. "Over your shoulder to the Public Turntable."

Nothing unnerves a slave as much as being tossed over a brawny man's shoulder, and up he went like a bundle of goods, and found himself upside down and sniveling and weeping uncontrollably. But it had lost that desperate edge of panic sound. It was the empty powerless weeping that I wanted.

The Place of Public Punishment was quiet at this hour though not deserted by any means.

The turntable was not engaged, though the whipping master was taunting the crowd to give him a partridge or a pork pie.

"Put him down on those steps," I said, and the guard deposited Stefan with appropriate roughness on the steps as Stefan's hands flew out to break his fall. This I did not mind as he had to go up using his hands and toes.

"Now up there, fast, and let me tell you, I want to see perfect composure on that turntable." I spoke loudly enough for the groom and the whipping master to hear me, but they knew my ways and what I wanted.

Stefan scurried frantically to the top, his cock bobbing, and then the groom at once gripped him by the neck and forced him into the proper position.

The whipping master picked up my angry tone, as he always did, with a wink for me.

"Hands to the small of your back now, handsome little pork pie!" he said. "And a nice crowd's gathering for you. You dare lift that chin off the beam and you'll learn what it means to give them a show."

I walked around till I could see Stefan's face or what the mask revealed of it. His lips were shuddering and the tears bathed his cheeks and chin, but he was not daring to cough up his sobs, and he cried like one utterly defeated.

But he wasn't utterly defeated.

And the crowd was pressing in, young couples coming round from the other booths and tents and amusements, glad to see some turntable sport. The groom was massaging the thick cream into Stefan's sore flesh, and his whole body quivered and jumped at the feel of the fingers on his backside. But he didn't dare to move.

"Can you see me down here watching you?" I called out. "I want an excellent show! You dare break form and I'll come up there and take that paddle myself!" I called out. The crowd gave a great approving cheer.

Ah, the wonder of it, the way his torso tightened and his whole frame shuddered, yet he did not remove his hands from the small of his back or try to get up from his knees. He had learned so much already.

Finally, the good sound spanking with the paddle commenced and the crowd began to chant the number of the blows.

I stepped back the better to enjoy the spectacle. The Captain of the Guard came up beside me with a cup of wine. I took it gratefully and drank. "Ah, that's so good."

"And who's the sleek piglet?" he asked.

"Let's just call him the Masked One for now," I said. "As the King and Queen wish it. The Masked One is going to learn more tonight about submission than ever he's learned in his whole life."

My eyes were fixed on him, watching every jerk and jump and shudder. His cock was beautifully hard, and soon his knees were jittering just as the crowd wanted, and cheers rose all around as he twisted reflexively trying to avoid the paddle which he had no chance of escaping.

It was a horrific paddling.

At last, I signaled to the whipping master, and the groom caught Stefan's shoulders and brought him up so the whipping master could take his arms and then hold him up by his wrists and turn him and twist him on his knees for the crowd to see the dark red and sore flesh of his entire backside. He'd been so thoroughly whipped and spanked, there was scarcely a bit of white flesh showing. And I could see he was limp, utterly pliant, utterly without resistance. His mouth was open in jagged breaths but he dared not make a sound. The gold coins and tokens flew from everywhere. And I waved for the groom to keep them. When I brought my slaves here for punishment, I never collected them.

The crowd was begging and chanting for him to be spanked again. I beckoned for him to be brought to me.

Finally the groom lifted him up and off his feet and shuffled him to the steps and down. I knew why. He was afraid Stefan was too weak to walk on his own, and I allowed this.

But when Stefan's feet hit the ground, I was immediately beside him ordering him to stand straight and march towards my townhouse. His gloved hands flew to the back of his neck without my having to say a word. It was as if he had no physical power at all to resist me.

"March with those knees high!" I said.

He rushed to obey, giving muffled choking groans that were low and spiritless.

I could scarcely find a spot on him that wasn't too red to spank, so I went to work on his calves mostly and not very hard. But I loved watching his scarlet bottom jogging and bobbing in front of me.

"March!" I said. "All your life you've seen slaves march! Do as I tell you!"

My quick impatient voice brought more whimpers and muffled wailing than the strap.

At last we'd reached my door, and my beloved night porter, Bazile, had it open for me. The little townhouse shone with dim light and polished paneling and furnishings.

"Strip off his boots and gloves," I told Bazile. I took a deep breath of the night air. I had planned to spank him up and down the high street, but he was far too worked over for that. His tender skin had had enough.

I turned to bid the Captain goodnight.

"Are we going to see more of these Masked Ones from the castle?" the Captain asked. He looked quite curious. "I think the crowd loved it!"

"Hmm, you think they guessed?"

"A slave with a golden mask? And such a fine delicate build? Yes, I think they guessed," he said. "Why else the mask? I've never seen a masked slave brought here before. Blindfolded, but never masked."

"I don't know, Captain," I said with a tired little laugh. "Maybe this will be the start of something. I have a good more in store for this young man tonight. I'll see you in the morning. Oh, and where is my Becca? I had hoped to whip her later tonight but don't think I'll have the time to attend to it."

"She's in the Slaves' Hall sleeping," he said. "She was paddled hard on the turntable at dusk, and then I whipped her through the village myself afterwards. You've done wonders with her. She belongs utterly to the one who wields the strap now, without reservation. She's as fine as she is beautiful."

We parted, and I saw Stefan on his hands and knees on the parquet floor, his reddened backside towards me. Bazile helped me off with my own dusty boots and I stepped into the cool air of the hallway.

I inspected Stefan's position. Perfect, and his sobs were silent convulsions now. Only tiny whimpers and moans came from him. I regarded him for the longest moment, thinking consciously of how many times I'd been in this same position, and how the rigors of the village had exhausted me, how I'd knelt like that, feeling empty and hot all over, my backside blazing with pain, yet longing, positively longing, for another crack of the strap as though I could not live without it.

I drew a long staff with a leather phallus on the end of it, out of the bin for such things by the door. At once Bazile held open a jar of scented cream for me and I smoothed the cream over it.

"Did you put the other slaves to bed?" I asked. I'd sent word that he was to do this.

"Yes, my prince," he said.

I slipped the phallus into Stefan's little anus and forced him up the stairs on his hands and knees. This was working wonderfully. He fled before me, his chest heaving.

I could see that already he had infinitely more self-confidence and control than before. He was learning faster than I'd learned.

He was moist all over from his exertions and I could smell the warm clean scent of his pampered skin as I forced him into the bedchamber.

"Up on your feet!" I said.

He obeyed. His hands went at once to the back of his neck. I had no idea how the room must look to him, so much smaller than the great bedchambers of the castle, or the larger rooms of Tristan's manor house, but it was finely appointed, and my three slaves were all abed belowstairs so I did not have to worry with them.

And so he stood, gleaming in the light of the oil lamps, dusty and full of ragged breaths, and I could see the glint of the light in his eyes.

I put my thumb on his chin. It appeared to quiet him.

"I like you like this," I said placing my hand on his flat chest, loving the way it heaved under my fingers. "All nice and warm and humble from your punishments."

I threw down the staff and the strap. I put one firm hand under his left thigh and grasped his chest with the other hand under his right arm and lifted him easily and took him to the bed and threw him down on his back. A ragdoll. A perfect ragdoll.

He struggled to keep his hands behind his neck.

Oh, how his cock was lathering, how it gleamed and how hard it was.

I opened my mouth and licked my lips and then I went down on it, feeling it hit the roof of my mouth, and I sucked it with all my skill.

He tried as all well-mannered slaves do to pull away gently before he came, but I held tight to his thighs and wouldn't let him and finally he spent with the longest most raw groan that had yet come from him.

I lay on my elbow beside him. Bazile brought me some very cold ale, my favorite drink at this hour, and I savored quite a bit of it from the icy tankard. How costly was this ice brought down from the mountains. But it was worth whatever it cost to put it in the ice cellar. I gestured for Bazile to leave us.

This was the first time I'd seen Stefan's cock in repose.

I leaned in close to him.

"I unseal your lips," I said running my finger over his mouth. I love to press on lips, to feel their subtle resistance. "Now you will call me prince or sir. After all your years at Court, must I tell you that?"

"No, sir," he said in a raw whisper. His cock was stirring again.

"Do you remember me?" I asked. "From years ago, when I served your cousin?"

"Yes, sir," he said.

I drank another deep gulp of ale. Then I kissed him. I pressed my lips gently to his, and to my amazement he kissed me back warmly, a soft sigh coming from him.

I mounted him and held his face in my hands and kissed him ardently. His mouth opened as if his soul had opened and his body was his soul. And suddenly I was driving my tongue into him and I was hard again, hard as when I'd sucked his cock, and I felt mad for him. I was crazed with images of his rushing before me in the dark wood, of him gleaming on the Public Turntable, of him years ago at Court, so handsome, so brooding, so silky, and so like the Queen, and here he was now, beautiful in a new and astonishing way.

His cock was bumping against me, and my cock was hard in my clothes.

I stripped off the mask and threw it to the side.

He stared at me with his pale blue eyes, such an opaque blue, so beautiful, and I kissed him again. "Put your arms around me," I said. At once I felt them enfolding me. We kissed and struggled and wrestled together, his cock against mine. Finally I could bear it no longer.

I turned him over with gruff thrusts and made him kneel up.

Bazile appeared as if by magic with the cream and I applied it to Stefan's anus and to my cock and then I drove into him, my greased fingers closing on his cock, pulling on it, gripping it, and I rode him and brought him to climax with me.

We fell down in a heap of hot and dusty clothes and limbs. I could not stop kissing him, smoothing his hair back from his face. How handsome he was, and how fine and how much a part of all that had happened to me—because he knew those times, knew me when I was very young and used to play with me now and then, laughing when the Queen spanked and tormented me, and I had him now, had him completely. I threw him over on his face again and looked at his red bottom. He flinched when I pinched him. I had to kiss him again, had to have his face beneath me.

Suddenly his eyes welled with fresh tears and I could see him silently begging me to kiss him. And so I did, and we were at it again, the two of us, men of the same age, men of the same story.

"I think I love you," I said, suddenly shocked to hear the words come from my lips, shocked to feel the increased heat of his kisses, the increased pressure of his embrace.

"And you, you . . . ," I asked.

"Oh, I am yours," he whispered. "Yours!"

Ah, what is happening here, I thought. But I didn't stop kissing his lean exquisitely modeled face. I'm to love this one? Not beautiful Barbara or Bertram or Kiera, or Becca? But this one.

"Oh, I remember you, remember everything about you," I said, "I remember when you sat and chatted with the Queen while I knelt at her feet, I remember your bright melancholy eyes and the way you surveyed the Court, so detached, so deeply troubled. . . ."

"Yes . . ." He cried softly. "I remember, and remember the day that you and Tristan were sent away, and I remember so many things, and then the years, the years were suddenly gone." He opened his mouth on mine again.

This I had not planned, no, not this.

"I mean to strap you to that wall, dusty and coated in sweat as you are, and have you tormented all the long night," I said. I gritted my teeth. "That's what I mean to do."

He gave no resistance.

I sat up and looked down at him. He'd closed his eyes. He lay there perfectly still. He had an elegance so like the old queen. His coloring and complexion were different, but it was from the same family mold that they came, of fine narrow features, only his eyes were larger and gentler than hers had ever been. Now he lay as if asleep, but he was not. And once again I touched his lips, marveling at how well made they were, and how softly pink, pink as the small nipples on his chest. What a fine thing he was, so much more delicately put together than Bertram, or so many other more eye-catching slaves. He was something hammered out of silver.

I called to Bazile.

"Strap him to the wall there, his backside against the wood, feet flat, legs wide, arms up, the X pose, the strap firm around his forehead to hold his head in place."

"Yes, sir," he said immediately.

Stefan gave no resistance at all as he was pulled off the bed. He did not look at me.

"But sir, don't you want him bathed, groomed?" Bazile said as he carried him to the wall.

"Not tonight," I said. "He's to be tethered the way he is. He's earned every particle of dust, every drop of sweat. In the morning, yes, he'll be thoroughly scrubbed and oiled."

I had my own attendants for this, my own bathing room for slaves belowstairs with its big bronze tub, and, of course, my own bathing chamber just down the hall on this floor.

Stefan fell against the wall without a bit of struggle. Again, he looked as if he were already asleep. And Bazile had him cuffed and locked in place within seconds. By morning, the dark shadow of his beard would be rough, sublimely rough.

"Now, call Kiera. I'm going to bathe. And after I'm asleep, you're to wake him every three hours, spank his cock and tease him, then drain it completely. By daylight, I want him sucked at least three times. I want nothing left in him. You know what I expect of you."

"Yes, sir." Bazile's lips curled in a secretive little smile, but not before I caught it. "And tease him plenty, whenever you have a mind to."

I cannot fall in love with you, I thought as I looked at him. But I wanted his cock in my mouth now. I wanted him moaning under me. I wanted to measure the tightness of that anus again with my cock.

Now who was being punished? Who was being tortured?

All the next day, he slept, and most of the evening.

No potion needed for him. Much healing ointment was put on his sore skin. Again my grooms and slaves suckled him and emptied him of tension and vitality. By the next morning, he was restless but utterly compliant.

A thick healing plaster was applied to the skin which needed more time under protection, and he was then placed outside the door of the house, back to the wall, hands tethered above to be the fabled Herm for the residence. His mask has been cleaned and refitted to his face. His hair was a shining mane, and his cock was alert.

I stopped to inspect him before I set out for the day's work. No shuddering, no weeping, just the silent helpless tears to be expected, and an obvious pride in his naked body, a tendency to straighten his posture periodically and to thrust his hips out as any well-trained slave should.

I felt crazed as I kissed him. I would go to the shop on the high street to order even more beautiful masks to be made for him to wear. Gold, silver, black leather painted with woodland designs. The shop sold everything a master could desire in the way of adornments. Surely they could make masks, elaborate masks, exquisite masks.

"By tomorrow, you'll be ready for the Public Turntable again," I said to him, kissing his ear. "And seldom will you ever be punished so harshly that you can't be taken there three times a day. Now I want you to pay attention when you go there."

He lifted his chin. He was listening with every fiber of his being. His nipples were as hard as his cock.

"In the old days whipping masters were not the colorful popular figures they are today," I told him as I pinched his nipples. "They're now in competition with one another to be remembered by the crowds. They are forming their own guild. Now, I'll see that you're spanked by three different whipping masters a day on the Public Turntable and I want to know later which of them you think has done the best job of it and why. Now answer: do you understand?"

"Yes, my prince," he said softly. No slave ever had a better demeanor.

But I was almost in tears as I left him. Because I wanted to be with him, wrestling with him again on the bed, and suckling his cock until he cried out for mercy, and I knew that he now had a permanent place in my heart.

It was bound to happen, I told myself as I went off to see to Becca, to take her to the Punishment Shop for her first taste of the gentle and loving old whipping master there. Such was bound to happen. And I would write to Tristan, of course, and tell him the truth. And so the course of my life spread out before me and torn as I was, suffering as I was, I could not help but be grateful and glad.

III

THE DESTINY
OF QUEENS

14

EVA:
HE WALKS
IN SPLENDOR
LIKE THE
NIGHT

i

I awoke before dawn. Something had changed in the room. Something had alerted me that I must wake.

I sat up searching the airy gloom for some sign of Severin, who should have been asleep on his pallet at the foot of the bed. Not there. And where was he and was it his disobedient comings and goings that had roused me before the rising of the sun?

Beyond the arches of the open windows, the sky was lightening and slowly giving up its great sweep of fading stars.

A man stood there, a man in a long belted robe with flowing hair.

I reached for the silver cover over the little night lamp and lifted it so that the struggling flame might show me just who this was—who had dared to come into my chambers without my welcome. It was not the King who might do so anytime he wished, that much I could see.

The light brightened and I made out the details of his face and form.

Skin like bronze, and great dark eyes, and curling waves that fell to his shoulders and a belted robe covered in embroidered gold and tiny twinkling jewels.

I rose from the bed and stood before him. I wore only a sheer white lace chemise but my appearance meant nothing to me just now. I picked up the small lamp and raised it so that I could better see his face.

His expression was one of awe as he gazed at me—of something beyond fascination.

His beauty was breathtaking, his dark skin flawless, and his jaw firm and strong. Set at the high border of his ornate tunic was a huge sapphire, perhaps the largest gem I'd ever beheld.

"How dare you come into my quarters like this!" I said. "Who are you?"

He shrank back as if I'd struck him and with his hands up imploring me he dropped to his knees.

His eyes feasted on me as before, boldly running over my face and my body and my bare feet.

Then he came forward with amazing ease for one so heavily clothed and he kissed my feet.

"Get out of here!" I declared. I moved to pull the bell rope.

"My lady, I beg you, don't send for anyone!" he pleaded. He had a sharp accent that gave his words a lovely resonant power. "I beg you to forgive me. I beg you, please!"

"Well, then, what are you doing here?"

"I dazzled and confused your servants," he confessed. His black eyes were almost too big for my taste, too powerfully etched by his thick black lashes, and his mouth was a dark rose color, natural, full, sensual, but not out of keeping with the general symmetry of his face.

"I'm Lexius, my lady. You have my many letters and I have yours," he said.

He knelt as before, hands raised, his heavy sleeves revealing a tight-fitting shirt of shimmering silk, and his fingers were covered in jeweled rings.

"I invite you to this kingdom, you a slave banished in disgrace, and this is how you repay my invitation!" I said furiously. "You dare to talk your way into my quarters at this hour and unannounced?"

"I felt my heart would break if I didn't see you," he said. "I arrived after you and the King and Queen had retired. I was going mad in my rooms. I had to see you, lay eyes upon, lay eyes upon the legendary Lady Eva who carries out the instructions of the great queen."

All this was said with apparent sincerity and the greatest politeness, but there was nothing obsequious in his manner. He was imploring me with the confidence of a highborn prince which is exactly what he was.

Now all the gossip, all the talk, all of the King's interest, made some new sense to me. He was magnetic, powerful. I could see this, and feel it. What a spectacular naked slave he must have been. And as the old steward of the Sultan, assessing and commanding slaves, well, he must have been a chilling wonder just as the Queen had said.

I pondered this, pondered him as he knelt there looking up at me with a steady gaze, and then allowed his eyes once more to take my measure down to my painted toenails.

"I could worship you, my lady," he said in a low voice, his eyelids quivering. "You are as everyone has said, a magnificent lady."

"In my chambers, I choose who offers me worship, Lexius," I said. "Stand up now."

He obeyed quickly as Severin might have done. And was Severin ever going to be punished for allowing this! I wondered where he was lurking and no doubt quavering in fear just now.

Lexius stepped back against the open windows. The sky was paling and the stars were gone. The soft silent rosy light of morning was rising.

"Oh, I have dreamed of this moment," he said again in that low secretive voice.

"And how so, my lord, and why?" I asked. "Why isn't the King or the Queen the object of your abject devotion? Are they not the ones who have drawn you here over land and sea?"

He didn't choose to answer. I felt a great desire to see the King discipline him for his outrageous behavior. But he was a returning prince.

"In time I will make all my secrets known to you," he said. "Will you forgive me that I've offended you, that in my zeal I've entered the temple as a clumsy pilgrim? Please don't close your heart against me!"

I moved towards him and closer to the window, causing him to turn to his right. Now the morning light fully illuminated him, and I saw the superb texture of his skin, and the taut perfect flesh of his face. Timeless, he seemed, timeless in the ways of Asian peoples, and with a regal air that suggested old Persian paintings of splendid courts and emperors of yore.

His hair was almost too long, spilling over his shoulders in serpentine waves and curls. And the rich colors of his beaded robe were visible now, the brilliant blue shining in myriad fragments behind thick golden and silver thread and emeralds and rubies and sapphires, sapphires like the magnificent sapphire at his throat.

He seemed to read my thoughts. Suddenly, he tore the giant sapphire from his collar and held it out to me, glittering like something made of water, in his hand. The sunlight found it and it became a light unto itself.

He fell hard on his knees and still held it up to me. "My gift to you, please, my lady."

"Save it for the King and Queen."

"Ah, but I have treasures aplenty for them, and wealth in other forms. This I give to you from my person. And I offer you my soul as well."

What did this mean, I wondered.

I took the sapphire in my left hand and gazed at it. I didn't need the lamp now so I put it back on the table and then took the sapphire to the windowsill and studied it, not because I wanted it or needed it, but because I hadn't seen anything quite like it. Stories came back to me of the jewels of India.

When I turned, I realized that he had prostrated himself full length on the floor. It had a ceremonial quality to it, the way that he lay there, his forehead touching the stone. Without a command from me he rose, sinking back on his heels, and then stood without the aid of his hands. His grace was like that of a dancer. And coming to his full height, he gazed down at me with the same rapt expression as before.

"Beautiful Lady Eva," he said.

"Enough. I accept your gift. Now, get out. I'll send word to Our Majesties that you are here, though no doubt they'll be told as soon as they wake. Go to the quarters given you and wait there until you're summoned. You've behaved like a thief or an invader."

"Please don't tell the King," he said softly. "Please. I am sorry. Forgive me this secret offense and you will have a friend in me forever."

"And why should I want that?" I asked.

"Lady Eva, give me time to earn your trust."

"Get out," I said.

He left without another word.

In a moment, Severin entered, and he was indeed quaking with fear as I expected.

"My lady, he said you were expecting him! He said if I didn't admit him the worst fate awaited me! He said terrible things, things I didn't even understand, that I stood between him and the sun and the moon, and no force on earth could keep him from his mission, he spoke of worlds traversed, of seeking a blinding light—"

"You ever let anyone into my chambers again like this," I said. "And do you know what I will do to you? You'll be on your knees naked in the kitchens below, the plaything of cooks and bakers for a year."

He was on his knees and kissing my feet immediately. My heart went out to him as it always did. He was so innocent, so tender of spirit.

"Now you listen to me, boy," I said. "This will be the end of it, but you never let him past the threshold of my rooms again."

"Yes, my lady, yes, please, please never send me away. Beat me, punish me, but don't send me away."

ii

"This is most strange," I said to Her Majesty. We sat on the open terrace above the gardens, having our morning meal together. She listened attentively as I recounted the words Severin had spoken. "And what does he mean by all this, this language, his 'mission,' and that he has traversed worlds to seek a blinding light?"

"Don't you know, Eva?" asked the Queen. She looked particularly lovely this morning in her gown of violet and silver with a silver necklace of amethysts and pearls.

Down below in the fountain court nearest the castle doors, the King was breakfasting with Lexius at a marble table. We could see them perfectly but not hear a word. Fountains everywhere gave a low whisper of sound to the morning gardens, and the day's relentless rhythm of entertainment and busyness had not truly begun.

Lexius was dressed as he had been to greet me, and in the bright light of the high sun he appeared a great god of the East encrusted with jewels. So rich and long was his hair he might have been mistaken at a glance for a woman. And his fine features would not have given his gender away. But his manner was now without reserve or any special obsequiousness and he was speaking urgently and rapidly, it seemed, with animated gestures to the King.

The King as so often had an air of contented patience as he listened. Never was he not outfitted for the eyes of the Court. His scarlet tunic flattered his complexion, but then what did not flatter him? He was smiling and nodding easily at Lexius.

I had not told the King that Lexius had invaded my private rooms. But from my blessed queen I held back nothing.

"Rip your eyes off our august visitor and answer me," said the Queen calmly.

"Oh, forgive me. You asked me whether or not I knew the meaning of his strange language."

"Yes, and surely you do know what all this means."

"No."

"Eva, you are the guiding genius of discipline in the kingdom," she said. Her voice was gentle. "You were that before we came! You are the shining representation of the old monarch and her exacting ways. The King may be the priapic guardian of the realm, but you are the prosecutor of our unique laws."

I was stunned. The Queen didn't say any of this in anger, nor did she seem to possess the slightest resentment of me, yet what could this mean for her to speak in this way?

"You are our queen," I said softly. "Your Majesty, this is called Beauty's Kingdom far and wide, and in the gardens during the revels and in the village and in all the rooms and hall of the castle, as a matter of course. Bellavalten has become Beauty's Kingdom."

"I am merely a symbol," she answered, "in a land of symbolic gestures and rituals and happy to be so. The old story of enchantment adds to my luster. But it is the King who rules Bellavalten and you who grasp the mystery of all we do and enjoy here, you who effortlessly command as others obey. This is not really 'Beauty's Kingdom.'"

What could I say? I waited. She was mistaken, gravely mistaken, if she thought my grasp of things exceeded hers. She fathomed depths of which the rest of us knew little or nothing. Her judgments were sound, and her decisions perfect. No scheme or design of hers had ever failed. The King marveled at this, as did I.

"Lexius has heard of you, Eva," she said, "heard of your unquestioned mastery, heard of your governance and your personal power—a power that cannot be bestowed on one by others. He's heard of your youth, and your strength, and your unconquerable soul."

"Perhaps," I whispered. "But my queen, why does this matter?"

"Eva, he would first and foremost be your personal slave."

"No, Your Majesty, allow me to contradict you. He is a slave by nature, that much is plain to me, but he is a proud prince as well. I venture to say he is a domineering prince. This morning, I felt two currents coming from him—extreme need and indomitable will."

The King rose from the table below and moved towards the castle doors. Lexius came after him, leaning close to him, slipping a bold arm around the King's back and talking urgently to the King as before. Out of view they walked together.

"Your Majesty, you've never been unhappy with me, have you?" I asked.

"No, Eva. Never. I would have told you were I ever unhappy. It's the opposite. I marvel that you can do what I cannot. I thought to rule Bellavalten properly I must at least understand what Eleanor understood so completely: how to punish and discipline with relish, how to savor the suffering of devoted slaves rather like savoring the fragrance of a great feast or garden of exotic flowers . . ." Her voice trailed off.

She looked out over the wilderness before her of handsome fruit trees and blossoming shrubberies, of ancient oaks here and there left as reminders of an earlier seemingly unconquerable forest—of dancing fountains and carpeted paths. She was sad.

The gardeners slave and free were appearing everywhere. Naked slaves bent to trim and tend the pampered roses and zinnias and oleander. Humbly clad peasants dug up the dark earth for new flower beds, and brought carts of mulch and rich black soil. She watched them as she watched everything.

"Do you fault yourself that you do not enjoy all aspects of this?" I asked. "But how can you fault yourself for such a thing?"

"Because I think that as queen I must. I cannot go out amongst my subjects as a naked slave, can I? I can't recapture what existed decades ago, not for myself. Oh, never mind, Eva. You have realized all my dreams for the kingdom. You have anticipated most of them. I envision, the King confirms, and you make real."

"Your Majesty, in your private chambers, you are free as any lord or lady of Bellavalten."

"I know that, Eva. I had dreamed of something exalted for myself, a reign to rival Queen Eleanor's, a face beneath the crown to strike terror in those who so long to be terrified, a manner to chill those who came to be chilled of their own will."

"Ah, but you possess these attributes, my queen," I said.

She did not believe it. She did not know. She did not realize the thrilling fear she aroused in all those around her. But how could she not know, she, who seemed so attentive to their anguished devotion?

"Your Majesty, the kingdom, such as it is, is your achievement!" I said. "You have a power over all of us, all your subjects, infinitely greater than Queen Eleanor ever had."

"How is that possible?"

"Because you are the iron mistress with the irresistible sweet smile, the absolute authority with the soft voice, the merciless queen who binds with more than mere chains!"

"Is it really so?"

"Yes. Oh, yes." I leaned towards her. I spoke boldly but in a confidential voice. "Your Majesty, the late queen's legacy was a great concept and a brittle refusal to carry it to greater and greater heights. Your genius with your slaves, your genius with Lord Stefan, your genius with all your subjects, is a marvel. Whatever you suffer inside, you make the kingdom what it is."

She did not respond. She stared out over the gardens.

"Why do you think we are all so devoted to you?" I asked. "Rosalynd and Elena live to please you with the gilded slaves of the nightly festivals. Your tender fillies are thrilled to their naked hearts to be delivered to your stables. Your little pets, both kittens and puppies, are in a swoon of torment to be near you. Your conviction is blinding in its brightness! You are every bit as potent in the ruling of this realm as our lord, the King."

She appeared to ponder this and finally she turned to me, her blue eyes soft and wondering, and her face as filled with sincerity as always. "I understand what they all feel, you see."

"I know."

"The King understands, but then the King understands everything!" She laughed.

"I know what you mean."

"It's as if every slave, no matter how lowly, how disobedient, how submissive, or how perfect is connected by a golden thread to my very heart."

"Yes."

"And I will be bolder in the sanctity of my chambers," she said. "The King has repeatedly urged me to be so. I will, from now on."

But this vow wasn't made with much spirit. I wanted to take her hand as she looked again over the bustling gardens. But this seemed presumptuous. I only watched her and waited. And then without turning, she reached out for my hand and clasped it warmly and then drew it to her breast.

iii

The King was always sending me presents. A robe of lavender-blue silk, a dress of plum-colored velvet, slippers of jeweled leather.

Now came the letter in the afternoon as I left the Hall of Postulants, weary from the day's work but quite encouraged. And the letter said simply for me to wear the plum-colored gown for him this evening, and that he had taken the liberty of retrieving from my quarters the blue sapphire given me by Lexius and that it was being set for me to wear in a necklace of gold.

The plum-colored gown was the King's favorite, by far. It was low cut to reveal my bosom, but with great flaring sleeves and heavy skirts. How many times had he knelt before those heavy skirts?

But I knew this was no summons to whip him tonight as I did perhaps every two weeks or so. This had to do with Lexius. Why else had he sent for the sapphire?

So I dressed with this in mind.

Severin hovered over me, helping me to rouge my lips; and my naked maids, lovely creatures—the Queen had been so right to say that naked slaves might be used for all manner of labor—did up my hair with ropes of pearls, leaving only the longest locks to fall over my shoulders.

The King liked bare necks and bare shoulders and as much of a bare bosom as a lady might dare to display. That is, when he looked away from his many slaves. Very well. I was more than contented with his taste. And I had a new pair of slippers from him with pointed toes and with the highest gold heels I'd ever worn.

I was dressed and ready quite early. I knew it might be an hour or two before the King's summons. In fact, I was sure of it as he was in the gardens now with the Queen, and Lexius was with them. Alexi had told me he would be seated with Lexius at the King's table. And the table tonight would be on the border of the Bridle Path so that the King and Queen and all their Court might pay particular attention to the slaves being paddled along by their masters and mistresses, boy, girl, boy, girl, as the King liked it. And I knew that Stefan, wearing a mask still, and unidentified to the Court, would be one of those boys. Dmitri would ride in the chariot to drive Stefan with the great leather paddle. Stefan was now Dmitri's obsession.

He'd returned the ravishing flaxen-haired Becca completely transformed into the most sensitive chamber slave for the Queen, and the Queen was most pleased with that. And though the Queen left the strict punishing of Becca to me, the Queen took Becca into her bed nightly.

The Queen was eager to see Stefan's performance tonight, to see his form.

Dmitri was toying with the idea of giving a new name to Stefan, a name to mark the trajectory of his new life when the masks were finally put aside. He was calling Stefan by the name of Xander, a nickname Dmitri particularly liked.

I would love to see Stefan for myself tonight, or Xander, and had no doubt that he would be perfect. Dmitri would never have brought him up to Court had he not been ready.

Indeed the strange "Masked One" was now a story in the village, and crowds gathered before the Public Turntable at the predictable hours just to see him whipped. It was the novelty of the mask, certainly, and the whispers that he was of the Court. But it was also that Stefan had become a paragon of decorum. Bad slaves from their pillories were instructed to raise their heads and watch Stefan being punished and learn from his poise.

Rosalynd had told me that it had been this way with Dmitri before he'd left the village years ago to be sent home. He had become the paragon of style on the Public Turntable where once he'd suffered so much. He had become the one whom the crowds gathered to see most especially. And now he had made of Stefan a rival for himself.

Rosalynd was brilliant. The Queen certainly thought so, and she was right. Rosalynd continued to supervise all the many gold-burnished slaves throughout the gardens, those bound to crosses and set in wall niches, and made into footstools, and those whipped in artful and extravagant ways and combinations for the Court. She was ever devising new motifs, new designs, new and artful combinations. She did all this so effortlessly and happily that she had time to spare. Elena was her natural assistant, her devoted friend. These two were the Queen's favorites.

But Prince Alexi was never far from the Queen either. Alexi longed for a special task, other than the examination and testing of postulants— something we all did—but his moment had not yet come. Strictly speaking, Alexi was charged with helping Rosalynd and Elena with the evening Court entertainments, but in fact, he did very little of this, other than wear the gold chain and medallion of his office which ladies found far too cumbersome and ugly to wear. He was a powerful symbol of authority, however. And the Court loved him.

We had our ceremonial rings from the King and Queen and that was quite enough. But I thought the chains and medallions very handsome on the men, and certainly this ornament added to the impressive quality of Prince Dmitri as he ruled the village punishments.

All these and other considerations moved through my mind as I waited for the King's summons. I sat at my writing desk and now and then made some note as to what I might do as to some difficulty, or scribbled out an idea that might prove amusing to the Court. And then I opened my diary and wrote my private thoughts.

Severin had been dismissed along with my maids for their shared recreation—a great novelty introduced by the Queen—in which they could loiter in a little private chamber among Eastern pillows and turrets and cuddle and play with one another and share secrets and confessions.

And though I'd wondered about this new custom, I had seen immediately that it was to be a great success. Slaves returned refreshed, more eager to serve than ever, and vying with one another to please. So what if they whispered about their "favorite" master or mistress in private? Or coupled with one another like little beasts.

There came a knock at my door.

Before I could rise, the door itself was opened and in came Lexius who immediately closed it behind him and advanced towards me with bold steps.

"What are you doing here, my lord?" I demanded. The heat rose in my face. I could hear my pulse in my ears.

He cut a powerful alluring figure. He was outfitted once more in Eastern splendor with more jewels sewn to his long tunic than I'd ever beheld in one place. Emeralds covered him and emeralds sparkled on his long dark fingers, and even in the lobes of his ears. But his eyes were his finest jewels.

He glared at me. I couldn't read his expression, and when he took another step towards me, I became furious.

"Explain yourself," I said. "Did I open the door for you? Did I bid you come in?"

"I must have you!" he said to me. His lips curled in a triumphant smile. He took another step forward, eyebrows raised and eyes quivering.

"Have me?" I asked. I came out from behind the desk and at once he stepped back. But the look of wild determination hadn't left his face.

Then he drew himself up and spoke again in a low menacing voice.

"I will have you, have you naked, have you here, have you stripped of all your authority and your finery." Once more he advanced.

"The hell you will!" I said. I slammed my fist down hard on the writing desk and he jumped back and his eyes grew large. "Whatever gave you such a preposterous notion!" I demanded. "You dare to come into my chambers and say these words to me? Get out of here, now."

He stood quivering all over.

"I will have you," he said in a voice that was almost a growl. "I will make you kneel to me."

He came forward as if pitching himself headlong into the gesture and reached out for me.

With the full force of my hand I slapped his face. Stunned he stood there trying to catch his breath. How lovely he looked—a dark god staring in wonder. I slapped him again and then again. I slapped him harder than I had ever slapped any slave. I drove him backwards in the direction of the door with my slaps.

And then with one mighty slap of my cupped hand, I caught him under the chin and slammed his head back against the door.

"Get out of here, my lord, before I drive you out on your hands and knees," I said. I was seething.

He didn't move. His face was bloodred from my slaps and his great dark eyes were blazing as he looked up and he laid his hands back on the wood of the door. His long luxuriant hair was tousled and lustrous in the candlelight.

"You are a goddess!" he said as he looked at me. His eyes were hungry.

"You don't know the half of it!" I said.

I reached out and caught him by the border of his thick tunic and dragged him forward so that I could open the door. Then I grabbed a great handful of his black hair and dragged him through the door and hurled him into the passage, so that he staggered backwards and nearly fell.

"I had to try!" he called out. He fell on his knees and threading his fingers together as he raised his hands, he implored me to understand. "I had to try, great Lady Eva."

"You did? You will rue the hour when you tried," I said. I slammed the door shut and threw the bolt.

15

ALEXI:
THE BRIDLE
PATH

It was the night on which the favorites of the King and Queen were
run on the Bridle Path, along with the favorites of the more powerful
members of the Court.

I stood at the door of the Bridle Path Hall where the glittering chariots were lined up, the various lords and ladies already mounted in them,
and ponies stamping their booted feet ready to pull them, and the poor
slaves chosen to be runners waited in line as well.

Rosalynd and Elena were instructing the grooms as they prepared the
slaves, adjusting coiffed hair or braided hair, brushing the bushy locks of
the boy slaves, and warning each and every one to run fast and hard.

"There is no escaping the paddle," said Rosalynd to the little thing
closest to her, "and if you pass the royal banquet table without putting on
the very best show, you'll find yourselves hung upside down in the gardens for the night."

The little thing was Sybil, stunning dark-haired slave already well
trained as a pony in the Queen's Stables, but she seemed at quite a loss
now, stripped of all her fine harnesses and ruthlessly exposed except for
her boots.

Nothing chastens quite like the Bridle Path, I thought.

Behind her came the tall and supremely lovely Blanche, Tristan's most attractive slave, and Tristan in his finest Court dress was already in the second chariot, ready to drive Blanche hard with the paddle for the frantic run of her life. Blanche had been run countless times and accepted her fate with downcast eyes, hands clasped to the back of her neck beneath her long hair, breasts heaving anxiously, though she was otherwise quite still.

Long ago, the girls had all had their hair braided, and we boys who had been run had had our hair combed back with oil.

But all slaves were ornamented now or they did not appear in the garden, and all lips and nipples were rouged or gilded, and hair was luxuriantly free.

Lord Stefan, behind a gorgeous gold leather mask adorned with rubies, stood waiting in third place. In the third chariot some distance away stood Dmitri, regal as ever, his blue eyes fixed on Stefan, though Stefan stood motionless with only the smallest twitch to the edge of his handsome mouth.

His punishment and training had been a great success, all knew. And several other members of the Court had since gone down on bended knee to Queen Beauty asking to accept "the Discipline of the Mask."

Of course Beauty, gracious and loving in all things, had said she wanted to ponder the matter, but that she fully understood their wishes. She and her closest advisors would give immediate attention to this idea of the "Discipline of the Mask," and she would have a decision very soon.

Was Stefan to become the first Disciple of the Mask? He was the lone such disciple tonight to be run on the Bridle Path.

I had my old memories of course of having been whipped along it near every day for the pleasure of Queen Eleanor (though she herself never whipped any slave on the Bridle Path; that was not for her) and always at what we called Festival Night. Now every night was Festival Night.

Stefan's sometime slave Becca, now the Queen's slave once more, who had seldom before been subjected to this ritual, stood waiting in fourth place. Dmitri had turned her into a gorgeous nymph and part of her bright shining hair was swept up and back into a thick silver buckle fitted with star garnets to reveal the special favor from the Queen with which she was now blessed. If Sybil pleased the Queen tonight, she would hereafter wear the buckle with the star garnets. And there were two other girls down the line so honored already.

Sweet Princess Lucinda, garbed in puce velvet, was already in her chariot to drive Becca. She flashed a loving smile on me when I caught her eye. A tall willowy figure with the most girlish smile, she would do an excellent job of it, of course, as she rode the chariot with the Queen's crest. It was her keenest pleasure outside of presiding over the Queen's Stables, and she drove one of the Queen's favorites almost every night. She was one of those imperturbable mistresses who saw to every punishment with great efficiency and unbroken decorum, never raising her voice.

I saw no end of sumptuous breasts and lavish pubic hair, of shapely legs turned out in tight boots, or downcast eyes and wet cheeks. Most cocks were erect and glistening, balls oiled to shine in the light of torches and lanterns, and gilded nipples everywhere twinkled like stars.

Then there were Dmitri's three darlings, Bertram, Kiera, and Barbara, all wearing his newly chosen signature jeweled buckles of gold and malachite. Would Stefan win such a buckle tonight?

Kiera and Bertram had run the Bridle Path many a time, and were only a little anxious, but Barbara was crying copious tears. She'd never been to Court before, ever. And though Dmitri could not return again and again to personally paddle all of his slaves along the path, he would double back to whip Barbara himself. I knew the terror she was experiencing now at the mere thought of his disapproval, how she trembled at the mere sound of Dmitri's steel voice.

I remembered how Dmitri had come to love her when he first saw her, and he had already created in her a slave of dignity and infatuating submission.

It seemed to me Dmitri's beauties lived in a delirium sustained by his capacity to frighten them and shame them which was as exquisite as any music ever played by horn or harp. His groom Fabien had been coming along as a household disciplinarian as well. Fabien's style mirrored Dmitri's style, and grooms of such personal will and force always fared well in the kingdom.

Dmitri did not so much as look at the others. The test for him tonight was Stefan, and his eyes were fastened to Stefan, but surely he was quite certain Stefan would not fail. Fabien stood against the wall watching Stefan also, as he'd apparently been told to do.

My eyes moved down the long row, casually inspecting others I knew by name and some I knew only by face and form.

There was juicy and curvaceous Cressida, another pony from the

Queen's Stables, with her flaming hair, crying softly as the grooms rubbed more rouge into her nipples and obviously coaxed her to stand up straight and proud. She had become fast friends with Sybil, in the stable yard at recreation. And the Queen favored them as a pair. But now Cressida was a quivering lily without the security of her customary bit and harnesses.

Then came Penryn, the sturdy and boyish slave of Prince Richard, who had never been brought up from the village before and was plainly very afraid. Prince Richard, who always cut a fine figure, was kissing Penryn and stroking his mop of yellow hair—a rare bit of mercy for a slave whom Richard drove relentlessly to be "as perfect" as any slave at Court, though Penryn spent most of his days in the village with his master, and was paddled in the Punishment Shops twice a day.

What was a special humiliation for most village slaves was daily life for Penryn because of Prince Richard's duties, and he lived to please Richard, often subjected to the worst humiliations if he failed. Whenever I spied Penryn on the Public Turntable I turned to watch, and I was never disappointed. The tender whipping master of the Punishment Shop called Penryn his favorite "dumpling."

After these and some others stood my own slave Valentine, sobbing bitterly, a precious gift given me by Dmitri who had bought Valentine from the village booksellers for the price of a precious volume of Horace.

Valentine had been bought for the village when he came to the kingdom. And had never dreamed he would become the slave of a prince. I found him sensitive and inviting in all ways, and loved that he cried unceasingly like an overflowing fountain. Blond hair, very pretty mouth. Almond skin. After the long boredom of belonging to a village scholar, he had found the ways of the Court terrifying in the beginning, cleaving to me when I walked him on a leash as if great peril might at any time befall him, but I had enjoyed training him, wiping his tears, pinching him, and making him jump, and he was polished enough now to be brought along with me when I went to dine alone with the Queen. Tonight, if he did well, he'd be bound to a cross in the gardens after and allowed to doze before adoring eyes. If he failed, he'd be hung on the stable wall with the bad slaves and punished and teased all night.

I wouldn't drive the boy myself on the Bridle Path tonight. Elena was doing the honors as the ride in the chariot thrilled her and the husky boy pony pulling the chariot was one of her favorites, part of the King's team—a punished pony who'd been promoted to a permanent pony on account of his great stamina.

At the very end of the present line—it would in the course of the night see many additions—stood César, the tall proud pony whom the King so loved.

I adored César. I was intrigued by César. I felt that his life story in the kingdom told us volumes about the minds and hearts of all slaves and that César ought to be studied in depth by those aspiring to be great masters and mistresses.

César had lived for two decades in the village stables, one of those slaves so attuned to pony life that no one ever thought he would be good for anything else. "Workhorse," "plow horse," those were terms used in the past for César. But the King, quite fascinated with César, had forced the slave to new heights.

Anyone could see why, and I certainly did, as César was not only extremely tall and powerfully built, but he had a face like a marble statue, just that perfect and just that large. He was one of those beings who looked splendid with his hair swept back from his forehead—indeed he had beautiful eyes and a beautiful forehead—and his hair was always brushed that way and with the forelocks gathered into a long thick braid to lie on the rest of his wavy mane as it fell to his shoulders.

But without the safety of his harnesses, and the butt plug and the horse tail, and without the comfort of the bit in his teeth, César was afraid.

This was the slave I'd drive tonight, and I went to him now. I walked back into the huge shadowy enclosure. Like all the structures of the new kingdom, it was a finely constructed building, and it was hung with many lanterns, and its soft earthen floor, so good for the slaves' horse-shoed boots, was swept immaculately clean.

I gave my handsome Valentine a kiss as I passed and then stood by César.

"What's all this weeping?" I asked. He towered over me, standing there with his hands behind his neck, and his face was as beautiful as that of a woman, with his soft tearing blue eyes. "Come on, answer me, César," I said. I poked him under the chin with the handle of my paddle.

"My prince, I've never . . . I . . . what if I fail?" Voices are very important when it comes to slaves, and César had a low, cultured, pleasing voice. Rumor had it that he had been a scholar in his early youth and much the prodigious scholar at that, yet he had taken to the pony life lustily and with utter abandon.

"Nonsense," I said reprovingly. I poked at his chin again making him lift his head. "You're not afraid of failing. You've been pulling carts for twenty years, and the King's fastest chariots for some ten months. You're in splendid condition. You could probably outrun the pony pulling the chariot tonight that carries me."

"Oh, no, my lord," he said, fighting his tears. "Your chariot tonight will be pulled by Brenn, the King's new favorite, and he's stronger even than I."

"More nonsense," I said. "He's as strong as you, yes, but he's not the King's new favorite pony, and you're to stop sulking at once. You put on a bad show tonight and Brenn just might become the King's new favorite, don't you realize that?"

I remembered him and when he came. He was not of royal birth, but of good gentry, sent to Queen Eleanor as a gift by parents who found his wit and verbal precocity annoying. She had scant interest in such slaves. Princes and princesses had interested her, and little else. And one look at this giant of a white-haired slave and she had condemned him to the village stables with a wave of her hand.

Of course he was not bigger than King Laurent. But he was as big, and that is saying something. And he was not merely beautiful, but he was pretty and fetching, and many at the Court had groaned to see him go.

But César had been happy in the stables. The grooms adored him. They hadn't seen a pony of his size since Laurent, who'd only lately gone home. And his hair was near white, and they loved this, and the villagers always stopped to watch him trotting past.

As he'd been an outright gift and not a tribute, the Queen had never bothered to ask about him again, and César himself had never wanted to leave. There have always been ponies like this—in particular, strong, muscular men of exceptional stamina who come alive in bit and harness and crave no other world.

Then King Laurent had discovered him, and marveled at his exquisite face and the smoothness of his skin. "Why is this jewel buried in the straw of the village stable?" he asked. And César had become a royal pony, elevated to the glamour of the new Bellavalten overnight. Now the King wanted more from César, and his courtly service to the King was beginning in earnest.

"I'll tell you what's wrong with you," I said. "You've been hiding all these years, hiding. You're terrified of the solitary exposure, of running with your head up, alone and without a team, and in fear of the inescapable paddle and hearing the Court cheer as you go past, you, César, inspected and admired for your own merits."

He squeezed his eyes shut and nodded, even though I still prodded him with the paddle handle. I gave one of his nipples a hard twist, and watched his chest muscles twitch.

"Oh, it's humiliating, all right, for a proud steed," I said. "I know."

I gave him a good hard crack on his powerful hindquarters and he jumped.

"But this is what the King wants!" I said. "And therefore you must want it."

"Yes, sir," he said, stammering and shifting his weight. He had always been very polite, well bred. When the King had discovered he was educated, he'd sent him books to read during his recreation—something that would never have occurred to anyone at all ever in the old kingdom— and César had enjoyed them, often curling up under an oak to read Ovid rather than jostle with the other ponies at rest in the yard. There was a special place in his stall for his books. Yet he had become a leader among the new Court ponies, teaching them many things, and the grooms came to him all the time with questions because there was nothing César didn't know about being a pony. I knew the King's taste. César and the husky and pretty-faced satyr, Brenn, were his favorites and one would not replace the other in his heart. Brenn was being trained to great versatility from the beginning and César must learn to be flexible and pliant as well. It thrilled me to think of how the King would turn César inside out in the months to come.

"Listen, the King loves you both," I said, now pressing close to him. "You're suffering over nothing when it comes to Brenn. Befriend him. That is what the King assumes you will do."

"Yes, sir," he said again. "Brenn is my friend. Brenn's been kind enough to me, has been since he came. I won't try to outrun him tonight, sir. I won't do anything to displease you or the King."

I squeezed his hard bottom. The paddle would barely faze him. His skin was alabaster smooth but tough.

I saw Elena hurrying towards me, looking quite tasty in her new black satin gown. The ladies of the Court were displaying new fashions inspired by the Queen. Breasts were often half bared, and waists were high and skirts full. Elena looked perfect in this new style, and wore ropes of pearls about her neck, given her by the Queen.

"They're ready to begin," she said. "They were all waiting on that strange wild-eyed Lexius and he is at last there."

I heard the trumpet sound for the first chariot and its passenger to whip the first slave onto the path. Sweet Sybil. I couldn't see from here. Though there must have been thirty in line, I knew things would happen now very fast.

Quickly, I went to Valentine and kissed him and embraced him. "Now you make me proud tonight," I whispered in his ear. He was crying as always but he answered me in the most gentle voice.

A groom came down the line, wiping noses and cheeks and making what last little adjustments might be needed to the slaves' boots. He was slapping cocks here and there, and pinching nipples to make them hard.

I headed to my chariot and climbed up and made sure of the reins. Brenn stood there, in full practical harness, arms strapped to his back, boots planted firmly on the earth.

"You ready to keep up with César tonight, Brenn?" I called out and Brenn gave me a vigorous nod.

He'd only been in the stable for three days, and yesterday after much training, he'd pulled the Queen alone in her smallest and most delicate chariot on her regular evening drive. The Queen had been completely delighted. She had had him turned out completely in red harnesses and had adorned his cock with red ribbons and golden bells. Brenn had shed a world of tears but was perfection to her and King Laurent.

When they returned to the castle she had given the reins to me to take Brenn back to the stables, and there I'd watched as Georgette unharnessed him, teasing him about being the only little colt among so many fillies.

She loved paddling him. She'd thrown him over her knee and asked him over and over again as she spanked him, "How much does the Queen love you, tell me! Tell me more."

Poor Brenn had sobbed and given the only acceptable answer, "I want to please her." After that I walked with the groom who paddled him back to the King's Stables for recreation. I had always hated those driving paddles and the humiliating spanks when a slave is merely being moved from place to place. But I knew that most slaves needed this. Slaves had to be maintained. Discipline had to pervade every moment of their lives.

Brenn's form was perfect. In the recreation yard, César had beckoned to Brenn to come join him and they lay on the green grass together, César reading his little book, and Brenn with his head on César's chest as he slept—and César playing idly with his black hair. But still, César was jealous. I knew this. I understood it.

Again and again the trumpet sounded as one slave after another was pushed onto the path.

I had a clear view of Dmitri lining up his chariot beside Stefan and I could see even from this distance that Stefan was as compliant as before. The mask looked so pretty. I wondered if we shouldn't do more with masks. But then the words came back to me, "the Discipline of the Mask." If it already had a meaning, well, then, we should develop that meaning, shouldn't we—of a highborn lord or lady within the kingdom submitting to rigorous slavery through the Discipline of the Mask. And surely the Queen was already contemplating this. She'd be asking our advice on it soon.

Dmitri and Stefan moved up to first place. The slave pulling Dmitri's chariot was Bastian, another of the King's own team. I wondered if the slaves hated this particular duty as they wore such plain brown harnesses with only a little brass here and there—nothing like the full dress when they pulled a carriage or chariot for the King.

Suddenly the trumpet sounded and Dmitri swung the paddle driving Stefan onto the path. I couldn't see if Stefan's cock was at attention, but I had seen it earlier and it was splendidly huge and red.

Off they went, Stefan marching with knees high and shoulders back, smacked again and again as they moved off and around the curve.

I listened attentively and could hear the distant roar of the crowd around the royal banquet table soon enough.

There were many slaves ahead of us now but César was brought forward and stationed to my right. He was now weeping frantically, and the groom again wiped his face.

César's backside was barely pink from whatever discipline he'd had that day. But his skin was tough, tough from years of the paddle and the strap, and I knew I had to paddle him hard to make the slightest impression and that I was prepared to do.

The leather paddle was long and broad and just the right weight. In the old days these paddles had been strapped to the arms of the lords and ladies who drove their slaves, but now we merely held tight to the handles. And there was a spare paddle in every chariot in case somehow one's paddle was dropped. I never saw anyone drop a paddle.

With a little time to kill, I jumped down and went up to Brenn. He was weeping as copiously as César. I checked his harnesses to make sure nothing was chafing. He wore a butt plug with a small decoration of flowers like all the ponies, and a long plain horse's tail of black to match his hair.

"Now what's all this sobbing?" I asked, but that only made him cry more. "You and César make a splendid picture. And I want pride now, not weeping." He did his best to straighten up.

I checked the bit between his teeth and it was perfect, soft, but good enough size, and of course connected properly to the reins.

"You set the pace," I said. "And César won't dare to outrun you." I kissed him and his eyes closed and then he glanced at me and I kissed him on his eyelids. "You're a lovely colt," I said. "Just the most beautiful." I rubbed his hair.

I went to César.

"Now, I'm going to pound that backside of yours," I said, "but you keep to the pace set by Brenn, you understand, no matter how hard I whip you."

"Yes, sir," he said.

"And let me tell you a little secret. When you find yourself running before the royal dais, when you hear the cheers of the Court, you'll love it. You'll stick out your chest and pick up your knees like never before."

I didn't wait to see all the tears that would gush after that, but got back in the chariot and took the paddle in hand.

Up ahead I saw Valentine spanked up to the starting line by Elena, who was a vision of sweetness in her black gown as she held the reins of her chariot in her left hand.

When the trumpet sounded, Valentine hesitated, but the paddle sent him scurrying forward and they were soon off, pounding down the path, Elena swinging the paddle lustily and Valentine running as if for his life.

A memory came back to me of being driven along the path in the last year of my time with Queen Eleanor—by the cold Lady Elvera who had been Laurent's mistress of those years. She was as sedate then as she was now. I knew she'd be at the banquet table on the dais. She always was. And I reflected helplessly on how very different everything was now.

Lord Gregory was forever seeking these days to draw her into his little world of grumblings and forebodings and bitter complaints: too much laxity; too much pampering; not enough maintenance of the hard and fast rules; not enough silence, isolation, hard punishment, and the like.

Lady Elvera tolerated him but she was more than content. She had the remote severity of the old queen.

We were nearing the starting line.

Only one chariot was before us, carrying the Grand Duke André in all his predictable splendor and, standing beside him, his precious slave, Princess Braelyn, who had been serving him for a year when Laurent and Beauty had come. She had a warm ruddy complexion and a wealth of reddish-blond hair. It was gorgeous as it fell down her back. The Bridle Path was nothing new to her. But I wondered what it meant to her to see so many new faces, new slaves, new courtiers.

We pulled up right behind them and I heard the Grand Duke, in his soothing voice, tell her that she must put on a special show tonight or she would disappoint him, but this was all the usual banter. He adored her.

When the trumpet sounded, he spanked her with a force quite remarkable for such an elderly man.

Off they went and we were in first place. I could hear César's sobs and I told him firmly to be quiet.

"Close your lips, as if you have a bit between your teeth!" I gave him a hard spank, but it was like hitting granite. Nevertheless he jumped as he always did, and he did quiet down. Veteran ponies can be remarkably sensitive to blows delivered by particular persons while becoming insensible to the endless whacking of drivers and grooms.

At last the trumpeter lifted his horn. There came the clear musical blast, and with a great hard blow I went after César, pounding him at least a good six times before we'd moved but a few yards. The reins were tight in my left hand.

Brenn ran as fast as he could, and César effortlessly kept up with him, and what a splendid pair they were.

Over and over I pounded César's hard backside, determined to make him feel something, and on he ran.

Suddenly we were nearing the royal dais and I could see the King had risen to his feet. He gave a cheerful wave to his favorites and blew them kisses, and a great roar went up from the crowd like a breaker on a wintry beach.

On the other side of the track was another dais, on which many were gathered, privileged to be directly opposite the King and Queen. And they too were roaring and cheering.

I paddled César harder than I'd ever paddled a slave in my life. He was running beautifully and so was Brenn. How that hard little butt plug must have jiggled inside Brenn's backside. I had no idea what it meant to run like this with a horse tail phallus or a plug inside me. My world had been made up of quieter things.

The royal pavilion was soon behind us. On and on we went past the countless smaller pavilions and tables, the waving arms and the eager faces, and finally we were in the last few yards before the new stables for the end of Bridle Path and the grooms waiting to attend both slaves.

As soon as I jumped down from the chariot, I took César in my arms. He was utterly broken down. I told him to embrace me and he did put his head on my shoulder and sobbed.

"You were magnificent!" I said.

A groom appeared and told us that César had to hurry, that the King wanted César rubbed with gold and mounted on a cross in the garden for the rest of the night.

Desperately his powerful hands clutched my shoulders.

But I pulled back and wiped his face quickly with my linen handkerchief and told him to do exactly as he was told. This had never happened to him before, being bound to a decorative cross in the gardens, and I knew he was afraid.

"In a few moments, you'll be strapped firmly in place," I told him, "just as firmly as ever you've been strapped to a chariot or cart, and then you can close your eyes and drift."

"Drift, my lord? What does it mean to drift?"

I laughed. "To doze and dream," I said. "Now go."

Brenn had been completely unharnessed and thrown over a huge overturned barrel to be scrubbed and bathed. He lay still with his eyes closed.

I waited until they had thoroughly dried him and then, unhooking the collar and leash from my belt, I went to him and told him to kneel for the collar. I snapped the leash to it, and told him he must walk before me, as the ground here was too rough for his knees.

"The Queen wants you for her pet tonight," I said. "They want to show you to their new guest, Lexius. Have you ever heard his name?"

"No, my lord," he answered. He was still winded and tired but clearly very at ease.

"Well, you will find him very pleasing to please," I said. "Your bottom's not red enough. But I won't spank you till we reach the garden."

"Yes, my lord," he said.

"And how was it for you, your first time pulling a chariot on the Bridle Path?"

"I hope I pleased, my lord," he said predictably enough. "I was running as fast as I was able. I knew César would run fast."

"You did well," I said.

When we reached the soft grass and carpets of the gardens, I ordered him down on his knees. I found a deserted table beneath a huge oak, somewhat out of the way of all the festivities, and I turned him over my knee and spanked his pretty quivering backside hard with the paddle I still carried till he was the perfect shade for the Queen's taste. After César's granite bottom, it was nice to be paddling a slave who flinched and sobbed with every blow. But he was as perfect as any slave who'd been here for months or for years.

I put him down on his hands and knees again and pulled him along. He followed at my heel without the slightest urging. Puppy or pony, he was excellent.

When I reached the dais, Beauty had a dish of cool wine and honey ready for Brenn and she watched with a smile as he lapped it up.

"That was all done very well, Alexi," said the Queen to me, "and my little Brenn was perfect, but I do long to see him smacked along the Bridle Path soon too. Perhaps tomorrow night."

"As you wish, madam," I said. "I'll drive him writhing and crying along the path with pleasure."

Brenn was hearing every word but gave no sign of it. I felt I knew Brenn's soul, knew the erotic delirium in which he was existing.

Lexius and the King were taking their leave.

"Where is Eva?" I asked. "I don't see her."

"I don't know," said Beauty. "Sit here beside me, Alexi. Thank you. I think the King will be busy with Eva and Lexius tonight."

I smiled. "That ought to be a splendid encounter," I said.

"Yes, and Dmitri's gone to be with them too." She put down bits and pieces of meat for Brenn to gobble.

"And what did you think of Stefan?" I asked under my breath.

"Oh, he was remarkable!" she said. "And he looked splendid. Dmitri drove him mercilessly but he never broke pace or form. I think perhaps the mask might come off soon. But then maybe again, he'll always wear it. Seems masks are most interesting to the Court and in the village. I'm giving much thought to the uses of masks."

I was not surprised.

"Come," she said. "Let's take a little walk through the garden." She tugged Brenn's leash as she rose and I took her hand. "I want to see some of the games. I haven't paid enough attention to the games."

That's our precious queen, I thought. I wished I could kiss her, take her in my arms and cover her in kisses, but I could not do such a thing here. But maybe later on tonight, I would be alone with her, if the King and Dmitri and Lexius and Lady Eva were busy as the hours passed.

If I hated anything in the kingdom, it was the King yanking me out of bed after Beauty and I had fallen asleep in each other's arms. He thought nothing of gently hurling me to the floor. Of course he was always in good humor when he did it, but there was a certain mockery in his voice when he said, "Out of my chambers, little monkey, and now."

Beauty roused me from my reverie. We were making progress slowly, surrounded by bowing courtiers on all sides.

"What do you think, Alexi?" she asked. "Is it splendid or not?" She gestured to the great teeming gardens around us.

"It's splendid, my queen, more splendid than I ever imagined it could be, and that is the truth."

"And you, my dear Brenn, what do you think?" She pulled him so that she might kiss him. "Is it all as splendid as you imagined?"

"Magnificent, my queen," he said. "I never in my wildest longing dreamed of such a paradise."

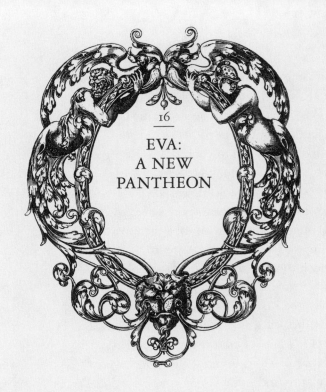

16

EVA:
A NEW
PANTHEON

Finally, the King's summons had come. It was very late, and I was
being escorted not to his private chambers but to those of "a guest."

My heart was tripping. All subjects in the kingdom served at
the pleasure of the King, and I did not know what this meant.

When the doors opened, and I saw Prince Dmitri and the King standing there with Lexius, I was intrigued, but resolved. I was a subject but
not a slave. When had the monarchs of the realm ever demanded that a
lord or lady strip and submit to them?

I walked into the room and made my bow to the King.

"Eva, kiss me," he said. His arms went out to me.

I embraced him warmly and looked up into his earnest and gentle
face. We kissed on the lips, and I stepped back, quickly taking the measure of Dmitri who stood with his hands clasped behind his back merely
eyeing me as if he were mightily intrigued with what was happening.

But what was happening?

As for Lexius, he was obviously deeply shaken. He regarded me with
timid near-worshipful eyes. He wore the same rich garments he'd worn
earlier, having changed only his boots for the golden slippers usually
worn inside the castle.

He was indeed almost as tall as the King, and in the many blazing candelabra of this chamber he appeared more comely and seductive than ever. This I could see with detachment. To deny him his godlike gifts in my heart would have been dishonest.

As for the room, it held the usual impressive coffered bed, but with space to spare for an extravagant scattering of stately chairs, and the fire was as always burning on the giant hearth.

Exotic scarlet hangings gave the room an Oriental feel, and I realized that the air was filled with the heavy fragrance of incense.

Dmitri was dressed as he always was when he came to Court, as a Russian prince in his heavy tunic and trousers. His expression was now grave, but then in his lusty dominance of the Place of Public Punishment, he'd become known for gravity or gravitas as the old Romans might have called it.

"My beautiful lady," said the King. "Prince Lexius has told me what he did, how he's twice offended you."

"Well, I'm most relieved to hear it, sire," I said. "Because offend me he has indeed done, and twice as you said, in ways I have never endured in this kingdom."

So far so good, I thought.

Lexius had begun to tremble. What is it about the vulnerability of such a tall and regal man that so stirs my blood?

I felt a great desire to treat him as he had treated me, but I had no intention of taking such liberties with any guest of the kingdom, or any lord or lady, or anyone whom I considered my equal.

"I've given Lexius my judgment on his behavior," said the King.

He was still dressed as he had been for the festivities in the gardens, in impeccable crimson velvet with lavish trimmings of gold, and he was as always a magnificent vision. It seemed that crimson or scarlet most flattered his dark face and his warm brown eyes and hair.

He went on:

"I have told him he must leave the kingdom at once," he said. "But he begs me to allow him to explain himself, to lay his apologies before you, and to confess to you why he has come here. I have summoned you to ask whether you wish to allow this."

"If Your Majesty wants me to allow it, I shall," I said. "In truth, I should like to know what prompted him—a man with much knowledge of Bellavalten in its old days—to behave as he has done with me."

"Speak then, Lexius. The lady's being gracious." The King shrugged and threw up his hands. "Perhaps you wish Dmitri to leave?"

"No, sire, please, let him remain," said Lexius. He had such an appealing way of holding himself, of inclining his head and extending his graceful hand in a feline gesture, that I found myself all the more intrigued. Why should a person of such manners have behaved so crudely?

"And you, Dmitri?" asked the King.

"I ask to stay, my lord," said Dmitri. "We have been friends, Lexius and I. As you know we know each other well. He has asked me to be here, and I am prepared for what is to follow."

The King nodded.

What is to follow? I pondered.

Lexius came forward and went down on one knee before me.

"My gracious lady, I beg your pardon for what I did," said Lexius. "And it is time for you and our gracious king to know why I came here. I did not come to return to life at Bellavalten. And if I have in any way misled anyone to believe so by my letters, I am sorry."

"Stand up, please, sir," I said. "I would look into your eyes."

He rose and stood before me, but everything in his demeanor suggested that he was still down on one knee.

"I accepted your invitations—yours, Dmitri's, and His Majesty's invitations to visit the kingdom, yes, but I came with a secret purpose."

"Which is what?" asked the King. He folded his arms, and gave a bit of a mock frown, but he was smiling. Only a person of immense self-confidence and inner strength, I thought, could offer such a facial expression to all this rather than cold suspicion.

"My lord, I come from the city of Arikamandu in India. This is a port city on the southeastern coast."

"I know of it," said the King. "So?"

"And I was born to a powerful family there. I say so that you may understand my position and my life. The members of my family have for generations been the protectors of a great secret, and that secret is a small realm that exists behind high walls in the jungles of my land two days' journey north of my home. This realm is known in legend and to those who people it and protect it as the Secret City of Khaharanka. It is a city-state of some two thousand souls who are dedicated to a way of life as unusual and sublime as that of Bellavalten."

"I see," said the King. "I suspected as much."

I was fascinated.

"Dmitri has visited Khaharanka," said Lexius. "And he can vouch for the truth of what I say of this city-state and its people. All my life I have been especially dedicated to the protection and nurturing of Khaharanka. Not all members of my family are chosen for this, only some. And having been chosen early I was sent to the sultanate to learn all that I could about its ways of pleasure slavery, its women and its men, so that I might better use this knowledge for the benefit of Khaharanka. The Sultan knew this. He knew that I was his guest. Yet at some time during my visit there he chose to treat me as a kind of hostage, demanding jewels and peacock feathers and gold and other riches from my family in exchange for my 'imminent' freedom. I was being held by force as surely as any slave when you came there, my lord, as a slave, and you brought me back here. Of course I permitted you to overwhelm me and make me your naked prisoner. And I allowed your Queen Eleanor to become my new teacher in the erotic arts, learning from her in ways I had never learned in the sultanate."

"I see," said the King again. "And of course you might have written to your family for help at any time, if you could have managed to get a letter sent on your behalf."

"Oh, that I could have easily done, but it would never have been necessary. Had I wished to leave, I might have put my case before the Queen and she would have immediately accepted a rich bounty in return for my freedom. I knew this, but I stayed on for all the reasons slaves of this kingdom always stay on, and so often return, because I loved serving Queen Eleanor, loved her, and loved my fellow slaves, and also because I had another purpose. And that other purpose was to bear in mind always that Khaharanka at any time might need a new and mighty monarch. You could say I lived a life of dizzying subjugation as I kept my eye out for the perfect soul who might someday mount the throne of Khaharanka."

"Khaharanka has no royal family of its own?" the King asked.

"No, sire, the monarchy is not hereditary. And the subjects of Khaharanka do not descend from families. The monarch of Khaharanka is chosen and always for life, and the subjects choose to be subjects—as the slaves of Bellavalten today choose to be slaves."

"And you came here now to look for a new monarch?" I asked. I had spoken without the King's leave but he was entirely accepting and seemed eager for the answer.

"I did," he said. "The last monarch of Khaharanka was chosen from Bellavalten."

"Sonya!" I said. "Your mistress, Sonya. But she disappeared years ago, or so you told Alexi."

"No, my lady, she did not disappear at that time. She disappeared only to the world from which she'd come, and was borne to Khaharanka, and I grieved for her because my family did not permit me to go to Khaharanka at that time to be her loyal subject. It was my task to find ladies of her mettle to serve as new members of her Court, and only two years later was I allowed to become Queen Sonya's devoted servant. And I have been Queen Sonya's obedient slave ever since."

"I see."

"Well, Queen Sonya has long wanted freedom from Khaharanka. She has been one of the greatest queens ever to rule the little city-state, and her Court has been perfection. But she would return now to Europe, and to Bellavalten, and when your many letters were brought to her, for me, from my family home, Queen Sonya allowed me to answer and she has sent me here to find a new queen for our people."

"A new queen!" I scoffed. "And you have selected me for this singular honor, have you? And for this reason, you burst into my chambers like a foot soldier in a conquering army?"

"Yes, my lady, I had to. I had to test your mettle. I knew your fame. I knew so much of your gifts and your strength that I did not question it. Yet I had to be certain of your unconquerable spirit."

"As if you and your blandishments and your crude assaults were the test of such a thing!" I said. "How dare you!"

The King was trying to hide his smile now.

"My lady, I worship you," Lexius confessed. "I am a poor person for such a test, I confess. I am. But your response to me gave no doubt whatsoever of your immense strength. Your indignation and fury were, how shall I say, natural."

I laughed. "And so your queen must be as resolute and merciless as Queen Eleanor," I said.

"Yes, my lady, and more so. Much more so, for she rules a most unusual realm made up of singular worshippers. And do understand, our queen is a goddess in our eyes, and all obeisance shown her reflects this. She and her Court of women are held to be divine beings of unquestioned authority."

"I see. Or I think I see," said the King. "You are saying that all those in authority in this Khaharanka are women."

"Yes, my lord," he said. "It has always been so and will always be so, and the great resources of my family provide the soldiers and guards of the secret city, and uphold the sacred authority of its female rulers."

"Certainly not all who serve are men!" I offered.

"Yes, my lady, all are male, but not men in the conventional sense."

"I have no interest in eunuchs, my lord, never have," I said. "I am a great devotee of the cock and balls of men. That's why I live in Bellavalten." I looked to the King. "Need we hear any more of this?"

"You misunderstand me, my lady," Lexius said. "There are no eunuchs in Khaharanka."

"Then what sort of men are these unconventional males?" I asked.

He bowed his head, and then he looked to Dmitri.

I couldn't see Dmitri, as he stood behind me and behind the King. I was before the King and facing Lexius.

The King could see that Lexius was struggling. Lexius's face was red, and in such a dark face, such a blush has a purple tinge to it, and tears stood in his eyes for the first time, not the gushing tears of disobedient slaves, but the hesitant and silent tears of someone engaged in a deep inner struggle.

"My lord," Lexius said, looking up at the King, "I cannot hope to fulfill my mission now, without revealing great secrets. Might I ask of you that no matter what you think of me and my quest, whatever you think of Khaharanka, that you hold inviolate the secrets I reveal here?"

"I cannot do that, Lexius," said the King, "without the Queen present."

Lexius appeared to think this over.

"Dmitri, go to the Queen and ask her if she will join us now," said the King. "I don't know whether or not she is still in the gardens. Likely she is in her chambers. Ask her to come alone with you here."

Dmitri went off at once, and the King continued to study Lexius.

"You do understand, don't you, Lexius, that it is Queen Beauty who actually rules Bellavalten?"

"I have heard it said, sire, that you have great love for one another which is the marvel of the realm and that you rule it together."

"That's a clever and agreeable response," said the King. "But it is the wisdom of the Queen that has rebuilt the realm. If you are asking Lady Eva here to go with you and become your sovereign, if you are to reveal secrets that I must keep, then the Queen must be here, as I keep nothing from the Queen, and cannot keep anything, and cannot continue to encourage you if she does not consent to it."

Lexius nodded. "Yes, my lord," he said.

"And do you also realize that my queen might be mightily displeased with you that you have come here with the express purpose of taking Lady Eva from us?"

"Yes, Your Majesty," said Lexius, "but I had hoped that you and your queen would both indulge my loyalty to my beloved Khaharanka, that you might look kindly upon our need for a great ruler, that you might extend to me tolerance and understanding, as we hold so many views in common."

"You've gone about this clumsily, sir," said the King. But he was not angry.

"I know, sire," said Lexius. "I have, but had Lady Eva not been the goddess described to me, well, had I not felt the need to test her mettle— Forgive me, my lord. I have indeed been clumsy, devious, desperate. . . ." He stopped as the doors opened.

Dmitri appeared with the Queen. She had obviously been in her rooms close by, as she was dressed now in a long rose-colored silk dressing gown. A bit of her lace chemise showed at her throat and at her wrists, and she wore a pair of silver cutwork slippers. Her flaxen hair was charmingly undone.

"My lord," she said, going at once to the King and taking her place at his right side. Once again Dmitri vanished into the shadows.

The King took Queen Beauty's face in his hands and whispered to her a few brief sentences which summed up the situation. I caught the name of the secret city, and the word "confidences."

"As you wish, my lord," said the Queen. "Lexius, I will respect your confidences as my lord respects them. But tell me, why is Lady Eva here? And why Prince Dmitri."

"Prince Dmitri can attest to the truth of all I say," said Lexius, and then blushing deeply again, miserably in fact, he said, "I have come to beg Lady Eva to become the next absolute sovereign of Khaharanka." Quickly but smoothly he reiterated much of what he'd said before.

It was enough.

The Queen had the picture.

She looked at me and I saw the sudden panic in her eyes. It was as if she were saying aloud, *Eva, I don't want you to go.*

I felt it deeply. A thousand thoughts crowded my mind. A moment ago, I had felt certain I would reject this outrageous proposal out of hand. Now suddenly I was more intrigued than resolute.

"Well, now, Lexius," said the King. "Will you explain further as to what characterizes the devotees of this queen of yours and her Court of women if your men there are not eunuchs?"

"My Lady Eva is well known," said Lexius, "for her potions, for the many kinds of potions she had developed in her alchemical studies. Perhaps the lady will understand as I explain. Those who would enter life and service in Khaharanka must be nourished by a special potion. Wild tales now shroud the discovery of this mysterious elixir. But it is the tradition in our family that after many trials and many failures it was developed by a clever doctor who tested it on numerous applicants before perfecting its final formula. Whatever the case, it is most effective and easy to produce and has no unintended or ill effects on the men who choose to imbibe it. And indeed, many who leave the kingdom—and who drink it no more—lose all the outward attributes they acquired under its influence. Not all however."

"So you are saying that these male subjects drink this elixir of their own free will?" I asked. "They drink it to serve of their own free will—just as slaves are here of their own free will now in Bellavalten?"

"Yes and no, my lady," said Lexius. "Some male slaves are brought as tributes—as these are the ways of war in all the world, and my Khaharanka is part of the world. But in the main, yes, the population is made up of those who have come of their own volition, and those who remain because they have embraced the elixir and the transformation it offered them."

A dreamy expression came over his face.

"It is not such a great thing, you see, this transformation." He smiled. I could feel his excitement. His anxieties were being burnt away in his zeal for what he was describing. "Yet at the same time the elixir changes everything! The genius of the elixir is that it feeds one part of a man while not starving the other. Some elixirs nourish one aspect of the supplicant but destroy another. Ours does not. It goes to the primal root of the being, and waters *all* the seeds meet for watering!" His eyes were bright and his lips were smiling. "And the end result," he said, "for those who dare to drink the cup to the dregs, is magnificent."

I said nothing. I could see that the Queen and the King were both staring at him in awe. And I too was much impressed by what he said.

"And what precisely does happen to the man who drinks this cup to the dregs?" asked the King.

Lexius looked at the King, and then his eyes moved to the Queen, and then to me.

He was quite the picture now, enormously improved by his zeal and the high pleasure he was experiencing at this moment. His face had the rapt expression of someone gazing into the heart of a miracle.

Slowly he lowered his eyes, and his hands went to his jewel-encrusted robe, and slowly he broke open a long multitude of hooks that were near invisible for the decorative gold and silver threads that concealed them. He opened his long robe a mere half of an inch and then he opened it all the way and dropped it to the floor to reveal his entire naked body.

Queen Beauty let out a gasp. I almost fainted. I have never fainted in all my life, but at this moment, I almost fainted.

There standing before me was a sight I'd never beheld in all my life except in statues or in old paintings.

Every inch of his magnificent skin seemed to shimmer in the light, and from his loins rose a cock nearly as big as that of the King, just as thick, and just as dark as it stood erect, but what had caused me to weaken and nearly collapse was not the dazzling beauty of all this, but of his breasts—his breasts which were as large as mine, as full and as round, and as high and as firm. His womanly breasts with their hard dark rosy nipples.

I was staring at a gorgeous androgynous god. And he regarded us calmly, his eyes moving from face to face, as we beheld him.

Queen Beauty gave another soft expression of shock.

The King wore a radiant smile, so like him, but his eyes were huge with obvious wonder.

I moved towards Lexius, this exotic being, this god, drawn as if by a chain, and then caught myself, caught myself as my hands reached out for his breasts.

"Oh, you may touch them, my adored mistress, if you wish," he said.

I did.

I went up to him and I felt them, felt them as I would the breasts of any fulsome female slave under my authority. I squeezed them gently assessing their firmness, my fingers pinching the dark tender aureoles and the prominent jewellike nipples.

And then I stared at the cock, the hard crimson shaft, and I felt the passion kindled uncontrollably. Never had desire ripened so fast as it did in this instant. I buried my face in his breasts, pressing them to my cheeks and my lips. I slipped my arms around his naked form and held him to me, nuzzling and feeding off his breasts. I could not resist his nipples, and as I squeezed them, twisted them, challenged them with the firm play of my fingers, there came another astonishing revelation.

Pale drops of translucent milk began to flow from them!

I lapped at them with my tongue! I was going mad.

I stepped back as if to save myself from some engulfing madness in which all restraint would be lost.

He merely gazed at me with narrow smiling eyes. His hands hung at his sides. "Go on, my adorable lady," he said softly. "Taste it. It is yours as I am yours."

And I did. I suckled him hard, embracing him again, and felt the sweet and salty flavor of it.

"The milk of Aphrodite," said the King.

I wrapped my arms around him, feeling his hard cock push against me, and I sucked and sucked as if I couldn't stop, and the milk now was the smallest part of it. My right hand went down and felt his cock, as my tongue lapped at the milk, as my lips drew hard on his breast, and my desire swelled and burned until I was moaning.

How I managed to turn away, I don't know. Except that I did. I remembered the King and Queen. I staggered away, and when I turned around again the King was making love to Lexius, kissing him, and kissing his breasts just the way he so often kissed mine, and he put his powerful hand on Lexius's cock. And the King was moaning as I had moaned.

The Queen stared in shock with both her hands up to her lips. But her eyes were vague with wonder. No horror. No condemnation.

I turned and looked at Dmitri who stood in the shadows. He watched me, he watched all of us, but he said nothing.

Then, as if he could not prevent himself, he unfastened his heavy tunic at the shoulder and let it fall to reveal his shirt and trousers, and slowly he undid the ties at his throat and opened his shirt.

"They are much smaller," he said in a small voice. "They are supposed to go away when the elixir is withdrawn. But they have never entirely gone away, and I conceal them, though I die every hour of every day for someone to touch them, someone besides me."

The Queen reached out for him, and Dmitri drew close to her. And only now did I see the remarkable similarity of Dmitri and Lexius, see the same shimmer of the skin, the same long full hair, uncommonly long and proudly long falling to the shoulders, and both seemed to me great gods of Eros, surpassing all ordinary beings in their pursuit of joys that make the rest of us cowards.

The Queen put her right arm around Dmitri, and with her left hand she touched his small breasts reverently, and gingerly she touched his nipples. The blush was burning bright in his face, as he looked down at her.

The King and Lexius were now bound together in a hopeless embrace as the King drank the milk lustily and hungrily.

I turned away. I couldn't contain myself. It was not only the desire thrashing inside of me like an angry serpent locked in the prison of my body, it was my soul, my heaving soul. *Magnificent.*

I went past the bed and towards the window. I sought the air, parting the heavy curtains, and I looked up into the night, the shining night of the half-moon and its drift of faint stars, and I sighed.

Behind me I heard the Queen's voice. "And all men who serve must take this form?" she asked.

"Yes, my queen," said Dmitri. "And how they throb with every wave of desire."

"Oh, but you see, I know," said the Queen. "For we share this, don't we?"

"Yes," he said. "Oh, yes."

I lay my head against the stone arch, and felt the warm caressing breeze of the night, my eyes closed and my mind filled with vivid images. *All men who serve.*

The heavy window curtains had fallen shut behind me. Yet I could hear the creak of the bed, of its boards, and I heard the sudden muffled rhythmic cadence.

Through the tiny seam between the draperies I peered and saw Lexius on his knees, his back to the King, his hands out to the coffered headboard of the bed, as the King rode him, the King's hands clutching at Lexius's breasts, his hands squeezing them with greater abandon than he might ever enjoy the breasts of a woman. A god and a god.

I turned back to the night, alone in my closet of velvet hangings.

The harsh and driving rhythms of the bed came suddenly to the pinnacle in a great explosion of cries and groans.

Then silence, and in the silence distantly, the Queen's sweet and subtle sighs and with them those soft shuffling indefinable sounds that meant another species of lovemaking. It seemed that in the very midst of this Dmitri was weeping.

In a ragged fervent whisper, he said, "My secret is yours, yours . . . yours."

I slipped from behind the curtain and, cleaving to the margins of the room, I went to the door.

I looked back. The King lay as if in a dead sleep.

The Queen and Dmitri were a hopeless and tangled shape on the floor in the shadows before the leaping flames of the fire.

How dare I leave without permission? And yet I had to leave. Had to go. I opened the door and ran down the passage, and when I reached my room, I fell down on the bed, my face in the pillow.

Severin had come. Severin begged to know what I might want. Severin took off my slippers.

"Go," I said. I was as one blinded by a fierce new light and could not just now look upon the old things, which had once seemed so wondrous.

17

BEAUTY: A FESTIVAL OF MASKS

Beauty waited. She sat by the fire. The night outside was mild and lovely as it always was, but here in this vast chamber the stone walls were damp, and the warmth of the fire, as well as its dancing light, soothed her.

Dmitri and Alexi sat with her in chairs opposite. Beside her sat Rosalynd, her beloved Rosalynd, buxom, pretty, and practical and truthful. Her slaves, Beauty had sent away, including her devoted Becca whom she already missed, but this was a time for privacy with her privy council.

I need them now so very much, thought Beauty.

Her farewells to Eva had been brief with unbridled tears and embraces. Eva had said again as she had so many times before, "I must go, Your Majesty. How can I not? How can I not go and see for myself!"

"Remember," Beauty had said. "Our guards will be with you every step of the way and shall not leave you in Khaharanka until you yourself dismiss them. You can always return. The cohort will remain outside the walls waiting for your word."

Beauty had cried but finally given her blessing. She had embraced Lexius for the last time as well, and as she looked into the flames she thought not of Eva or Lexius but of the future.

How am I to rule without her, without the one who made all my designs into reality, the one who carried out with vigor those proposals that were dreams to me?

Dmitri, Alexi, and Rosalynd had assured her that they would take the place of Eva. Elena was committed to this as well. It was Elena who had presided over the evening banquet, receiving the new guests, and showing her generous appreciation of all the special entertainments.

The slaves of the realm were at peace. None could guess how thoroughly Lady Eva had constructed the world in which they suffered and loved and thrived. But Beauty knew.

At last the King came into the room. He waved for all to remain as they were, no bows now in private chambers.

"Well, I did my best," he said. He walked to the great fireplace and rested his hand against the stone, looking down into the flames. "I begged her not to go. I reminded her of all the inevitable perils. I assured her that I would seek to rescue her if I received the message. But how can any of us know what is to become of her? And I cannot raise an army to cross such vast seas. I'm afraid for her."

"Have they gone?"

"Yes," said the King. "I implored them to go tonight. I implored them not to let another sun rise on the same talk, the same pleading, the same tensions. They won't go far tonight, but they're gone, once and for all. It's been the most trying week since we came. I'm glad it's over."

"Yes, and you did all that you could," said Beauty. She looked at him, marveling at how untroubled he was, how certain that the future would not be changed by Eva's going, his certainty that the kingdom had a great destiny as before, and that what Eva had chosen to do could only hurt Eva.

But this was the way with Laurent. Beauty knew this. Yes, he loved with a special love. But he was not to be undone by Eva. As he had said, Eva's work had been completed. It was Beauty who had introduced the greatest innovations, and the staff which now presided over all the kingdom was as dedicated and efficient as always.

"Now, Beauty," he said, turning to her. "I won't hear any more of grief or doubt. You are to give up at once on this mad idea that Bellavalten will suffer without Eva. The kingdom is too strong for such a thought. And the love of our subjects for you is too great for you to doubt it. Not another word on this."

"Yes, my lord," said Beauty. She gave him her most knowing and taunting smile. It was the smile she always reserved for such moments, when he was dictating to her in the presence of others as to how she must feel in her soul. But she loved him. Loved him so much, and so unwaveringly.

He shook his head and gave back his own reproving smile and then he bent to kiss her.

"Queen of my heart," he said. "In a matter of months you will wonder why you ever feared the loss of Eva."

He rose to his full height again and stretched and then shook himself all over. He looked at Dmitri and Alexi.

"Who wishes to agree with me?" he asked. He was to some extent teasing, but it was like all teasing in that there was a truth to it.

"I agree completely, sire," said Alexi. "What this means is more meetings, more councils, a few more appointments. And that is all. We shall miss her but she leaves no ragged hole in the fabric. The fabric has already begun to mend."

"Yes, that is what I wanted to hear," said the King. "Now if there is nothing more for me to do here, I'll go down and join Elena." And with one more kiss for Beauty he was gone, leaving the room with the same easy stride with which he'd entered it.

How long, thought Beauty, shall I keep them here, my beloved companions? Is it really their task to comfort me when I'm beyond comforting? She had heard their many predictions and assurances all week long.

"No one expects you ever to pretend to feel that which you do not feel!" Alexi had said over and over again. And Dmitri, more reticent but of the same mind, had said more than once, "You rule with perfect grace. That is what matters."

So why did it matter so to Beauty that she could not experience raptures when she exacted alluring shudders and whimpers from her charges? Why did it trouble her that from the throne she did not know the exaltation she had known when she had been a naked slave of others?

It was unseemly to her to call some cruel and demanding master to her private rooms, as Laurent had done so easily with Eva. She did not want that, the inner shame of being the Queen naked and on her knees before another. Indeed, what she knew in Alexi's arms and in Dmitri's arms was rapture beyond imagining. It was different, that was all. Different, their caressing, their play, their shared enjoyment of the slaves she kept for her own amusement. So what was lacking?

She resolved she would not again complain of losing Eva.

"I have a thought," she said. "An idea. Something I would like to see, something special, not for every night but for one very special night."

"Ah, I can't wait to hear it," said Alexi.

"Your wish is my command," said Rosalynd.

Ah, she loved the soft informal voices of those who trusted her and were close to her.

"We have talked a lot of the Discipline of the Mask," she said. "Explain how it goes just now with those who ask for it."

"Well," said Dmitri, "there are five so far, three lords and two ladies. And they wait as before for your permission. I've spoken to each of them, as you ordered, and I think they are apt candidates—all in fit condition, comely, and with an undeniable aptitude for service."

"You want to tell me now who they are or must I drag it out of you?" said Beauty, but not in a mean voice, no never in a mean voice. She made a little gesture of welcome with both hands as she smiled at Dmitri.

"Lady Juliana," said Dmitri. "How long ago did she return? It's been six months, I think?"

Beauty nodded. "Lady Juliana. What a fearsome creature she was when I first came here and such a friend to the late queen. But you know, she did originally come here as a royal slave, and as a royal slave she was sent down to the village for punishment, only to be elevated and made a lady-in-waiting by the Queen. And that is what she is with me."

Dmitri nodded. Alexi had his usual slightly mocking and knowing smile. He certainly hadn't forgotten the beautiful blond Juliana who'd driven Beauty on the Bridle Path the first time long ago.

In those days Juliana had worn her hair in long thick braids threaded with pearls. And now she wore a great braid encircling her head behind which her blond hair was exquisitely coiffed in waves, and the old threads of pearls were there and her face was as pretty as ever, and her voice just as lilting.

"So she wants to take the Discipline of the Mask," said Beauty. "Prince Roger will find that most interesting, as they were once slave runaways together. And she was elevated to the Court without him." Prince Roger was fast friends with Prince Richard in the village.

"Yes, Roger is aware and he does find it amusing," said Dmitri. "And they've spoken of it as openly as you and I are speaking now. She knows what she wants, my queen. I have no doubt that she'll do well with the Discipline of the Mask. What we need are rituals . . . how to anoint these Disciples of the Mask, and what rules to apply to their tribulations."

"I have many ideas," said Rosalynd. "I say we need a special day on which such persons can appear naked and masked before the Court to be anointed."

"I like that idea," said the Queen. "As it was in the old days with Midsummer Night."

"Yes, and we might have more than one such festival; perhaps three or four a year," said Dmitri. "Perhaps one every two months. We could see how it goes as more of the old royal slaves return to the kingdom."

"Another is Princess Lynette," said Dmitri. "You might not remember her, my queen. She ran away and was never caught. Well, she's been back more than once. The Queen pardoned her and welcomed her to Court ten years ago."

"I remember her," said Beauty, and well she should since she had received her with Laurent. But it was quite impossible to remember all the names and faces of those they received nightly. The Lord Chamberlain had his lists, his proper titles, his little histories. And that was a good thing, for Beauty could not recall right now just what precious Princess Lynette looked like.

"But you know who she is, don't you?" she said to Alexi.

He laughed. "I certainly do."

Lynette had featured heavily in a long story Alexi had once confided to Beauty—of how he had been broken and taught to please the Queen. Blond hair, blue eyes. Yes, that much Beauty now remembered.

"I would say she knows what she wants too," said Alexi. "We've both spoken with her and Lady Juliana. They're ready for the mask. They're asking only for a limited time, say six months of slavery, and then a chance to renew their vows, like all the other slaves."

Beauty nodded.

"Now for the three lords," said Dmitri. "The first is Prince Jerard, the blond one, who was a pony in the stables after you left. And he knows perfectly well what he wants. No doubt about him. He understands that once he dons the mask, he will have no choice in the matter of where he's made to serve, but he wants to be a pony again. He's fit enough. And frankly handsomer than he was in the old days. And then there is a young duke, Claudio, only lately come to the kingdom. He's very innocent but he's spent the last eight months here and knows well what all this means."

"Yes, Claudio," said Beauty, "of the auburn hair, rawboned, tall, but utterly enchanting. We've had him at the royal table countless times. He keeps the most piquant little slave, Isabella."

"Yes, well, I'm for letting him do it," said Dmitri. "In fact, I'd love to acquaint him with the rigors of the village myself, as I did Stefan. Now as for the third, well, this is young Lord Lysius, grandnephew of the old king at our border, and I think he is being hasty. He does not realize what it means to be anointed a slave. He thinks he does, but, well, all I can say is, he does not. He's a dreamer, a poet, in love with the kingdom but not ready to serve others."

"I agree," said Alexi. "Lord Lysius should be refused. And if we do have four ceremonies of acceptance a year, well, he could be put off for a certain period of months with the promise that he might apply again."

"Seems you have it well in hand," Beauty said. And she believed it. But she was not so sure young Lord Lysius should be refused. She knew him. He was a lad of sensitivity and great imagination. He knew what the slaves felt as he punished them. Why shouldn't he take the mask? But she would press this later.

"But what special night, what festival, should be the occasion for these presentations?" asked Rosalynd.

"A Festival of Masks," said Beauty. "I have been thinking of it for some time. A great and beautiful Festival of Masks when all the Court shall mask as well, and all free men and women of the kingdom."

"Ah, lovely," said Rosalynd.

"A great night of masked dancing and frolicking when all wearing clothes shall wear masks to embolden them to celebrate the freedom of Bellavalten," said Beauty. "Something like the old celebrations of Perchta at Midwinter." She smiled to think of Perchta, the old goddess of spinning.

And it had been a spinning wheel that had been Beauty's long-ago undoing, when as a girl of fifteen she pricked her finger on a spindle and fell asleep for a hundred years.

But what did Perchta mean for all the world?

Didn't matter. She was seeing a more complex and wholly original festival.

"And in our festival," said Beauty, "all naked slaves of the village and of the Court and of the kingdom may frolic as well in the castle gardens for that one night, free of restraint and punishment, to dance and drink and embrace one another, along with their masked lords and ladies. We shall all celebrate the freedom of the kingdom."

"A form of Saturnalia," said Dmitri.

"The only naked slaves who shall wear masks on that night," said Beauty, "will be the five who are accepted for the Discipline of the Mask, and they shall wear their masks thereafter for six months, at which time they may remove them and return to Court or become slaves indefinitely."

"Perfect," said Alexi. "Simply perfect."

"And that settles it," said Dmitri. "Stefan should wear his mask for six months from the time he put it on."

"That is my wish," said Beauty. "And as for young Lord Lysius, the decision is his also."

"Ah, this will be wonderful fun," said Rosalynd, "but what great ritual will lie at the center of it."

"I'm coming to that," said Beauty. "You, and Dmitri, you were both on the ship with me and Tristan and Laurent as we sailed to the sultanate. Do you remember an early feast on board the ship in which Tristan and I were gilded lovers?"

"I remember it vividly," said Dmitri.

"So do I," said Rosalynd. "And we spoke of it often afterwards. We saw other such reenactments in the sultanate. It had no great meaning for them, but I am seeing what meaning it might have for us."

"I was painted in gold," said Beauty, "and surrounded with fruit dipped in honey, and my body filled with such, and I was laid out on a great bier as if I were a feast myself, and then Tristan came, and ate the fruits with which I was filled and coupled with me."

"I can see this," said Alexi.

"Yes," said Beauty, "but now imagine it with our gracious king agreeing on that night to remove all his clothes and adornments—except for his mask—so that he, of his own will, couples with the gilded female slave offered to him on a great platter. Imagine it, the great ceremonial coupling of king and kingdom."

"Oh, so splendid," said Alexi. "The marriage of king and kingdom. Yes, this would be a great and sacred moment."

"I can hear the harps and the drums," said Beauty, "and see His Majesty rising from the throne at the sacred moment and stripping off his fine clothes, with only his mask left—perhaps a mask that has the horns of Pan or the horns of a goat—for he would be the goat god, the god of wine, the god of fertility, the god of rampant celebration—and imagine him approaching the bier on which the gilded female slave is offered to him."

"Breathtaking," said Alexi.

"Yes," said Beauty. "She would be all painted in gold, and she too would be masked because she represents all slaves of the kingdom—all slaves, not her single solitary self—as the King couples with her."

"Yes," said Dmitri. "The King should eat the fruit from inside her and then take her. Ah, the great wedding of all who rule with all who serve!"

"But how shall you figure in it, Beauty?" said Alexi. He had forgotten to address her as "Queen" or "my lady," but Beauty didn't care. If anything she wanted all of them to be less formal.

"Well, the Queen must watch from behind her mask on the throne, I would imagine," she said. She had chosen her words carefully. But she was thinking of something else entirely.

"Do you think our beloved king will do it?" asked Dmitri.

Beauty laughed. "If ever there was a king who would, it is Laurent. I can see it now, see his ruddy flesh and the gilded flesh of the prone slave, and see the two masks, his decorated with horns, yes, and hers perhaps with green leaves and purple grapes painted on the leather, and the whole platter, the whole bier, decorated with such Bacchanalian foliage."

A moment of silence passed.

"My queen, you keep dreaming the dreams," said Rosalynd. "We can easily make of this a perfect reality. I'm ready now to make drawings, the plans. We will need many more musicians, vats of the finest wine, and all the naked slaves shall be encouraged to dance on that night with utter abandon."

"All shall dance with utter abandon," said Beauty.

"But the masked girl, the slave chosen to represent the kingdom," Dmitri pressed. "Who should she be? Someone very special. I mean this should be a very special honor, to be chosen for such a ceremonial wedding. Should she remove her mask afterwards?"

"Remove her mask? Why should she? For she is everyone," said Beauty. "And I do have someone very special in mind, but you must let me ponder that now on my own for a while."

Her eyes drifted and she saw Dmitri looking up dreamily as he envisioned this. But Alexi's eyes were fixed quietly on Beauty, and Rosalynd too regarded her with a secret smile, gazing at her out of the corner of her eyes.

"Announce the feast. The night does not matter. We make a new custom here, and shall hold such a feast as soon as we can. And we shall make the date a memorial. Announce it shall be the night when the accepted Disciples of the Mask will step forward and be taken off by Prince Dmitri at the end of the night to the village to begin their servitude. Perhaps they shall be ceremonially bound for their journey. Make a great raised dais for this great platter or banquet table on which the slave girl shall lie after she is brought in. And make sure the dais for the King and Queen is above it. And leave the King to me. I will put it to him so that he will do it. And the Queen shall preside as always from her throne as the ceremony is accomplished."

For an hour they spoke of nothing else but the feast which now had the title "The First Festival of Masks," and Rosalynd at Beauty's writing table scribbled down many ideas and drew some scant pictures.

At last Beauty dismissed them all except for Dmitri.

The bolt was thrown on the door, and in the warm shadowy chamber, they both removed their garments. How marvelous to shed the heavy trappings of royal attire and stand naked on the bare floor.

The size of Dmitri's nude breasts astonished Beauty. He seemed as accustomed to them as Lexius had been to his. And he showed not the slightest shame as Beauty drank him in with her eyes.

"And this is only one week on the elixir?" she asked.

"Yes," said Dmitri, gazing at her with the serene face of a statue. "And Lexius left us plenty enough for many to imbibe if they wish. Matthieu has no difficulty with the formula. He will soon be able to make as much as we like."

"And how do they feel to you?" Beauty asked, though she wanted above all to know how they might feel to her.

"Tender," he said. "Firm, but exquisitely sensitive."

"In time we shall talk of this," said Beauty. "Of those who might want to drink this potion. For now, you do as you wish."

She was so glad that Eva had not asked to take her alchemist, Matthieu, with her, and that he remained still in his workshop producing potions and pastes, and lotions and perfumes.

Matthieu was quiet and solitary by nature, and took no direct interest in slaves, though he used them all the time in his experiments. It was amusing in fact to watch him feeding a passion potion to a female slave and then feeling her soft little pubic patch for the telltale moisture. He took note of this as a tailor might of a measurement and wrote it down directly. He never so much as glanced at the faces of the slaves strapped to his walls as he went about his work.

Beauty drew near to Dmitri and stroked his breasts. She could resist no longer. His cock came to life immediately. Dmitri thrilled and intrigued her as no other being in the kingdom just now, and he seemed to have grown in grace since he'd taken more of the potion that made him the great enigmatic god who stood before her.

She led him to the bed and they lay down together.

"Ah, this is so splendid," she said, lying beside him, facing him, studying him, stroking him. "If I could only grow a cock only for a night." She was lost in his eerie beauty.

"My queen, you have no need of one," he said. "You are as much a man and woman as I am a man and woman."

They pressed close to each other, their breasts crushed against one another, and he kissed her lips tenderly. She felt a throbbing in her breasts and in the little chamber between her legs. She felt herself melting against him, against his silky skin.

"And you, you alone, behold me as I truly am," he said to her in a voice rich with feeling that deeply touched her. "You and you alone see and feel these ornaments that make me doubly your conquest."

"I alone?" she asked in a low purring whisper. "Not even Stefan sees these luscious gifts?"

"Stefan wouldn't want to see them," said Dmitri. "And no, he shall never. For now, they belong to you."

Beauty pressed Dmitri down on the pillow so that he lay on his back. She straddled him, and rising up received his cock gratefully. Such a divine sensation, that of the hard cock going deep into her, widening her vaginal mouth, rubbing harshly against her burning clitoris. Reaching for his breasts as he reached for hers, she moved up and down on the wet shaft of his cock, slowly finding the inevitable rhythm. Her eyes closed, her hands kneading his breasts cruelly, her thoughts filled with flaming bits and pieces of dreams, she came—crying Dmitri's name. She felt the hot semen inside her.

Tumbling down beside him, she fell into an easy sleep, now and then nuzzling into his breasts or feeling his lips graze her forehead and cheeks gently.

Suddenly an unfamiliar impulse came over her. She motioned for him to turn over on his face. Drowsily and wordlessly, he obeyed, his eyes closed, his face serene and soft against the pillow.

She explored his hard firm back, his small waist, and the bones of his narrow hips, and then her fingers stroked his soft backside, and pried apart the cheeks of his bottom so that she could see the pink little anus there. He offered no resistance to her. Seldom had she ever examined this part of a man, which so delighted others in the kingdom. Now she studied the tiny wrinkled mouth. She pushed at it with her fingers. Dmitri was awake, she was sure of it, but lay silent and still. She felt the desire to find a wand with a phallus on the end of it, the kind used for driving pets in the garden. She had never used those wands. She'd always pulled her little puppy, Brenn, along by a leash. But she thought now that next time she would examine Brenn's nether endowments with greater interest, and she would drive him with such a wand, and maybe Dmitri as well when the mood came over her. Yes, she might drive Dmitri around this room, and it would be interesting to see how his backside looked at the end of the wand, how his shoulders would look, and his face, yes, his face, when he was made to crawl about in this manner for her. He would love it. She knew that he would.

She lay back down to sleep once more.

In the quiet bedroom with only the flames of the fire for light, the King's step sounded. The door shut.

She opened her eyes to see his face as he raised his eyebrows and looked down on Dmitri.

The Prince awoke, and dutifully left the bed, snatching up his clothes before disappearing into the antechamber.

"How now, my little damsel?" said the King. "I'll drive that princeling from your mind with every thrust!" He tore off his garments and let them drop. Then he mounted her and she felt the great familiar crush of his cock inside of her. And looking up in her delirium she saw the handsome face that had guided her waking life for decades, and guided it still.

"King of my heart," she said. Falling away from him, she pushed her face into the pillow.

"And this little queenly bottom is still all mine," said Laurent softly in her ear. "No one else has whipped or spanked it." She felt his large warm hand closing over her buttocks.

"No, my lord," she whispered sleepily in reply, "and I do not think anyone else ever will."

"But if you wish . . ."

She smiled. She was so sleepy. He had never said this before.

"If you wish, you know, it is your prerogative. . . ."

"Hush, my lord," she said. "I do not wish. Go to sleep."

Hours later, Beauty fell into a vivid dream. The great fairy wise woman, Titania of Mataquin, was talking to her and they sat together in a great grove of multicolored flowers and gentle green willows by a small sparkling stream. This was the fairy queen's realm.

Titania spoke to her.

"Ah, but don't you see, the laws that bind you are yours to change to your own purposes. You are mistress and slave of all the realm."

18

BEAUTY: THE MARRIAGE OF THE KING AND THE KINGDOM

It was the most glorious night in Bellavalten that she had ever experienced. The garden was thronged with masked revelers in festive attire, and naked slaves dancing together in circles both great and small, and in pairs and in chains as they rushed singing through the many scattered little pavilions and tables.

Every fountain had been emptied, cleaned, and filled with the finest wine. And vats of wine were everywhere positioned for those who would dip their goblets or tankards.

The spectacle of the masked people of the village and the Court was splendid and exciting even beyond imagining. And the musicians from far and wide played the gayest and lustiest tunes and dances.

Never had there been so many torches, lanterns strung in the limbs of the trees, or so many candelabra burning against the walls, or lamps shining on the countless tables.

In the spirit of a Saturnalia, citizens served themselves from the huge tables laid out with every meat and fruit and delicacy. And the slaves feasted as well.

The grooms and attendants on duty wore masks, though they worked always to see that tables remained clean, that all had what they needed, that nothing ran short as the feast continued hour after hour. Yet even they partook of the delicious food and wine, and had their turns at dancing and singing.

Beauty sat back, comfortable in the immense gilded throne looking down on the dais prepared for the great marriage ceremony directly before her. All the Court could see the dais and see the masked king and queen as they smiled down on their subjects.

The King had danced over and over, and the King and Queen many times, and the Queen with her beloved Alexi and Dmitri.

The thumping of drums, the peal of pipes, and the strumming of lutes and lyres filled the air, along with the cries of the excited merrymakers.

No slave pets tonight, no slaves bound to crosses, no slaves driven on the Bridle Path—only the shared gaiety of all the realm who gave no thought to tomorrow.

It was now the eleventh hour.

Very soon the gilded maiden would be brought in, and the King would rise to be the lord of the grape, the lord of the fields, the lord of plenty and celebration—and take his bride in his arms for the great ceremony. Of course he had been willing to do what his beloved Beauty had asked of him. What did it mean for him to strip naked and perform before his worshipful subjects? He had said at once, "What a great pleasure and what a small request."

Beauty had loved him for it. Behind his ornate gold mask with its slanted eyes and horns he appeared deliciously frightening to her. As for her mask it was large and concealing as was his, and she wondered if her mouth seemed as lush and inviting to Laurent as his did to her. Ah, what masks did to faces and to souls.

Rosalynd appeared before the banquet table and nodded. Beauty knew her by her hair as well as her brilliant purple gown, and by her demeanor, of course, as she knew many in spite of their masks.

She rose at the signal and slipped away.

"To refresh myself, my lord," she said. "I'll be back momentarily. And I want to see to the gilded maiden, that all is as I want it to be."

She and Rosalynd rushed through the shifting crowds, Rosalynd leading the way, clasping Beauty's hand tight as Beauty struggled to keep up with her.

There before them stood the white tent, on the soft green grass beyond the Bridle Path.

They crossed the beaten earth where so many slaves ran to the tune of paddles every evening but this evening.

And slipping inside, Beauty stopped to catch her breath. For a moment her heart beat too fast, and she knew fear, a new and delicious fear that she had not known in many years, a fear that brought the color to her cheeks and made her smile to herself before she turned to take the measure of her surroundings.

There lay the great wooden platter, wondrously wrought with hammered gold leaf, and on it the narrow silken bed on which the maiden would lie—the whole resting on a bier ready to be carried to the ceremonial dais.

Six grooms with gilded masks stood ready to carry the bier when it was ready.

Another small cluster of grooms with the gold paint and oil and other adornments waited to go to work. Elena stood by with Alexi and with Dmitri, and there quite alone it seemed was Beauty's beloved naked slave Becca.

Becca's gorgeous flaxen hair had been coiffed exactly like that of Beauty tonight, with ivory combs and opals and pearls, and she stared at Beauty with soft blue eyes, a smile on her coral lips, waiting. How seductive she appeared in her nudity with such elaborately dressed hair.

For a moment, Beauty only gazed at her, and the throbbing music rose in her ears, the distant uneven chorus of song and laughter.

Very well, thought Beauty. I am going through with it!

Quickly she commenced to remove her violet-and-silver gown, and at once Rosalynd and Elena stepped up to help her with its many fastenings.

"Come here, Becca," said the Queen, and the girl hurried to stand before her. At once the gown was put over Becca's head and pulled and fastened to fit her easily if not perfectly. Beauty kicked off her slippers and removed her mask and Becca received the mask as a groom helped her into the discarded slippers.

Now the mask was in place and Becca stood before Beauty, garbed as Beauty had been garbed, coiffed as Beauty had been coiffed, and masked as Beauty had been masked.

"Perfect!" said Rosalynd with a long sigh. "Utterly perfect."

"Now remember, don't attempt to imitate my voice," said Beauty. "You won't fool him. Simply take your place beside him and smile. You will do this just as the bier is being brought in and there won't be time for talk anyway."

Becca nodded.

"Yes, Your Majesty."

"She could fool anyone!" said Dmitri.

Becca moved back to the far corner of the tent, her disguise complete, and she waited.

Only now did Beauty realize that she stood utterly naked and barefoot before her closest friends, her privy council, her most beloved supporters.

"Quick, we should hurry, lest someone come to see if we're delayed," said Alexi, taking Beauty's hand. He helped her to the long hard gold platter.

Four of the grooms surrounded her and began to rub the gold-pigmented oil into her skin. Another groom began to paint her lips gold and her eyelids and her nipples.

Beauty closed her eyes. There came back to her the sweetest memory of that long-ago night in the hold of the Sultan's ship when other attendants had performed these same ministrations so reverently. She felt the pins and combs being drawn out of her hair, and the hands busily working on her most secret parts, fingers rubbing the gold into her pubic hair, and into the crevice of her bottom.

A great throbbing relief weakened her all over and she felt every fiber of her naked skin, every fiber of her naked soul once more as she'd felt it long ago, for so many days and nights.

At last it was done. She was covered in gold as she had been once before on that strange night—and Alexi and Dmitri lifted her along with the grooms as others gently laid out the bed of silken cushions beneath her. Rosalynd gathered up her hair. Elena began to paint her toenails.

Now came the final preparations. Dmitri lifted the glistening handfuls of fruit, quartered melons, red cherries, bits of ripe apple, soft slices of fresh peach and plum, and began to put these inside of her. Her sex awakened and throbbed as the fruit was pushed into her. Her clitoris hardened and she closed her eyes for one precious moment, fighting the rising orgasm that threatened to overcome her.

The grooms brushed her hair out over the pillow in waves, sending tingles through her scalp. Alexi held up a glistening date for her to see and then placed it in her navel.

All around her the grooms packed the fresh fruits against her, from her feet to her neck. Garlands of grape leaves were strung through the fruits. Between her legs lay more fruit. She sighed and twisted comfortably on the silk, her vagina deliciously full and gasping, it seemed, gasping as if to devour the fruit inside her.

Dmitri held up the small loose cluster of grapes, such glistening purple grapes, and Beauty opened her mouth to receive it, to hold it with her teeth.

Suddenly it seemed her breasts would burst with the delicious pressure rolling through her, through all her limbs, through her face. Again, she closed her eyes for one vital second.

Then she looked up to see the maiden's mask before her. It was as she had designed it, a light shield of leather with oval eyes, gilded and painted with bright green leaves and purple grapes like those she held in her teeth.

Carefully Dmitri placed it over her face, smoothing it to fit, and then lifting her head, he ran the strap around it and positioned the jeweled buckle just behind her left ear. Now she gazed out of the almond-shaped eye openings, and all the world seemed a little less clear and she seemed a little more safe, and her heart pounded with renewed excitement.

"You are gorgeous to behold," said Alexi. She knew he wanted to kiss her painted lips but they were for the King tonight.

What more was there to do—the piling of the platter with more polished fruit, more soft ripe fruit, more leaves.

A silence fell within the tent.

Only the music was audible, the great tantalizing beat of the drums and the high-pitched cry of the horns.

"They are ready."

Again came the fear, the thrilling fear, so secret and so sharp and so exciting. And there came back again the splendor of that long-ago night and how trusting she'd been to the fire burning inside her. Well, she was trusting now to that fire. And it burned hot, and as she felt the bier lifted, she knew that she was ready.

And now they are carrying me, naked and gilded and prepared, out under the stars and through the gardens of my own kingdom. And I am queen and slave in one. I am the ruler who has ordained these things, and I am the slave, the abject slave, the devoted slave of all my subjects!!

On and on the grooms in their gilded masks moved with the bier. The Princes walked beside her as did her two ladies. And there was Becca, she could see her plainly in Beauty's raiment, Becca now the perfect image of Beauty.

They had come to the area behind the royal banquet table. She could hear the gasps and exclamations of those who had glanced behind from their chairs above.

"Now go up, my queen," said Alexi to Becca, "and sit beside your husband and smile and say nothing."

A signal had been given. Silence. All music had ceased.

Then the drums were beating a cadence, the deep drums, the drums that send their deep-throated voice through your bones.

And as the bier came round in front of the royal banquet table, as Beauty looked up at the masked face of the King smiling down, she heard the horns begin and the lutes with them. It was a rhythm of reverence, of expectation.

The great bier was carried up onto the dais and a great loud exclamation came from the crowd as a body. Beauty did not need to see them as they undoubtedly struggled to see better the great ceremony. A great hush had fallen over the spectators and only the music spoke now for the crowd, only the music announcing a moment of supreme importance.

Beauty turned ever so slightly on the silken pillow. She looked up at the King who had risen to his feet. His stately masked queen was seated to his right, her head turned slightly towards him.

The King stepped up onto the table, and then down onto the planks beneath it and in front of it. He unfastened his great scarlet cloak. And then opened his long tunic and let it fall away from him. His attendants took his boots, and took the ceremonial chains from around his neck, and even the handsome bracelets from his arms as he held out his hands.

And there he stood naked except for the gleaming horned mask, his cock hard and ready.

Down the carpeted steps he came to the dais that held Beauty.

He stood above her gazing down on her, staring down at this masked maiden who she had become, and now the music became rapid, wild, exhorting, and pounding. He dropped down and with his hands caressed Beauty's breasts and kissed the mouth of her sex, kissed it and began to gnaw at and extract the fruit that filled her.

She felt his tongue against her clitoris again and again as he dragged the juicy dripping fruit from her, until at last his tongue searched the cavity for the very last bits and juices as her desire maddened her and made her toss her head ever so gently, her hands clawing at the silk and the fruit, her eyes closing.

But she wanted to see. She wanted to see him.

He was above her, his powerful arms like pillars beside her, his eyes glittering behind the mask, his lips curled in the old familiar smile, as his cock plunged into her.

She sighed, and lifted her hips. She could not stop it.

In a daze she saw all the faces above at the royal table; she heard the music pounding on her ears; she heard her own heart throbbing in her ears and her eyelids.

"My beloved, my kingdom, my realm, my soul!" the King whispered. Beauty could scarce control herself, writhing under him, his cock stroking every fiber of her vagina, as it plunged again and again, and finally she gave a loud cry as he tossed his hair and closed his eyes and groaned above her.

On and on he pumped into her, and then at last he was still.

A deafening applause rose from the crowd. It rose all around them, and seemed to come in waves from all quarters of the garden, washing over them like water.

The King rose to his feet. The applause became a raging chorus of cheers, unending as it drowned out the drums and the horns. She looked up to see Laurent holding up his hands as the cheers grew even louder. It sounded as if the whole realm was cheering, and again the applause broke out, coming in great waves, and the mingled cacophony of music and clapping and voices lulled Beauty into a trance as the shivers of desire continued to wash through her.

The King looked down, and then he reached for her hand.

She rose up and allowed him to pull her to her feet.

"Our kingdom!" he roared. And the crowd once more applauded him. He turned to her and said, "Let me take off your mask, beautiful maiden of the kingdom. Let them see the one who has lain here beneath me as the symbol of the realm."

"Are you sure, my lord?" she said. "You want to see me? For if you do, I am more than willing. I am more than willing that they know how much the Queen loves them."

He stared at her, that was plain enough, eyes glinting in the eyeholes of the mask, his mouth slack with astonishment.

"Beauty?" he said.

"Yes, my lord," she said. "For you, and for them, I am the kingdom."

What did he think? What would he say? What was going on behind the ornate and shimmering mask?

Then came the smile, the slow easy smile, the great smile, the beloved smile.

She lifted her hand to her mask and he lifted his hands to assist her, pulling it loose from her and casting it aside and holding up her hand in his.

"My queen!" he called out. "The eternal maiden of the kingdom, Beauty, my queen, queen of my heart, Queen Beauty of Bellavalten!"

It was madness, sweet madness. In all directions Beauty saw the dancers leaping in the air, clapping, the naked slaves jumping up and down like children, the torches blazing, as the voices came louder and fuller and all the more jubilant with unstinting praise. Alexi and Rosalynd and Elena were dancing before them, Alexi clapping his hands wildly over his head. From left to right, Beauty looked, and behind her—at the smiling figure of Becca above—and before her. The Captain of the Guard was on his knees looking at her with upraised hands. And Princess Lucinda was there in her unmistakable gray velvet waving her hands as she danced. Tristan and Roger and Richard were waving with both arms as they swayed back and forth.

The five naked Disciples of the Mask were brought forward by Prince Dmitri and stood with their heads bowed waiting to be given over to their six months of irrevocable bondage. In a frenzy the crowd danced around them, closing in on them and then backing away from them, and then dancing near to them again—clapping and cheering, and then again raising their hands, countless hands, hands wherever one looked, to the King and Queen.

Solemnly the King gestured to each of the humble supplicants and then with his open hand to Dmitri who might now take them away. Beauty nodded, raising her right hand in blessing as well.

As the five were led away, Beauty saw Dmitri looking back from the midst of the frenzy. On and on went the dancing and cheering, and the drums thundered and the pipes broke into a wild dance.

Suddenly right before her she saw her beloved Brenn and Sybil. They were leaping with their arms raised, and Brenn shouted:

"Beauty's Kingdom!"

"Beauty's Kingdom!" sang out Sybil in a high-pitched jubilant voice.

"Beauty's Kingdom," they sang together.

Lovely Princess Blanche was also dancing before the dais, and with her the pretty slaves Penryn and Valentine, and countless others, all singing out "Beauty's Kingdom!" over and over again.

"Beauty's Kingdom!" cried Laurent. He held up Beauty's hand with his. He swayed in the dance, both arms raised, his right hand clasping her left hand. "Beauty's Kingdom," he cried again, and the cry was taken up all around. "Beauty's Kingdom!" From everywhere voices echoed it, and repeated it until it became a roaring chant.

Beauty's Kingdom.

And I am your sovereign, Beauty thought as she looked out over the endless wilderness of happy subjects, naked and clothed, unmasked and masked. And I am naked before you because I choose to be, and yes, I am the kingdom. I am you all. I will serve you always; I will give you all. Demand what you will. Need what you will. *This is my destiny, my submission, my true surrender.*